SUPERCONNECTED SERIES BOOK 1:

BY 27

This book is dedicated to the three men in my life:

Russell McAteer

For whom I wrote this story down

Tony Materniak

Who listened, even when it was gibberish

And

Joseph Tapp

My life long friend who has never been afraid to tell me when I was wrong, and to tell me in great detail.

Also the people who made me me:

Jeannie McAteer
Jodie and Gonzalo Camelo
Hiten Shah
Tricia Arnseth Black
Drew Hollywood
John Kenneth Fisher
Michelle Beaver
Karen Rancont

3

3 Months Ago

I grew up thinking the greatest sacrifice you could make was to lay down your life to protect the one you love. What did I know, all my learning came from books. I wish I had someone, anyone, to tell me it wouldn't be that easy.

I could hear water running. I awoke, sat up in bed and looked at the clock. 5:00. Only in Vegas did your boyfriend get home from work at 5am.

I yawned and stretched as my eyes started to focus on the dingy white walls and the cracks in the plaster. I smiled. This motel room may be rough around the edges but it was the closest thing to a home I'd had in years.

I rose to find Luke in the bathroom with a swollen face, bent over the sink trying to wash blood out of his only work shirt. I wish this was the first time this had happened. I wordlessly went down the motel hallway and got some ice, wrapped it in a towel and held it to his cheek. He had called himself "lucky" once and I had adopted it as a pet name. I reached down to brush Lucky's rust-colored hair away from his eyes. The side of his handsome face was very badly bruised.

"Are you okay?" I asked.

"Me? Sure, I'm fine," he answered just a little too quickly. "You should have seen the other guys." He forced a laugh. He didn't want me to worry.

This wasn't the first time one of us had been jumped. Teenage runaways like us were often victims of brutal crimes. Assailants knew we wouldn't go to the police.

They picked the right one to attack. If it had been me, someone would have gotten hurt. I mean seriously hurt. I wasn't your ordinary little girl. From the day I was born my body seemed to overproduce electricity. It was like a constant electric overload coursing through me. Growing up you couldn't touch me without getting a static shock. My father dropped me off at an orphanage but somehow paid to retain custody of me. This only served to prevent me from loving foster homes and adoption. The orphanage separated me from the other children and an endless parade of doctors arrived to perform tests on me. Nothing was conclusive and finally they all stopped coming. The difficult years from 6 to 14 I spent in relative solitude. Then a turn of fate brought me to Lucky. Just two years older than me at 16 he was far more worldly and wise than anyone I'd ever encountered. His hard work and patience had helped me gain some control of the electric charge that was raging inside me. Lucky helped me to see static electricity as an advantage, rather than an affliction. I would do anything for him.

"Tell me everything," I pleaded.

Lucky sighed. He launched into the story of his assault. "I left work around 3." Lucky had a job as a busboy at one of the fancier Vegas hotels. "I was still in the alley behind the hotel when I got jumped by a gang. Two guys held my arms while a third searched my pockets. When he found my cash he backed off and the other two let me go. My fight reflex kicked in."

He had no formal training to speak of, but Lucky had been practicing different techniques of martial arts for most of his life. He knew where to hit, when to kick, and how to do the most damage. "I kicked the guy in front of me in the ribs, he went down. I jabbed the guy to my right in the face. The guy who had been on my other side used his body weight to force me back against the wall of the hotel. This dude started hitting me hard in the face. That's where all this bruising came from. I used the wall for leverage and kicked with all my force. When the guy backed up a few steps it created an opening for me to escape. I dodged the guy, sidestepped the one I'd punched and ran quickly to the one who had my money."

"That mugger had recovered from being kicked in the chest. He was back on his feet and counting the wad of cash he had taken from me. I ran straight at the guy. He expected me to punch him so he put his hands up to block. I ducked down, and swept the guys legs out from under him, knocking him on his ass. I grabbed whatever money he dropped and kept running. Now all three were after me."

"I got out of the alley and ran to the front of the hotel. I rushed past the rich hotel guests and slipped into the back of a cab. I didn't know what to do so I had the driver circle around the city for two hours to make sure the muggers weren't following. The cabbie dropped me off a few blocks away and I made my way here."

"Would you like some soup?" was all I could think of to say.

"Yes, please," he responded and stepped into the shower.

While he was showering I picked up the tub of soup and took it down to the lobby of the motel where there was a beat up old microwave. I heated the soup and returned to the room just as Lucky was toweling off. There were cuts and abrasions all over him. I said nothing.

Lucky gobbled down his soup and then crashed out on the bed. I cuddled up next to him for a bit but was unable to return to sleep. He would tease me if he knew I was worried.

Lucky had this good natured way of making the best of everything. When we first ran away together we slept on the ground, under bridges, you name it. Cutting across a field one morning I slipped and found myself knee deep in mud. As he reached for my hand Lucky smiled and said, "Rich people would pay a lot for this mud bath." Another time we had spent the night at a bus stop to get out of the rain. The early morning bus flew passed and drenched us with a spray of dirty water. When I looked up at him in dismay he said, "Just a flower covered in morning dew," and kissed me on the forehead.

Lucky always knew how to keep my spirits up. Together we crossed the country. I taught him how to read (since English was not his first language) and he taught me, well, everything else. Most importantly, he taught me how to survive on the streets. We would walk for days, sometimes weeks, from little town to little town until we found somewhere big enough to stop for a while. It was always easiest to find jobs under the table in a city, but there was much more likelihood of having a run in with the cops. We weren't criminals; we worked very hard to live honest but we were runaways. I was a ward of the state in New York City and Lucky had illegally come overseas. Neither of us ever wanted to go back.

The first thing we would do when we got to a new city is dye our hair. Lucky's hair was naturally black (a color I never even got to see except at the roots.) He would always pour a big bottle of bleach over his head. Often he'd leave it blonde or he favored a reddish brown that I secretly considered "Lucky's color." My hair was naturally blonde so it really needed to be hidden. We tried to dye it red but it turned into a dazzling orange color that attracted more attention, not less. We settled on a chocolate brown that Lucky said was "yummy."

Besides finding work, hiding from cops and trying to stay safe, our lives were pretty free. We walked from town to town so we saw a lot of the USA. Everywhere we went we met people. We never told our real names or where we had come from, but other than that we were honest. Our lives were rich and full and we were happy. All we needed were some aliases and some good fake IDs and we could start living a normal existence. We had been chasing a group known for their excellent forgery for months. We located them in Chicago, followed them to San Francisco and eventually found them here in Las Vegas. Now all we needed was the $6,000 cash they demanded for the IDs. Lucky had been doing odd jobs until he found work as a busboy. The first few weeks we were here I had gone to restaurants at closing time hoping to get some leftovers. While I was waiting out back I would always tend the alley, taking out the trash, anything I could do to thank the restaurant. A place that sold only soup invited me to come back and work for money under the table. I'd been there every night since. They paid me cash and still let me bring home the leftover soup for Lucky.

The fleabag motel we stayed in was frequently robbed so Lucky thought it would be better if we kept our money on us at all times. I walked around with almost a thousand dollars. Lucky carried over three thousand. It was only a matter of time before some criminal got wise.

The past few hours had drifted by and it was time to wake Lucky. He stirred and grumbled groggily. "Maybe you shouldn't go to work today," I offered. I already knew what he would say.

"Are you kidding? This is the best job I've ever had. I'm not going to risk losing it over something stupid like this. Can't we cover the bruise with some makeup?"

I didn't really own any makeup but I volunteered to run to the store to get him what he needed. When I returned I caught him coming out of another hotel room. My stomach tightened and my knees felt weak.

"What were you doing, Luke?" I asked intensely. I never called him "Luke."

"I just stopped by to ask Camino some advice," he said, avoiding eye contact.

"That guy sells drugs and weapons. Which were you buying?" I asked, not sure that I wanted to know the answer.

"Look, you're just going to have to trust me. I don't want to hurt anybody, but more than that I don't want anyone to hurt us."

"It's only money, Lucky. If we lose this we'll make more. Let me hold onto it, all of it. Thugs don't hang around the soup café," I pleaded.

"No way!" Lucky shouted. "That is the last thing I would ever do. My job is to keep you safe. Giving you the money is like putting a target on your chest. It won't be long before they figure out you're my girlfriend, Stephanie. Go to work, come straight home and don't answer the door for anyone." Lucky had never yelled at me before. I thrust the cover-up in his hands and ran through the parking lot and away from the hotel.

I went to work that night and smiled at everyone but I couldn't get Lucky off my mind. These past two years he had taught me everything, showed me infinite patience and kept me safe. I felt bad for not trusting him.

When work was over I got a nice tub of steaming hot soup to bring home to Lucky. I went straight home just like he told me. When I got to the parking lot I could see the lights on in our motel room. He must have decided not to go to work after all! I was so excited I ran to our room and threw open the door.

What I saw shocked me to my core - the place had been ransacked! The bed had been torn apart, lamps pushed to the floor and nightstands and chairs knocked down. There were three men in the room searching through the rubble. One stood up and addressed me. It was Camino, that scumbag arms dealer.

"Where's Luke?" he demanded.

I didn't answer. I was trembling in fright. My fear was far more dangerous than the men tearing our motel room apart. I mentioned my body overproduced electricity, but I didn't share the details of my unending struggle with it. The power itself was hard to keep in check from moment to moment but when my emotions were out of control, my power too became uncontrollable. I was scared and I could feel the unmanageable electricity rising inside of me.

The men looked up from destroying my property and were now on either side of me. A short, sweaty guy lunged for me. I turned to run but he grabbed me by the shirt and pulled me further inside as the other guy closed the door.

I knew I had to think quickly. I handed the steaming hot soup to the sweaty guy. He reflexively took it from me. I spun around to the other guy and kicked him hard between the legs. He bent forward in pain and I caught his chin with a swift strike of my palm, knocking him down. The sweaty guy now dropped the soup and let it cascade all over the floor. He grabbed me by the arm. I gathered as much static electricity as I could muster and shocked him. His face twisted in pain and his whole body trembled as if he'd been struck with a taser. He shook a bit and then collapsed to the floor.

I wasn't going to give the third guy a chance to attack me. I opened the door and ran as fast as I could. I didn't know where I was running, I just kept going. The last guy, Camino, gave chase for half a block and then stopped and went back home. I was relived he had given up.

Sometimes I can be so stupid.

I wandered around the city for an hour or so trying to figure out what to do. I knew I didn't want Lucky to go back to that ransacked motel room so I decided to make my way over to his workplace.

I walked into the luxury hotel through the front door. The sweeping marble entranceway and glittering lights were breathtaking. I felt

12

exhilarated as I made my way to the ballroom where Lucky worked. There was no one standing at the door so I slipped in and hid in the corner. I saw many elegant couples dancing gracefully across the wooden floor. The tables behind them were cluttered with dishes and the busboys were working rapidly to clear them. I made my way to the kitchen door and stood against the wall waiting for Lucky to go by.

"What are you doing here?" Lucky hissed when he saw me. "I told you to go straight home."

"I needed to talk to you," I pleaded. "I wouldn't come here unless it was important."

"Go around to the back. There's a door that says 'Employees Only.' Wait there, I'll be out in 5 minutes." Lucky instructed. He turned away without saying goodbye.

I made my way to the back of the hotel and found myself in a dark alley. This must be where Lucky was attacked last night. I felt a chill wind down my spine. There were bodies hidden in the shadows. I plodded forward, desperate to reach the back door.

I heard whispers and grew more uneasy with each step. I slowed my pace and turned around to run.

"Grab her!" I heard from a low, scratchy voice and then suddenly the shadows were alive. Men jumped in front of me and behind me. They were all grabbing and pushing. I charged up and released as much electricity as I could. It knocked a few thugs back, but two seemed to be holding me tight. They were the guys I had faced in my motel room and both were wearing bright rubber gloves meant for dishwashing. They looked ridiculous but the gloves were very effective, my static charge did nothing.

The back door opened and Lucky stepped out. Immediately half a dozen guys rushed him. Lucky was forced hard into the cement wall; I saw blood begin to trickle down his face. Guys seemed to rush him from everywhere, hitting from the back and the sides. I tried to break away from the two holding me but I was frantic and unfocused and they seemed to have learned my moves from our previous battle. They pulled my arms behind me and pushed me face down to the floor.

I looked up to find Lucky and I noticed something peculiar. Some of the gang members had started fighting each other. It was dark and loud and I couldn't see much from the ground. I managed to twist away from one of the guys and pull myself up to my knees.

Gun shots!! It was impossible to tell where they were coming from in but suddenly the gang members were all racing out of the alley. In the panic I was getting kicked and pushed and battered. In the midst of the fray it seemed to get very quiet. All I could hear was a ringing in my ears. I felt warm and tired all of a sudden. I thought if I could just lie down and rest for a moment I would feel much better, and I closed my eyes.

The next time I opened them, I was halfway around the world. I had come back to consciousness a few times, all characterized by confusion and pain. When I finally awoke, I was in my own bed. In my own bed? I sat up in a flash. I was back in the tiny closet in the orphanage where I grew up in New York City. How is that even possible; just yesterday I was in Las Vegas with Lucky. I stood up and pain shot through my right side. I lifted my shirt and saw a neat bandage on my left side about 6 inches above my hip and 2 inches in. I pried the bandage open. "Oh my god,' I said aloud. "I think I got shot." I dropped back on the bed trying to figure things out.

I thought it had been a dream, a bunch of person sized blurs hovering around me. They must have fingerprinted me in the hospital and called someone from the New York state department to bring me back here. I desperately longed to see Lucky again. Then it really sank in where I was. "Will I ever see sky again?"

Chapter 1

Two Years Ago

Stan was nervous. He was fidgeting and sweating more than usual and he was a pretty fidgety guy. There seemed to be some urgency as he led me away from the orphanage and straight to the game shop instead of the usual route to the alley with the dirty mattress.

We came upon two tall buildings before we hit the game shop. Stan stopped in the space between them and backed me up against a chain fence. He was staring down at me through that mop of brown hair with those harsh grey eyes.

"I need your gaming deck," he told me and started rifling through my pockets.

Stan was 15, a year older than me, and had been tried as a juvenile for a series of petty thefts. He was assigned community service and twice a week was my court ordered companion. For the first few weeks we said very little to each other but then Stan revealed he was obsessed with a trading card game and taught me how to play.

The game needs two opponents. Each person has a deck of cards. On each card is a picture of a person, a weapon or a magic spell. You must lay out the cards to simulate a war. You try to destroy the other person's army and hit points. The person with the best strategies and the best cards wins the game. Turns out I was a pretty good strategist.

Even though I only had Stan's leftover cards to create a playing deck with, I built a championship deck in no time.

I found my deck wrapped in an old cloth to protect the cards. Stan snatched it from me and as the cloth fluttered to the ground he started tearing through the cards. "Whoa, whoa" I waved my arms frantically, "what are you doing?"

"Well the Regional tournament finals are this weekend," he said, out of breath. "And we had to register our decks, not our names."

"Right." I already knew this.

"Well, my deck didn't qualify." he told me. It was a manly way of saying he lost.

"Oh Stan." I felt sorry for him. "All champions have their setbacks. Don't worry Stan, I'll avenge you! I'll win for both of us!"

"Are you kidding?" Stan asked incredulously. "You've been playing this game for what, a few months? I've been doing this for years! You wouldn't even be here if it wasn't for me." What was he thinking? Was he going to take my deck to compete with?

"True Stan, that is so true – I owe everything to you. I really appreciate everything you've done for me," I grabbed wildly for my deck. "But I've worked hard too and this is my big chance. You know that." Didn't he realize this was my one chance to spend an entire day outside the orphanage? "I know how much this means to you Stan but I need to stand on my own, for once."

Stan reached out and backhanded me right across the face. I sprawled back against the chain link fence and slid down to my knees. My nose was bloody and tears sprung to my eyes then rolled down my cheeks. Stan took off for the game shop.

As Stan pulled the door open, several guys poured out the front to smoke cigarettes. I could see them from where I was, sunken to the concrete. I didn't want them to notice me, so I stopped my crying and tried to make my breathing as silent as possible.

No luck, one of them was coming over. "Hey?" he reached out softly. "Hey, are you alright?"

I turned completely away from him. "Here," he said and reached over my shoulder to pass me a cloth. It was the one I had held my precious cards in. I took it from his hand. I wiped away the tears first and then blotted at my swollen nose.

"The bleeding will stop faster if you tilt your head back," the stranger told me. "Believe me, I've had plenty of bloody noses." I wasn't sure what he was telling me to do so I held still, hoping he would just back off. He didn't. He came around and hovered in front of me. I kept my head down and didn't make eye contact. "Turn your body so that your back is against the fence," he told me. I obeyed and scooted around. "Now tilt your head back." I wasn't sure what he meant. "Lift your chin up," he told me and reached out to touch under my chin and guide it in the right direction.

The second his fingertips made contact with my skin there was a static explosion! The force jammed my head back hard into the fence and the guy was blown back several feet. His hand definitely took some trauma. When I looked up at him, he was cradling the hurt hand in his good hand. He was staring down at it incredulously. I was terrified that he might really be hurt.

"Whoa," he said, his voice a little shaky. "You ok?" he asked me. I was too terrified to answer. How badly had I hurt him? I should just get up and run all the way home.

"Now I've heard about sparks flying between two people, but I never realized they meant that literally," he said with a huge smile on his face. "I guess we were made for each other!"

I wasn't sure what he was talking about and I was certainly thrown by the smile. Every person I had ever shocked was furious or doubled over in pain. "You're ok?" I asked with surprise and doubt.

"Yeah, sure," he said. "It was just a static shock. I'm more worried about you. Has your nose stopped bleeding?" He took the cloth from my hand and folded it around to hand me a clean edge. "You don't have to tilt your head back but I assure you it helps."

Who was this guy and why was he so nice to me? I'm sure he wanted something. I didn't want him to try touching me again so I put my head in the position I thought he wanted. He seemed satisfied with that.

"So how did this happen?" he asked, looking critically at my nose before squatting down next to me.

"Oh, you know." I had no idea what to tell him.

"Look, I'm not from around here," he told me. "But I have a feeling it had something to do with a bushy-haired emo boy who busted past me in the hallway." My shoulders slunk. "Is he your boyfriend?" I shrugged. I really didn't know.

"Has he hit you before?"

"No, but..." I betrayed myself.

"But what?" he asked.

"There have been times..." I trailed off.

"As bad as this?" He gestured to my nose.

"Worse," I said, "but in places you can't see." I wrapped my arms around my stomach.

We fell silent. After what seemed like ages, the guy took out a cigarette and lit it. He took a long drag, held it a moment and then a long exhale. I tilted my head back to normal and removed the cloth. My nose had stopped bleeding. He offered me his cigarette. It smelled very good, not like any other cigarette I had been around. My curiosity was piqued.

The guy seemed to read my mind. "You've never smoked before, have you?" I shook my head shyly. He laughed. "Oh, the first time is the best!"

The stranger became very animated. He started explaining how to inhale but that there were many different muscle groups in the body so that you could continue to inhale six or seven times to really breathe it in. "This is more important with pot than it is with cigarettes."

"Pot?" I questioned. I didn't know a lot of slang.

"Yeah, you know, like marijuana," he replied.

"Oh, you mean drugs." I remembered a radio commercial that had been on when I was a child. The knowledgeable sounding voice would tell us "If you take drugs, you'll be living on the street." Maybe no one had told this guy. I would educate him. "Drugs are bad. If you take drugs..." The words caught in my throat.

"I'll be what?" he smiled. "Living on the street? Ha ha, I remember that old commercial," he grinned.

I took a moment to look at him. Wow. He was the most attractive guy I'd ever seen. He was near my age, but a few years older, I thought. His hair was kinda spiky and coming off his head in all directions. The hair was dyed a reddish brown but it had been dyed some time ago and you could see the black roots at the base. Both his hair and his skin were scorched by the sun. He had big, honey brown eyes that had a laughter of their own. I looked down at his clothes. He must have been wearing 7 different shirts in different colors, one on top of the other.

"You do live on the street, don't you?" I asked.

"Yes, Princess, I do."

I didn't know what to say. I didn't know anything about homeless people. I could tell he was waiting to hear what I would say next, waiting for rejection. I knew that feeling, the waiting. For me it was knowing that no one wants a lifetime full of electric shocks. Maybe his life had been full of rejections too?

I boldly reached out and took the cigarette from his lips and puffed on it.

"So..." I started. Our heads turned and our eyes met. We looked at each other hard. Something happened, something unspoken passed between us. Here, sitting on the sidewalk in front of a chain link fence, nursing my swollen nose, looking into these eyes. I felt right, I felt like I belonged.

"What's your name?" I asked.

We held our gaze solid for a few seconds more and then he burst into a huge smile.

"What's my name?" he asked. "You sure you want to know?"

"Try me," I dared.

He stole back the cigarette I was smoking and took a long drag. "My name is Luke Clove. It's a name I made up. I have a couple others that I use but that is mostly what I call myself. I got the name Clove on my trip from Japan to America. On the boat, there were all kinds of people. We were at sea for over a month, so I got to meet a good many of them. There were some guys from India and every night they would smoke these hand rolled cigarettes made from an herb called 'clove.' I was hypnotized by the smell. After a couple days of my poking around, the guys invited me to smoke with them. I didn't know a word of their language and they didn't know a word of mine, but we sat there, night after night, smoking these cloves. I don't know how it worked, but somehow we were communicating. We were ascending, reaching a new level of understanding that didn't require words. It was almost ecstatic. I made up the name "Clove" so that every time I introduce myself it would remind me of that feeling."

Wow, who was this guy? He was thoughtful, intelligent and a total hottie. This was the best night of my life!

"Was Luke your real name or did you make that up too?" I asked, forgetting myself and getting absorbed by this stranger.

"Uh, yeah," he stammered. "Well the lead singer of my favorite band Stroke 9 is Luke Esterkyn so that's where I got the idea, plus Americans love..." He covered his face and breathed deep and loudly.

"Luke, I am your father!" Luke said in his best Darth Vader voice.

I laughed and clapped a little. "That's perfect! It's a perfect American name," I told him in support. "So are you Japanese, then?"

"Half Japanese. My father was an American soldier. I came here to find him but...I only found disappointment," Luke's face clouded over with unhappiness. "I haven't talked to either of my parents in years and I don't intend to. I've started over. I'm Luke Clove now. I didn't exist until I first set foot on US soil."

"So what's your real name?"

"Luke is my real name."

"No, the name you were born with."

"Maybe that is the name I was born with."

"Just tell me your real name already!" I shouted in frustration.

"Oh no!" He laughed. "I'll never tell! Never. They will bury me as Luke Clove!" he claimed defiantly, looking me right in the eye. I giggled. "Whoa, I think I kinda saw like a really small smile going on there," Luke said, moving closer to me.

"Please don't get any closer," I begged him.

"I'm just being friendly," he tried. I looked defeated. "Ok, ok. I'll back off," he said as he literally backed off. "Now it's your turn pretty girl. What's your name?"

Did he just say I was pretty? Stan had never said anything like that. Maybe Luke was just being nice. "Well my name is made up too, only I didn't make it up. When I was surrendered at the hospital they didn't have a name for me. I wouldn't stop crying so a volunteer named Stephen took me for a walk in the park. By the time I returned they had started calling me 'Stephanie Park.'" I relayed the embarrassing story.

"Ok, turn this story back to page one, Princess. You were abandoned as a baby?" his eyes held genuine concern. "Do you even know who your parents are?"

I was so used to this story; I had long ago hardened my heart. In fact it was just a story to me. "I don't know anything about my mother." I replied. "My father knows who I am but I've never actually met him, or if I did I don't know it."

"So you grew up on the street?" he asked, slowly and gently.

"No, no way. In fact I've barely even been outdoors. I grew up at an orphanage."

"That doesn't let you outdoors?" he questioned with traces of sarcasm.

Suddenly I halted. What was I doing here? This guy had been kind to me. Did I really want to embarrass myself and frighten him with the truth about me? I started tracing patterns on the concrete with my fingertips. Luke crushed out his cigarette.

"Look," he said jumping up. "After I walk you home I'm going back to the game shop and I'm going to beat the crap out of your boyfriend."

"No!" I shouted, jumping up myself.

"Don't play this abused girlfriend card. He's bigger than you, he's stronger than you and long after he's killed you, he'll be beating other girls," said Luke in a huff.

"He has a lot of friends," I said, trying to scare him off.

"Doesn't matter," he said, lighting another cigarette. "After Saturday I'm gone, and I'm never coming back to New York."

Gone! Forever? "You don't live here?" I asked. It never occurred to me he might not live here. I'd never met anyone who didn't live here.

"Nope, just passing through," he told me.

I felt crushed. Soon I would have to be back at the orphanage and this amazing stranger would be gone from my life forever. I thought for a moment. "You're here for the tournament?"

"That's right, Peaches."

"So what do you do, wander from town to town competing in tournaments?"

"That's exactly what I do," he said. "Or try. Sometimes I can't get to a town in time for the matches. In that case I'll go in after and challenge some of the winners to play for money. Usually they're all hyped up from winning and it's an easy sweep. If I can't find any gamers or the towns too small I'll do odd jobs or whatever I can to survive."

Wow. Luke was really out there on his own, surviving. "How long have you been on the streets?"

"About 4 years now."

"4 years! You were still a child!"

He laughed "Yeah, pretty much. I had ambition and I had nowhere to go so I started wandering. I've met a lot of amazing people, had some crazy adventures, done things I never could have done otherwise. I don't regret a second of it."

God, he was so brave! He seemed so powerful, so in control of his own destiny. Up until tonight I had only known the guys at the shop and they were all just spoiled gamers. This guy was different in every way. This guy was amazing.

He chatted on about some of his adventures and I took it all in. His brown eyes sparkled as he talked and I was hypnotized. He leaned in during a dramatic moment in his story and an enormous static charge jumped from my arm to his. The blast definitely knocked him off his balance, but he said he wasn't hurt. He started laughing and said that we had gotten to the "shocking" part of the story. I loved the way he made little jokes about my static discharges. Other people had freaked out or just ignored them all together, but Luke, Luke noticed, acknowledged them and then continued. He was recognizing the taboo part of me. No one had ever been so accepting.

"So let me walk you home," he brought the subject up again.

"Believe me there is nothing I want more, but it has to be Stan. He's the only one who can come get me, he's the only one who can bring me back."

"So what if a different guy shows up to get you?"

"No, they won't let me go. Stan had to be fingerprinted and he went through like a training class and such. He's the only one that can come and get me."

"Do you live in an orphanage or a prison?"

I decided to take the plunge. I would tell him the truth. "The truth is...it's kind of both."

"What?" he cried. I could see he was bewildered by the statement. I prayed to God that he wouldn't run away. "You've got to be kidding me!"

I swallowed hard. "You know the little static shocks I've been giving you? Well they will keep on coming. I don't know what's wrong with me but I seem to make my own electricity. The orphanage says I'm a danger to myself and others. To protect the other kids they moved my bed into the supply closet. That's where I've lived my whole life, in one tiny room."

"I don't know what to say," Luke told me honestly. "That's pretty hard to believe."

I reached into my pocket and pulled out the cut plastic band that Stan had removed after picking me up. "Do you know what this is?" I questioned, putting it in his hands.

Luke turned the piece of plastic over in his hands for a minute. "I know what this is," he said. "It's a trash bag tie. You can also use them for handcuffs. You can tighten them all you want and they can't come off,

28

am I right?" I nodded. "So these things, and the bloody nose before - these are just games you and your boyfriend play?" What! Oh my God, that couldn't be further than the truth! "I get it," he said and crushed out his cigarette. "I'm out of here." He turned and started walking back to the shop.

"Wait!" I called after him. I started following him when down the road the door to the game shop opened and Stan stumbled out with a few of his friends. Stan noticed that Luke was walking away from me and got his attention. "Hey!" he shouted to Luke. "Were you talkin' to her?"

"A bit," Luke said. I could hear everything from this distance. "She's a real piece of work," he said.

"Tell me about it," Stan started. "Not my problem anymore though. I am sick of that freak. Tonight is it. I'm gonna make her do whatever I want and then I'm gonna dump her on the steps of that crummy orphanage and say 'Sayonara'!" Stan and his friends laughed. "Did she tell you what a freak she is?" Stan asked Luke. "She says the human body produces its own electricity and that her body makes too much. If you don't watch out she'll give you a bunch of electric shocks. Boy did that get annoying fast. I can understand why her parents abandoned her. I mean, I'm happy to get rid of her myself."

"Dude," one of Stan's friends was trying to get his attention. "If this is your last night and all, maybe you could, you know - give us a turn?" Stan's other friends, five in all, seemed really excited about the idea.

Stan was seeing a big opportunity opening up before him. "OK, yeah, I could do that, for a price," Stan schemed. "Say 20 bucks a piece?"

Luke had been silent up until now, but he needed some questions answered. "Ok, you're dumping her tonight, but first you're going to pimp her out to all your friends? How do you know she'll do it? Does she do that kind of thing all the time?"

"Well no," Stan admitted. "Up til now it's just been her and me. But she'll do it; she has to do everything I say."

"Is this some kind of game you guys play?" Luke asked in earnest.

"No man, nothing like that," Stan said lighting a cigarette and then leaning forward to light Luke's too. "Ya see at the orphanage they keep her in this closet but it's always locked up so it's practically cage," he began.

"A cage?" Luke asked dubiously.

"No I'm serious; she needs to stay in there so she won't shock anybody."

"That seems a little hard to believe, that they would keep a growing girl in something like that."

"I know, man," Stan continued. "They explained it to me but I really didn't get it until I saw it. It's real small, too. Just enough room for her bed, a couple of shelves of supplies and the plastic tray she uses for a desk. She's got books and papers everywhere, her dumb plastic radio and this stupid guitar she's always trying to play for me. Like every song she knows is from the 70's. I guess that's what kinda sheet music they were throwing out that day," Stan said with a laugh. His companions all laughed along. "Why are you so interested anyway?" Stan stared pointedly at Luke.

"Just never heard anything like it man. It's wild."

"She's wild alright," Stan paused, making sure all the guys were listening. "It took ages for the orphanage to agree to let her leave the house at all. They only let her come to this game shop for 2 hours every Wednesday. She said that before that she hadn't left her closet except to use the shower for the past 8 years. Eight years! Isn't that crazy? So like I'm feeling kinda bad for the girl, right? She's not bad looking. So it's the first time we're out, she's all staring at everything like a mental patient, telling me about how she imagined this thing and that thing when she read about that in books. Books, man! This girl like never even had a TV. So she's just freaking out over everything and people were totally looking at us and that is when I just decided to cut off that stupid plastic trash tie," he said triumphantly.

"So it wasn't for her freedom, it was just so people wouldn't stare?" Luke asked rather sarcastically, but Stan didn't seem to notice.

"Oh yeah, man. She was already getting enough freedom in my opinion."

"You really are a selfless individual," Luke told him.

"I know, right? Anyway, after everything I've done for her, I say she owes me a little something."

"I still don't see how you can just get her to do whatever you want," Luke stated.

Stan was happy to be the center of attention. "Oh, one little word from me and she'll live out the rest of her days and die in that stupid closet. They think she's dangerous, I'll give them dangerous. I could just say she attacked me with her electricity or like that she walked past a window and the stuff inside exploded." Stan had clearly spent some time dreaming up ways to frame an innocent girl. "Are you ready for the best one?"

"Can't wait to hear it," answered Luke.

"There are like a hundred, maybe a thousand homeless people in this city who die every day. They OD, or freeze to death or just get old, whatever. Anyway, all I have to do is find one. Then I bring her back to the orphanage and tell them 'It was horrible! This poor old man just asked us for some change and Stephanie ran up and used her electricity on him and killed him!'" Stan widened his eyes like he was shocked at the brutal crime. "One tale like that and they will lock her up and throw away the key."

Luke was dubious. "When they check out the body they will know he wasn't electrocuted. I mean can she even do that?"

"Trust me, there won't be an investigation. That orphanage is just looking for a reason to get rid of her," Stan smirked.

"You know, that's kinda hot," Luke said, lighting yet another cigarette. "I'd be into checking her out myself."

"Wish I could, buddy, but we only have a little bit of time and I already promised my buds," he said, gesturing to the sleazy group around him who were now all licking their lips and checking me out.

"I think I have something that might change your mind." Luke reached into his pocket and pulled out the small metal tin that held his gaming cards. He pulled one out. It was the first part of a two card combo. The combo was so rare and powerful it almost assured victory for the gamer. The first card was pretty common. You could purchase one for about $25.

"Whatever, dude," Stan said. "My friends offered way more than that."

"I'm not finished," Luke said. "Give her to me tonight and I'll give you this card right now. On Saturday you and I will go to the orphanage and pick her up. Let me use her all day and I will give you this card." Luke dramatically removed the top card to reveal the precious card beneath. It was the second part of the combo. There were less than a dozen of these cards in existence; no one I knew had even seen one up close. This card was easily worth $500. Stan's eyes were wide as saucers. "You're going to give that to me?" he drooled.

"I'm not going to give it," said Luke. "It is payment. No one but me touches the girl tonight and you get her for me on Saturday. Do this and the cards are yours. Fuck it up and there is no deal."

"Oh no, man, you've got a deal, you've got a deal for sure." Stan reacted like he'd won the lottery.

"I'm coming with you to pick her up on Saturday, and then you'll get your card," Luke confirmed.

"Sure man," Stan was quick to agree. "Whatever you say."

"Alright," Luke started. "I'm gonna take the girl now but I'll head back here after and we'll make plans for Saturday," Luke said, handing him the first card.

Stan giggled like a schoolgirl when he looked at the card, no doubt imagining the powerful combo he would soon possess. "Stephanie," he called to me. He shouted pretty loudly, which meant he must have thought I couldn't hear him all this time. "This guy Luke is going to walk you home. I'll be there on Saturday to pick you up for the tournament, so be good until then."

"Can I have my deck back?" I asked barely above a whisper.

"I'm going to hold onto it," Stan told me. He didn't even make eye contact with me. "Luke, my man. The orphanage is four blocks down and six blocks over. If you cut across the alley after the 3rd block there is a stairwell with a nasty old mattress on it. Don't lie down on it, it is covered with vomit and blood and all kinds of things. Protect yourself man - make her lie on it. If there's a homeless guy on it, just give him a dollar to get lost, unless you want him to watch or something. There are a couple hooks sticking out of the wall and you can hang her by her plastic handcuffs if you want. She'll probably start bawling like she does and asking you to stop, but just ignore it. She's inexperienced but I'm sure she'll do whatever you tell her. I know she's really excited about going to the tournament on Saturday." Stan turned to me. "You listen to whatever the fuck this guy tells you and you'll see the light of day on Saturday. Got it?"

"Got it," I nodded. I was now terrified of Stan and Luke. I heard the awful things Stan had to say, but what was Luke planning? It had to be something pretty serious for him to offer up that card. I tried to get a sense but he wouldn't look at me. He walked right past me and gestured for me to take the lead. As we walked away Stan and his friends started to hoot and holler about what a "good time" I would be. I hung my head and trudged on.

Luke followed behind me silently. We arrived at the little alley with the dirty mattress. I stopped at the entrance. Luke pushed past me and walked forward to the mattress. He reached up and grabbed the ladder from the rusty fire escape above and yanked on it, as if testing its integrity. The whole thing shook. He looked down at the scuzzy mattress and kicked it with his worn, dirty boot.

"This is for real, isn't it?" he looked at me. "He puts you down on this and forces you..." his voice trailed off. He started speaking again but this time he wasn't really asking me, more like speaking aloud to himself. "You really are an orphan. Anybody who tries to touch you gets shocked...or worse. You will live in a closet cage forever because you have been stripped of your humanity and therefore all civil rights." He squatted down, wrapped his arms around his knees and hid his face.

"Murmur me me me," were the sounds I heard but the true words I couldn't understand.

We were silent for a moment.

He looked up. "Run away with me."

Run away...does he understand what he's asking? Does he realize I am a freak of nature? I have never had a friend, never belonged to a family, never gone to school. I have lived out my days as a prisoner in a wooden cell even smaller than a true prison cell. I have been ignored, neglected, mistreated. Yet never once did I ever entertain the idea of running away. Here was this boy before me. This kind, attractive, intelligent stranger was asking me to run away. Wait, that's not the whole truth. He was asking me to run away WITH HIM! I was certainly thrown; I thought he had just bought and paid for me with some pricey cards for sexual favors. What was his plan?

He was staring me down. "C'mon, you haven't said anything. What are you thinking?"

"Is it even possible?" I asked.

"You're kidding, right? He looked at me incredulously.

"I ran away from Japan when I was twelve years old. I stowed away on a cargo ship that was dirty and full of dangerous men. Some of whom would be pretty excited to get their hands on a little boy." I shuddered at the thought. He continued. "I had to trade away anything I had that was of value just so I didn't starve to death on the boat. When I arrived in San Diego I had no money, no skills and spoke broken English. I did a lot of physical labor at first like picking crops or landscaping - anything where you didn't need ID. I learned from the other immigrants that there was a shelter where you could sleep at if you were homeless. There were soup kitchens to get food at. I discovered that some restaurants were willing to give you their leftover food if you showed up at the back door when they were closing. I always tried to do something nice for them like take out the trash or sweep the walk."

I could just imagine a tiny 12-year-old Luke dragging enormous garbage bags half a city block to a dumpster. He really wasn't afraid of hard work.

"When I wasn't working I had nowhere to be so I would just wander through the city. I ended up at a game shop one night and watched all the guys play the trading card games. Those games had been big in

Japan so I already knew how to play. It was just a local get together at a game shop for fun, but every month they had a small tournament and 1st prize was $200! I was working from sun up to sun down and I wasn't making $200 in a week. I decided at that moment to become a champion card player."

"Wow, did you become a champion?" I asked excitedly.

"I do alright," Luke said. "I learned quickly that I couldn't do the really high profile matches because I am an illegal alien and I couldn't risk a run in with the cops." That made me sad, the thought that he might be good enough to be a champion but that his life on the run made his dream impossible.

"Listen," he said, his voice taking on a gravely serious tone. "If you leave with me, this is the kind of life you can expect. We will always be dodging the cops. We'll have to move from town to town quickly to avoid notice. You will spend most of your nights sleeping on the side of the road. You will sleep out in the rain and you might have to sleep out in the snow, although that hasn't happened to me yet," he said with a half-smile. "You will be hungry a lot. You will be betrayed by those you thought were your friends and you'll be helped out by the kindness of strangers. Do you understand what I'm saying?" As he was talking I was picturing myself in all the situations he described. Despite the harshness with which he spoke, he also seemed kind of proud of his existence.

"It's not all bad," he told me. "You see a lot of amazing sunsets and sunrises. You'll see trees and fields of unrivaled beauty." He stood up and walked over to me. "And sometimes..." he began. "Sometimes you meet some amazing people." He was looking in my eyes, but I saw him square his shoulders and brace his body. Before I even knew what he was doing, he reached out and grabbed my hand.

The static charge burst like a firecracker between our hands. I was blown back a couple feet but he only backed up a single step. My hand was raw from the static shock and his must have been too. Still he walked back up to me and reached for me again. I pulled away; I didn't want to hurt him anymore. He reached forward gently but firmly and grabbed my hand again. Again there was the tiny glittering explosion between us. This time, however, the force of the blast wasn't quite as powerful - he managed to keep a hold of my hand. I looked up at him, surprised.

"It's just like I thought," he said with a cocky smile. "You probably have a limited amount of electricity. The first blast you gave me tonight was really strong, but the last two have gotten progressively weaker. If we could learn how to get the electricity out of you all day, you'd practically be a normal person by night."

Normal person? Me? Could this be true? I was a danger and a monster and one day might end up a...killer. I looked down and saw his red raw fingers wrapped around mine. I could get used to this.

"You'll just have to train yourself to keep it in control," he said, thinking aloud. "It won't be easy, but it has to be better than living in a box forever."

I was still staring down at his hand holding mine. This offer he made me: "run away with me." This was more than I ever dreamed of. Hours ago I lived in misery and now I felt like a princess from a fairy tale. I looked up from gazing at our joined hands and locked directly with his smoky brown eyes. "We could do this," he told me. "What do you say?"

"I don't want you to get hurt," I said.

"I know," he responded. "You'll train; you'll learn to control your power." Power? He was making me sound like a superhero.

"I don't have any money or anything."

He smiled. "I figured as much."

I wanted to make sure he knew the truth, the real truth of what he was getting into. "I don't really know...anything. I've been in just one room for the past 8 years."

"Look, no one knows anything when they start out. You live, you learn. I just need you to decide before..." his voice trailed off.

"Before what?" I asked nervously.

"There's no going back, once you've decided. That's law. There's no changing your mind."

"Well, tell me this before thing," I insisted.

"Have you decided?"

"I want to go," I said. I had never been more certain of anything in my life.

"Oh good," he said, exaggerating relief. "That's it. It's done. On Saturday we leave New York forever."

"So what was this thing you mentioned before?" It was worrying me.

"Oh. I needed you to decide...before I messed things up."

"Messed things up?" What was he talking about?

"Yeah. You've decided. You've gotta go whether you want to or not."

"I want to, I want to!" I insisted.

"There's something that I've got to know." He tugged my hand and stepped forward and drew me into an explosive kiss. Whether it was the static charge I released or just the connection between us, pleasure shot in every direction through my body.

Luke walked me home and went over the plan again and again. He kissed me once more before I reached the front door. As I turned to leave I prayed to my guardian angel that Luke and I would be together again.

The plan was to pack up whatever clothes I could and any money or things I could sell. To be honest, nothing I had was worth much. I'd never had anything new in my whole life.

The days passed in a blur, I was too nervous to eat or sleep. In a few hours I would be free. Free to do what, go where? I didn't know anything beyond these orphanage walls.

Finally it was time. Stan arrived and met me at the staircase. Over Stan's shoulder I could see Luke standing on the curb. Luke's back was towards me and he was wearing a beat up brown leather jacket and a raggedy, faded black backpack. This really was going exactly as Luke had designed. My heart started pounding in my chest.

I stepped away from the orphanage. The entire movement seemed in slow motion. Color filled my eyes. Everywhere was brilliant with sunshine bouncing off of cars and windows. I had to squint just to see. It was more beautiful then I imagined.

I stepped off the shaded stoop and immersed myself in sunlight. Stan walked right past Luke and hailed a cab. He opened the door and glared at me. I scrambled down the steps and into the cab. I looked over at Luke. He was very nonchalantly walking around the cab and he slid in the front seat next to the driver. There was a plastic partition between us and Luke. I wished I was sitting up there with him. He was talking to the driver but I couldn't make out what they were saying.

After we'd been riding a minute, Stan cleared his throat. "I believe you owe me something," he said to Luke.

Right!" Luke agreed. "I just wanted to tell the driver a shortcut." Stan seemed satisfied with that. "Give me a minute and I'll jump in the back, so pick your bag up off the floor, Stephanie." I did as he instructed. We came to a stop at a light. I was looking out the window filled with more terror and excitement than I'd ever known. The light turned green but the driver didn't move. Suddenly Luke jumped out of the front seat and tore open my door. He grabbed me by the arm and pulled me right out of the car. He slammed the door shut and the cabbie peeled away with a bewildered Stan in the backseat.

"I don't know how smart Stan is so we better run, ok?" he asked. I nodded, bewildered. Luke grabbed a hold of my hand and we started running. He led me to the first subway station he could find.

We raced down the stairs, Luke first, shielding me from the people passing by. I could feel static building up between me and everyone I was passing but the discharges were small, so no explosions. Luke dropped in a token and went through the turnstile. He dropped another token in and turned the turnstile with his hand while guiding me through. He certainly wasn't taking any chances of me having a reaction from contacting with the metal.

The train was pulling away. "Run!" Luke shouted to me and pulled my arm so that I was moving in the same direction as the train. He dropped my hand and jumped from the platform onto the train, wedging his arm between the tightly closing doors. Sensing the pressure, the doors sprung open. Luke reached his hand back out for me. "C'mon!" he yelled. Everything was moving so fast, I wasn't even sure what was going on. Did he want me to jump on the moving train? That's crazy! I've never even seen a train before. I'd kill myself. The train was picking up speed and I was nearing the end of the platform.

"Don't think, just jump," Luke screamed. He was hanging out the door of the train holding on to the doorframe with just his fingertips. "Run towards the train!" he shouted. I was so terrified I couldn't even think. I held my breath, turned and ran right at the train, knowing that whether the train killed me or the orphanage locked me up forever - either way I was already dead.

It seemed like immediately Luke was there, scooping me up. He pulled me inside the door seconds before the platform came to an end. He released the top of the doorframe with his fingers, allowing the train doors to close. Then he swung around and pulled me tightly into my first real hug.

 "I can't believe this worked!" Luke exclaimed.

"Neither can I! You must be a genius!" After what he just pulled off, I truly meant it.

"Genius? No way." He ran a hand through his hair. "I'm just not afraid to take a gamble. If anything, you can call me lucky."

"I will!" I giggled. "From now on you can be America's Luke but you're my Lucky. You won't regret taking me with you, I'll learn fast."

"Well you've already mastered lesson number one: never pass up the opportunity to be rescued by a beautiful stranger."

^ ^ ^ ^

We changed trains a couple times and by the following day we were in Pittsburgh, PA. Lucky figured it was far enough from New York City to give us a head start if the cops gave chase. Also, we were completely out of money. It was time to start living on the road.

Chapter 2

The next two years were filled with adventure. I really learned to love traveling. I was always excited to get to a new town and I never minded doing odd jobs. At night Lucky and I would work on my electricity problem. At first the electricity just built up and released on its own. Slowly and carefully I learned more control until I was able to build it up and release it at will. I would release as much as I could in the morning and then again at night. I started to feel like a normal person.

We both greatly enjoyed the city of Chicago and lived there for several months. We found counterfeiters who could provide us with fake IDs but they skipped town before we could get them the money they demanded. We planned to stay in the Windy City but after a run-in with the mob we decided we'd get back on the road and track down the counterfeiters.

We trailed them to the city of San Francisco where I met someone who changed my life.

Lucky and I were at a gaming shop that was holding a huge tournament. Now the tournament was huge but the gaming shop itself was pretty small. The gamers were wall to wall, stepping over each other and spilling out the front door. I was hanging out front getting to know about the city from the locals. All the while I watched Lucky through the store window as he advanced and advanced again. I had dollar signs in my eyes thinking about the $300 first place or even the $150 second place prize. We both desperately needed new clothes and we had talked about getting a small tent and living right on the beach.

Hours went by and the tournament dragged on into the evening. I had to go to the bathroom for most of the day, but I was waiting until the crowd thinned out inside. I had been slowly gaining control over my electricity but I still never wanted to take chances. After a time a whole group of gamers filed out the door. I didn't wait to see what they were up to, I just hightailed it to the restroom. When I was finished I saw outside that a large truck had pulled up and they were unloading a massive arcade game. I tried to get out of the game shop as soon as I could but it was already too late, the delivery guy was wheeling in the game and the crowd was filing in behind him. As these kids raced past me each one created a friction between us and passed me a little static charge. All these static charges were building and building as I raced for the door. The static built too fast for me to control. Suddenly it started sparking from my hands and feet. I tried to reel it in but it was no use, the static was too much for me. I screamed as it overwhelmed me and released an enormous static explosion. The lights in the store started exploding as well as any other electronics that were plugged in. Lucky leaped over the game table and wrapped me in his jacket. He pushed everyone out of the way and pulled me out the front door. "Can you run?" he asked. I nodded. We raced down the block and around the corner away from the game shop.

"Wait," one gamer yelled following behind us. "I have a car," he said holding up the keys. In his other hand was Lucky's card deck. Those cards meant money to me and Lucky. We decided to follow the guy to his car.

When we got there we both got in the back seat and the stranger started to drive.

"My name's Julian. I saw the explosion, it came from the girl," he told us. Lucky and I said nothing. "I won't tell anyone," he continued. "I go to that game shop all the time. If they ask why you ran off I'll tell them you got into a fight or something and just happened to run off at the same time as the explosion." He looked at me through the rearview mirror. "You're...special, aren't you? I want you to meet someone, my cousin. He's special too. Prepare yourselves though, he kinda lives in a cage."

Lucky and I looked at each other. All color drained from my face. Another kid raised in a prison for being different?

We arrived at a rundown house in San Jose. We had to wait a little while until the stepfather went to work driving a cab. Then we crept around to the back of the house and went in.

Inside the living room was an enormous cage that stretched floor to ceiling. There was a bed and some books, a TV, computer and some video games. The cage was bigger than the closet I had grown up with but worse in a way because it had actual bars. I assumed the inhabitant was going to be some kind of creature. I was amazed when he greeted his cousin Julian with "What's up dude?" He backed into a shadowy corner and pulled a blanket around him when he saw me and Lucky. He turned to his cousin in fury. "You know you're not supposed to bring people over!" he screamed.

"I know, I know but this girl is different," Julian explained. "Remember how you said you wanted to meet someone *different*?"

"Hey, I'm Stephanie." I waved.

"I'm Jage," he said hesitantly. Poor thing, his name even rhymed with "cage."

"I grew up in a place just like this," I said gesturing to the cage.

"Yeah, right." Jage said.

"They said I was a danger to myself and others, even though I never hurt anyone." I told him.

"Hey me too," Jage agreed. "Well I hurt someone once, but it was an accident."

"Why don't we step outside for a cigarette," Lucky said to Julian and the two disappeared.

"So what, you grew up in a cage and then they just let you out?" Jage asked.

"Hardly," I scoffed. "I ran away. I'm kinda on the run, living on the streets right now. That guy I'm with is my boyfriend, he protects me.

"My cousin Julian thinks I should break out of here too. He said we could get an apartment together. I could make money on the internet." Jage sounded hesitant.

"That sounds great, why don't you do it?" I asked.

"That's easy for you to say, you're pretty. Hey what is your mutation anyway?" Jage finally questioned.

"Reach out your finger," I told him. I built up a charge in my hand and pushed it out my index finger and shot it straight to his. The shock wasn't enough to hurt him but definitely enough to sting.

"Man!" Jage shouted. "You're like E.T....on steroids!" the two of us started laughing. "That doesn't seem so bad,"

"Ask your cousin how he found out about me - while I was running for my life after practically blowing up a store. No one got hurt though. I'm not dangerous. Well maybe a little." I smiled. "Ok," I said in a commanding tone. "Your turn."

Jage slowly and hesitantly stepped into the light. I could see his eyes, blue like mine. His hair was light brown, maybe ash blonde on top. It was all ratted up like an 80's hair band but I suspected it just hadn't been brushed in years, if ever. It hadn't been cut either; it rolled down his back and past his waist. His fingernails too were badly groomed, long and sharp. He was wearing shorts so his legs were easy to see.

50

They were enormous muscular legs like tree trunks. Behind him resting on the ground ... was that a tail? It was at least 3 feet long and reached from the small of his back to the floor with a few inches dragging on the ground. It looked to be made of muscle and it was covered with Jage's normal human skin.

"What are you thinking?" he asked timidly.

"Dude. I can't get over your huge, powerful legs. What do you do like 1000 squats a day?" I was truly curious about his amazing legs.

Without warning Jage exploded on me. "Am I supposed to believe for a second that you care about my legs when I have a huge freakin' tail," he thundered.

"Sorry, I didn't know it was my job to gawk at your tail. I mean the tail is cool I guess but it's not the big deal you think it is. Now the legs are far more interesting to me. Lucky and I walk all day long and our legs are solid but they're nothing like yours." I confessed. "How do you get them that way?" Jage was definitely thrown by my lack of interest in his mutation.

"Well my tail has a lot of muscle in it. I can turn myself any which way and I need my legs to keep me stable." With that Jage leaned back and lifted his feet off the ground. The tail acted like a little stool beneath him. I could see the muscles of the legs straining to stabilize Jage. That's how he kept them so strong.

"Show me something else!" I cried with excitement.

Jage tilted himself further back on the tail until his legs were in the air. He was almost lying on his back, it looked like he was in an invisible armchair. Then he pushed his tail forward and kicked in the air with his feet. It was an epic move.

"Oh My God Jage, I bet you could kill somebody with that move!" I told him.

"I sure could," Jage said with pride. "That's why they keep me in this cage. I'm too dangerous. You see when I was a kid I wasn't allowed to leave the house. My mom didn't want anyone to find out about my tail. My cousin Julian would come over and tell me about birthday parties and movies and the shopping mall. I wanted to go too! I developed an anger problem. I would scratch, kick and bite my mother and step-father all the time. One day when I was seven, I got so furious I rolled back on my tail just like I'm doing right now and I kicked my stepfather in the face. He survived but he was in the hospital for almost two weeks. That is when my mom had this cage built and I've been in here ever since."

"They never let you out?" I asked, my heart breaking for the guy. Punished forever for one mistake?

"Nah. I've broken out a few times just for a challenge. Never went further than the backyard though. My mom got smart, now there's an electronic lock so I can't undo it."

"Electronic, that's my area." I followed Jage's gaze to a break in the bars where the door was locked. I took a look at it. It couldn't be any simpler. I knew if I just pulled a little extra juice through it the whole thing would fry. I gave it a try and in less than a minute the lock popped open.

"Come on," I said to Jage opening the door. "Let's go get some air." Jage didn't move. He looked at me hesitantly. "I don't want anyone to see me," he said. I looked around the room and found a large raincoat hanging near the door.

"Put this on" I told him. He cautiously took the raincoat and put it on. You could see a bulge in the back but you couldn't tell what it was. He followed me out the back door to find Lucky and Julian.

Julian jumped off his chair when he saw his cousin outside. "She's got you outside already? Wow this girl means business."

"We wanted to take a short walk. I saw a reservoir only a block from here when we pulled up." I told the guys. "Do you mind?" I asked them both but looked directly at Lucky.

"Do what you gotta do," Lucky said.

Jage however was not so cool about it. "I'm not leaving the backyard," he said obstinately.

"Look Jage, you have the rest of your life to hide in that house if you want but you only have tonight to spend with me. I'm going to the reservoir. I know you're brave enough to come with me, even if you don't want to." I reached out and grabbed his hand. He trudged gradually forward.

Slowly but surely we made it to the reservoir. The night sky was glittering with stars. Jage picked up a few pebbles and tossed them into the water. I walked along the reservoir for a bit and then turned to look at Jage. He looked like a regular guy, just in desperate need of a haircut. "I don't want you to go back to that cage," I confessed. "People like you and me, we have to work harder to blend in with the real world but this is where we belong. I know you're scared that people won't accept you. But even if they don't, even if they make you feel terrible - isn't it better than spending a life sentence in prison? I don't know your mom or step-dad but I do know they're wrong about you. You are different, not dangerous."

"Can I come with you?" he asked. "I mean two freaks, and we're the same age. What if there's no one else on earth like us? We should stay together."

"I would love to have you with us Jage, but Lucky and I are running from the cops. Get that apartment with your cousin. Live like a regular person or hide inside if you want, just choose for yourself. As long as you live free, we'll find each other again someday." I knew the guy wasn't up on the hygiene but I didn't care. I reached out my arms and gave him and very long and sincere hug.

We made our way back to the backyard. There were a dozen cigarette butts on the ground. Lucky only chain smoked when he was nervous. "Julian is going to give us a ride to the bus stop," Lucky told me. "If you're going, I mean." I looked at him quizzically. "Well now that you found someone else like you, I thought you might want to stay." Lucky looked at the ground, terrified I was going to leave him.

"You know, he seems like a nice guy but Lucky's really a jerk." I told Julian and Jage. I watched both of their jaws drop. "Terrible, horrible, no good at all." I think I heard Lucky's little heart break. I gleefully went on. "When a guy's that bad it would just be cruel to unleash him on the women of the world. It's my job to stay with him and protect all those innocent girls." I started laughing. Lucky pounced on me and picked me up.

"I knew you were messing with me," he said as my legs kicked fruitlessly in the air. I squealed with laughter until he put me down.

I gave Jage one final hug. "I can't tell you how great it is to know I'm not the only freak. Your secret's safe with me. I know I was pushy, but I was only trying to help you. I don't want you rue the day you met me."

"I'll rue whatever the fuck I want," Jage snapped, finding his voice for the first time. He tilted his head back and shouted into the night sky. "I can regret the rest of my life, if I want to. It's not about making the right choices, it's about making my own choices."

Chapter 3

The great escape Lucky and I made, traveling the country, meeting Jage; all that was behind me now. I was back in the orphanage I loathed with people who wouldn't touch me. Every day was exactly the same; eating cold food, listening to the laughter on the other side of the door. For the first month I was too depressed even to play my guitar. I tried breaking out of that closet any way possible. I used physical force and then I tried blasting the joints with the highest voltage lightning I could produce. The best it did was to break the little glass window the staff used to peer in at me.

My body healed much quicker than my heart. I was lost without Lucky. I spent hours tracing over the pattern of my shiny new bullet scar. It was shaped like a snowflake or a sunburst and was pretty big, taking up most of my left side.

I'd been back 3 months when I got my first outside visitor. He was a biologist, I think, who introduced himself as Mr. Gerard. His eyes looked vaguely familiar, as though he might have peered at me through the glass before.

"I've read your file and seen your charts. It seems your body produces an excess of electricity," he told me. He was in his 40's, not a bad looking guy. Brown hair parted on the side. His jacket, pants and coat were all brown too. The only thing that wasn't brown were his blue eyes. His clothes looked expensive and he was wearing gloves even though it was spring; a tell-tale sign he was rich. I was immediately uneasy. He was still talking, but I think he could tell I had stopped listening.

"Stephanie, you have an abnormality of sorts. I have been studying irregularities like this for many years. You aren't the only person with one."

"I'm not?" I asked dubiously.

"No, in fact I have been studying odd cases like yours since med school and I have been trying desperately to bring this to light in the media. I've even written two books on the subject but no publisher wants to touch them. I have the accounts of over a dozen kids like you in my journals. So you thought you were the only one, huh?"

I nodded yes as if I had never met Jage. I had no intention of exposing my friend.

"I don't want to beat around the bush, Stephanie. I want you to help me show your natural gifts to the world," he said with a grand flourish of his hands. "Think of all the poor kids growing up in captivity just like you. We need research, we need support groups. We need to recognize this condition. You could help people all over the world."

"What do you want me to do?" I asked with hesitance. I had a feeling whatever it was, I wasn't going to like it.

"I want you to become really famous overnight. Let's get the world's attention, make it impossible for them to ignore us anymore. I've got the goal, but I'm not sure how to pull it off. You play the guitar but becoming a pop star or joining a rock band would take years. The same is true for becoming a professional athlete. We could publish a paper under your name but that wouldn't give you the type of fame I'm looking for. Every idea I've had is either out of reach or would take too long. I want your face on a magazine cover and I want it as soon as possible." Gerard smashed his fist on the wooden door for emphasis. This idea was painful for me to hear. "You've found the wrong girl," I protested. "I'd rather be in the shadows then the spotlight. I don't want to be famous. You said there were other kids in your studies. Ask one of them." I spent my whole life hiding who I was, what I was. Now this guy wanted me to tell the world.

Mr. Gerard didn't seem daunted at all by my negativity. "I'm prepared to do something for you. If you and I can come up with an acceptable plan to make you famous, I'll petition the courts to let you out of this orphanage and have you come live with me. Once you turn eighteen you will be free to do as you please. Thanks to your electricity problem the orphanage has permission to keep you until you're twenty one, and you're too old to be adopted. Consider my offer, it may be your only escape."

In the instant those words were said I knew he was right. My dad was never going to show up. Even if Lucky did come back for me, we'd still be fugitives. Mr. Gerard was my only chance.

After that visit I began to spend my every waking moment thinking of a way to get famous. I had missed my last two years of home schooling while I was on the road so academic and political pursuits were impossible. I didn't know how to get my own reality show or how to make a great viral video (I'd never even touched a computer.) I'd love to get famous saving someone from a burning building but there was no way to predict when something like that was going to happen. I could try to break a world record, but which one? I started spending time standing on my head just in case.

I hadn't heard from Mr. Gerard for more than a month when he finally he came to see me again. I'd thought about nothing else but becoming famous and still didn't have a viable option.

"I've got it," were the first words out of his mouth. I let out a sigh of relief, but as soon as he spoke I realized I sighed too soon.

Mr. Gerard laid out his plan. "I am on the township committee for my hometown of Mayville. We needed to cancel the Miss Mayville pageant this year but we are still able to name a girl Miss Mayville.

"I…influenced the committee to select you. I want you to enter the Miss New York pageant, make it to the final round and tell the world on TV about these irregularities. Tell them that you're special."

"No way! No! I won't do it," I ranted. "A beauty contest? That is far worse than anything I could have imagined. Can't I just stand on my head until I break the world record? "You want me to prance around in high heels and not to trip over my own feet? Waste my time worrying about makeup and bathing suits. My scar is way too big for me to wear a bikini. How is this supposed to be helping people? I won't be in a beauty pageant. I don't know anything about them and I am not beautiful or graceful."

"You'll get sponsors and we will hire trainers and such to help with that. All I'm asking from you is a little patience and courage." Mr. Gerard put his hand on the plastic wall between us. "Let's get you out of here."

It was an offer I couldn't refuse. In just a few hours I was out of the orphanage with all my things. We drove away from the city and through grassy fields to get to Mr. Gerard's house. It was a nice big house, where I would have my own room. Before we went inside I had one more question to ask Mr. Gerard. "Are you my father?"

Mr. Gerard coughed as if he were choking. "This is a temporary guardianship Stephanie, temporary. I'm not adopting you.

"That's not what I'm asking. All my life I couldn't be placed into foster homes because my real dad maintained custody of me. I'm sure they needed his permission to let me leave with you. Unless you are my real dad and could just come for me whenever you wanted."

"Stephanie, I have a daughter. She is quite grown now and has exceeded my every expectation. She is my one true progeny. All the other children in my life have been nothing but experiments," he said in a tone that clearly indicated the end to the conversation.

I was eager to learn about these "experiments" and Mr. Gerard gave me access to all of his files. It was fascinating to see all the different abilities these people possessed. I felt like I was reading through a comic book.

After dinner, the doorbell rang. Thanks to some sort of mix-up, Mr. Gerard's fourteen-year-old nephew Drew was visiting for the week. He entered and immediately planted himself in front of the TV with a big stack of video games. I couldn't get over how much he looked like Mr. G with the same brown hair and blue eyes. I didn't look anything like them, yet still couldn't deny the possibility that Mr. Gerard might be my father.

I spent the next few days trying to make myself useful to Mr. G. I tried making dinner but ended up making a mess. When I tried to clean up the mess, it resulted in a bigger mess. Mr. Gerard asked me instead to entertain Drew. All Drew wanted to do was play video games, so that is what we did all day. When I first left the orphanage I wouldn't dream of being so close to electronics. I had worked hard learning to control my electricity and especially my power surges. Now I felt confident touching a TV or game controller.

Mr. Gerard didn't seem to have any free time and was thankful that I could entertain his nephew. "Are you and your Uncle close?" I asked Drew. Drew shrugged. "He and I both like to be left alone. He never talks to me and that's the way I like it."

In our conversations throughout the week Drew and I realized that we both liked trading card games. I told him how Lucky and I used to play for money. We started searching the internet and discovered that a convention was currently being held in the city. Drew begged his uncle to take us. Not surprisingly, Mr. G didn't have the time. He gave us some money and a map of New York City and dropped us off at the train station.

Drew and I were excited! We bounded off the train when we hit Penn Station and ran off to our convention. Our excitement quickly turned to aggravation as we became lost in the city streets. We asked a passerby for directions that only served to get us more lost.

Even though I had lived in New York all my life, I had never walked around it. I was making my way to the corner, struggling with the giant map. Frustration took over and I crammed the map into Drew's hands. "You figure out where to go," I said. We were standing on the street waiting for the light to change. I looked up to see the person on the curb standing next to me. Looking back at me was a pair of emerald eyes and a giant smile. It was a small boy, no older than 12.

"Wow, you look pretty lost," he laughed, pointing to our map.

"Do I know you from somewhere?" I asked.

"I don't think so," he giggled. "Think that map is big enough?" he asked jokingly.

I looked over and realized Drew was simply lost in the giant map. I blushed. "Well, we are terrible with directions."

Drew finally pulled himself out of the map and looked up at the boy standing on the curb. "Whoa," he started and jumped back. "Dude, we do know you."

"You do?" the boy asked.

"We do?" I questioned simultaneously. I turned to look at the boy. He was now watching me very intently.

"Your brother is Keith Mal - the game designer!" Drew thundered triumphantly.

Oh, man I realize it now. Keith Mal was always in the front of the pictures, but just behind him and a little out of focus was the brown haired cherub standing next to me.

Drew was waving his arms so frantically, he nearly dropped the map! "Oh my god!" he squealed. "You must be Kyan."

"I am," Kyan smiled, clearly delighted at being recognized. The light we were waiting at signaled to cross, but nobody seemed to notice.

"We're here for the gaming con," we told him.

"Is that what the map was for?" We nodded, he laughed. "Well, you're going to wrong way, I was just leaving it. It's right down the street there," he said, pointing to the exact place that we just came from.

"Thanks," I said, my cheeks flushed with embarrassment. I lived in New York almost my entire life and get hopelessly lost, and this little kid finds his way with no problem.

My brain jumped back a second, "How come you're leaving the convention?"

"Oh my brother didn't want to leave the hotel. He's always busy, so I told him I would make an appearance for him. I thought I could go in and talk to a couple gamers but there were hundreds of people lined up at our gaming booth. They were all screaming for Keith, so I got out of there. Now I'm heading back to the hotel to tell my brother all about it."

"Hotel, huh? I take it you don't live here," I said.

"We've been living in Silicon Valley for the past few years so that Keith could develop his games. Now that he's started his own company we're moving here to get things going," Kyan told us.

"Here? Like New York?" Drew asked. "That's so cool."

"Well," Kyan started. "I've only been here about 2 weeks but..." he paused, not sure if he should continue. He took a deep breath. "School sucks, none of the kids like me. Also, they pick on me, because I'm so small for my age. They call me 'kindergartner.'" He looked up with fear and concern in his eyes. "Don't tell my brother!"

As he was opening up to me I could feel his electricity grow intense. Usually I would step away from someone when this happened but being near Ky felt so good, so natural. He seemed so ashamed of being picked on, I wanted to comfort him. Before I even realized what I was doing I stepped up on to the curb and pulled him into my arms. Our energies swirled together like nothing I'd ever felt before. As I hugged him tight our energy seemed to make a whirlwind around us and through us. Now I know my body's electrical field is in overdrive but I'm pretty sure Kyan was just a regular human. Why then this connection? Although it was like a tornado around us, inside was calm. I felt safe, at peace. I looked down and saw the little boy was hugging back with abandon, his little eyes squeezed shut.

"Um, what's going on?" Drew asked. "What's with the hugging?"

I remembered myself and let go of the child. We backed away from each other. Did he feel what I did? No, I'm sure he couldn't have. Kyan looked up at me with those giant green eyes. I wanted to say the right thing. "Those kids...don't listen...they're stupid. I know martial arts!" Wow, I can't believe I got through that sentence, but I hit upon something good.

"Martial arts, like karate?"

"Yes! Exactly!" I replied enthusiastically.

"So you are going to beat up the kids at my school?" Kyan asked.

"Not me, you!" I answered. Wait, that's not what I was trying to say. "I don't mean beat them up, I just mean defend yourself."

"By beating them up," added Drew.

"You're not helping!" I glared at Drew.

By now the traffic light had turned countless times. I figured we should leave before I made a bigger fool of myself.

"Thank you for helping us, we probably would have been lost all day." I turned around and faced the direction of the convention. "It was a really nice to meet you."

"Wait, don't go," Kyan stopped us. "I have some passes you can use to get into the convention; save your money."

Kyan held up the pass he was wearing. "These will also get you to the front of the lines for everything." Drew and I shrugged and started following Kyan to his hotel. He took out his cell phone and called his brother. From the bits of conversation we could hear, it was clear he was going to give us the passes but we would have to wait about an hour. "Um, my brother is in the middle of a meeting…he said we should get some lunch. I know this crazy restaurant that's just down the street; we've got to go there!"

"Drew and I brought peanut butter and jelly. It's probably not as fancy as what you're used to but we brought plenty. Why don't we just find a place to sit."

"Sure," Ky said with a smile. There was a short wall in front of a nearby building and we helped each other onto the ledge. As we sat and munched our sandwiches Drew decided to bring up the one subject I wished to avoid. "Hey," he told Ky, "did you know Stephanie's a beauty queen?" he laughed.

"Oh wow!" Ky started to get excited.

"It's only by default," I told him. I can't believe Drew brought that up! I felt like I should relate the whole story. "Some drunken teenagers crashed their car into the Mayville assembly hall the night before the pageant. The city council held an emergency meeting and decided to cancel the Miss Mayville pageant and just submit one of the girls as the winner in order for Mayville to be represented the statewide "Miss New York" pageant. Mr. Gerard, my guardian, is the head of the city council so he picked me to be Miss Mayville.

"Well, Mr. Gerard probably thought you would have won if the pageant had happened," Kyan said.

"That's the weird thing; I wasn't entered in any pageant. I was still locked up in the orphanage at the time. I didn't know anything until he told me I was already Miss Mayville."

"Let it go Steph, my uncle probably had good reason for what he did," Drew entered.

"Let's just forget the whole thing," I told them.

"You know, you've been ignoring it all week," Drew said, sounding mildly irritated. "You better get it together. You were supposed to find yourself a sponsor and get yourself some real training. I heard you in your room fiddling with the guitar and you don't sound pretty or

67

polished. Also, you dress like me, in hoodies and jeans. You don't know the first thing about picking out a nice dress or walking down a runway. You've got to get moving or you'll be a joke at the competition."

"I already feel like a joke," I said glumly, "and I really don't want to be in any competition." How did Drew observe so much about me? We'd barely spoken all week."

"You know this isn't about you, Stephanie," Drew said, his eyes narrowing and his voice taking up a serious tone. "I know what my uncle wants. You've got to speak for his patients, those who have no voice. You are going to be the first one to reach out, to make a difference."

"I don't think I understand," Kyan stumbled. "Reaching out?"

Was there any easy way to tell this little boy that I was a genetic freak and I was trying to reach out to other freaks like myself?

"Don't even bother, it's just stupid," I told Ky. I wish Drew had never mentioned it." I was trying to end this now but the little boy pressed on.

"What's a sponsor? Can they teach you how to win a pageant?"

"The sponsor is just like a company that gives you money to get lessons or whatever. You go to their events and stuff and let people take pictures with 'Miss Mayville' and then they cross their fingers and pray that I become Miss New York and then I become free advertising for them. I have actually tried writing the proposal but..." I trailed off.

"It's just so embarrassing. I can't even imagine standing in front of the CEO of a company and saying 'Please give me money even though I have no chance of winning this pageant. *Please sir, I need all the help I can get.*'" I said like little orphan Oliver. The boys laughed.

"So don't be like that," Drew said with a plan. "Bring your guitar, be confident, think of your mission. All the other girls in this pageant are in it for themselves but you are in it to change the world. People who don't even know you yet are counting on you – do it for them!" Drew shouted triumphantly; you could practically hear the Battle Hymn of the Republic behind him. "I really think you can do it!" he told me confidently.

"I think you can do it, too!" Kyan chimed in. Suddenly those big green eyes were staring up at me again. "You're pretty and you're nice and I'm sure you could help a lot of people."

Poor kid, he didn't even know what we were talking about but he was enthusiastic anyway. Sitting next to him on the wall was weird. I mean it wasn't romantic, but it was powerful. He had this energy that really just flowed with mine. I'm 17 now and in my travels with all the tournaments and night clubs and concerts and such, I'm sure I've met hundreds, maybe thousands of people. I've had connections before, some physical, some emotional, some mental. This was electrical. I felt the magnetism, the pull. Some electrical force was influencing us to stay near each other. Had it brought us together?

We finished our sandwiches. I definitely didn't want to talk about the pageant anymore (or ever again.) Kyan told us a little more about what he had seen at the convention. We figured enough time had passed and headed to Ky's hotel.

Chapter 4

We arrived at the statuesque building of one of New York's most elite hotels. I was nervous even looking at the building. When you are homeless you learn to fear nice places and fancily dressed people. It is an easy assumption that you don't belong and they don't want you around. Since being in the wrong place at the wrong time can get you arrested, you try not to hang out in places where you clearly don't belong. This was the epitome of places I didn't belong.

There was something else. I didn't mention it to the boys but I had already met Keith Mal. I only met him once and boy, did he leave an impression. It was following one of the trading card tournaments I went to after Lucky helped me escape from the orphanage.

Lucky participated in the tournament and was doing well. The two of us were really excited. First prize was $500 in trading card merchandise and with some luck and Lucky's natural salesmanship we could probably turn that into $1,000, at least! That's nothing to sniff at when you're homeless. It meant food, maybe a bed in a hostel for a few days, maybe a change of clothes and bus tickets to our next destination! Although we made the best of every situation, riding a warm bus always trumps sleeping on the side of the road.

Lucky had made it to the finals, and was backstage preparing. I tried my best encouragement speeches but Lucky was so buzzed he didn't seem to hear. I reached behind my neck and unlatched the subway

71

token necklace Lucky had made for me. I took the necklace and smashed it into his open palm, then covered it with his fingers. "I want to be up there, with you." Lucky paused for a moment looking at the closed fist that held my greatest treasure. He rose from his chair and crushed me into an embrace.

The tournament went well and Lucky made it to the finals. He climbed onstage, behind the giant podium, listening to all the screaming fans and loving every second of it. He played his best, but lost. We gathered up our things and left. We were half a city block away when I felt around my throat. My necklace! I ran all the way back to the arena. When I got there, the trading card companies had already left and now they were setting up some giant screens for video games. I made my way to the podium to find a guy there, not much older than me. He had already positioned a laptop on the podium and looked to be orchestrating the set up. "Excuse me," I interrupted. He turned around and I nearly exploded. He was an amazingly good looking guy, the only one I'd ever met who could stand up against Lucky. He was thinner and taller than Lucky, but still well built. His hair was a medium brown, darker strands strewn throughout. It was long on the top to about his ears, then completely shaved down the rest of his head and neck. It was the sexiest hairstyle I'd ever seen. I was definitely rocked by his good looks and he seemed to appreciate me as well. When we looked at each other I could feel the static building between us.

I paused for a minute, just taking him in. "I think I might have left something at the podium," I said, making eye contact with him. The electricity was so strong between us I could almost see it.

He seemed a moment behind is his response as well. "There was nothing here when I got here, but you can look," he said, stepping away from the podium. As I stepped forward and closer to him, the hairs on the back of my neck were standing up. I think if we had brushed against each other it would have caused an explosion so colossal that it would have taken down all the equipment in this room. I scanned the podium but couldn't find my necklace. I got on my hands and knees and looked everywhere in case it had dropped but it was nowhere to be found. I turned back and Keith Mal was just staring at me. "You didn't see a necklace, did you? It was a NYC subway token on a black cord?"

"What if I did?" he asked.

"Well if you did, could you please tell me where you saw it? It's very important to me."

"How important?" he asked. The electrical field around him was growing more powerful. "I mean what would you be willing to do for it?" Now he was either flirting with me or being a real jerk, and I didn't care for either.

"If somebody got in the way of me and my necklace, I wouldn't want to be that person. Let's just say I have a lot of talents for causing pain." I didn't really use my talents that way, but the statement was true.

"Promises, promises," he mused. Ok, now I was pretty sure he was flirting.

"Well, if you have my necklace could you just give it to me?" I asked in desperation.

"And lose my only bargaining chip? I mean if it wasn't for this necklace you wouldn't even be talking to me, so if I want to keep you around, I better make sure you don't get that necklace," he teased with an amused smile on his lips.

"You're the biggest asshole I've ever met!" I screamed, throwing my hands up. "Just tell me if you've seen the necklace or not."

"I think that's the first time in years anyone has dared insult me," he said still smiling. "You've got guts."

"Yeah, I've got brains too. Enough to know that you don't have my necklace," I said as tears started to fall. "Sorry for wasting your time." I broke into a run for the front door.

That was how we parted two years ago. I was praying he didn't remember me.

Kyan opened the huge hotel suite doors and showed us in. There was a big couch and a big screen TV when you first walked in. On one side it had a kitchenette and a door which must have been a bedroom and opposite that on the other side of the suite was another such door. Next to that was a giant L-shaped desk with several computers on it. Hidden behind the very last computer was a guy. I'm sure that was Keith Mal.

Kyan ran over to the guy. "I want you to meet my friends."

He put down the screen of the laptop in front of him and reached out his hand to Drew. As they shook, he looked up at me. I couldn't tell if he remembered me or not. He didn't bother to greet me but he kept his eyes locked on me.

"The passes are next to the television," he told his brother. Drew and I proceeded to thank him. He just held a hand up to stop us and said, "I wasn't using them anyway." Kyan walked us to the door.

"Listen," Keith told Kyan. "Why don't you go back to the convention with your friends and I'll take you guys to dinner when it's over."

"Oh no," I started. "We couldn't."

"Why?" Keith interrupted us. "Am I too big of an asshole?" Ok, he remembered me.

"You know what," I said, knowing that I was not going to win this one, "dinner sounds great."

Drew and I finally got to the convention with Kyan leading the way. The three of us had a blast! Kyan knew all the game companies and got us t-shirts and toys and even free video games! It was spectacular.

When the convention day was over we met Keith at this awesome restaurant called Jekyll and Hyde's. The place was horror themed. Ky, Drew and I were having a blast scaring each other, although Keith didn't look happy.

"Not having a good time?" I asked him.

"I'm fine," he replied.

"He never smiles anymore," said Ky.

"I have you to smile for me," the big brother told the little brother.

Kyan was sitting next to me in the booth and I grabbed him and started tickling him. I started talking to him like he was a dog a little "Is that what you do?" I asked rhetorically as he screamed from the tickling. "Is that what you do? You smile for two?" I was laughing too, this little boy was awesome!

"Kyan, why don't you show Drew the bathroom door that only opens if you pull the right book?" Keith suggested. The boys scampered off.

"So you've got me alone, isn't that what you wanted?" the big brother asked.

"What?" I said, shocked and a little insulted. "I came to dinner with Kyan."

"Right, right," he said with sarcasm. "Ky already told me why you're really here. You want my company to sponsor something."

"That's not true. Ky put that together himself and it isn't true. I wouldn't even take your help if you were giving it."

76

"I find that hard to believe," Keith drawled.

"I'm looking for a sponsor that can benefit from my mission."

"Mission?" Keith laughed. "I thought this was the Miss New York pageant." I knew this was the first of many people who were going to laugh at me. A beauty contest does seem Neanderthal, but Mr. Gerard didn't really give me a choice. I had to become someone that everyone liked so when they found out the truth about me they would support me, not turn on me. Once the public accepts my oddities, it will open doors for others. That was the hope, anyway. That was why I agreed to this whole crazy thing. "Well, it is a beauty pageant, but that's just a tiny part of it," I tried to explain. Keith was still laughing. Wow, he was turning out to be even more of a jerk than I remembered.

The boys returned from the bathroom. Keith immediately pounced on Drew. "Stephanie won't tell me her mission."

Drew looked surprised and a little irritated. "I don't know what you're talking about," he said.

"I'm just trying to help her," Keith said innocently. "If she wants to sign a sponsor she's going to need to be honest about what she's doing."

"Are you not being honest about something?" Ky lifted up his green eyes questioningly.

"It's not that," I told him. "It's just my secret is very, very dangerous and people could get hurt if I open my mouth."

"So first it's a mission, now it's a secret," leered Keith.

I stood up. I had enough of his crap. "You know what Keith Mal, you're a jerk!"

Keith grabbed me by the wrist and pulled me back into my chair. "You don't want to make a scene do you? That's not the way you treat your new boss."

"New boss?" I questioned. "Wait...so you are going so sponsor me?"

"Maybe," he responded. He was infuriating!

"Just tell me right now are you going to sponsor me or not?" I demanded.

Keith smiled. "What, tell you now and lose my only bargaining chip?"

Something was happening. I'm not sure what but all of a sudden I felt like Keith had all the control and I had none. We finished our dinner in silence. Afterwards Keith hailed a cab and put Drew and me inside.

"Give me your address," he ordered. Drew told him where we were staying. He passed a handful of cash to the driver.

I rolled down the back window and leaned out to give Ky a hug.

"We're friends, right?" he asked, a little scared to hear the answer.

"Best friends!" I told him. Whatever strange bond I was feeling this morning had only grown over the long day.

"Enough," Keith snapped and pulled us apart. I waved goodbye until the cab pulled out of sight. We rode all the way home without saying a word.

When I arrived at Mr. Gerard's house he was already on the phone with Keith Mal. Were the Mal brothers really coming here tomorrow? I was bewildered but excited and that made it hard to sleep.

It was well past noon the next day before I caught sight of them. Mr. Gerard had me reading a book about a farm that was run by the animals who lived there. I was interested, but not enough to stop me from daydreaming about the Mal brothers. Keith was mean but seemed so smart and exciting. Kyan was like the little brother every girl dreams of: sweet, understanding and fun. I climbed the big tree in the front yard and waited for them.

When their cab finally did pull up, I stayed hidden in the tree so they wouldn't know I was waiting for them. As I watched them go inside I wanted to count to 100 and then follow them. I only made it to 27, but I decided that was good enough.

When I entered the house Keith was already speaking with Mr. Gerard. I stepped through the doorway and everyone turned to look at me.

"Here's our girl. Blonde hair, ice blue eyes, perfect muscle tone. She's every culture's idea of beauty," Mr. Gerard said and put an arm around me. It was the first time he'd touched me since I'd been here.

"You've met Mr. Mal and his brother Kyan." Kyan and I smiled and waved frantically to each other.

Keith stepped forward to introduce the last gentleman as his lawyer.

"Let's get straight to business," Mr. Gerard began. "Stephanie, Mr. Mal is interested in becoming your sponsor for the Miss New York Pageant. He's here to hear your platform." Just tell him why you want to be Miss New York."

"Well..." I started hesitantly. I looked at the floor. I didn't have room to be nervous, I needed to nail this. I took a deep breath, planted my feet and let electricity buzz and flow gently from my hands and skin.

I looked up at my audience. The three guys and Drew had pulled chairs in front of me so I felt like this was a real performance. As I said the first few words, I could already feel my blue eyes flashing.

"I was born with a deformity, a mutation in my body. This mutation attacks a series of specific genes, but in unpredictable ways. My mutation causes my body to create and conduct greater amounts of electricity than a normal person. Although I was diagnosed as a child, there was no treatment or even research for my condition. I was placed in a storage closet to make sure that I could not give static shocks to people. This room was floor to ceiling wood with a little plastic window at the top of the door for things to go in or out. I lived in this room from ages 6-14 without ever getting to use a bathroom or a shower by myself. During those 8 years I saw the orphanage care takers and I had several religious visitors. I never saw an animal, plant or even sunlight. No human being, not even the doctor touched me. It was thought, but never proven, that I might be a danger to myself and others." I involuntarily wrapped my arms around myself as I spoke. "At age 14 I began receiving visits from a young man who would eventually facilitate my escape from the orphanage. I ran away and lived on the streets for two years. During that time I was never a danger to myself or others. I did, however, meet another child with a similar deformity. His family's silly, groundless fears that he was dangerous drove them to keep him in a cage his whole life, just like me."

"This genetic mutation I have, I am not saying it is a huge, global problem but it is a problem. We need to acknowledge this situation and begin funding for research and support. We need to help these poor people hiding in shadows. Growing up I had a right to leave my room, I had a right to go to school and I had a right to all the same advantages that any child gets. Let's work together to make sure this never has to happen to anyone else." I had been concentrating so hard to say the right words I hadn't noticed that several tears had formed and streaked down my cheeks.

Ky tumbled out of his chair and ran to hug me. I just held him and cried.

"When was the last time you saw that awful place?" the lawyer asked.

"Oh, about a week ago when Mr. Gerard got me out," I said, wiping my eyes and nodding to the man who had rescued me. This was obviously much sooner than the lawyer or the Mal brothers had guessed. All three seemed to do a double-take.

"So a week ago you were imprisoned?" Keith asked incredulously.

"And still last night you had the nerve to yell at me in a restaurant? If I had called the police you would have been sent straight back there."

"Story of my life," I grumbled.

"I'll take her," he said to Mr. Gerard as if he was buying a piece of furniture. He gestured to Ky and me. "You two go pack her things. She'll be staying with Harlan for a while. Keep yourselves busy, the grownups need to talk business."

Ky and I scampered upstairs. It took me about 5 minutes to pack all my worldly possessions.

"Who is Harlan?" I asked.

"Oh, one of Keith's friends. I think he's like a model or something. I think he's supposed to train you for the pageant."

Oh good, that should be helpful.

"Your speech was really good," Ky told me. He sounded proud but sympathetic too." Did all those bad things really happen to you?"

"Yeah, they did. I was born with an anomaly in my body and it made me a pariah my whole life. No one would touch me."

Ky reached out and grabbed my hand. "I'm not scared," he said, looking up at me as a static snap rocked his little frame.

"That's because you're so brave!" I shouted and tackled him to the ground. We wrestled and tickled and pushed and poked each other and never once did he complain about being shocked. Mr. G was right; kids like me were being punished for no reason.

We went downstairs where the guys seemed to be signing an awful lot of paperwork.

"Please protect her," I heard Mr. G asking Keith Mal. "She really is a simple creature."

When they finished a cab was called and I happily put my bag in the trunk and prepared myself to move in with someone named Harlan. I stood before Mr. Gerard and bowed deeply. "Thank you for EVERYTHING you have done for me, Mr. Gerard. I won't fail you. I will do well in the Miss New York pageant and get my fellow oddities the funding they deserve." Mr. Gerard still didn't touch me, but he seemed very, very proud. I climbed in after the Mal brothers, closed the door to the cab and started the next chapter of my life.

Chapter 5

I didn't say a single word during the cab ride. Keith and his lawyer

talked very loudly about things I didn't understand. Somehow Kyan

was able to take a nap and I just watched him sleep. .

We stopped in front of a large skyscraper. Keith looked down at the

sleeping Ky. I seemed to know what he was thinking.

"Don't wake him," I said. "I can find my way." Wordlessly Keith closed

the door to the cab and they drove away.

I found the name on the mailbox in the lobby and began making my

way to the elevator and up to the apartment on the top floor. I didn't

know if this guy was expecting me, or if he knew I was a freak. Come

to think of it, I didn't know anything about this guy.

My hands were shaking a little as I reached up to knock on the door.

"Come in," answered a masculine voice from inside. I opened the door

to utter darkness. There was a small fireplace gleaming in the corner of

the room.

A presence was distinct. You couldn't see him but you could almost tell

he was sitting in an armchair in front of the fire. I tried to speak but I felt

my throat catch. "Just leave the groceries at the door and take the

money on the table. You'll find I've been more than generous, so

please - no hassle."

I swallowed the lump building in my throat. "It's not the grocer, Mr. Caruthers," I called out to him, my voice wavering. "My name is Stephanie Park. You were hired to train me for the pageant."

Without getting up, Harlan Caruthers craned his neck to get a look at me. "Come closer so I can see you," he said. I hesitantly took a few steps toward him.

"You know things would be much easier to see with the lights on," I muttered.

He bowed his head. "Not very lady-like are you Miss Park?" Oops, I guess he heard me.

"These days I try to stay out of the light. The light exposes too much, you know?" He paused, then said solemnly "In time you'll understand."

I noticed an empty wine bottle next to an empty glass. That explains so much, you know.

Harlan raised his head again and beckoned me closer with his hand. He grabbed me on the shoulder and seemed to position me the way he wanted me to stand. "So now let me look at you." I stepped close enough to the fire and for the first time since I arrived here, I was able to see him too. He had sorrowful gray eyes that looked like light glinting through a piece of cloudy glass. He had neatly trimmed blonde hair. I could see why he was a male model; he was handsome in that very together way, even if he was drunk and sacked out in the dark.

"I don't want to sound negative, but you'll never make the top five in any pageant: your hair is limp, your skin is sallow, and your posture is atrocious. Your figure is nice but you are far too muscular. I'll do what I can but I'm no miracle worker." That was his version of *not* being negative?

"Keith wants you to stay here until he gets a bigger place. You and I will train every day so it will work out well to have you close. Your room is back there." He turned around and pointed behind him.

My eyes had adjusted to the darkness and I could see the apartment. Dear God! It was an absolute pigsty. There were old newspapers and wine bottles on the floor. The countertops had empty Chinese food cartons and plates with food dried on them. Everywhere were sloppy piles of unopened mail. This guy was letting me stay for free, so I was going to clean all this up for him, but I really wasn't going to enjoy it. I followed where he had pointed to a bedroom he had obviously been using for storage. I guessed if I turned the light on I'd be grossed out so I just cleaned off a space big enough for me on the bed and went to sleep.

I woke up the next morning ready to get started learning how to be a beauty queen. Harlan was asleep in the armchair I'd seen him in the night before. I worked on cleaning his place for a few hours until he awoke. When he woke up he screamed "I'm late!" just like the White

Rabbit in Alice in Wonderland and changed his clothes and dashed out of the apartment without saying "goodbye" to me.

I decided to head over to Ky's hotel suite. I knocked on the door and Keith opened it. He looked past me and asked "Where's Harlan?"

"I don't know," I said truthfully. "He took off without telling me."

"Just as well, I need to talk to you anyway." Why did he never make eye contact with me?

Ky came out of his room and ran into my arms for a big hug. It seemed like every hug felt better than the last. Keith sat Ky and me down and addressed us.

"So now that there's 3 of us; this hotel suite isn't going to be big enough. We need a house, something out of the city. Tomorrow you two are going to buy it."

Ky and I looked at each other with shock. "We're going to buy the house?" Kyan asked incredulously. "You're just going to let us pick it?"

"Well," Keith started. "You'll be spending more time there than I will, so I'm sure it matters more to you. Plus it's not like I'll let you pick any house. I already told the realtor what I want and she's limited it to 13 choices. You can pick one of those."

Wow, I can't believe I get to decide where I'm going to live! "I can't wait!" I exclaimed.

"Good. We'll start tomorrow at eight." Keith said.

The next morning I arrived at 7:30. Keith was already sitting at his computer with a huge mug of coffee. "He's sleeping," he told me. I stood in the doorway for a moment looking at Ky's closed door. "You can wake him up," Keith said. I nodded, put down my things and made my way into Kyan's room.

The next thing Keith heard was my bloodcurdling scream followed by an even louder scream from Kyan. He dashed across the hotel suite in horror and raced into the room. He found Ky sitting up in bed and me beating him mercilessly with a pillow.

"That's not funny," Keith started with the lecture. "You only scream like that if you break something, got it?"

"Keith dropped the pillow on the floor and stormed out.

"Awwwwww," I squealed loud enough for Keith to hear me. "Your big brother was worried about you Ky." I reached out for him and gave him a hug that was more like a squeeze. "Oh no, Ky, I'm losing my balance," I said as I purposely dropped my weight on him, bringing us both crashing down on the bed. We both cracked up. It was fun to have a playmate!

The realtor came by and started showing us the houses. Nine houses later we were stuck in the back of the limo with the most uptight real estate lady ever. She yelled at me for standing up on the kitchen counters to check out the cabinets at the first house and she yelled at Ky at the fourth house for starting a fire in one of the fireplaces to make sure it worked. He didn't know you had to open the top and the room filled with smoke. The alarms went off and we ran for the exit. We were all choking but I was also laughing so hard I could barely move. Ky grabbed my leg and pulled me to the door. I used my static to push myself off the ground to make it easier for him. When we got outside I shouted "My hero! You saved my life!" We had to wait for the fire department before we could go to the next house. Ky and I just laid back on the front lawn and watched shapes form in the clouds.

So, back in the limo we had already seen 9 houses. We liked two of them but we were waiting to be "wowed." We entered the next house. Wow.

The hallway floor was marble. Upon entering you were treated to a magnificent curved stairway. It started with a short staircase which brought you into the living room, complete with fireplace. Turn to the left and you were in the kitchen. Floor to ceiling, everything in the kitchen was stainless steel, even the table and chairs. "It's like a hall of mirrors," I said to Ky, which of course made us break out in a host of funny faces in front of the fridge and dishwasher.

The kitchen and living room were the only rooms on this level. The house was a split level and the curved staircase connected the living room to a platform upstairs. At the top of the stairs was an open sun room. The small square window panes went from floor to ceiling, even curving at the top to make a partial roof. On the left side there were

French doors leading out to a beautiful balcony. The balcony was huge, more like a raised patio with a giant round tent on the far end. We went back through the sunroom and there were hallways going off in both directions. We followed the realtor as she showed us the master bedroom. "Perfect for Keith," we both thought. The giant bedroom was gray with white highlights. In the top left hand corner there was a large platform displaying the bed. Now the private bathroom attached to the master bedroom was downright mesmerizing. The artist who created it used those little glass squares that let in all the light, but somehow you can't see through them. Everything was swirls. There was a dark grey tiled floor and all the accents were either metal or glass. The entrance to the bathroom was just an open gap between two giant swirls. One held a glass/metal rack for towels, the other encircled a rack filled with bathroom supplies. When you first entered there was a giant bathtub raised two feet off the ground. It was outlined in blue and green glass squares. Then to the left the spiral concealed a large stall shower. To the right of the tub was a spiral you had to walk almost completely around to find the toilet. It was amazing, there really was no door but still you had complete privacy. Ky and I were in heaven wandering around this bathroom.

"Let's check out our rooms," Ky said. Wow, I paused. This is really happening; we can live in this house, and this can be our home.

Across from the master bedroom was the "second master suite." This one was decidedly different. Whereas the last one had been very modern with cold, hard lines, this room was very cozy. It was a giant mustard yellow room with a big wooden four-poster bed. All the furniture matched the same dark wood. The bathroom was cream colored with red fixtures. There was a separate room for the toilet to ensure privacy. There was an enormous red tub right in the center of the bathroom, a stall shower behind it and some sinks lining the wall. "So," I said, playfully to Ky while I climbed into the tub, "is this where we're going to take our bubble baths?" He followed me into the empty tub and snuggled into my arms. "We're going to have all kinds of adventures here."

"Yes, this will be our home," he said, sounding a little serious for a 12 year old.

"You ok?" I asked.

"Yeah," he said. "I just wish things were different and we were living with my mom and dad."

I sighed. Poor little kid. If anyone deserved a loving family it was definitely him. My heart sank. What could I possibly offer him? "I'll bet things would be way better with a family than having to live with me," I said sadly.

He sat up. "That's not what I meant. I mean I wish we all lived together. That would be perfect. And everyone would be happy and no one would yell or..." a look of fear flashed across his face. "No one's ever gonna hurt you or make you feel scared, I promise." I pulled him back into my arms and hugged him fiercely.

The real estate agent stepped into the room. "Would you like to see the rest of the houses?" She asked.

"No need," Ky said. "We've decided on this one. Do what you've got to do."

Chapter 6

The agent needed to draw up some paperwork, so we headed to the hotel to meet with Keith. He was still in his chair behind the same computer.

The agent tried to sell him on the house while he was signing.

"A charming home," she gushed. "Hot tub and outdoor swimming pool, a complete workout center and only ¼ mile from your own private beachfront. " Wow, Ky and I looked at each other with surprise. I guess there was a lot more to the house than we realized.

As they were finishing up the paperwork there was a knock on the door. I jumped up to answer it. Looking dapper in a very expensive suit was Harlan.

He looked me up and down. "Come with me," he ordered. I didn't even say goodbye to the Mals, I just followed closely behind Harlan.

"I'm taking you to meet two girls. Now they are graceful, elegant, stylish. I want you to watch the way they hold themselves, the way they move, the way they hold a glass - everything. You must get this down and fast. Remember for the pageant you have to be even more graceful and elegant than the rest." He was right; nothing about me was graceful or elegant. I would study those girls, I would become them.

Harlan led me into an extravagant lounge in the hotel lobby. He sat me down at a table with two very sophisticated young ladies. "Stephanie

Park, this is Christine Coulter," he said gesturing to the brunette, "and Eve Eden," he directed towards the redhead. Eve Eden! According to Ky that was Keith's girlfriend. She hadn't been very nice to Ky and I disliked her immediately. I guess my anger flashed across my face. "Ms. Park you must maintain a look of serenity at all times. Feel your face, relax your face. You squish it up like you just ate a lemon," Harlan instructed. I tried to look completely blank.

The brunette, Christine, looked from me to Harlan and then back to me. "Oh no," she said. "You're not teaching her how to become a model, are you?"

"Worse," Eve interrupted. "She wants to be 'Miss New York.'" The two ladies busted into hysterics. I guess Eve knew about me.

"Oh that's rich," Christine said, unable to control herself.

"Ladies, really," said Harlan, trying to calm them down. I just tried to keep my blank mask on my face.

"Do you know what Mal calls her?" Eve asked her eyes wide with excitement. "A tax deduction!"

"So you're going to be Miss New York?" Christine asked me while eyeing my jeans and blue "I Love Ponies" t-shirt. She and Eve were wearing stunning dresses, clearly prepared for a ritzy night ahead.

"I'm going to try to, yes." I was using my body to copy hers exactly, the way her feet were crossed at the ankles, legs sweeping up to her body curved off to one side of the chair. It was an attractive pose and it looked like it hadn't been on purpose, although I knew it was. Christine and Eve babbled on about gossip and nonsense. I spent the next half hour imagining my body was a snake and it was twisting gracefully into one sophisticated pose after another. I was hoping Harlan was watching and approving. He kept looking past me like he was studying the room. I tried to keep my mind clear and not focused on how much I didn't like Eve.

Keith entered the room. He was wearing a very nice shiny blue suit with an alien green collared shirt underneath. He looked amazing and I thought I might have drooled a little. He walked right over to Eve and started kissing her like they were wrestling. My stomach felt ill. Why did I care? I stood up to leave. Harlan stood up too. "Tomorrow we'll work on your presence some more. I liked what you did tonight."

"You weren't even watching," I said glumly. Keith walked over to join the conversation.

"I wasn't watching you," Harlan said. "I was watching you get the attention of every man in this room."

"Really?" I was doubtful but excited.

"To be honest," Harlan started, "It's already changed the way I'm looking at you. You may have a chance, kid." I blushed at Harlan's words. "Now don't let it drop, keep it going out the room and back upstairs. Hang here, I'll pick you up when I get back tonight." I said goodnight to the guys and girls. I thanked them for their time and I ignored their snickers as I floated gracefully out of the lounge up to the top floor.

"You have to help me, Ky," I said as he let me in the suite. "You have to make sure I stay graceful and ladylike all the time. I want to be just like Eve."

"Blechh," Kyan made a vomiting sound. "I don't want you to be anything like Eve. I hate the girls my brother dates."

"I'm sure you don't hate all of them," I said.

"ALL of them!" he corrected. "They all think they're so great and they all talk to me like I'm a baby. I just don't get why someone nice like my brother would go out with girls like that."

"Ky, those are the girls everyone wants," I informed him.

"Well, not me!" he said emphatically.

"Can I get that in writing?" I asked. We both looked at each other and laughed. We had some snacks and then watched TV until Harlan came to get me. The next few days were busy. I didn't see Kyan at all. Harlan had me up early to jog, then yoga for grace, then he would teach me walking and standing and everything I'd need to do. Finally on Friday Ky got me on the phone. "Don't forget, it's our anniversary tomorrow," he said. Wow, had it only been one week? I felt like a lifetime had passed.

"We are going out to dinner and then we are going to see the opera!"
Ky told me. I was silent. "I know it sounds stupid but Keith said you
would like it. Are you happy?" he asked, looking for my approval. He
got it.

"I'm ecstatic!" I told him. The one sucky part was that I needed to buy a
dress. Luckily Harlan didn't trust me on my own and made me send
pictures to his phone of all the dresses. I ended up leaving with 3
dresses for future social occasions.

I was so excited as I got dressed for my big night. Harlan left to pick up
his date and I was meeting him at the Mals' hotel.

I arrived at the Mals' and I knocked on the door. No one answered. The
door was locked with a key card. I mean it's no effort on my part to
break in; just a tiny magnetic charge from my palm and it's open. I
zapped the lock and the door sprung open. I took a few steps inside.
Keith came racing out of his room. Oh My God. He was glistening from
the shower and barely covered by the towel around him. He had a
muscular body for someone who sat behind a computer all day. His
arms were like bands of iron and he had a washboard stomach. His
hair was damp and hanging in his eyes. We looked at each other and
the electricity started shooting off me. It turned on his stereo and TV.
The lights started coming on and off. He was looking hard at me and I
know I looked luscious in my sleeveless, scoop necked gold dress with
a cranberry ribbon tied right below the bust. I had gold glitter eye

shadow and cranberry lip gloss. My heels were a cream color with gold trim. My hair was partially pulled into a very loose, sexy bun; the rest of it falling softly on my shoulders.

Keith and I just stood by his front door and stared at each other. It wasn't chemical between us, it was magnetic. We were slowly drawing closer to each other. I could feel the pull from deep inside my body. Keith and I were inches away from each other now. I tilted my head so our lips could meet. I could feel his breath softly on my face.

Ding-dong. Of course. Of course! The doorbell rang and we quickly pulled away from each other like we'd been stung. I don't know why that almost happened anyway. I guess I'd never really seen a man half dressed except for Lucky and it had been a while. Keith was certainly an attractive guy. He darted back to his room to get dressed and I answered the door. When Keith returned he didn't even say hi to me and he didn't make eye contact. He talked and laughed with Eve and Harlan (and whoever Harlan's date was). I paid my attention to Kyan.

Chapter 7

Nobody really said anything to me or Ky in the limo or at the restaurant so we talked about whether it would be better to live on a different planet or live under the sea. When we arrived at the Metropolitan Opera House my eyes nearly fell out of my head! This place was a palace. The chandeliers, the velvet seats, it was all more luxury than I had ever seen. The usher took our tickets, led us into a personal elevator and then escorted us to our seats. Keith had purchased an entire opera box for us!

The opera was "La Boheme." It was a tragic love story. At first Kyan was having trouble reading the subtitles but I told him just to watch and listen to the music and I would tell him what was going on. At the end, when the heroine died in her lover's arms I wanted to cry. I looked at Ky sitting next to me and I couldn't help but feel grateful for the past week.

When the show ended the Keith and Harlan led us downstairs and out the front doors. There were hundreds of people in fancy dress milling on the front steps.

"There he is," Keith said and pointed at some guy. "He's turned down the alley. Harlan let's go." The guys took off down the alley.

"Good luck," Eve said after them.

"Where are they going?" asked Ky.

"There is an important businessman Keith has been trying to get an appointment with. We found out he has a box at the opera, that's why we came here tonight." Just like Keith, always working an angle.

"It's strange though, this businessman is a really rich guy. I wonder why he turned into that alley," Eve pondered.

"Isn't that how Batman's parents died, they got mugged in an alley after the opera?" I asked.

Eve just turned and looked me in the eye. "You're a freak," she said. She and Harlan's date moved themselves away from me and Ky. I stared glumly at them and wished I was invisible.

There were still plenty of people around but the crowd had started thinning. As Eve and her friend were chatting a man in a tattered trench coat approached them. Both girls looked surprised and then afraid. I followed their eyes. The man had his hand in his pocket, simulating a gun. I gently reached up and beckoned a static-y hand towards his pocket. If there had been any metal his pocket would have lifted towards me. The gun was just a ruse. Eve and her friend slowly passed their purses to the crook. He backed away and then turned to run. To get away he was going to need to pass me and Ky. I squatted down and when he was upon us I stuck my leg out to trip him. It worked! He tumbled to the ground and all of the opera guests gasped and turned to stare. I climbed onto his back, keeping him on the ground with my weight. He tried to pull himself out from under me with

100

his arms but couldn't. He rolled over onto his back, forcing me onto his chest. This was just what I wanted.

"Give back what you stole," I told the mugger.

"I have a gun, I'll shoot you," he said.

"I know you don't have a gun," I told him. "Give back the purses." The mugger didn't move. I leaned forward and slid my knees until they were on either side of his neck slowly choking him.

"Here," he shouted and tossed the purses at me. I slowly moved to get up. A crowd member grabbed my arm to help me up and the mugger got away from me and ran. The opera patrons applauded. I immediately made sure Ky was completely safe.

Keith and Harlan had seen the crowd gather and they had made their way over. Eve was crying and Keith was comforting her. Both Harlan and his date were on cell phones describing very loudly what happened. My sweet Ky was standing, watching the man go.

"He won't come back," I said, putting my hand on his shoulder. "And even if he did, I'd protect you."

We made our way to our limo. From everywhere opera patrons were patting me on the arm and back, telling me what an amazing thing I'd done. I stopped a crime and I helped out Keith's girlfriend. I felt like a million bucks.

As soon as the limo door was closed, Eve turned on me. "You know they're not going to let a gang banger be Miss New York," she huffed.

"I saw you kick that guy. You've been in fights before," she said as if she was unmasking me.

"What you did tonight was dangerous and stupid," Keith yelled at me. "That guy said he had a gun. He was just going to walk away but you had to mess with him. What if he decided to shoot Ky. You just put my brother's life in danger!"

"Didn't I just do something good? I stopped a crime. The only person that was in danger was me. Well, and the thug." I smiled at Ky and he smiled back.

"Stephanie, you need to understand that when you do reckless things like that you put everyone around you in danger," Keith scolded.

"Keith, you have to get rid of her. You can't let her represent your company," Eve started whining.

"Get rid of her?" Ky looked up at me with surprise in his little green eyes.

"Listen to me, Kyan. Now that I've found you I'd fight an army to keep us together." I rubbed his hair reassuringly.

Eve just whimpered. "She probably would fight an army with her bare hands. She's crazy, Keith, and she's just using your poor little brother to get to you."

"Eve, enough." Keith tried to silence her. "I'll handle my own business. Anyway, MalAdjusted has a contract with Stephanie."

"But she doesn't have to live with you," Eve purred. "Let her stay with Harlan. I'll come keep you company at our big new house!"

"It's our house!" Ky yelped and jumped off his seat to wrap his arms around me.

"Look!" Eve screamed. "She's even coming between me and Ky-am!"

Whoa. We all just looked away after that one. Any credibility Eve was trying to build was washed down the drain.

"She just misspoke," Keith piped up. "She knows it's Kyan. It's been a stressful night for all of us so everyone just shut the hell up."

We dropped Eve off first. She argued and begged Keith to stay with her but he said he really needed to take care of Ky and that he would call her in the morning. Harlan and I followed the Mal brothers to their hotel suite. Keith handed me one of his button-down shirts to sleep in then headed straight for his computers.

It was about 1:30 in the morning but I was pretty wired. "We need some snacks," I told the Mals.

"Kitchen's closed downstairs," Keith said. Ky and I groaned. I started poking through the fridge.

"So it looks like just alcohol and a bottle of chocolate syrup," I said, pulling out the latter.

I popped the cap on the syrup, turned the bottle upside down and started drizzling it on my fingers. I place one chocolaty finger in my mouth. "Not bad," I mused. I held my chocolaty hand out to Ky. "Try it."

"Ewww no," Ky said. "I'm not putting your hand in my mouth. That's gross."

I didn't see what was so gross about it. "You're just uptight."

"I am not!" Ky screeched.

"Then eat my dessert," I said, trying to force my hand into his mouth. Of course he got up and ran and I had to chase him around the suite. "Eat your dessert," I said. "It's a Steffy Sundae!" I grabbed him and tried to force his mouth open. "Steffy Sundae, Steffy Sundae!" He broke free and ran towards his brother. I gave chase, but Harlan opened up the front door and I nearly ran into it! I lost my balance and tumbled to the floor.

"Oh good God," Harlan said a reached down to pick me up off the floor.

"Steffy Sundae?" I offered, holding up my syrupy hand. He looked at me coolly then rolled his pale gray eyes.

Keith went into Ky's room to tuck him in bed. "Me too?" I asked carrying in a pillow from the couch. "No," Keith said. "I need to talk to you."

I went back into the main room and sat down on the couch. Harlan was shaking the martini shaker. He poured two glasses full of clear liquid. Did they drink vodka or gin? Keith headed right for the drink and stood there and swallowed the entire thing. Ok, well I guess he's upset about something. He didn't leave me guessing for long.

"What the hell was that tonight?" he said quietly, but with rage. He didn't want Ky to hear I guess. "I can't have you endangering my brother's life!"

"What? That's the last thing I'd ever do. I'd protect Ky with my life."

"Why? You've know him a week. I've no reason to believe you. I think you are reckless and dangerous," he spat. "Ky is already immature for his age. What could have happened tonight would have scarred him for life."

"I was in control the whole time. That guy didn't have a gun."

"So you're a psychic now too?" he thundered.

"No, but I can sense electrical fields. Your brother is safer with me than anyone else because I do have quick reflexes, heightened senses and…"

"And what?" he shouted, getting right in my face. "Tell me why the hell I should trust you? Because right now I am hoping you walk out that door and never come back!" he shouted, pointing at the door. Something took over me. It only seemed to happen when I was pushed to my breaking point. I got up and walked past the TV to the windows behind. I opened up the curtains. The windows stretched from floor to ceiling. "Those windows have alarms on them," Harlan pointed out. I reached up my palm to the alarm, synched my electrical frequency with the alarm and then disarmed it.

"Oh my God," Keith cried. "You're a criminal too!"

"Keith. I am so many things it would blow your mind." I walked into the kitchen and grabbed the aluminum foil. I wrapped it around my feet and ankles like foil boots. I returned to the window. "You want me to prove myself to you, win your trust – come here."

He looked at me like I was diseased. He slowly made his way to the window. I was standing in the open window frame. Below was nothing but a 30 story drop.

"I'm not coming any closer," Keith said.

"Just lean your head out. If you want to trust me, I need a little faith from you."

Keith Mal looked very, very wary, but came closer to the window. "Now poke your head out," I told him. Slowly he leaned his head over the edge. Before he could react I reached up and let my hand land with full force on the back of his neck. I pushed him out! He let out a bloodcurdling scream.

I remember Lucky teaching me about the magnet trains in Japan. With a click, they would come screeching alive. They could move thousands of pounds in seconds in one quick magnetic push. With another click and a rapid magnetic pull they could come to a screeching halt. This was the same principle I used here. I let Keith fall just enough to get in front of me. Then I gave a quick electric charge to my foil boots and sped right past him, catching him under the arms as I went. When we were inches from the pavement I reversed the charge, pushed against gravity and we went springing straight upwards. I swiftly pulled Keith

with me and we rebounded right over the building.

I stopped the charge to my "boots." As we started heading back down

towards the hotel I played with the charge until we gently touched

down on the hotel roof. My arms were still around Keith and I could feel

his heart pounding. I let go of him and took a step back as the two of

us tried to catch our breath. Keith spun around and pulled me into a

fevered kiss. I was surprised and overwhelmed. I had never been

kissed like this before. My entire body was wrapped up in this kiss.

Electricity started to snap, crackle and pop right off of me. My static

field was catching particles of dust in the atmosphere and causing

them to burst into luminous sparks. Oh my God, this was amazing! I

felt Keith break off the kiss and back up. I opened my eyes to look into

his and had just enough time to see his fist heading straight for me as

he knocked me out.

Chapter 8

I woke up on a bed in a dark room. I had a splintering headache. What happened? The last thing I remember was Keith Mal and I...wait, we were kissing. We were kissing each other like crazy. Was I in his room? I was still in his blue and white striped button-down shirt. Maybe he was coming back to seduce me.

I went into his bathroom to collect myself. I snapped on the light and looked in the mirror. Whoa, there's the cause of my headache, the whole left side of my face was completely swollen. Now I remember-- Keith punched me. What the hell was going on tonight?

I left Keith's room and headed into the main room of the suite. Harlan was asleep on one of the couches. Keith was sitting at one of the computers, the sun was rising behind him. He looked like he hadn't slept. "Sit," he said when he saw me. I obeyed. He brought me some ice wrapped in a towel for my swollen face. It's not often that your attacker tends to your wounds.

I had to ask. "Why did you punch me?"

"Because," he said. He was authoritative and I felt it was in my best interest to behave. "You need to understand. You do not put my life, you do not put anyone's life in danger just to prove a point." Oh, snap. He was right. I shouldn't take chances like that.

"I was wrong, I admit it."

"Good. Now I never want to have that conversation again, understood?" he said glaring at me. "I'm your boss and I want you to treat me that way in all aspects of your life."

I shrugged. I had nothing better going on. I respected Keith and he took such good care of Ky, maybe he would take care of me too.

"Am I going to be your girlfriend now?" I asked shyly.

He got up and walked back to his computer.

"No," he said. "I didn't want you to date anyone; that includes me. You need to focus on the pageant, you need to win."

"To win, I just needed to make it into the top 5." I said. Man, that would be hard enough, winning – that was just impossible.

"You need to speak for those who have no voice." Suddenly Keith was sounding shaky. "You need to fight for those who are too afraid to come forward. Who knows, there may be thousands of freaks out there and you will be the person they all look to, they all turn to, to make them feel normal. To make them feel okay with being different." He hesitated, but continued.

"You can make the world a better place, you know. You have this way about you, it's magical. I knew it from the first time I saw you all those years ago."

I got up and walked over to him. "It's just electricity, nothing more."

"No, it's more. You have to believe it's more, I do," he said, sounding incredibly unsure.

109

I sat down next to him and put down my ice, exposing my battered face.

"I'm sorry I hit you so hard," he sounded sincere.

"I'm sorry I pushed you out a window." Wow, that sounded funny when I said it aloud. We both laughed a little.

"So you can fly, huh?" He seemed amused.

"Oh, I wouldn't say that, I can bounce, really. Push and pull my energies."

"I would like to train you. I've been doing a lot of research on the physics behind electricity and I have some ideas."

"The physics behind electricity?" I didn't even know that existed.

"Yeah, physics is kind of my thing. My brain works a little different than most. Do you know anything about quantum mechanics?"

I really wish I had, but I shook my head no.

"Well, there is a quantum physics concept that one thing can possibly exist in multiple places at the same time. My brain kind of works like that. I can see things from several angles at once. That's what makes me such a good game designer."

"So you can think two or three completely different things at the same time? Wow," I said dryly, "sounds like an anomaly." Now it was all coming together. Why he was sponsoring me for the pageant, why he wants me to live with him. He needs to guard his secret by having me expose mine. "And Ky? Is he a genetic freak too?"

110

"I suspect he will be someday but I haven't noticed it yet. My dad was pretty specific that Ky needed to be protected, so I assume he's more than just a regular human."

"Your dad?"

"Another story for another time," he said, clearly ending the subject.

"Keith," I said and put my hand over his. "I want to protect Ky too. I know it has only been a short time, but I love him. He's everything to me."

"I believe you genuinely care for him, but don't get him mixed up into anything questionable, got it? Try thinking before you act," he lectured.

"What about us?" I asked, trying to catch his gaze.

"There is no us. What happened on the roof tonight, forget about it, please." Over his shoulder, the city shone with morning gold. "Get to bed," he instructed. I would do what he told me, but I couldn't forget our wicked chemistry together. I climbed into bed next to little Ky but it was his big brother I was dreaming about.

The next few weeks passed quickly working with Harlan in the morning to get ready for the pageant, guitar and voice lessons in the afternoon and playing mutant guinea pig to Keith every night. They had opened up the New York office for MalAdjusted Games. Keith's office was on the top floor and an emergency exit got us out to the roof where we could work with my "powers" without being noticed by anyone. Keith came up with a million different tests and trials for my electricity. He made up names for everything I could do so that he could command me precisely. He was ruthless, but truthfully I thought we made a good team.

It was finally time to move into the new house!!! Harlan and I were only going to meet a few times a week now, so I thanked him for letting me stay with him, packed up my stuff and headed outside to my waiting car. Keith had hired several drivers so that he could get back and forth from the new house to the new office. The drivers would also be in charge of bringing Kyan and me back and forth to school, which started in just a few days!

The house was fully furnished when I arrived. Some of the things were here when we picked out the house and some of the furnishings were new. "Hello," I yelled out. No answer. Guess I was the first one here. I ran upstairs to unpack my things in my new room. I made a right at the top of the staircase and walked past the couches in the small circular room at the top of the landing the realtor had called a "solarium" because of all the windows. Sooo cool! There were only three bedrooms at this end of the hall, the two master bedrooms and the tiny room, probably for a maid or something. I went to the tiny room, just big enough for a bed and a dresser. It took me less than a minute to unpack, I just had one bag of stuff and the dresses Keith had paid for. The driver brought up my guitar and placed it on my bed. "This place is a palace and you get this little room. Now that's unfair," he said.

"No, I picked this room so I could be close to Ky," and Keith I added silently.

I picked up my guitar and walked out the balcony off of the landing. I sat on one of the lawn chairs and played through some of the songs I knew. "Sounds like you're going to need a new guitar for the pageant." Keith had snuck up behind me.

"I didn't know you were home." Home? It sounded weird coming out of my mouth. The last place I called home was a nasty hotel. "Is Ky with you?"

"Yeah, he ran off straight to his room. Listen. I don't want you in that tiny room. There are plenty of bigger rooms; you don't need to be there. I've gone and had one of the rooms on the other side of the hall refinished for you. It should be done in a few weeks. When it's ready I want you to move over there," he said in his no-nonsense voice. "Now tomorrow you and Ky are picking up your school uniforms at the tailor and then I want you to go to the music shop and get yourself a better guitar."

"Oh, no thanks, Keith, I'm good with my old one," I said. His generosity made me squeamish.

"No, your old one sucks and we have a competition to win; am I right? You're no good to MalAdjusted if you lose." He was right; over the past few weeks I had done some photo shoots for MalAdjusted games. I needed to win to make my face more valuable to Keith. It was all

113

coming down to that. I did want to help the other kids like myself, but I really didn't want to be a beauty queen. I just wanted to make myself valuable. Every night Keith and I practiced together for hours and I could feel the chemistry between us. It's been a long time since I've seen Lucky. Was I still his girl? All I know is that Keith Mal was generous and kind to me. He provided for me, cared about me and worked daily to improve me as a person. I noticed. I noticed everything he did for me. They were like silent "I love yous."

The next day Ky and I did our shopping. We picked out a nice, but not too nice new guitar and went to Central Park where I played the songs I had been practicing for the pageant. "What do you think?" I asked Ky. Kyan scrunched up his little face. "They're good," he told me, "but none of them sound like you." My heart sank. I really needed my personality to come across to the judges. "Why don't you write your own song?" he suggested. With 10 weeks to go before the pageant? I guess even if I play the wrong song really well I won't do any better than if I play the right song really badly. "I'll give it a try," I told him.

That evening Ky and I ordered pizza and sat on the floor of our new living room and tried to write a song. We struggled to combine my funky 70's music style with some solid lyrics to make a hit. We wrote down what we came up with, but really none of it was usable. After a frustrating night I tucked Ky into bed and crossed the hall to my little room. It was only the 2nd night here at the new house and this place was a fortress. I think I heard every little creak. I got into bed and tried to fall asleep.

A short time later I heard Keith arrive home. I jumped out of bed to go greet him, when I heard a high, haughty girl's cackle. Eve. I'd managed to avoid her since the night of the opera. Ky told me she was getting more and more pushy about her relationship with Keith. I couldn't understand how Keith could deny the clear attraction between us and continue his relationship with Eve. What did he see in her?

I heard them pass my door on the way to Keith's bedroom. I flopped back down on my bed and pulled my pillow over my head. Please go to sleep I prayed. They didn't. I could hear their coupling right through the wall. I wanted to scream! I wanted to punch the wall my bedroom shared with Keith's until it shattered into a million pieces.

I grabbed my guitar and stormed out of my room and through the landing to the balcony. At least I couldn't hear them out here. I started banging on my guitar working through my frustration by creating a really angry song. Little by little it started coming together and I realized that anger was a good inspiration. I went back into the house and returned with a notebook and pen and started scribbling everything I was thinking. More than an hour passed and I had cobbled my thoughts together into a coherent song.

"I thought I heard you out here." Oh great, it was Keith. Done banging your stupid girlfriend so soon? "What were you playing? It sounded good."

"Ky thought I should write my own song for the pageant, so I was working on it," I told him. I prayed to God he didn't ask me to play it.

"Play it for me," he commanded.

"It's not even a song yet. I'd rather wait." I started blushing.

"You don't have to be shy in front of me," he said. Did you ever notice the person who tells you not to be shy around them is the exact one you should be shy around? Duh Keith, not only are you my boss, but you are also my secret crush. Was it even a secret? I'm pretty sure everybody knew. Anyway - do the math!

"Look, you're the only one on the planet who knows *my* secret. I've never even told Ky." What secret, that he had a mutation? I didn't even know that was a secret. "I'm just saying you can open up to me." He seemed sincere. God this guy was so hard to read. I didn't think Keith was going to let me off the hook so I just decided, cheeks flushed, to play the song.

I started my song, an up tempo piece called "You'll Remember Me." It started off as an angry list of my good qualities that would disappear when I left, but evolved into a stirring tribute to why I am more memorable than the next girl. I thought with a little work it might be something that could stand out to the judges.

116

Keith just stared me down with those piercing green eyes of his. "Wow; that sounded like a real song. I expected something pretty terrible, but you have some real talent. Play it again." I protested. "C'mon, I'm your boss and I said play it again." He really loved to push this "boss" thing. I ended up playing the song a few more times and Keith seemed to enjoy every one. I went to bed with a smile on my face.

The next morning I awoke to Ky's little face in front of mine. "My brother wants us to come downstairs for breakfast," he told me. I grabbed him by the arm and pulled him down next to me on the bed. Again, I tickled the poor kid.

I threw on running clothes and trotted on down to the table. Everyone was waiting for me, the Mal brothers and Eve. As soon as I sat down Keith started talking. "I have changed my trip to California so that I will be leaving after breakfast this morning. I know that means I'm going to miss your first day of school, and I'm sorry." He sounded genuine. "Eve will be coming with me. She wants to see the original MalAdjusted Games headquarters. Now do you think you can handle things for a few days or should I hire a sitter?"

"I think we can manage to not burn the house down," I said with a smile. I don't care if Keith is going to California with her - he paid all his attention to me last night! "I appreciate your trust in me and will do my best to be worthy of the honor," I said and bowed my head. Eve snickered. My "friend", she didn't even pretend to like me.

117

I went for my morning run. Then Ky and I discovered if you walk far enough through the thick woods that are in the back of our property, you come to the beach! Wow, our own beach! We would have to find a way through those woods that took less than 45 minutes and didn't leave us covered in scratches. Still, we had a beach! We walked back to the house, ate some lunch then crashed out in a nap on the couch. When I woke up I was feeling antsy. I wanted to find a dance floor and let off some steam. Since both Ky and I were underage and couldn't get into clubs, we decided to go to an all-ages rave. We got dressed up in some wild clothes and headed out to New Jersey. We heard about a party with DJ Pauly in a big club on the Jersey shore.

Ky and I had a blast! I taught him how to dance and boy did he pick it up quickly. Girls were all over him and guys were challenging him to dance battles. We had a seriously good time.

Before heading back home we stopped in a diner for a bite. Ky rattled on and on about what a good time he had. Then he got strangely quiet.

"Do you like my brother?" Oh man, I knew this talk was coming.

"Yes, I like your brother very much," I told him.

"Me too," he said. "Not a lot of people like him you know, we're special." He smiled the world's cutest smile.

"Eve likes him," I said, and immediately wished I hadn't.

"Nah, Eve doesn't know him the way we do, it's not the same. He hides himself from her. She's just the girlfriend but we're his family." He was saying such sweet things but they weren't melting my icy heart. A single teardrop fell and landed on my cheek. "You like him, like him don't you?"

There was no point in lying to the boy. "Yes, I really do. I think we are amazing when we're together."

"What about Lucky?" I knew that question would be hard to answer.

"I don't know," I said truthfully, my soft blue eyes brimming with tears. "It has been a long time since I've seen Lucky, what if I never see him again? I still love him...but I love Keith too. I love them both." With that the tears just burst forward and I didn't even try to hold them back. Ky walked around the table and scooted into the booth next to me. He grabbed hold of me tight as I cried. Have you ever noticed that one trigger can make you start crying, but once you start all the other things that are buried inside want you to cry for them too? I cried because Keith refused to notice me, because Lucky had been missing for so long, and then I started really crying as I thought about Ky, this sweet little boy with his arms around me who had no parents to take care of him. I had no parents either.

Ky and I headed home and watched the sunrise from our balcony. We held hands as Ky drifted off to sleep in the chair next me. Thanks to my electro-charged muscles I was strong enough to carry him to bed. I tucked him in, but couldn't bear to leave the room. He said we were a family.

Chapter 9

The next few days passed quickly and soon it was my first day of school! Keith had found us a private academy with grades 6-12 so Kyan and I could attend the same school. Ky held my hand like he promised and we went straight to the assembly hall. From there they assigned us to homerooms. When I arrived at my homeroom everyone's eyes were on me. The glamorous girls waved me over. I was really glad I took time to do my hair and makeup. They asked me about myself and I told them about living with the Mals. I also told them about the Miss New York pageant. They seemed impressed. I was fitting in!

The teacher entered and told us to get our seats. He handed out our school schedules. "Let me see yours," said Lyn, one of the popular girls and snatched it from me. "Oh my God," she said in a very serious tone. Lyn held up my schedule and announced to the class, "She's in almost all freshman classes!"

Everybody gasped and laughed. Freshman classes? My cheeks flushed with shame. I took back my schedule. I had gym class and lunch with the senior class. Somehow I had tested into AP English, a college level class, but for everything else I'd be lumped in with the freshmen. The bell rang and I could hear everyone whispering "dumb blonde."

My morning was pretty rough. The kids adapted a joke of talking extra slowly to me, like I was too dumb to understand.

At lunch Ky dashed over to me; obviously his day was going well. "I've made two friends already, Max and Mac."

"Are they twins?" I joked.

"Huh?" said Ky. "They aren't related. Everyone at school is talking about you."

"Yeah, I figured," I said glumly.

"They all think you're smokin' hot," he said cheerfully.

"But dumb as a doornail," I concluded. Ky shifted his weight from foot to foot and avoided my eyes. "Go have lunch with your friends, tonight we'll go swimming." He smiled and then took off.

I struggled through the rest of the day. I performed well in gym although the girls laughed when I asked the rules to field hockey. I was thinking maybe if I studied hard I could retake the entrance exams. I was advised that if I needed tutoring, there was a girl named Jeannie I should track down. Jeannie had already been accepted to Yale, Princeton and Colgate but decided to finish out her senior year at high school while she made her choice. It turns out she was in my Advanced Placement English class. Jeannie was a pretty girl with long silky brown hair and an ivory completion. She looked really smart in her glasses. She was happy to help me for free but I insisted on paying her. We agreed to meet every day at lunch. Yea! Now I could sit with Jeannie and her friends and not be alone at lunch.

The first few days of school were a nightmare. Jeannie was the only cheery face in my dismal days. After only a week of tutoring, Jeannie told me something wonderful. "You know, you're not stupid."

"I'm not?" I asked in disbelief.

"No, not at all," she said. "Just look. The tests you did the worst on were history, science and math. These classes are all based on cumulative knowledge. Since you've never studied these subjects, you couldn't have passed. Now the reading comprehension and vocabulary are tests that work your mental abilities rather than just your stored knowledge, and you aced them! So here's my idea. We study math, straight math until the PSAT. I bet you'll do fine. After that we'll worry about advancing your other studies, just keep up with your freshman classes for now."

Jeannie was a natural teacher. She really made me feel confident with my studies. Now confidence in other aspects of school was another thing entirely. I couldn't seem to make a single friend on my own. I excelled in gym class but none of the girls would talk to me. All the kids in my freshman classes laughed at me and every guy who talked to me was just looking to get laid. I was way too embarrassed to talk to anyone about the pageant. I finally confided in Jeannie. She thought the whole thing was barbaric and told me she was not going to waste her time tutoring me if I was going to end up as a trophy wife. I promised that I cared about my studies, I told her I was tired of being a dumb blonde. Then Jeannie tried to make *me* feel better. Wow, that was just the kind of person she was.

I showed up for school one morning and Jeannie wasn't there. I sent her a text message and she texted back that she wasn't feeling well and wouldn't be at school. It was going to be a long day.

I got laughed at by my history class because I could only name 11 presidents. I thought about what Jeannie told me about not being stupid and I managed not to cry. I lost it in gym class though. When I got out of the shower my lock was missing and my locker was open. Sure enough my clothes were missing! My anger exploded and static charges started radiating off me. I had to get under control. I grabbed the locker next to me and blasted off the lock. I grabbed the uniform inside and threw it on. Sorry to whomever I stole this from. I grabbed my backpack and ran down the hall and straight out the side door of the school. I kept running and running. I probably ran for miles. When I finally looked up I was in a pretty seedy part of town.

I walked a few more blocks. I was still afire with rage. I also stuck out like a sore thumb in a bad neighborhood with my bright white button-down shirt and plaid skirt. As soon as I realized I was a target it was like my sensors went off. I sized up every person I walked past. I was pretty much begging them to start something with me. I didn't have to wait too long. A tall guy with a lot of muscle who reeked of bourbon came up behind me and draped an arm around me. "You better be careful, Sweetie, it's dangerous down here. You're lucky I came along. What's a sweet thing like you doing in this neighborhood?"

"I was just looking to make a few bucks on some cards, know where I could get some action?" I reverted back to my street smart days.

"A gambler, huh? Yeah, I know a guy." He left his arm on me and guided me a few blocks away and down a normal looking alley. There were a couple guys gambling. I was an ace gambler and took all their money in less than an hour. The guy running the deal wanted his money back. He asked me if I could handle a serious game. He took me to a door in the back of the alley. We went down a slippery flight of stairs into a very dark, damp basement. In the corner was a blue lamp and a few guys beneath it gambling.

These guys were heavily mutated. The first guy was huge, and the one next to him looked like he had horns. The third guy just looked like a regular guy and the fourth guy was in a trench coat but I think his skin was greenish. Since I had been with Mr. Gerard I had known that mutants like these existed, but I had never met any. I knew on sight that I was in way over my head. "I've changed my mind," I told the guy I came with.

"Oh no you don't, missy!" he shouted, getting the attention of everyone in the room. I turned to run up the stairs and out of there. By my third step, the guy who brought me here grabbed my leg and pulled it swiftly

out from under me. I fell straight down, knocking the wind out of me

and hitting my chest and my chin hard on the stairs. My legs were

scratched and scraped and started to bleed.

The guy had a mean hold on my right ankle. I tried a swift, direct kick

from my left foot to his face. Success! My kick loosened his grip on me

and knocked him down. I pushed myself up off of the stairs and began

to run again. The mutants who were in the corner of the room were

now right behind me. I flew up the steps and started running through

the alley. The huge guy and the green guy were on my heels. The

huge guy caught up to me in a flash. He pulled up on my right side and

swung his left arm. The impact turned me and pushed me right into the

brick side of the building. I felt pain everywhere. Blood was flowing

freely from somewhere; the blood drops on my shirt were multiplying. I

started to get scared. The huge guy brought his giant body up behind

me and pushed me harder into the wall. He wrapped each hand

around one of my wrists and held me prisoner. He turned me back to

face the other guys. I was an open target.

The guy with the greenish skin was standing in front of me fumbling

with something in his pocket. He pulled out a black plastic rectangle.

He gave it a squeeze and two metal darts attached to long wires shot

out and attached themselves to my hip. A stun gun! I felt the electricity

start to flow into me. I could feel the big guy holding my wrist getting excited. I guess this is how they got their victims. They were going to get a surprise.

I started absorbing the electricity from the stun gun. I trembled and twitched like it was getting to me. All five guys in the alley came close, circling me like a pack of wolves. I built up an electrical charge in both of my hands. I let my body go limp. The evil crowd gathered around me. The ogre loosened his grip on my wrists to hand me over to his gang. The second my hands were free I started releasing electricity in two huge bombs coming off my palms. I don't know if it was enough to hurt these guys but it was definitely enough to stun them. I squeezed right between the green guy and the huge guy and raced down the alley and back out in the sun. I ran right into the street and hailed a cab. I dropped into the backseat and looked back at the alley. I don't know if the blast had knocked them down, or just startled them. Either way they weren't following me.

I had won more than enough money to take the cab from the city all the way home. I paid the cab driver and hobbled up the front stairs and into the house. My shirt was covered in blood, I would need to stash my clothes first, then clean and dress my wounds. If all went well I could get back to school in time for Tim to pick me and Ky up and no one would ever know anything. I could blame the injuries to my face on gym class or martial arts training. Oh, no need to make up elaborate schemes. Keith was blocking the stairs.

We opened our mouths at the same time. "What the hell happened to you?" he shouted as I asked "What are you doing home?"

He answered first. "I got a call from the school. They said someone saw you leave the grounds. Did this happen to you at school?" he looked very seriously at my injuries.

"Not exactly," I said, avoiding his gaze. I remembered what he had said about staying out of trouble. I wondered if he was going to send me away.

Keith gave me an angry, fierce, furious look. Then he just kinda dropped it. "Let's clean you up and get you some food." With that he slipped his arm under my shoulders and one under my knees and picked me up. Keith carried me up the stairs and into his room. He brought me into his private bathroom and sat me down on the ledge next to the sink. He handed me a robe and turned as I removed my bloody clothes. I was in so much pain I was numb. Keith carefully cleaned and dressed each cut and scratch. He went out into his room and brought back a chair and helped me off the ledge. He leaned me back in the chair and washed all of the blood out of my hair. I had no idea he could be so gentle, so tender and caring. Well, this is the guy who raised Ky, after all.

I started to forget my bad day and my injuries. All I wanted to think about was Keith. He pulled out the blow-dryer and handed me the plug. "Can you charge this?" he asked. A month ago I couldn't have

127

given it a charge without blowing it up, but Keith was teaching me control. The blow-dryer came alive in his hands. "You did it," he said and flashed me a smile. I just about melted! With my hair cleaned and dry and my wounds dressed I thought he would start grilling me about my day, but he didn't even bring it up. Instead he told me he had something he wanted to talk about.

My ankle was still swollen so he carried me out through the solarium and onto the balcony. I guess the balcony was like my special place in the house, where I felt safe. After all those years locked up, the open air represented freedom to me. He set me down under the tent in one of the comfy, cushioned chairs he had recently brought up here. Without a word he turned and left. Just like him.

He returned with a bottle of wine and a pair of glasses. I suddenly got very, very nervous. "Cool down," he snapped immediately.

"How did you know…" I started but he cut me off. How did he know I was nervous?

"You light up like a Christmas tree. Remember we are working on energy control. Take a deep breath and get your energy together." He had this way of talking to me like I couldn't think for myself and I needed him to think for me. Strangely, I found it comforting. It made me feel like what I did mattered to him, like he cared. He poured the wine and handed me a glass.

"Just try to be quiet for a couple minutes. This isn't easy for me to talk about." He sighed. "I can trust you, right? I mean, I let you around my brother, you live under my roof. What I'm about to tell you - you tell no one, got it? Especially not my brother." He ran a hand through his hair and looked intently at me. What kind of secret was he keeping from his brother?

"You have done so much for me. I'll keep your secret. Even from Ky."

"I never want Ky to know," he said with intensity. I nodded. He downed the entire glass of wine then grabbed mine out of my hands.

"Kyan is my half-brother, we had different mothers." He looked ashamed. I was glad he took the glass from my hand, I would have dropped it. I was glad he asked me to keep quiet; I had no idea what to say.

"My childhood was awesome. I grew up in California, in a modest house in a nothing little town. My parents were amazing. My mom Eleanor was sweet and caring; she always made me feel loved and safe. My dad Kaden was my total hero; he never talked to me like I was a child. My mom used to say "he'll never understand you," but I did, I mean not every word that he said but I really got it. He really kicked off my love of learning, my love of art. He was just an amazing man, he was so happy to be alive. There was a light around him. Just like you."

Like me? I blushed.

Keith struggled to say the next words. "One day when I was seven years old, my father disappeared."

I gasped. "Just disappeared?"

"Yeah," he said. "He didn't take anything, no clothes, no money. He didn't even take the car. We thought he had been kidnapped or murdered. Life became one giant nightmare. It turns out my dad had been living off the grid. He had no social security number, no fingerprints on file. For all intents and purposes he didn't exist."

"I know a little bit about living off the grid. It doesn't mean your dad was a bad person." I tried to be comforting.

"I don't think my dad was a bad person. He may have lost his mind…Let me finish. My dad had been missing for about three weeks when he just showed up at home. My mom had picked me up from karate and we pulled up to the house and he was sitting out front. I think that was the happiest I've ever felt, just so relieved. I ran to hug him and…" he stammered. He finished the wine in my glass and then poured two more glasses. He handed one to me and this time I chugged it straight down. This was a crazy story, but I've witnessed some messed up things in my little lifetime. I didn't think Keith would lie to me.

"I ran up the front walk and my dad was holding this little baby. He grabbed me and hugged me so tight. I was so happy to see him. My mother, on the other hand…" He was shaking his head in disbelief.

130

"She was so angry. She just walked up to him and asked 'Is that baby yours?' My dad just went to pieces. He tried to tell her that he hadn't cheated, that the baby was somehow from a failed romance long before he met her. I know it was impossible but I wanted to believe him."

"The shouting went on all day, it was impossible not to hear them. Eventually my father asked 'It doesn't matter where the baby came from, can we raise him together, alongside his brother Keith, like a family?' My mother absolutely refused. The baby was fussing and crying. My father picked it up and brought it into my bedroom. He sat down on the bed and gestured for me to sit next to him. He told the fussing baby 'This is your big brother Keith, the one I told you about,' and placed the screaming baby in my arms. Immediately the baby quieted down. That pretty much won me over." I smiled; little Ky was always the charmer.

"'Keith,' my dad said, 'this is your little brother Kyan.' Immediately I asked if my mom was his mother. My dad told me, 'She is now.' He got very serious and said, 'Keith, you and your little brother are very special and because of that you always need to stick together. Now you are the big brother so you need to protect your little brother. Protect him with your life, Keith.' Then my dad just started crying. It was the only time I'd ever seen him cry. He kissed me on the head and walked out of my room. I heard him tell Mom that he was going to fix things and to just watch the baby until he got back. Then he walked out the door forever."

I couldn't believe what I had heard. "Oh Keith," I started but he just held his hand up.

"Just shut up and let me finish," he said, his voice full of pain. "From that day on my life became a nightmare. My mother hated and resented Ky. She was never there for him; she barely took care of him. I'm the one who helped him learn to walk and learn to read. I was a child myself and yet I was raising a child. I hated my mother. I know my dad walked out on us, but I always felt like it was she who betrayed us. She would ignore us as if we weren't there and she had like a million boyfriends who would come and go and most of them would live with us for a while. A lot of them would knock us around."

"Like hit you?" I cried in shock.

"Yeah. I always tried to protect Kyan. No matter what if I was able to stand I would be standing between danger and Kyan. He's my brother, you know."

"I knew Ky wasn't Mom's son, but she didn't have to treat him so bad. After a while I felt like I wasn't her son either. When I was about 13, Ky was like six, Social Services took him away. He was gone for a year and a half, living in foster homes. I begged and pleaded with my mother that if she got him back I would take him away and she'd never hear from us again. When I was 15 I got legally emancipated from my

132

mother. I got a job and an apartment and Ky came to live with me. We only went home when the social worker came to visit, to pretend we were a loving family. Even then I'd bring money to my mom to make sure things went smooth. On my eighteenth birthday she signed custody of Ky over to me and we haven't heard from her since. Ky still thinks she's his mother and he still tries to reach out to her. I promised him we'd go see her for Christmas." He finished sounding bitter with a little hint of wistfulness. "You love Ky, right? I mean you really, really love him?" He looked at me with questioning eyes.

"Of course I do. I love him more than anything. From the minute we met he's been the center of my whole world." I meant every word.

"Then you've gotta stop this shit," he said, gesturing to my injuries. "You've got to stop thinking of yourself. You've got to always stay healthy, always stay alert, always stay strong. You have to always take care of the baby," he said, giving me a lot of insight into why he was so gruff and rigid with me. There was never any room for failure in Keith Mal's life. He wanted me to be tough, just like he has always had to be. He wanted me to be good enough for Ky.

Chapter 10

After the incident, Keith didn't make me go to school. He hired Jeannie to tutor me 4 hours a day. The rest of the day I worked with Harlan, a singing coach and a guitar teacher to get ready for the pageant. Sometimes in the afternoons Keith would work with me on my static. He would give me exercises to practice, mostly exercising my control. I wanted to focus on my power, really see what I could do but Keith thought control was important above all things.

MalAdjusted Games had just taken over two floors in a Mid-Town Manhattan building, so they had a bunch of empty rooms. Keith designated one for me. It was pretty empty, white walls, two long brown tables and some chairs, Keith brought in a stereo to cheer up the drab room, a kindness he immediately regretted.

"Could you turn that down, I am trying to work on the other side," Keith burst into the room a few days later sounding pissed. He crossed his arms in front of him. "What is this? You've been blasting it all week."

"Um, Thomas Cunningham," I said shyly. I didn't know he could hear it from his office.

"Is it really that great?" Keith demanded.

"Yeah, it's phenomenal. It's pretty mellow but he really expresses a thought whether it fits the pattern of the song or not. You have to appreciate passion like that. I could switch to Dispatch. They are great, also very chill. If I want something a little fiercer I'll put on Shades Apart or Our Lady Peace. I also love harder rock like Silverchair and Linkin Park.

"You seem to know something about music. Did you teach yourself this at the orphanage?" Keith asked.

"No, I learned it from Lucky actually. He loves music," I said smiling, thinking about Lucky rocking out.

I unplugged the mp3 player and handed it to Keith. "I made a great Linkin Park playlist. Give it a listen."

"You know I only listen to the Beatles, right?" Keith asked sounding skeptical.

"Well maybe it's time for something new. Linkin Park has a way of giving a voice to your silent feelings." Keith left with the player and never said another word about it.

When she was feeling better Jeannie came back and started drilling 4 hours of math into my head a day. She tried to keep it fun and interesting although I found the whole thing altogether painful. While I was working on my exercises she took over the stereo and popped in a favorite CD of hers. I was expecting something from the Lilith Fair and was more than a little surprised to hear a blaring rock groove. I was even more surprised at how good it was. I had one of those moments, you know, when you know you're in the presence of something great. Jeannie noticed I wasn't doing my work. "Is something wrong?" she asked

"Yes, something's wrong," I said. "Who is this band and why haven't I heard them before?"

"Oh, It's the Eric Stewart Band," she told me. "They come from Brooklyn."

"Really?" I raised my eyebrows. Brooklyn's just a stone's throw away. "Are they old school? They have such an awesome sound, classic rock and sometimes country. Why haven't I heard them on the radio?"

Jeannie laughed. "I wish you were this excited about math. ESB is pretty modern, I mean they're still making albums. They aren't on the mainstream radio because they're unsigned."

"Unsigned? But they're so good!" Wow, they must really be artists! Does that even exist anymore? So dreamy. And this music…I think it dipped a finger into the pool of my soul and stirred me up.

Jeannie promised to take me to an Eric Stewart Band concert if I got a 1200 or better on the PSAT. Wow, now I had some incentive to study!! The weeks raced by this way, my days jam packed with lessons, my nights with the Mals. Keith would go out with Eve most nights, leaving me to babysit for Ky. We learned early on that I couldn't cook anything without burning it so we survived on delivery pizza and cold sandwiches. Ky and I managed to entertain ourselves night after night. We built tents with the bed sheets and made constellations by holding tin plates over the flashlight and poking holes.

One day we got into a fake battle and I found out that Kyan could really fight. He told me it was a secret and that he and Keith went to training in the wee hours almost every morning. I had never even heard them sneak out. I promised I would keep the secret.

Every moment we spent together just made me love Ky more. Some nights Keith would hang with us and play video games or watch movies. He always approached everything with a stern countenance but Ky and I knew how to make him smile. I'd fall asleep dreaming that Keith and I were married and Ky was our son.

Before long the day of the pageant arrived. I stood in front of the mirror and stared at my reflection. I didn't see a beauty queen. All I saw was a girl.

My hair was a blonde I never liked. I hadn't bothered to cut it in a long time and it was almost down to my waist. My eyes were a watery blue instead of the honey brown I admired so much in Lucky. My body was kept lean by my extra electricity but I worried that my build was too muscular. Too late to worry about it now, in a few hours it would all be over. What I needed to do was get my electricity flowing the way Keith had told me to do the night of the opera. If I could do that I could surely attract enough attention to make it to the top 5. After that, well after that I would make history.

I headed downstairs and got into the limo with the Mals and Harlan.

"Nice energy," Keith said immediately. "Think about the control exercises we worked on and keep that, ok?"

I nodded.

Keith smiled warmly. No kidding, he really smiled. He started touching the long locks of my hair. "If you make it to the top 5, I will let you be the MalAdjusted Games girl. If you win the crown," he leaned forward to whisper in my ear. "I'll give you a kiss!"

Now my head was spinning! We rode the rest of the way silently. We arrived at the hall and everyone wished me luck and said kind things.

Ky gave me a long, strong hug. "We already know that you have the patience and the quick thinking to handle this and your talents will speak for themselves. All that's left is just to do your best."

"You are my greatest treasure," I told him. I took off before I said too much.

It was the Monday before Thanksgiving. Win or lose I still had to go to a gaming convention on Friday and Saturday and maybe be the MalAdjusted Games girl.

I arrived at the theater where the scene was already chaos. The pageant officials read the schedule and they told us about the prizes but I had already tuned out. We rehearsed the dance numbers, practiced where we were supposed to stand and pretty soon it was time to get ready.

So many girls fussing in the dressing room with hair, makeup and clothes. They were pushing past me and reaching over me and all the friction was building up my static. I waited until the last minute before getting ready myself. I didn't have the time or a place to discharge so I had been holding in the static these girls generated.

When I got to the mirror, I gasped. My skin was radiant, my eyes and hair electric! All this static build up was like a super makeover for me. I had never imagined I could look so pretty. I suddenly felt confident. I walked out under those lights to confess to the world my most private secret.

The pageant began without a hitch. The dance performances went great. I kept my poise and smile through the evening gown and swimsuit competitions. I kept my hand strategically placed over my bullet scar as Harlan had instructed.

The judges cut us down to the final 10. The talent competition was a little tougher but I know I rocked it. They cut us down to the final 5. This was it, this was the reason I was here. I hadn't noticed the cameras too much up till now, but they seemed to be breathing down my neck.

The emcee read off my question. "What group of people did you come here to represent?" Wow, it was the perfect question.

"The people I speak for live in the shadows and can't speak for themselves. There is a genetic disorder, a mutation that afflicts hundreds, possibly thousands around the world. Those afflicted have hidden themselves in shame and because of that, they have never gotten the medical treatment or even the humanity deserving of a person with such an affliction. I came to this stage tonight to let you know, New York, there is a race hidden among your citizens. I got up here so that my voice could be heard by all people with genetic deviations. All of you, hiding out there, I'm asking you to come into the light. We must stand together. You don't have to hide, you don't have to be alone anymore." Tears started trickling from my eyes.

"Ladies and Gentlemen, I have an unexplained genetic disorder. And though it does grant me special abilities, I have struggled for equal treatment all my life. Instead I was caged like an animal. This is America and I stand here and say those with anomalies come forward. We are Americans too and we need to believe in a land where there is no ridicule for us, no inhumane treatment, a land where we can seek medical assistance, attend public schools and contribute to society. We need to believe in each other and we need to believe in ourselves. We need to believe in a land with liberty and justice for all. Thank you!" The theater erupted into applause. I saw Mr. G jump to his feet and pretty soon everyone was standing. I kept bowing, saying "Thank you" and brushing away the tears. Finally the pageant went to a commercial and I was able to get myself together.

Only a few moments later the lights were back on me again as the top 5 took their place for the crowning. The emcee started droning on about the history of Miss New York and I started thinking about what just happened. Did anyone hear that? Did it affect anyone? I think that Mr. Gerard's attempts with this pageant were to get some exposure for the mutant cause, but also so that the first visible mutant would be a young, pretty blonde girl. I think he thought that was an image America could handle and not my dear friend with the prehensile tail swinging himself across the living room. I had to chuckle at that one.

I had gotten so absorbed in my thoughts that I wasn't paying attention. Suddenly a light was on me. Oh man! I think I won one of the crowns. Take that Keith, 2nd runner up! I was going to get my kiss and there was no chance I'd have to be in the Miss America pageant. I was actually kind of proud.

Suddenly there was a circus of flashbulbs, ticker tape and people screaming. I must have taken a million pictures, my face hurt from smiling.

When everything was finished the reporters and photographers followed me backstage. The reporters had some interesting questions. "Are you an alien?" "What can you do with your powers?" "Are you here to take over the world?" were just a few. I honestly couldn't answer a lot of them. Was I an alien? That would explain a lot.

I made several appointments with reporters to get my full story. I was also appearing on Good Morning New York at 6 am and on the NY News later in the morning.

I was so excited to finally leave the pageant hall. Ky was waiting for me. He told me that Keith and Harlan had left for the party and Mr. Gerard had gone home to blog about the pageant. I wanted to take off my crown and sash but Ky insisted I keep them on until I got to the MalAdjusted party.

We arrived at a really swanky hotel downtown where Keith had gotten us rooms for the night. Keith had also rented out a ballroom and had put giant plasma TVs everywhere so that the MalAdjusted staff and their guests could watch the pageant. We walked in the room to thunderous applause. Now getting applause from strangers is cool, but it is way sweeter when it comes from people you know. Even though the pageant had been over for hours it seemed like every TV had a different news show on and every news show was talking about me. Wow. I saw my face on a dozen different screens. Honestly, it made me queasy. This thing was a lot bigger than I had realized.

I looked around for Keith but I didn't see him. Everyone at the party was swarming me. I wasn't excited about all the attention. I just wanted my kiss from Keith and a good night's sleep.

I made my way over to Harlan and Eve. Eve looked lovely in her green dress. When I looked into her eyes though, I could see pure jealousy. As soon as she saw me, Eve's wheels started turning. She asked loudly for everyone's attention. She raised her glass. "We're very proud and more than a little shocked at dear Stephanie's victory tonight."

That was mean. I could feel a blush warm my cheeks. Eve seemed a bit tipsy. "Is Keith here?" she asked looking through the crowd. He was still missing. "Well MalAdjusted is happy to announce that Keith Mal and I are getting married!" Harlan's eyes widened and his mouth dropped open. Eve squealed and pushed her hand forward. In the center was a big, flashy emerald surrounded by smaller diamonds and some brilliant purple stones.

My heart swelled like a balloon filling with too much air. I couldn't breathe, couldn't see straight. I felt dizzy and disoriented. I got away from the crowd and stumbled out the door into the hallway. I tried to climb the stairs to my room but I only made it a few steps. I dropped to my knees right there on the stairs and vomited. Tears started pouring out of my eyes. There was nothing between Keith and me; it had been all in my head. I was just a fangirl. I was nobody to him.

I sat there on the steps and sobbed. I knew someone would hear me but I couldn't keep it in anymore. My heart was breaking. Did I really do a great thing tonight by exposing all those mutants? Was Eve going to keep me away from Kyan?

I won, I won in that stupid pageant. Everyone in New York loved me. Everyone but Keith. I broke off the crying and headed to my room. I didn't even bother to hang up my evening dress or my sash. I just stripped off my clothes, brushed my teeth, got into bed and cried myself to sleep.

I don't know how much later, but someone sneaked into my room. I didn't hear anything so he must have had a key card. I didn't even know someone was there until I could feel them climbing into bed with me. "Ky?" I asked out loud. No answer. "It's Keith," the voice said. Ok, now I must have been dreaming because there is no way that Keith Mal climbed into my bed, on purpose. I was naked but he was still wearing all of his clothes. It was dark so we couldn't even see each other. "You better get back before your fiancée misses you," I told him tartly.

"Listen," he started. Such a smooth talker, Keith Mal. "I bought her the ring but it's just a present, it's not an engagement ring. I didn't ask her to marry me."

I knew what he was doing; he was trying to play both of us. How did I get myself into this mess? "Just get out!" He didn't move. "I said get out!"

"Ok," Keith purred. "I understand you're a little cranky. We'll talk in the morn…wait, are you naked under there?"

"Keith! I am going to kill you!"

"Okay, okay. I'll get out of here, it's just…don't you want to know where I've been the last few hours?"

"No, I don't care."

"You really will like it, please?" he begged like a child. Who was this guy? Was he just playing me? I really didn't understand.

144

"First you tell me why you fuck around with me. Do you like me or not? Just answer the question." I was sick of his games.

"Of course I like you, I like you a lot," he said. "It's just that things between us are kind of...intense."

I had to agree with that.

"I need to keep my eye on the prize, I need to take care of Ky," he said earnestly. "I already waste too much time on you."

"I'm a waste of your time?" I asked, my heart sinking.

"It's not that. Just turn on the lights, I have something I want to show you," he ordered.

I kinda waved my hand and the light overhead went on. It surprised me that it happened so effortlessly. Keith was taken aback as well.

"Wow, you seem to have a lot of control when you're pissed, I gotta remember that." He sat up in bed. I was still naked, hidden under the sheets.

"Get out of here so I can get dressed," I hissed.

"Don't bother, this will only take a minute." He scooted over next to me on the bed. We were so close we were touching and I could breathe in his sexy, masculine sent. I thought you could only get weak in the knees if you were standing, like gravity increasing on you. Guess you could feel it lying down.

What was he doing here? Waking me up in the middle of the night? Climbing into bed with me? Didn't he know he was torturing me?

145

"I'm sorry I missed your party tonight but I was working on something for you." He held up a notebook. The page was filled with numbers, like math formulas.

"I created an algorithm for you. To be honest, I've been working on it for weeks now. I just wanted to get it done so I could teach it to you." He seemed very proud of himself.

"I don't even know what an algorithm is. What does it mean?" I questioned. It just looked like letters and numbers to me.

"It's a plan of attack. It uses your abilities in different tactical situations to determine what will always be the best possible move to stop a situation or an enemy using the least energy needed to do the most damage possible." He paused, trying to read me. "I thought if you got into trouble again it would help you."

Wow, he really put some time into this. In fact, in a weird way it was one on the nicest things anyone had done for me. Helping me protect myself was really just his way of protecting me. My anger dissipated. "I love it," I told him. "I can't wait to learn."

"Great!" he broke out into a toothy grin. "I was thinking that Kyan has two weeks off for winter break, I thought the three of us could go somewhere warm, maybe tropical where we could be away from other people. You and I could practice these theories and I could take Ky fishing. It'll be a lot of work, but it will be fun too. What do you think?" He had definitely put a lot of thought into this.

"I think it sounds like heaven," I answered honestly.

"Great! Well that's what I wanted to show you. I'll let you get some sleep,'" he said, but hesitated to move. "Steph, I'm really proud of you. I think you really did a great thing tonight. You opened a door tonight a door for...for people like us. As soon as you told me about the pageant, I knew you'd do great. Why do you think I was so quick to sponsor you? I just hope that now that you're famous, you won't forget about me and Ky." He actually sounded concerned.

"Forget about you? You're all I think about." Oh my God, I did not just say that out loud!

Keith cleared his throat. "Yeah, I guess it's pretty obvious we've been crushing on each other."

We both fell silent. I just listened to the sound of his breathing.

"Remember when we kissed on the roof?" he asked.

"Only every 30 seconds or so," I answered. He laughed.

"I LOVE your honesty," he said. I had a long day, and a long couple of months and I felt like saying something I knew I was going to regret.

"Keith, man," I turned and looked at him like I felt bad for him, having to hear what I was about to say. "I love your *everything*. I love the way you look, the way you smell. I love it when you're nice to me, and even more when you're a jerk. I love how smart you are and how you're always trying to challenge yourself. I love all the charities and causes you donate to and how you really care about the world. I love how you're into classic rock and how you worship the Beatles. But the thing I love the most about you..." before I finished, Keith turned to me and grabbed the back of my head and swept me up into a mind blowing, passionate kiss. My energy radiated out in all directions, turning on and off lights, the TV, the radio.

The lit bulb over us exploded showering us with tiny glass splinters and blanketing us with darkness. Keith didn't waste any time. He shucked his clothes without breaking our kiss. He slid under me. "I don't want you to get cut by the glass," he told me. I didn't need any convincing. I leaned in for more kisses.

Sex between us was everything I'd imagined. It was fierce with biting and hair pulling, passionate kisses. Everything between us was electric! I could hear things tumbling and breaking in the hotel room around us. I tried to reel in my energy but somehow Keith noticed. "Don't hold back," he told me.

Things got furious between us. The electricity was flowing right off the walls, like some giant Tesla experiment. I was in a shell of pure bliss coupling with Keith. The energy in the room reached a frenzy as Keith and I did. As I climaxed everything in the room seemed to explode. I mean really explode. The mirrors all over the room shattered and the fragments filled the air, covering Keith and me on the bed as they fell. The glass and tubes burst out of the TV, the refrigerator and desk ended up on the other side on the room. The blinds were ripped down and thrown and suddenly Keith and I were bathed in light streaming through the windows from outside.

"Are you okay?" I breathlessly asked Keith. I would die if I hurt him.

"Actually, I'm impressed. I guess you can't call yourself a good lover until you make a girl blow up her hotel room," Keith giggled. He actually giggled, I swear. I started laughing too. I felt so great, everything was so perfect.

I lay down on top of Keith and he brushed the glass off my back and picked it out of my hair. We started kissing and almost immediately Keith's phone rang. I guess it wasn't fried in the chaos. It was Ky's ring. "I have to answer it," Keith said.

"Of course." I would have answered it too. It was probably 4 in the morning, why was Ky awake? I was concerned. I listened to Keith's side of the conversation; it didn't sound good.

"I'll be there in a few minutes. Ky, do you want me to send Stephanie to stay with you? Ok, I'll get her. I'll be right there." Keith hung up and sighed. "It's Eve, her father had a heart attack. He died." I gasped. There was no love lost between me and Eve but my heart went out to her. I've never know what it's like to have a father, let alone to lose one.

Keith sat there on the bed. "I don't know what to do," he said in earnest. "I mean I was going to break up with her the next time I saw her. Now I just don't know what to do."

"Is Ky okay?" I was worried.

"He sounded shaken up. I told him you would stay with him." He gestured to the destroyed hotel room, the wreckage of our escapade. "You certainly can't stay here."

"Go, comfort Eve. Do what you think is right." I hoped being a friend to her and then choosing me was what he thought was right. We dressed quickly. I had a bad feeling watching Keith go. He walked out the door without a word, without looking back.

I grabbed my things and headed down to Ky's room. He was standing in the hallway between his room and the one Keith and Eve were sharing. "They're going to the airport," he told me immediately. "He asked me if I wanted to go. I said I wanted to stay with you." He was about to lose it, I pulled him into his room and closed the door. We sat down on his bed and he started to tremble. I knew exactly what he was thinking because it was the same thing I thought when I heard the news.

"It wasn't your dad. Your dad is out there somewhere and he's doing just fine. You're going to find him someday."

"You really think so?" he asked, his eyes filled with hope.

"Oh, heck yeah. I bet your dad and my dad are best friends and all day long they talk about how much they love us and miss us and can't wait to see us again." That sounded plausible.

"That's just stupid." He sniffled, but he did stop crying.

"I can't wait to meet your dad. Remember that picture you showed me of him and your mom when Keith was little? I bet he's awesome just like you are. I know he's gonna find you someday. I really believe it." After the story Keith told me I knew their dad would come for them. I looked at the clock and sighed. "I hate to tell you this but I have to start getting ready for "Good Morning New York." I'm going to jump in the shower and get dressed. Why don't you go say goodbye to your brother?" He jumped off the bed and headed to the door. "Hey," I called out. "Until he gets back I'm not going to leave you for a second." He smiled, I think he was reassured.

Chapter 11

The interviews were the same all day. What was I? How many of us were there? How many did I know? What were their powers? Could I show them my abilities? Keith told me just to let a spoon dangle like an inch away from my hand as a demonstration and to conceal my real powers. I also gave one of the TV hosts a loud but painless static shock as a demo.

Ky and I crashed out as soon as we got home. Keith called to check on Ky and to say he would be home Wednesday night. He didn't ask to speak to me.

The next day wasn't any better, with more interviews and some photographs. I really couldn't believe how much attention I was getting. Mr. Gerard called several times a day. He said I was doing great and to just hang in there and be likable. He had finalized all the paperwork for his charity so I made sure to mention it at every interview. I knew Keith would be home soon and I missed him terribly. I couldn't wait until we were finally together. Another call to Ky revealed that Keith and Eve could not get a flight and would now return on Thanksgiving. I started getting concerned and tried phoning Keith but he didn't pick up. Thanksgiving arrived. Keith had promised to take Kyan to the Macy's parade. Even though his brother was nowhere to be found I wasn't going to let the little boy down. We woke while it was still dark to get a good spot at the parade.

The parade was a blast! The Macy's Parade was the parade of parades! By the time we got back home it was almost 4pm. Kyan and I still hadn't heard from Keith. We had pre-purchased some Thanksgiving trays for us to heat up. We gorged ourselves on food, then wrapped up plates for Keith and Eve to eat when they got home. Ky and I cozied up on the couch and dozed off. We got a call at 10pm from Keith saying they had landed and would be home in an hour or two. We waited up but two hours turned to 3, then 4. I made Ky go to bed, since we had the gaming convention in the morning. I lay down in his room with him but I couldn't sleep.

At about 2:30 I heard them come in. They were drunk and they were laughing. I didn't know what they had been through so I reserved judgment. Keith went directly to check on Ky. I pretended I was asleep. I'd have all day tomorrow to talk to Keith and figure things out. After they had closed the door I decided to get up and go sleep in my own room. I walked out into the hall and heard something. They were having sex! I couldn't believe it! Keith said he was breaking up with her, he said he wanted me. Was that just a lie so he could screw me? I thought I was going to burst into tears right there in the hall and then ran and hid myself in my room.

The next day was the gaming convention. We all woke early to get ready. I skipped breakfast so I wouldn't have to see Eve and Keith together. No big deal, soon Eve would leave and the three of us would have the next two days together.

Yeah, right. "Eve's going to tag along with us," Keith said as they were getting in the car – not giving us a choice. We rode to the convention in silence.

We got there and set everything up. Keith had hired a woman to do my hair and makeup. I sat with her for a good hour while she taught me some ways to style my hair. I was wearing a glittery lilac evening gown that made me feel like a princess. When we were done she turned me to the mirror. Wow, I looked like a model!

The guys from Keith's office had gone all out. There were huge plasma TVs to play games on a little area that people could take pictures with me in front of the MalAdjusted Games logo. The photographer would instantly print up the digital pic so the gamers had a souvenir.

I put on my crown and my sash and went to work. From start to finish, all day long there was a line of people waiting to take pictures with me. I really couldn't believe it. One guy said he waited 2 hours to take this picture. I laughed and joked and tried to get to know a little about everyone in line. I'm going to meet thousands of people in this life and I want to make each meeting count, for them and for me. Towards the end of the day one guy grabbed his print out and ran back up to have me sign it. After that I autographed every picture. Autograph – me – can you believe it?

Keith and I managed to ignore each other all day. I think I made it an art form. Everyone was so busy with the big crowd at our booth anyway. It didn't escape Ky's notice though. He was visibly upset by the end of the day. Keith needed to stay behind and finish up some work before the convention opened again tomorrow. Ky, Eve and I ended up in the limo together riding back to the house.

"You did a really great job today. You brought a lot of attention to MalAdjusted," Eve said to me.

"Thanks," I said quietly.

"Keith told me about the two of you." My eyes widened and my jaw dropped in shock. "I'm not jealous or anything," Eve continued. "I think it's a great plan, you and Keith will make a great couple." Did Keith really break up with her? Oh my God, this is a dream come true!

"What's going on?" Ky asked.

"Your brother is a genius and he's going to make a lot of money," Eve said excitedly. "Keith and Stephanie are going to start dating," Eve said.

Ky exploded with excitement! He grabbed me and gave me a squeeze. "That's awesome, why didn't you tell me?"

"I wasn't sure myself," I said truthfully. 'It's all happening,' I thought. I won the pageant, I have a great best friend in Ky and a beautiful home and now I'm going to have Keith Mal as my boyfriend! My life is perfect. I put one arm around Ky and snuggled him close.

"Now we will really be a family," Kyan said.

"Awww, Ky, I think you misunderstand," Eve said. "Keith will still be *my* boyfriend. The relationship with him and Stephanie is just for publicity." Ky and I just sat there frozen from her news. She went on, "He told me he showed you the plan after the pageant. Didn't he go up to your hotel room with that notebook full of numbers?"

"My algorithm? What does that have to do with this?" I was starting to feel numb.

"Well sweetie, I don't know what he told you but that was his formula for how to cash in on the MalAdjusted beauty queen. He told me he kissed you so that it wouldn't look fake in public." Now I was sick to my stomach.

When we got home I went straight to my room without dinner.

Ky came to check on me. "Is it true you kissed my brother?" he asked.

"Yeah, I did," I admitted. "I thought he really liked me, Ky."

"So did I," Ky said forcefully. "It's just not like him. Maybe Eve got it wrong. You should talk to him."

"No sweetie, I just want to let it go. I have to see your brother every day, live with him, work with him. I don't want to mess it up any more than it already is."

"But it's not fair!" Ky thundered. I was starting to worry about him. He was really starting to fly off the handle when it came to me and his brother. I curled up in his bed and let him sleep in my arms for the night.

The next morning I got up really early went to the con by myself. The hair and makeup woman wouldn't be around for a while so I started just walking the floor and talking to the game industry folks. I met some cool people and learned a lot about the industry that I was now part of. I even met a girl from Ozgon Gaming, which was the company Keith worked for before starting MalAdjusted. She told me he had the reputation of being a womanizer even back then as a teenager. Figures.

Everybody started arriving and the con got underway. The Mal brothers didn't arrive until almost 2 hours later, and they were looking pissed. On my lunch break I finally got a minute alone with Ky.

Ky exploded. "My brother is furious. First he heard that you were giving your number out to guys yesterday by writing it on your pictures. You didn't do that, did you?"

"What? No! No way. I was just giving them autographs." I never would have thought of such a thing.

"Well this morning at breakfast Eve said you were just coming to the con early to get in good with the other gaming companies. She and my brother started arguing and then she told him that you said you only liked him because he was rich and you wanted to get something out of it. I said that wasn't true and even Keith said you already had

everything he could give you so it seemed really unlikely. Eve told me
to shut up and then Keith told her not to talk to me like that, it was a
mess. So I went to my room and my brother comes in and I told him
that you really like him and he told me "Well she'll just have to wait until
I'm ready."

So that was it huh? Wait until he's ready? How much can a girl take? I
thanked Ky for telling me everything and went to go find Keith. He was
at the booth talking with some colleagues. I waited until they were
finished and then politely asked him if we could talk for a moment.

"I don't think that's a good idea," he said curtly. I asked him why not?
He said, "I need you to take beautiful pictures and it's not going to
happen if you start crying."

"I just think we should clear up a few things…and why would I start
crying?" I asked.

"I said no," he snapped. "I'm working and you're supposed to do the
same. Go, work." He brushed me off. I took the hint, five more hours of
smiling for the camera coming up. My face was starting to hurt.

The day went by and it was time to put the sign at the end of the line
so no more people would line up for pictures. I just had 20 or so to go
and then I could go home and bravely face whatever Keith had to tell
me.

There was guy in line who was grinning like a madman. As he got closer to the front I didn't know if I should be scared or not. Finally it was his turn. "What's the big smile for?" I asked him.

"You're gonna remember me," he told me. "Said the guy who gave me this," and he held up a folded piece of paper. We took the picture. "Can I get like a kiss or something for delivering this?" Again he waved that paper around. I leaned forward and kissed him on the cheek. "Good enough," he said and handed me the paper. I opened it to see what his fuss was about. It read:

"Yesterday's a dream, I face the morning crying on a breeze the pain is calling..."

Barry Manilow lyrics? Who even knows Barry Manilow?

The only sound I could hear was my heart pounding. It couldn't be! I felt like the room was spinning. I tried to look around me and saw nothing. I was having trouble breathing. I didn't know what to do. On instinct I hiked up my dress, got a running start and hopped on the booth's counter. I looked into the crowd, there were hundreds out there, thousands maybe. I had to do something. With all my might I started to scream "LUCKY!!!!"

Everyone turned to look. Off in the distance I saw a furious wave. I jumped off the counter and started running. I was pushing through a thick crowd of people. It looked like the waving guy was pushing his way through too. People kinda got the idea and just parted and there we were like 100 feet away from each other. Our eyes met and we broke into a run. We crashed into each other. We wrapped our arms around each other and squeezed so tight, I never wanted to let go. I was surrounded in that old familiar embrace; he had that same manly smell. My Lucky had returned!

It seemed that everyone in the room was watching, including the Mal brothers. Lucky and I took a step back to look at each other. He still looked amazing. The bleached blonde hair was now the reddish brown it was when we met. He seemed taller, almost the same height as Keith. Lucky gave me an approving once over glance. Then, with no words he swept me into a passionate kiss. The floor erupted into applause.

Stunned, we made our way back to the MalAdjusted booth. I wanted badly to introduce Lucky to Ky but one of the guys said Keith had dragged him off during the kisses. Great, as if Keith wasn't pissed at me enough. I still had pictures to take.

Lucky sat by my side while I posed with fans and filled me in on his journey from when we parted in Las Vegas until we met up now. He had waited a month in Vegas after hearing on the street that I had been arrested. He was hoping to get the IDs in place before leaving but the whole thing had fallen through. Lucky had traveled back across the country hoping to find me. He said he expected me to be locked up in that orphanage and figured the "Miss New York thing" had something to do with that. I told you he was smart! I asked him how he found me and he told me, "Oh, it's real easy now that you're famous."

"Oh I don't think I'm famous, just a little local popularity," I said gesturing to the gaming fans.

"No Sweetness, I was in Atlanta on Tuesday and you were on the front page of the paper. Turns out your mutation announcement dropped a big bomb. Everyone in the country is interested."

Wow, I really had no idea. It was pretty creepy, all these people knew something about me but I didn't know anything about them. I finished with the pictures, thanked everyone and then tried to look for the Mals. I found my limo driver and he said they had already gone home. I tried calling Ky's cell phone but there was no answer. I was a little worried, but I forgot it quickly when I turned back to Lucky.

As we walked to the limo, I let Lucky know my situation. I told him of my attraction to Keith and the state of things now. I didn't know if Lucky was looking for a romantic relationship with me. I told him I needed to sort things out with Keith and then we'd see. Lucky said he could wait. Then we got into the limo. Then he started kissing my neck. Then we started kissing, there was some removal of clothing and Bam! We had sex in the back of the limo. It didn't mean anything, I think it was sort of a relief thing because we hadn't seen each other in so long and we were glad the other was ok. Really. Then we did it again, this time just for fun.

161

We got dressed as the car pulled up to the house. "This is where I live," I told Lucky.

"I figured Keith Mal would have you in a mansion. I bet everything's all fancy inside," he huffed.

"Well it sure beats sleeping on the street!" I pointed out.

"Amen to that, my sister," he joked. This was going to be the start of something amazing!

We'd barely opened the front door and could immediately hear Keith and Kyan arguing. I had never heard them fight before. They were at the top of the stairs and they were pretty loud. Ky already had tears streaming down his precious little cheeks. I ran to the stairs to comfort him.

"Stop!" Keith shouted. "Don't even think about coming up the stairs. Just stay in the foyer with your boy-toy." Keith turned around and marched into my room. He came out a second later with an armload of my stuff. He walked straight to the top of the stairs and dropped my things to the floor 20 feet below. I heard things break and scatter. What the hell was he doing? Lucky and I just stood there stunned. He came out of the room again, this time with my clothes, including the dresses he bought me. He dumped them all over the side.

"Keith, what are you doing?" I yelled up to him.

He came out a third time, his arms full of toiletries and such.

Ky screamed "No!" and ran over to stop him. Keith snatched the things away and shouted, "You go to your room now, you hear me?" Ky backed up but didn't leave.

"Keith, please," I called from downstairs where he had told me to stay. "Calm down, we can fix this."

"Don't talk to me!" he shouted. "Don't ever talk to me again. You don't live here anymore. You don't live here! And you're fired from MalAdjusted, get it, you're fired. I don't ever want to see you again. Now take your shit and get out!"

I was worried about Ky, but I didn't know what else to do, I started picking up my things.

Keith ran back into my room and came back with my guitars. He took the pretty new guitar he just bought me and without hesitation, smashed it against the wall. The wood splintered into thousands of pieces. I felt like it was my heart he was smashing.

Ky ran over and grabbed my shabby old guitar, the one I've had all my life.

Keith put a hand on it. He stared down Ky and told him "I thought I told you to go to your room?"

Ky continued to cry. "Big Brother, please don't do this. We're a family."

"No, we're a family," he gestured to the two of them. "This," he holds up my guitar, "was just a waste of time." I gasped. Keith smashed the guitar against the wall. The other things I couldn't care about, but that guitar – that was mine. I never saw this coming.

No one said a word.

"Ok, ok I get it. I'll get out and I won't come back. I'm just going to come up there and say goodbye to Ky." What was I going to say to the poor kid?

"Absolutely not!" Keith shouted and pulled Ky behind him. "You will never see him or speak to him again."

"Keith, no!" Kyan screamed. "She's my friend, she's my family."

"She used us and played us Ky, never again!" Keith was seriously insane. I knew he wasn't going to calm down with me here so I backed out slowly.

"I'll fix this, Ky. I love you more than anything. I'll fix this. We'll find a way to be together." I felt desperate inside, could this really be the last moment for me and Ky?

Keith leaned over the balcony and said, "I promise you will never see or talk to my brother again."

"Brother, please!" Ky cried, he really sounded shaken.

"No! No 'please'. She was a mistake that we are erasing. She no longer exists. She doesn't exist!" Keith shrieked.

"Brother, when did you get so cruel? You're not the guy I look up to, you're not the guy I trust." Ky really didn't sound like himself anymore.

"I need her and if you send her away, I'll die. I will, I'll just die."

164

"I will not be told what to do by a child!" Keith yelled. Didn't he realize he was a child himself? Ky came to the edge of the stairs and looked down at me. I tried to mouth "I love you" but he had already looked away. He ran into his room and slammed the door.

Lucky I and had gathered up my stuff and headed out the door. I turned back and told Keith gently, "Thanks for everything."

"You were my worst mistake," he said.

Chapter 12

Lucky and I walked out to the limo and dumped my stuff in the trunk. When Lucky returned a few hours ago I thought this might be the best day of my life. Now I was pretty confident it was the worst.

I shrugged off Lucky's comforting touch. "I can't leave without saying goodbye to Ky. You guys drive down the road a little so Keith thinks we left. I'm going to break in."

Lucky pulled me into a reassuring hug. "Be careful," he said.

As they pulled away I floated myself up to one of Ky's windows. I balanced my electricity with that of the alarm and then safely opened the window. Ky's room was dark. I whispered his name but there was no answer. Keith was sitting out in front of the door trying to patch things up with his brother. As my eyes adjusted I realized Ky was not in the room. I opened up his walk in closet but he wasn't there either. I went into the bathroom. There was my little Ky collapsed on the floor! Inches away was an empty bottle of aspirin. I screamed! Keith heard me and broke down the door. He rushed in and found me leaning over the body.

"What did you do?" he asked incredulously.

"He did this. He's still breathing, we've got to get him to a hospital!" I screamed. "Call an ambulance."

"There's no time," Keith said, the color fading from his face. "You've got to go now. You're got to take him."

"I don't know what to do" I felt completely inadequate.

"Do something! Use your anomalies. Use your powers." Keith grabbed my arm and dug his fingers forcefully into my shoulder. "Save my little brother." He got up. "I'll get the foil."

Ky was white and clammy, his pulse was faint and his breathing shallow. Oh dear God punish me, punish me and not this little boy.

Keith returned with the foil. We hurried to wrap it all around my body.

"Keith, I've never done anything like this before. I don't think that I can do this."

He stopped wrapping and pointed to his brother. "Without him, I have no family."

I grabbed Keith by the arm. "Without him, I have no family too. Please don't take him away," I said and started crying.

Keith grabbed my chin. "No time for this. You have to make him safe. The hospital is 20 minutes by car but you can get him there in 5. I know you can do this. I believe in you." He knelt down and lifted Ky's tiny unconscious body. "Save my baby brother, please." This time it was Keith who had tears in his eyes.

Covered in foil like some bad robot costume I held out my arms and Keith handed Kyan to me. He looked so peaceful, like he was sleeping. I couldn't waste another second. I held tight to Ky, walked to the window and stepped out.

I used the static electricity of my body to balance over the ground. I let the electric waves bounce off of the ground to keep me in motion. I was able to stay about 40 feet up. I tried to remember what Keith had taught me about super positioning. As I pushed against the ground, I pulled myself forward and pushed myself forward at the same time. The strict concentration I needed kept me from being scared. I seemed to be gliding over trees mostly and some dark houses. I don't know if anyone saw me. We could explain that later, all that mattered now was saving Ky. I did make it to the hospital in 5 minutes.

I put myself down about 50 feet from the entrance and broke into a run. Keith had called the hospital and they were waiting. They took Ky from my arms and put his little body on a gurney. Then they whisked him away. Would I ever see him again? I just stood there in the doorway, covered in tin foil, feeling more helpless than I ever had in my life.

I snapped out of it a little and went to the bathroom to remove the foil and splash water on my face. I took a seat in the waiting room. Wow. I knew Keith was rushing here as fast as he could but it seemed to take forever. Every minute that passed could be deadly for Ky. If I hadn't been there, if I wasn't a static freak...

I dropped to my knees right there in the waiting room and for the first time in my life, I thanked my guardian Angel for making me a mutant. If it never did anything good for me my whole life, this anomaly helped me do the most important thing I've ever done, protect someone I love.

I was on my knees praying when Keith rushed in. MUCH to my surprise, Lucky followed him!

"Where is he? What'd they say?" Keith demanded.

Lucky helped me off the ground. "They just took him..." I said. "He was alive when we got here."

The three of us just sat down wordlessly.

It seemed like an eternity until the doctor came out. He explained to us all the lifesaving measures they had taken. The little boy's life still hung in the balance. The doctor didn't seem too positive. "He is very young," he told us. "So that indicates a good chance for recovery. It's just...his will is weak. If he doesn't start fighting..." The doctor sighed. He told us they had moved Kyan to Intensive Care. We brushed past the doctor to find our little boy.

The room was tiny, we were only allowed in one at a time. Keith went first, of course. I just sat in the hallway and caught Lucky up on the past year of my life. His life had been an adventure too. He had spent a few months in Atlanta hanging with a gang. They called themselves The SilverSword Alliance and they were attempting to change gang violence by promoting swords instead of guns.

We talked to fill the silence as we sat in the hallway for hours.

Keith finally got up and walked out of the ICU. He looked like a skeleton. His eyes were hollow with dark rings around them and his face was ashen. He walked right over to me and talked without making eye contact. "I want you to stimulate his brain," he instructed. "Get some activity going, ok? Get some electrical charges in there and keep that brain alive. Just take your time and be really, really careful. He's surrounded by a lot of machines. One wrong step and you could blow us all up." Great, no pressure.

Amazing, it seemed like Keith always had a strategy on how to use my abilities. He thought about them more than I did. It was like all the work on control we had practiced had prepared us exactly for this night, for this procedure.

Lucky squeezed my hand. "I believe in you," he said.

I entered the little room and sat down on the bed. Ky seemed so tiny and helpless with all those tubes and machines attached to him. I tried to think of the best way to send electricity to his brain without blowing us all up. I was thinking standing behind him putting my palm directly on his head would work best. I started moving around the machines so I could get behind him. I heard Lucky and Keith talking in the waiting room.

"Look man, whatever you were pissed about, you were wrong," Lucky said.

"Excuse me?" hissed Keith.

"Back there, that fight. You smashed her guitars."

"I remember," Keith snapped. It had only been a few hours.

"Well, you were wrong. Whatever it was. Stephanie didn't run out on you or betray you or anything. She's the real deal. Maybe the only one." Lucky sounded sincere.

"It's complicated," Keith said.

"Yeah, usually. But not in this case. You know I'm telling you the truth. Whatever you believed, it was lies. Stephanie can't manipulate because that would be for personal gain and she has never felt a second of entitlement. All she does is love and she does it with her whole being. I'm sure you've seen that."

"For God sakes will you shut up! My brother might be in there dying and I hate you!" Keith thundered.

"Hate me? Nah, the way I see it, we're like the best friends ever," Lucky said calm and confident.

"What the hell do you mean?" Keith was ready to explode.

I could almost hear Lucky grin. "Well, we're both good looking guys. We both have seen a little too much for our age. We both love classic rock, won't take any crap from anybody but we know how to dish it out and we're both in love with the same girl. The way I see it, we're soul brothers."

Keith was silent for a change.

"I'll tell you something else, your brother is going to be okay." Lucky stopped.

There was a moment as if Keith was deciding whether to trust Lucky or not. Finally Keith asked in a quiet voice, "How do you know?"

"Because she's in there with him right now," Lucky was speaking of me I suspect. "All she wants is to help that little boy, and she doesn't fail."

The two were quiet for a while.

"Do you ever just resent her?" Keith asked Lucky.

"Oh yeah," Lucky replied. "Do you ever wish you never met her?" Lucky asked.

"All the time," said Keith. "I swear she is so clueless sometimes it's like I have to live her life for her."

"Oh tell me about it! I did that for two years. Come outside and have a smoke with me," Lucky said cheerfully.

"I detest cigarettes," Keith growled.

"Good thing that's not what we're smoking!" Only Lucky would smoke weed at a hospital! "Don't worry, if anyone asks we'll say we have a prescription!"

Keith peeked his head in to look at Ky. "Any change?" he asked with concern.

"I haven't started yet," I didn't want to tell him I'd been eavesdropping. "I'll let you know."

I was ready to begin. I tried giving a small shock through his head. I felt the energy dissipate when it hit his skull. I tried to ramp it up a little harder and my flicker drew a spark from one of the machines.

172

Suddenly all the bells and buzzers and flashing lights went off. Three nurses pushed into the tiny room. I had to tell them that I set off the machines. Two of them looked pretty pissed at me. The third, a quiet woman with a maternal manner to her stayed and checked all the machines and hoses.

"How does it look? I mean, do you think he has a chance?" I asked, fearful of the answer.

The nurse looked at me warmly. "Sweetie, his brain activity is very low. Talk to him, there's always hope you'll get through."

Keith returned. He smelled like a hippie but he did seem more relaxed. I told him about my failures with brain stimulation.

"Well the brain makes its own electricity; just try to pull that up into your hand." I took a deep breath and tried. After a bit, I could feel the electricity Keith was talking about. I put my other hand under Ky's chin and got a good circuit going. The motion registered on the machine! I called the guys in and showed them. They were hollering like farm boys. They told me to keep at it. I pulled electricity through his brain for more than two hours before taking a break. All the while I told Ky that I would protect him, that I would never leave him.

For the next day we took turns standing by the hospital bed and talking to Ky. I would give him as much brain stimulation as I could stand. I tried to eat to keep up my strength, but couldn't. Sleep wouldn't rest my tired body either. We just waited. It had been more than 24 hours

173

already. If Ky didn't start getting better...I really didn't want to think about it.

Every time I walked out of Ky's ICU chamber, I saw a guy further down the hall glancing over at me. As soon as I looked back he'd look away. I mentioned it to Lucky. "He probably just saw you on TV. Leave it alone," he told me. But that guy was grating on my nerves, I couldn't just leave it alone.

After a few times, I had enough. I stormed over to him and asked, "Do you have a problem?" As soon as the words escaped, I wish I'd kept my mouth shut. This guy was a mutant, and not a normal one like me. His energy was powerful, it swept out in all directions. I felt it surround me as I walked towards him. He was tall, brunette, looked like he was in his late 20's. Not a bad looking guy, but his energy was strong and it frightened me.

The guy looked up at me with big green innocent eyes. "Do I know you?" he asked.

I wasn't about to let this guy play games with me. "Let's step outside." I kinda asked him but mostly told him.

"I've seen you all over the television the past few days," he started. "You told the world about your powers."

"Yes, I did." I wondered where this was going.

"Do you really think that was smart? You made yourself a target you know." He didn't look at me, just kept looking straight ahead.

"Someone needed to speak for those who have no voice," I said.

"Yak, yak," he cut me off. "You synergies have been roaming the earth since the dawn of existence and suddenly now you want attention for it. I would think you'd be eager to hide it."

"Attention for what, and what are synergies, what are you talking about?" I was bewildered.

"Wow, you really don't know much about yourself, huh?" he looked smug.

"Maybe not," I said hesitantly. "Stephanie Park," I announced and put out my hand.

"Lord Eric," he said and shook hands with me.

"Lord...Eric? Is Lord your first name?" Was this guy for real?

"Just Eric is fine."

"Eric, what are you doing here? Why is a mutant of your strength sitting in a hospital waiting room staring at my friend's doorway like the Angel of death?"

Eric sighed. "I really like you, but there is so much that you don't know and if I explained it, you'd be lost."

"Try me," I said gently putting my hands on top of his. He started speaking so fast I could tell he was going to tell me all along.

"When people die, their souls go to heaven or hell," he said firmly.

"Well I'm not a Christian," I told him. "I don't know if I believe that."

"I'm not talking about belief, I'm talking about the truth. When a person dies their soul materializes in heaven or hell. When it dies there, it becomes part of the collective unconscious. When a child is born, a soul from the collective unconscious is incarnated in the child. If we didn't reincarnate, existence would be overrun with souls."

"I guess that makes sense," I said. I was understanding him, but I don't know if I was believing him.

"Well last night when Kyan Mal died, his spirit briefly materialized in heaven."

Ky actually died? "Wait," I thought suicides go to hell," I interjected.

"No, that's Christian philosophy again. There are very strict guidelines for getting into heaven, just because it's so small. It's just a few that get into heaven and most go to hell. This is the essence of why I'm here. I need to make sure that Kyan Mal goes to heaven."

I wasn't born yesterday. "You're here to kill him."

"Well yes," he said without a hint of remorse. "It's the only way to be sure."

"I won't let you." I turned to him, my fists blazing with electricity. Lucky and Keith had been watching us through the window. They saw me power up and they ran to catch up with us. The two sped outdoors and got behind me, staring down "Lord Eric."

"I have my own team of fighters and they far overpower your abilities. I'm going to take Kyan no matter what, but you don't need to kill yourselves over this. Especially you Stephanie, I've been watching you all your life. I like you. I think you have a lot of potential."

I didn't care what he was saying, all I heard was he wanted to kill Ky. If it was a fight he wanted, it was a fight he was going to get, I was definitely in the mood to kick ass. "Call your boys," I told Eric.

"Please don't do this," he begged. "Ky is going to die no matter what, but you don't have to."

"Just get them here!" I was furious and I wasn't waiting long. I would cut down anyone standing between me and Ky.

Eric looked around us. There was no one in sight. He turned away from us and breathed deep in focus. He lifted his hand, palms forward and created a small, floating ball of light. In an instant the ball burst and spread upwards and downwards simultaneously. It seemed like a glowing crack in the earth. He parted his hands like a sorcerer and the crack seemed to spread out like a giant glowing door. I couldn't see anything but the glow.

"Go on through," Eric said.

Who was this guy? How was he doing this? I turned to him. "They stay here," I said and nodded towards Lucky and Keith. The two immediately started protesting. I darted through the glowing door. I landed on soft dirt on the other side. I turned back to the glowing door and watched it rapidly fade and disappear.

With the door gone it was easier to see my surroundings. I was in a park it seemed, definitely late at night. Behind me was a park bench with an attractive couple talking to each other and ignoring me. I approached them. "Do you two know a guy named Eric?"

"Um, you mean Lord Eric?" the girl responded as if I was the dumbest person alive. She was cracking on a piece of gum. She had glossy, strawberry blond hair pulled back in a ponytail. She was wearing a shimmery top and a pirate necklace.

"Is he really a Lord?" I asked.

"And then some," said the guy. He was an old fashioned brawler, you could tell by the muscles. He had shaggy dark brown hair that grew past his ears. Right now his head was tilted and I couldn't see his eyes. I'll bet he was sizing me up. I could tell right away these were Eric's fighters.

"I'm Stephanie Park," I introduced myself. They didn't seem too interested.

"I'm Sam, this is Jenni," the guy established. "We're waiting on Steel."

Oh, I didn't know they were waiting for someone. I guess I should be lucky they didn't bum rush me as soon as I walked through the door.

"So what?" I asked. "Are you just hired killers?"

"Don't you dare," Sam hissed. "We're warriors, and we're the best of the best. We protect Earth and Heaven. Lord Eric is the only guy in Heaven with any balls, so we back him up when he needs to come to

178

Earth to deal with pathetics like you." Sam certainly seemed devoted to his Lord.

"And you what…nuzzle each other until I get nauseous?" I was trying to rile Sam up so he would fight. It wasn't working.

"Do you have any idea who you're talking to?" the girl Jenni was addressing me. "Sam knows absolutely everything about war craft. He once battled for 45 days straight. He's not scared of you. Heck, he better let me go first or I won't even get a taste of you."

She turned to Sam and changed her tone. She spoke condescendingly to me but with Sam she begged like a child. "Maybe we can get started, and be done with this before Steel even gets here." Jenni pleaded. "Steel's crazy! He's too powerful for his own good and one day he's just gonna turn on us and kill us!"

"If Steel's such a bad ass why does he paint his fingernails?" Sam asked Jenni.

"I told you, that's just his Fiend race," Jenni seemed exasperated explaining. "Members of that clan naturally have blue hair and fingernails, he doesn't paint his!"

"Ok, ok," Sam scooped Jenni into a hug. "I know you're scared of Steel." Sam leaned forward and gave Jenni a tender kiss. "I don't see why we can't let you get started, I mean it's not like Steel's a team player anyway. Plus he's late and he knew he was supposed to be here." Sam glanced at me and sized me up. "This butterfly doesn't

179

appear to have much power anyway, probably won't last too long. I say

go for it Jenni!"

Jenni squealed with excitement. She seemed to have a small black

case with her. She opened it to expose a small white piece of canvas

and half a dozen colorful paints. I stood still; I would let her attack first.

She dipped a brush in the black paint and gracefully drew the outline of

a woman. "What do you think?" she asked me, holding up the figure.

"Is that supposed to be me?" I asked.

"Of course!" she smiled. She then drew two beautiful Angel wings on

the figure. She added little butterfly antennae on the head and a long

curly tail coming from behind. The picture was adorable and Jenni

herself was charming. I had completely lost focus on why I was here.

Jenni held up her picture for me to see. "Now comes the fun part!" she

squealed. She reached up and joyfully ripped the picture, tearing one

of the wings right off. My body actions mimicked those of the picture. A

deep, wide cut appeared on my back as if I truly had wings and one

was ripped from my flesh. I screamed out in pain! Before I could even

move a step, Jenni ripped an antennae off of the picture. This caused

a blinding pain in my skull. I couldn't see straight, my balance was off. I

knew I had to get that voodoo drawing from her and fast.

As I used my static to help me stand straight, Sam decided not to

watch from the sidelines but instead get into the game.

I was standing tall and about to rush Jenni and grab that painting when I got blindsided by Sam who tackled me to the ground. I fell on the side with the cut from the painting wing. I screamed out in pain. Sam rolled me onto my back and held down my legs and arms with his. I struggled but didn't have a chance against him. While he had me pinned he brought his knees up so that he was kneeling on my chest. I couldn't breathe! He let go of my arms to sit up and put even more pressure on my chest. If I didn't do something soon I was going to pass out and they were going to kill me. Wait, my arms were free. I held one palm behind another and focused out my electricity. I released it point blank on Sam. The shock threw him right off me and about 15 feet straight back into a tree. The impact to his head was hard and knocked him out before he hit the ground. I heard Jenni scream as she watched her lover go limp and unconscious.

I forced myself up and turned to Jenni. She looked at me with horror then grabbed her paints and ran over to protect Sam. With the paints in one hand and the painting of me in the other, Jenni was pretty much defenseless. I made a break for the painting and at the same time held my hand out towards Jenni and sent a static charge to knock the paints out of her hand. Everything worked, maybe not as well as I would have liked. When I went for the painting Jenni dived to keep it out of my hands. My static push did knock the paints out of her hands. Because she was diving to keep the painting from me, the paints tumbled and spilled out all over the two of us. I was not prepared for the burning sensation which exploded from every part of my body the paints touched. These were not washable paints, this was a mix of toxic chemicals. Jenni and I both started screaming from the pain. She curled up in a ball and shook. Desperate I looked for a pond or something we could wash off in. No such luck. I saw a fire hydrant, that'll do. "Jenni, you need to get up!" I yelled. She was still curled in a ball and now she was crying. I didn't know what else to do. I picked her up and carried her to the hydrant. I used my static to knock it open. The water came flooding out. I kneeled in front of the spray and pulled Jenni on my knees in front of me. I tried to rinse the toxic paint from both of us.

When I had gotten off as much paint as I could I carried her back to the tree. I placed her down on the other side of Sam, away from the paints that were now seeping into the earth. She wordlessly crept across him and picked up the torn, battered painting she drew of me. Oh my god! Even this weak and hurt - she could still kill me! I held my breath as I watched her look intently at the painting. Then she reached in her pocket and pulled out one more jar of paint - a white one. She placed the painting on the ground and poured the white paint over it. She dropped the jar and her whole body went limp, cuddled next to her beloved Sam.

I took a step back to catch my breath. This whole situation was crazy.

Who were these people? Was I really fighting for Kyan's life?

"Not bad," I heard a deep voice say. I looked up and saw a guy

lounging on that same bench just a few feet away. When did he get

there? I hadn't heard or seen him arrive.

"I guess if I'd shown up on time, they wouldn't have lost." He was

looking down at Sam and Jenni, but he looked amused. "Not that I've

ever seen them lose before," he grunted. "I don't say this often, but I'm

impressed." He looked up at me with crystal blue eyes.

"You must be Steel," I said. Getting him talking would buy me time to

rest.

He threw his head back and laughed. "Yes, I'm Steel. I can't seem to

go anywhere without my reputation proceeding me." He had the look

and the build of a teenager, maybe around 15 and well-muscled. He

had blizzard blue eyes and short spiky royal blue hair with matching

fingernails. He looked like a wannabe punk that had missed out on The

Clash. Looking at him I had no idea what Jenni was so afraid of, but

when he spoke, he sounded I don't know, authoritative to say the least.

"How old are you?' I asked.

"I don't come from a world that keeps track of things like that." A world?

What is he talking about? Well I did come through a glowing door,

maybe I was in another world.

"Are we in your world right now?" I asked and gestured to the park we were in.

"Are you retarded?" he asked and punctuated it with a look that clearly showed that he thought I was in fact retarded. "I think we're like a couple miles from your house."

"Well Lord Eric made this glowing door thing," I started but Steel cut me right off.

"Oh yeah, isn't that cool. You know there are only 5 beings in existence that can transport through dimensions like that? God, Lord Eric, his stupid cousin, Lord Quarreon and my girlfriend Princess Jodie Jhira," he told me with pride.

"Your girlfriend is a princess?" I asked.

"Yep," he said, pretty pleased with himself. He put his hands behind his head and put his feet up on the bench.

"So if you marry her..." I didn't even get the words out when he ripped into me with venom.

"You girls, you're always like 'get married.' Leave a guy alone, seriously. She knows I'm with her okay, that's all that matters; there is no need to get married. Look who's talking anyway, like you're one to advise on relationships. 'Oh poor me, I'm a beauty queen and I'm in love with 2 idiots," he said mockingly.

"How do you even know that?" I was pretty stunned.

"Are you kidding, Eric watches your life like it's a soap opera. He thinks it's destiny that you got tangled up with that soul he's been looking for." He must have meant Ky.

"How does Lord Eric watch me?" I was utterly bewildered how a total stranger knew the intimate details of my life.

"You have got to be kidding me. Are you the stupidest synergy alive? You don't know much, do you?"

"Tell me more about this soul you're talking about," I commanded.

A big smile spread across his face. "I don't think I like your tone. First of all, you never order me to do anything. You can ask, but I'll only comply if you have something that I want. Second, I think I've let you rest long enough, don't you? I don't want Eric to come back and find you still standing." He stood up from the bench and drew a long sword he had been concealing. "Your world doesn't use swords anymore. A weapon for gentlemen. You guys are all about your dumb noisy guns. I hope you have one on you, you're going to need it." He thought for a second and then looked very impressed with himself. "No wait, it won't help, I can dodge a bullet," he said and with that he disappeared in front of me only to immediately emerge behind me. His sword grazed one of the scars from the "wings" Jenni had given me and the wound burst open. Oh my God, that pain again!

How do I fight an enemy so fast? He hit me again, a shallow cut to the left thigh. I blasted off a few big thunderbolts hoping that one of them would catch him. Everything missed. I could hear him laughing at me. He came in closer and slashed the top of my right arm just below the shoulder. The pain was blinding. I tried dodging his attacks but he just seemed to appear all around me. 'He's too fast,' I thought. I was in so much pain I couldn't think of a strategy.

"You're gonna die here you know," Steel said to me with pleasure. "I know you're better than this. You're over thinking! Don't think, just MOVE!" he screamed. I pushed at the earth with my static and rocketed straight up.

"Now that's what I'm talking about!" Steel shouted from beneath me. "I didn't know you could fly; this changes everything."

Yeah, it gives me a minute to think. I could stay up here until I came up with a strategy. God this is the worst possible timing. I was so worried about Ky I hadn't slept or eaten for two days. Fighting Jenni really sapped my energy. How was I supposed to battle this guy? Ow, I think I just got hit with a rock. Sure enough Steel was using his lightning speed to hurl rocks at me. Okay already, I was heading back into the fight. I was feeling these sharp pains in my arms and legs. The rocks were just a distraction! The true attack was a series of ninja stars he had thrown which were now lodged deep in my skin and ripped flesh and muscle with every move I made. I had to get them out. I fired off a full blast of electricity coming from every point in my body. The pressure did force out the ninja stars. Since the energy was coming

186

from all directions, I unexpectedly managed to hit Steel. It didn't do much but slow him down for a second, but at least I knew how to hit him!

I didn't have enough energy to continue releasing from everywhere in the hopes of hitting Steel again. What I did think of was to try again at full power, hit him long enough to stun him and then grab his sword. It was a bold plan. I needed all of my strength and speed to pull it off. Steel was smart enough to know I would try a full blast again. He moved far away from me to plan his own strategy...

I figured if I pushed myself up, gravity would help bring me down quick. I didn't need to land on Steel, just get close. I used the static from the ground and pushed about 6 feet into the air. Sure enough, gravity was tugging down on me and I released the charge and came crashing back down. I managed to land a few feet from Steel. Before my feet even hit the ground I let out an enormous lightning bolt. I only needed a semi-circle since I knew where he was. He ran and the static still caught him just like I hoped. I reached forward with my palms and grabbed the sword. The blade was dull! Steel wasn't planning on hurting anyone with this. I grabbed the blade with all my might. Steel pushed down on the blade so I countered. I walked right into his trap! He let the sword go and I wasn't quick enough to stop the hilt from hitting me right in the face. The impact knocked me on my ass.

The sword fell on the ground. Steel reached in to get it. He knew that if I was touching it I could send a charge through the metal. What he didn't think of was that I could do the same from a distance. As soon as he got his hand on that blade I sent the biggest shock I could create. The electric spark was sucked up by the metal sword and buzzed right through Steel. He roared with pain on impact. I could smell his hair burning, he was electrified!

"You dirty bitch," Steel uttered and turned to me. "You think you're hot shit, don't you? I'm going to teach you a new meaning of the word 'pain.'" Steel sounded like a psycho killer.

"Bring it on, you big baby," I goaded him. I held out my palms in front of me. I could see electricity leaping off them like never before. I held my hands out to attack.

"Stand down," we heard in the distance. I was going to ignore it.

"It's Eric," Steel said. "Stand down." I stopped my attack but I didn't let my guard down.

Lord Eric stepped through his portal with a stern countenance. I held my guard.

"Oh my God," Steel started screaming. "You didn't do it. I can see it all over your face. You chickened out. What the hell, Eric. I distracted her just like you said." Lord Eric looked uncomfortable.

"So Ky is going to be okay?" I asked. Lord Eric just kind of nodded. Tears filled my eyes. Without thinking I ran to Lord Eric and wrapped my arms around him. "Thank you. Oh thank you." I blustered.

"Oh now I see," Steel sneered. "You let him live so that you have an excuse to hang around the girl. Pathetic."

"Right, like I care what you think. You're one to talk about relationships. Tell me Steel when do you plan on telling Jodie's parents about the two of you?" Lord Eric said snidely.

"Oh man, you haven't met her parents yet?" I laughed, wiping tears of relief from my eyes. "How long have you been together?" I asked.

"It's not that big a deal," Steel protested. "We're just waiting for the right time to tell them. We've only been together a couple years."

"Try like a couple hundred years," Lord Eric taunted. Steel growled. I was stunned.

"You're kidding me! You're over a hundred years old?" I asked, stunned.

"100?" Add the better part of a millennium to that," Lord Eric said with authority. "I would say he's somewhere between 600 and 700."

"Years old?" I questioned. "I'm just not sure I can believe that."

"There you go again with your 'beliefs.' Here's my advice: Stop worrying so much about your beliefs and start opening your mind to the truth. I told you when people die they go to heaven or hell, right?" Lord Eric seemed to be instructing me. I nodded, heaven or hell, I get that.

"Well, when people came into existence and started dying they went to heaven and hell. These are actual, physical places, not just concepts. And being that they are real places, it would make sense that they already had their own inhabitants. Heaven was populated by Angels and hell was ruled by Fiends. Humans were the first creatures to be made of two parts, the body and soul. So humans get to live two lives. One here on earth until their body dies and then they go to heaven or hell until they are reincarnated," Lord Eric said with absolute certainty.

"I think my head is going to explode," I said, dizzy with the knowledge he had just spilled. Could he be telling the truth? "Earlier you said I was a 'synergy.' A synergy of what? What does that mean exactly?"

Lord Eric enlightened me. "The actual definition of synergy is: an interaction of two or more agents or forces so that their combined effect is greater than the sum of their individual effects. Hence when an Angel or a Fiend has a child with a human it is called a synergy. It is far greater than just a normal human. That's what you are, my dear."

"How can you tell?" I wondered.

"Well one clue is the eyes. If you have green eyes then there is Angel blood in your background. Blue indicates Fiend. Brown eyes are the trickiest because they could hide either Angel or Fiend," Eric taught. "It doesn't matter too much, most people have Angels and Fiends so far back in their lineage that the eye color becomes meaningless."

"I'm a Fiend? My parents were from hell, like the devil?" I was the bad guy? It was almost too much to bear.

"Look, don't take it so hard. No one said Fiends were bad. I know a lot of Fiends who are fine, upstanding individuals. And 'hell,' well that word covers 28 different worlds. Some of them are the most beautiful places I've ever seen. No one is saying heaven is that great either. You really need to let go of what you've been told all your life and open your eyes. Existence is a vast and complex place. There is good and evil everywhere."

It was all too much to think about. "Is Keith Mal a synergy too?"

Eric shook his head like he was talking to a child. "All of your so-called 'mutants' are synergies. You'll find most of them are orphans or with a single parent. Angels and Fiends don't spend much time in this world. It's too dangerous for them," he stopped abruptly. "We'll have to finish this some other time. It's time for you to get to the hospital; your injuries need medical attention." He was right, I was getting woozy.

"I want to know more!" I wanted to know everything.

"I'll come by in a few days. We can talk then," Lord Eric said, as if he was any other guy and just wanted to hang out. "Now tend to those injuries."

That blinding door appeared again. I stumbled through and it disappeared. Lucky was waiting on the other side. I took two steps toward him and just completely passed out into his arms.

Chapter 13

When I awoke I was the one in a hospital bed. They had patched me up pretty well; I was still all drowsy with painkillers.

Lucky was bent over watching me intently. As soon as I opened my eyes he scooped me up and whisked me down the hall. I had a good feeling.

Lucky carried me right into the ICU and right over to Ky's little bed. Sitting upright, eyes open, trying to drink a glass of juice was Kyan Mal. Lucky dropped me right on the bed and I crawled over to wrap my arms around Ky. I think this was the happiest I've ever felt.

Ky looked like hell. He definitely looked like he had died and come back. Keith was standing over him with a big smile.

Ky took one look at my bandages and got worried. "Are you ok? How did you get hurt?" I guess no one had told him anything. Was I supposed to tell him the truth?

"It was a test," Keith piped up. "Apparently Stephanie passed or did well at least. A guy named Eric said that she was going to be your guardian, Ky." Guardian of what?

"Sweet!" Kyan said. "That means she needs to stay with me. She can't guard me if you make her leave."

"Ky, Luke and I think it's best if you move back into the house," Keith said to me gruffly.

"Oh you and Luke think so? Since when are you and Luke such good friends?" I drawled.

"Mind your business! Do you want to go back to living on the street?" Keith sounded pompous.

"What makes you think I'd be out on the street? I'm Miss New York runner-up now, I'm sure someone will take me in."

"Ok, well I'm your boss and I say you're moving back," Keith snapped.

"You're not my boss anymore, you fired me," I pointed out.

"I am your legal guardian," he countered.

"I'll just go back to Mr. G," I told him.

"Well, I'm your boyfriend and I'm telling you you're moving back into the house," he sounded triumphant.

"You're my what?" I asked stunned. I looked at Lucky, who was looking at the floor.

"Well, Keith and I thought it would be best for Ky, well, best for the situation really..." Lucky stammered. He took my bandaged hand and looked up at me with his beautiful brown eyes. "Look, you're in a good place here and it would be wrong for me to take you away. I mean this guy's totally loaded and well, did you see the algorithm he made you?"

"I just don't get it. Remember like two days ago when he destroyed all my things? Keith is a psycho and I...I want to be with you," I told Lucky though I knew in my heart he had already made up his mind.

"I just think that right now this is what's going to make you happy," Lucky said earnestly. "I'll stick around for a little bit and make sure he's nice to you."

"What about you?" I asked full of concern. "This isn't like you, walking away. Don't you want me? Aren't you going to fight for me?"

"I'm cool. I wanted to see you again but this whole Miss New York runner-up thing is a little too much for me. I've kinda got my own thing going on in Atlanta," he confessed.

"You know you're my best friend in the world," I told him. "After Ky."

"Yeah, yeah. Just make sure Keith marries you and bam! Divorce him and take half, then run away with me." Lucky grinned.

"It's a date," I promised. "But this time when you leave, cell phones, plane visits. I don't want to lose touch with you ever again," I stressed.

"Yeah baby, you know you can't live without me!" he laughed. I playfully smacked him.

"Ok you two, enough," Keith broke in.

Ky, Lucky and I started laughing when Eve poked her head in the room and motioned to me and Keith. My heart sank.

"You are never going to believe what happened," she told us. "This whole "synergy" thing has started a frenzy. The Mayor is going to address the city and he wants Stephanie to be there with him!"

Wait, what? The Mayor of New York? Wants me there, whatever for?

Eve continued telling us what she had heard. "Apparently the government wants to learn more about this. This could mean charities and scientists. They might be able to help all these folks who were locked up just like you."

I nodded, still bewildered by what I was hearing.

"This could help a lot of people. At least run it past Mr. Gerard, ok Steph?" Keith asked. I nodded again. Keith continued, "Mr. Gerard has had some big plan from the beginning and we are all just playing into it. It's time we make him tell us what's really going on."

"It doesn't matter," I said. "If the government is going to seek out the synergies, they are going to do it whether it's in the eyes of the public or completely secret. If the people really trust me like you say, they'll be less scared if I'm leading the way. Whatever the Mayor wants, we cooperate." Keith headed back into Ky's hospital room when Eve grabbed my arm.

"You know he doesn't love you, right? Keith just hates to lose. He saw your old boyfriend show up and he got a little jealous. That's all." Eve gave me a look that was pure venom. "Before you were Miss New York's runner-up Keith wouldn't lay a hand on you. He loves the celebrity, not the girl." I pulled my arm from her grasp and walked away without saying a word.

I went back into the hospital room and pulled Ky into a hug. "Whatever kind of guardian you need, I'm going to make sure you have it. You can count on me."

"I want to protect you, too," sweet Ky whispered, pulling me into a hug. He made me feel strong and safe. Lord Eric was right, Ky did have a special soul.

"Oh hey," I started. "Did you guys know there are other worlds?"

The hospital released me with a stern lecture about fighting, but they kept Ky for a few days. Keith and I spent every minute of visiting hours by his side. When we were done at the hospital, my driver Tim would drive me up to see Mr. Gerard. I told him the secrets that Eric had shared with me. Mr. G coached me on exactly how to respond to the Mayor and what message to send my fellow synergies. He also warned that the Mayor might just be trying to cash in on my new found fame. He showed me dozens of websites that had shown up in the past week since the pageant. All of them about me, none of them accurate.

"You're using the term 'synergy' now. Where did you get that word? A synergy is a blend of two things. What are you the mix of?" Mr. Gerard mused.

"I don't know. I guess a human and a..." I didn't know exactly, and maybe I didn't want to know.

I had several days to kill before my actual meeting with the Mayor. My head wound was going to heal in time but I needed to keep covered from head to toe while the rest of my injuries mended. I got pretty banged up in the fight with Eric's goons but it seemed like my electricity helped me heal.

I moved back into the Mals' house. This time I would be down the other hallway on the opposite side of the solarium from the Mal brothers. My new room was the one Keith had prepared for me. I don't know what he was thinking but the room was floor to ceiling in purple. The walls, bed and carpet were all a lavender shade and there were two huge sets of dark purple curtains covering the two tall windows. I'm a girl who likes blue so I was definitely taken aback but if this is what Keith thought to create for me then I was determined to appreciate it. I had my own master bathroom with a huge tub in the floor, a stall shower and a pair of sinks, all off white. It certainly seemed majestic.

We set Lucky up with the room across the hall from me. That one was a simple off white with a green carpet. There were still 4 more empty rooms on our side of the hall.

It felt weird every night when Keith would claim his boyfriend privileges. I was so excited to finally be with him, I wanted to give myself to him completely but part of me was holding back. Part of me definitely still belonged to Lucky. Also there was something else that was bugging me.

197

"Keith, when you dated Eve I was beyond jealous. I wanted you desperately," I confessed. "Now that I have you, I love you with that same desperation. I love you but it feels so passionate and crazy. When I was with Lucky it was nice and happy. With you, well, I'm scared of the way I feel."

"Being with you makes me uncomfortable too," Keith said. I wasn't quite sure we were feeling the same things.

Ky came home from the hospital! I went to the party store and decorated every part of the house! I even got Lucky to help me hang some of the banners. "Can't you use your synergy powers to do this?" Lucky asked.

"I suppose I could," I realized.

"Well then, see that you do. Practice with them all the time. What if you get into another fight like with Eric's team? I really don't want to see you get hurt," Lucky instructed. It was so great to have him here looking after me again.

Chapter 14

Pretty soon it was time for me to meet the Mayor. All week long the "mutant" situation was the hot topic on the news. I went for an interview myself and introduced the word "synergy." Now everything was "synergy" this and "synergy" that.

I ended up standing on the steps of City Hall listening to the Mayor reassure New Yorkers that synergies were citizens like everyone else and there was nothing to fear. He did say he would like synergies to identify themselves to the city via a secure website. This way, the city could provide help and treatment for any synergy that needed it. I smelled a little McCarthy era witch hunting, but under the circumstances it was to be expected.

After the Mayor's speech I stuck around to sign autographs and take pictures with the citizens. There were way more people than I anticipated and I started getting nervous and retreated back towards City Hall.

Suddenly it seemed like a small riot broke out between security and the crowd. Some of the security backed up to protect me; the others started pushing back the crowd. Somehow one guy managed to get through. He was running straight for me, screaming my name. One of the guards reached up and hit him with a taser. As he was being electrocuted, I could see his face clearly. Jage! Oh my God! Jage was the first mutant I had ever met. He made me realize I wasn't alone.

Now his face was twisted in pain from the taser. "STOP! STOP!" I

yelled. "I know him, he's with me." I fell to my knees and pulled Jage

close to me. "Are you okay?" I asked.

"Not really," he answered.

"I'm going to bring you back to my house, ok? You just rest until then."

I don't even know if he heard me before he passed out. The security

guards carried him to the limo, apologizing profusely.

I ran to tell the guys about Jage and they followed me back to the limo.

As we headed for home Lucky and I told the Mals how we met Jage in

San Francisco and how as a child Jage had been caged up just like

me, though in his case it was an actual cage, bars and all. He was a

synergy and he had himself a tail. It looked like a kangaroo tail and

allowed him to lift himself up and bat things away. He was wearing a

big, floor length coat which hid his tail completely. What was he doing

in New York?

We carried him in and put him on the couch in the living room. Keith

started heating up some dinner and I watched over our guest.

Jage's hair was light brown with natural blond streaks through it. It

looked like it had been neatly cut some time ago and was now a bit

overgrown. It had been wildly overgrown when we first met him,

looking like it hadn't been touched in years. I thought the wild hair had

added to his sexiness. Lucky just thought I was a groupie for guys with

tails.

Jage came to with a start and sat straight up. I had to hold him down.

"Relax," I commanded. "I'm so glad to see you," I told him.

"I need your help," Jage said frantically.

"Calm down," I told him, but he was clawing at me, too worked up to calm down. "I'll do whatever I can Jage. Tell me everything."

"My girlfriend Ari, she's in danger. We need to rescue her." He really seemed afraid. "I left her behind to get help. God, I'm so worried about her!"

Keith reached out grabbed Jage by the collar choking the poor guy.

"Calm the F down already. We can't help her until you tell us everything so stop being an ass and tell us something useful."

You gotta hand it to him, he wasn't a nice guy but Keith sure knew how to control a situation.

"Here it is," Jage began. "I met Ari almost a year ago in a chat room. It was a group who would pretend they had super powers and figure out different ways to use them. After a few months everybody had crazy impossible powers and we stuck to what we had first joined the group with. We kind of found each other then. We met up a few weeks later at a rave. I couldn't believe how beautiful she was. Bright red hair, eyes that were cerulean blue and the sweetest shy smile."

I interrupted him. "You were pretty shy when I met you too."

"Yeah," Jage blushed a little bit. He continued, "Anyway, by the time you showed up at Miss New York there was so much stuff about

201

mutants flying around. We heard about this group that would help you out discreetly. A few days ago they were having a meeting and the special guest speaker was Stephanie Park. I told Ari that I knew you and we went and checked it out. The meeting was interesting and the special guest did look very much like you, but obviously it wasn't you. I took her aside afterwards and told her I knew the real Stephanie Park. She told us her name was Alexis and admitted she created this con the day you became Miss New York runner-up because it was hard to get kids with anomalies to come out in the open. Ari and I had coffee with her. Turns out her ability is pretty insane. She the closest thing you'll find to a shapeshifter. She can change her hair and eye color, even her skin color, but not her body shape."

"So Alexis has this house not far from here. She said it was a sanctuary for synergies. Alexis told us all she wanted was to help synergies like us find our place in the world.

Ari and I packed our things and headed out here to New York. When we arrived at Alexis' place, well nothing was what it seemed. The place was a dump. There were four other synergies there, all guys. They were nice but they were, I don't know, goons. The leader calls himself 'Destroyer' and he seemed like a decent guy, all about making the world safe for synergies and such. The first night Ari and I wondered if we made the right choice."

"The next day Alexis said she needed to take Ari with her to meet someone. I spent the day with the guys training and such to keep the area secure for when more synergies joined us. Alexis and Ari didn't come home that night. I was really worried. The next day I tried to call Ari's parents but I couldn't get reception on my cell and there was no phone line at Alexis'. Her house was in the middle of nowhere. It seemed like a safe place for a sanctuary, but I realized there was no escape!"

"Why would Alexis want Ari?" Lucky asked. Jage looked away from us.

"Jage," Keith started his tirade. "I'm imagining that this story is going to end with you asking us to put our lives on the line to save your girlfriend. Am I right?" Jage swallowed hard and nodded. "We need a little faith buddy, tell us what we're dealing with."

"Ari has an incredible power," Jage admitted.

"Now we're talking!" said Lucky. "So what can she do? Walk through walls? Start fires with her mind? Turn water into wine?"

"She can tell if someone is a synergy." Wow, that shut us up. "There's more. Synergy energy emits a light pattern depending on the evolution of its particles. In essence there is a color coded system to how powerful a synergy is. Ari can see all of that. In the wrong hands Ari's power could be used for terrible evil. You can't leave her in Alexis' hands!"

Keith, Lucky and I huddled up.

"Well, we've been talking about building a legion of superheroes. This could be our big break," Lucky said, pressing his fingertips together like some evil villain.

"And who are you supposed to be?" I asked him. "You don't even have superpowers!"

"You know, I'm that human guy that everyone fears and respects because I'm the only human bad ass enough to command a legion of super synergies!!" Lucky laughed with an exaggerated maniacal chuckle.

"Luke is right, no time like the present to see what we're made of. I'll assume command for now. We'll have to come up with a plan." Keith was quick and decisive as always.

I, however, had a little more to say on the subject. "Don't either of you care that this is a person we're talking about? That Jage is a friend of ours?"

"I don't care. Keith?" Lucky said and looked to his friend.

"That's what we have you for," Keith told me. "You're the girl; you do the worrying and the hugging and stuff. Now make yourself useful and go tell Jage we'll do it!"

"We *will* rescue your girlfriend," I told Jage and in doing so told everybody else. "But not because she is a powerful synergy. We'll do it because you're our friend, Jage." Jage looked at me with surprise and then pulled me into a hug. Keith and Lucky just looked at each other and nodded.

"Thank you, oh god thank you!" Jage whispered.

"So where is Ari now?" Keith asked, needing desperately to formulate a strategy.

"Alexis said she didn't come back with her but I know that she did! I heard her. There is only one room in the house that Alexis keeps locked, I think she's in there." Jage still seemed shaky.

Keith took charge. "Ok, Jage, you need to get online and find me that property. I want maps, satellite photos, whatever you can get. Lucky, start searching this place for anything that can be used for weapons or armor. Stephanie, I want you to contact Harlan, he's going to watch Ky tonight. The time is about 9pm. I'd like to be ready to leave here by 1am, understood?"

"Yes sir," we all kind of answered and scurried about. Keith grabbed Jage by the arm. "I'll need a breakdown of all the people on the property and what they are capable of." Keith stopped for a moment. "Jage, I know that you're worried, but on the battlefield I need you to be tough as nails, do you understand? You need to pull it together."

"I will," Jage promised.

I took Kyan over to Harlan's in the limo. "I want to help!" Ky declared.

"You are helping," I reassured him. "What do your brother and I worry about most?"

"Me?" he asked.

"Yep. So knowing that you're safe and sound is the most important thing for both of us. When we're done I'm going to need a great big hug, and you know who I'm going to!" I used my fingertips to creep along the car seat and up Ky's side until I was tickling him. He laughed and squealed like a little boy without a care in the world.

When I got back to the house the guys were pretty much ready. Keith had planned out a strategy. I was to lure the synergies into the woods and the guys would free Ari. Keith would drive the getaway car. Lucky had found some metal pieces from a MalAdjusted video game trade show. It was a medieval video game and the pieces were supposed to be plate armor. They were long metal strips that went over the head and protected the front and back almost to the knee. There were no sleeves, though. Jage threw one on. It fit fine and didn't disturb his tail. He put his long overcoat on top and he looked like a modern day knight. Lucky, Keith and I were all impressed. We tried on the other pieces. The metal fit together in zigzag rows.

"Like snake skin," I murmured.

"Ok, we all need codenames," Keith instructed. "Stephanie you will be 'Spark,' I will be 'Sharp,' Jage will be 'Rue,' Luke will be..."

"Wait, stop right there!" Jage commanded. "Roo, like kangaroo? What, 'cause I have a fucking tail? No way. You are not calling me that."

"No man 'Rue' like 'rue the day?'" Keith asked. "Stephanie said that was your thing. The kangaroo part is just a hilarious coincidence." He and Lucky were looking at each other trying to bite back laughter.

"Whatever." Jage seemed miffed about the name. "Just save my girlfriend."

"What's my name?" Lucky asked.

"I was thinking 'Assassin,'" Keith announced.

"How come everyone else's name is one syllable and mine is three? Are you planning on calling me Ass?" Lucky asked suspiciously.

"No," Keith chuckled. "Well, maybe. The word assassin came from the Persian word Hashshashin which means hashish user." Everybody giggled. Perfect for Lucky. "The Hashshashin were highly capable but weren't strong enough to go head to head with their foe so they developed covert tactics to accomplish their goals. I figured since you didn't have any synergy powers..."

"Yeah, I get it," Lucky broke in. "It's awesome, I love it! Assassin. Bad ass!"

"Are you sure you are all ready for this?" Keith asked us. I was nervous, to be sure, but I knew what it was like to be locked up against your will and I would put my life on the line to help this girl.

We didn't have a car of our own so Keith grabbed the limo. He went over and over the plan the whole ride. The guys had decided to stop the car a safe distance and sneak in through the woods. Keith held me back a minute to give me kisses. "Thank you for helping Jage," I told

him.

"Hey, we need to build allies, right?" Keith smiled. He acted like he was

always working an angle but I knew underneath he was just a big

softie. I gave him the most passionate kisses I could and then headed

off to catch up with Jage and Lucky.

The guys had scampered off quicker than I thought. I was trying to

follow them, but it was hard to find their trail. I continued on in the

direction they had gone, hoping to reach them. Suddenly I heard them

in the distance. I ran to catch up. It wasn't them! This was my first

mission and I was so green. The noises in the woods were the enemy

fighters. Oh crap! They were closing in on me! I turned and ran deeper

into the woods. If I could distract a few of them it would keep them off

Lucky and Jage.

I tried to count how many there were. They were hiding in the trees

and it was hard to make out. I looked around for something metal to

send electricity to. No such luck, we were deep in the woods. My only

metal was the armor I was wearing. If I could get these guys close

enough to touch it…no, wait. I didn't know how good these fighters

were. They might kill me before I even had a chance.

I decided the best possible plan was to try to lure them forward and

take down one at a time. I would take down the fastest one, then

continue running until I isolated the next guy, then take him down too and so on until they were gone. They were all keeping a pretty good pace so I started building up a static charge from the friction of running through the grass. I saw the shadow of a tall lanky male on my right and I struck out with an unsteady lightning bolt. I hit! I heard the guy topple to the ground and stop running. One down. I started gathering up electricity and pulled the same maneuver on the guy to my left. Nice! Knocked him down, too. I realized there could only be one or two left so I stopped running.

"Come out and fight," I shouted into the trees. A moment later a figure in motorcycle leathers wearing a plastic biker helmet with the visor down stepped out of the shadows. Who the hell was this guy? His body was completely protected from my electric attacks. Was he a psychic? How could he even know who he was fighting? What he didn't know about were my decent hand to hand skills.

He circled me for a moment. I wanted him to make the first move. He seemed a little dazed. I decided to strike. I put my fists up to protect my face and went at him with a lower leg kick to his right thigh. He dodged! Oh my God he was fast. I tried again with all my force. Again he dodged! I decided to strike. I took a left jab right at his face. He effortlessly pulled away and my punch went right past him. This guy made me look like I was standing still. I bent forward and charged him, hoping to get him on the ground. Success! I did knock him down but not in any position where I could dominate him. Still, he fell to his side and I kicked off the helmet. Holy crap, he was a kid! He couldn't have been more than 16. His body was so well muscled I had definitely thought him 10 years older.

I knew I couldn't get anywhere with him on his side, so I jumped back to my feet to try striking him again. The challenger also got to his feet.. Messy blonde hair that hung past his ears and intense ice blue eyes. I was spellbound for a second. He was looking at me approvingly as well. Maybe I could use this to my advantage. "I don't want to hurt you," I said holding my fists up again.

"I wouldn't worry," he laughed. "I don't think you could hurt me if you tried."

I threw a right hook with all my might trying to catch him. I missed. I faked another right and threw a left instead, still he dodged. This guy was lightning fast. I didn't know what to do.

"I admit you're better than me," I told him trying to throw him off.

"That's why I'm the leader of this crew," he said with pride.

"Leading a crew of villains, that's something to be proud of," I snapped. I punched again with my right, this time he caught it! He actually caught my fist and just held it there.

"First off, you're the invader here. Second, I haven't thrown a single punch. You're clearly outclassed here; I'm being a gentleman by not fighting."

Before I knew it he was leaning in to me. Was he trying to give me a kiss? Some gentleman! I kneed him in the stomach, dropping him to his knees. The only exposed flesh on his body was his face so I pressed his cheek to my armor and let the static buildup transfer to his face. He twitched from being electrocuted and I could smell his hair burning. I pulled the charge away before I fried him. He was still alive when I let him fall to the ground. I could hear Keith's car nearby and I ran through the trees hoping to find it.

I caught up to the limo in under a minute. I was happy to see that Lucky and Jage were okay. In Jage's arms was a pretty red-head I could only assume was Ari. In her arms she clung to a mass of folders and paperwork.

Lucky filled me in on their part of the mission. They had gotten into the house but found the locked room already open and empty. Ari had freed herself and gathered up all of the information she could find. She made her way down to the docks on the opposite side of the house from where we had entered through the woods. While she was hiding she noticed Jage and Lucky skulking about. The two took out the lackey who was left to guard the house, while I was stuck in the woods fighting the other three. After that Ari ran up to them, they signaled Keith, and everyone got away. Pretty lucky for our first mission.

We all went home and hit the showers. After we were clean we raided the fridge like maniacs. I was a little disturbed about my fight. I brought it up with Jage and Ari.

"You must have been fighting Destroyer," Jage told me. "He's been with Alexis for a while now, captain of her guard. That kid is amazing, quick as lightning and strong, really strong." Ari just shook her head in agreement with Jage.

"It just doesn't make sense. If I was the infiltrator, why didn't he pummel me first and ask questions later?" No one could answer me. It was time to turn our attention to the files that Ari had stolen.

"These were Alexis'," she said meekly. It was the first time I'd heard her talk. "These are the synergies she is trying to sign up. She talks a good game but her motives are sinister. All of these people are in danger!"

Keith looked at the stack of files a bit and then threw them down on the table. "This is where we recruit. These synergies are in danger and we need body guards. Tomorrow morning we'll go through these and see who we can save."

Chapter 15

There were a lot of files, each one a life of a young synergy not knowing where their power comes from or what they are truly capable of. I didn't know what we were going to do, if anything.

The next morning Keith tucked the files in his briefcase and Jage, Ari, Lucky and I accompanied him to work to do some research and strategy. We took the limo first to Harlan's to pick up Ky. He gave me a hug as we dropped him off at school. "Can I hug Ari too?" he asked.

My little Angel! Ari was only too happy to give him a hug.

As soon as Ky left the limo, the guys started talking about the files they had selected. There was no plan on how to convince these new synergies to join us except to say that we didn't want them to fall under the influence of Alexis, which was the truth.

We arrived at the building and poured into Keith's office. Keith went immediately to open the curtains behind his desk. He had just begun to let the light peek through when he dropped everything and thundered, "How did you get in here?"

We all ran to the desk and saw that sitting in Keith's chair was the leader of the synergy group we fought last night. Jage immediately jumped in front of Ari and everyone else took a defensive stance. This guy might be capable of killing all of us. He didn't look so much like a killer though. He was relaxed in the chair with his hands folded behind his head. His face was badly burned from our altercation last night.

"What are you doing here?" I asked with trepidation.

"Changing sides," he told us.

Huh? What? Did he just say he was changing sides?

"I saw your little operation last night and I can tell you could use a fighter of my strength. I broke through this building's security this morning to show you I'm smart, too." His blue eyes were sparkling.

Lucky wasn't taking it for a second. "Get out and don't ever come back. Don't test me!" he got right in the stranger's face and shouted.

"You can burn in hell for what Alexis did to Ari," Jage sneered.

"Ok calm down," the stranger was starting to lose his confidence. "Alexis duped me too. I thought she was the good guy until last night. I never knew Ari was being held against her will. I thought we were working together to rescue all the world's synergies. I thought I was being a hero..." his voice trailed off.

"What changed your mind?" Lucky asked.

"Well truly it was seeing Stephanie. It was hard to believe that Miss New York #3 was out to harm us, synergies I mean. We were told that anyone found on the premises was after us and that we needed to protect the files of our mutant brothers and sisters. After we let Ari go Alexis went nuts screaming at us and I was like 'Ok, something is clearly wrong here.' I talked it over with the other guys but they wanted to stay loyal to Alexis. She really roped us all in, you know." Ari and Jage looked at each other. You could tell they agreed with the guy.

214

I reached over to the stranger and took one of his hands in mine. He had been through far more than he was telling us, that much was clear. "What's your name?" I asked gently.

"Uh, Destroyer," he mumbled. I remember hearing it last night.

"Not your code name silly, your real name." He looked away.

"I, uh. I walked away from that life. That name isn't me, I don't want to hear it." He looked genuinely upset. Suddenly Lucky could identify with the guy too.

I took a second to look at him. I'm sure he would say he was 18 but he didn't look more than 16. He had dirty blonde hair with sun bleached highlights that told me he was outdoorsy or that he had traveled a long way to be here, maybe even hitchhiking and such. He was in a gray t-shirt with a navy blue warm up jacket and jeans. He was such a good fighter for his age, which suggests he came from a city. Maybe an abusive parent too.

While the stranger and I were conversing Jage, Lucky and Keith gathered in the corner to discuss this outsider.

The stranger kept on talking. "So, do you have a boyfriend?" he asked very enthusiastically.

"I only date guys with names," I cracked.

"Ug," he grabbed at his heart. "I told you it's De..." I reached up and put my hand over his mouth to stop him from repeating that silly nickname.

215

"Look, give me something. A first name, a last name. A middle name. One of your legal names. I promise we won't call you by it."

"What are you going to call me, then?" he pushed back. He certainly had a lot of spunk.

"Um, Zeal," I declared. "We'll call you Zeal."

"Zeal," he repeated. He thought it over. "Ok, that's fine. I'll give you my initials, but not my name."

"Good, that way when I take the witness stand I won't have to lie." We both laughed, but there was something still bothering me.

"I really messed up your face. Aren't you mad at me? You can tell me the truth." I braced myself for the worst.

"You put everything you had into freeing your friend," he said. "I'll do the same thing someday for the people I care about." I couldn't help but smile at that.

"Ok, those initials," I gestured with my palm like he was going to physically put the initials in there.

"W.......S. And don't ask what they're for! This was a trade; I never want those letters arranged in that sequence again."

"Ok, ok, never again. From now on it's Zeal." I flashed him a smile. He flashed one back and then looked over to the whispering group. "Thanks for being so cool to me. Doesn't matter much, your man's kicking me out anyway."

Huh, how could he hear them all the way in the corner? And how did he know which one was my man? We turned toward the group.

"He's right Steph," Keith said. "He's too strong and we don't know if we can trust him. He's one of Alexis' goons, maybe he's spying for her right now. It's just not safe to have him around."

"But he didn't fight back last night! Doesn't that mean something?" I could tell there was good in this guy.

Zeal jumped up from the chair. "Well, I don't want to be anywhere I'm not wanted." He bowed to the group. "Thank you for your time," he said. He kissed my hand. "We'll meet again, I hope."

He walked away as Keith's cell phone buzzed with a text message. "Freeze," Keith shouted as Zeal headed for the door. "What the hell is this?" He pushed his phone in Zeal's face. Zeal looked shocked.

"Dude, I don't know nuthin' about this, okay? I'm the good guy, remember? I would never hurt a kid."

Hurt a kid! What are they talking about? The phone got passed to me. On it was a picture of little Ky tied up and gagged! Tears sprung to my eyes. What was going on? The phone started ringing in my hands. The caller ID said it was "Kyan." I shakily handed the phone to Keith. He answered with the speakerphone so that we could all hear but gestured for us to be quiet. "Keith Mal," he answered.

The woman who spoke was clearly Alexis. "I don't think I have to tell you how much danger your brother is in, do I?" she snarled. "Let's

217

make this easy on all of us. Send Ari and Destroyer back to me with the files and I will gladly hand over your brother. No one needs to get hurt; we're all on the same side here."

Everyone in our group started panicking. Only Keith, the guy with the most to lose, kept his calm. Keith began negotiating his brother's release while protecting his team. "Jage and Ari skipped town immediately last night. They're halfway to California by now. I'll be happy to trade you the files for my brother."

"I had a feeling Jage and Ari would hightail it, but I know Destroyer is with you. He practically wall papered his bunk with pictures of wannabe-Miss New York. I should have known he'd run after her the first chance he got, so if he's not there now he will be soon. Wait for him and I'll trade the child for my man and the files." With those final words she hung up.

I was terrified. Ari started to cry. We reached out and hugged each other tight. Keith was silent for a moment and then he started to speak. "Well, we've copied the files. I'd consider changing the information before giving them back to her but I really don't want to take the chance that Alexis will notice. She's a smart woman, we're lucky she let the Ari thing drop. We've isolated the synergies we're going after, and we'll try to warn the rest by phone. We'll just have to leave tonight as soon as this thing is over." Keith spoke calmly and rationally but there was fear in his eyes. He continued on detailing to us the plan that was forming in his mind.

"Stephanie and..."

"Zeal," I finished for him.

"You two will go in to exchange the files for Ky," Keith told us.

"You don't have to put her in danger, I'll go alone," Zeal stated.

"Look, never mind that this is my little brother we're talking about. I'm the leader of this group, I tell you what to do!" Territorial pissing between the two had begun.

"Alexis wants you back. If you walk in on your own, she'll know you're on our side. If we send you in with Stephanie - then it looks like you are returning and Stephanie is there to get Kyan." Keith was definitely enjoying barking the orders to Zeal. It might just work out having this new guy on the team.

"Now Zeal, tell me about your forces. If Stephanie walks out the front door with Ky are you going to be able to break out of there or is she going to have to go back for you?" Keith wondered.

"No problem, I can handle those guys. Let her take the kid and I'll be right behind," Zeal said breezily like he staged daring rescue operations on a daily basis.

Lucky got in the middle of the two and pushed Zeal. "What if he's lying? What if this is a trap? I'm not sending Stephanie in there to get snatched or killed!"

Keith broke it up before Zeal could retaliate. "Chill, Luke. Stephanie is famous, remember? That's why she worked so hard to get that way. She can't be touched. Every citizen in New York would be out for blood if something happened to their precious beauty queen. Alexis knows that. She's a sociopath who thinks she is helping synergies; she's not looking to kill us off. She really does care, that's why she was able to dupe intelligent people like Jage and Ari."

"And Zeal," Zeal muttered.

"Let's go now. I'll drive the limo. Luke, you're with me. Jage and Ari - you stay here. Luke, give them your mobile. Get all the information ready for the police. If you don't hear from us in 3 hours I want you to call 911 and then destroy the files, understand?" Jage nodded his head. I knew we could count on him. I wasn't going to let it come to that, though. I was going to save Ky.

We got in the car and I realized Mr. Gerard might be able to help us.

"Mr. G. it's Stephanie. We're in a lot of trouble. Do you know a synergy named Alexis? She's kind of a chameleon."

"Alexis Munroe," Mr. G confirmed. "I knew her personally, she was my girlfriend for a little while."

"Well she's kidnapped Kyan. I need you to tell me everything you know."

Mr. G sighed. "I tracked her down a few years back. I was hoping she could be the one mutant I could introduce to the public. It was always

220

my idea to win hearts and create sympathy for our cause. Alexis had grown up thinking she was the only mutant in the world, like many of you. When she found out there were hundreds, possibly thousands she wanted to band together and force the world to pay for mistreating and discriminating against her."

"She became obsessed and I had to break up with her. She broke into my lab a few days later and ran off with a stack of my research files. I guess she's been using them to hunt down synergies," he paused. "This is bad Stephanie. Those files are some of the most powerful beings on earth. If Alexis recruits them, she may really have an army on her hands."

"Right now I have to worry about Kyan. That's all I care about. Alexis can have her stupid army." I said angrily.

"Please," Mr. Gerard pleaded. "These people are innocent just like Kyan. Don't let Alexis recruit them."

I thanked him and hung up the phone. I relayed what he had said to everyone.

Keith and Lucky went back to talking non-stop in the front seat. They plotted and planned while I just hung out in the back and felt panicked. Zeal tried to help me calm down. He offered me a giant piece of bubble gum. I declined and he popped it into his own mouth. "She's not going to hurt the kid," he said, putting his hand over mine. I wished I knew that was true.

The drive seemed to take forever. Finally we were in front of the house. Keith had laid out a very specific plan. First we get Ky safe, then me, then Zeal. I didn't like the plan at all and I told him so. Keith reminded us that it was his little brother; we would do what he said. All four of us got out of the car. Lucky and Keith would stay put unless they thought we needed them.

There were about four men waiting in front of the house when we got there.

"New recruits?" I asked Zeal.

"Not my guys," Zeal told me. He blew a bubble with his chewing gum. We slowly made our way to the door. The house was much bigger and shabbier than it appeared last night. Being right on the water had rotted out a lot of the wood.

"Looks like a fire hazard, wouldn't you say?" Zeal asked me. "Alexis would never let us smoke inside. We might catch the whole place on fire." Shut up Zeal, why was he so chatty?

We walked in the front door. The front room was big and it had three exits, a back door, a doorway to a living room and one leading to the staircase upstairs. There was a mutant posted in every doorway. These were Zeal's men. He nudged me and then made a point out of waving to each one of them. I followed his fingers; he was showing me there were metal reinforcements on each of the main beams in the room. This was going to be like taking candy from a baby.

"Alexis know we're here?" Zeal asked one of the toadies.

"She'll be right out," the guy replied. "Who do you think you are running out on us like that?"

"C'mon guys, I asked who's coming with me but you all said no." While the guys were distracted Zeal put a matchbox in my hand. He opened it and pulled out two matches, then closed it and left it in my hand. He continued to talk to the guys asking if Alexis had hurt the little boy. He nudged me again and I noticed a ninja star lodged into one of the walls. I could tell that he wanted me to get it. I raised my hand and pointed to the doorway nearest the star.

"Is Ky in there?" I asked, walking toward it. Everyone started immediately protesting and telling me to back up. No one even noticed as I magnetized the star and pulled it into my hand. I returned to my position next to Zeal. He took the star from my hand and started playing with it, spinning it on his fingers like it was no big deal.

A few more minutes went by. Alexis finally emerged. She had two big guys guarding Ky, still tied and gagged. When she entered the room, everyone turned to look. Zeal took advantage of the distraction. He took the gum from his mouth and pressed it to the ninja star. He snatched the matches and ran them across the box in my hand to light them. He blew quickly on the matches and they blazed. Then he stuck the matches to the piece of gum and attached them to the star. He threw the star straight up hard and it stuck. His movements were so fast, so swift even I couldn't follow them. I looked up to the ceiling; it was slowly catching fire. This would cover our tracks!

Alexis came forward for the files. "I'm sorry to have to force you back like this, Destroyer. I'd like to give you the time to realize on your own that this is a mistake, but we really need you. With Ari's help we jumped forward on our goals and now is the time to save our synergy brothers and sisters."

"Like this?" he asked, walking over to Ky. "By torturing children to get what you want?"

"I did this because I care," Alexis shrieked.

"I care too," Zeal said. "And that's why I'm telling you all to run. Stephanie is about to bring the house down." Zeal made a sweep with his foot and knocked Ky to the ground. Zeal covered the boy, signaling me to pull the metal shanks in the beams. I started magnetizing and pulling them all at once. I backed up into the doorway and ripped down all the main beams of the house. People were running and shrieking. There was wood and dust everywhere. The entire house began collapsing. In a flash, everything started catching on fire. Zeal waited until it was safe and then jumped off of Ky. He grabbed the little boy and ran for the door. Ky looked fine but Zeal was totally beat up. He had really taken this one for the team.

Chapter 16

Once in the car I pulled Kyan into my lap and began to untie him as his big brother sped away. "Did she hurt you?" I asked Ky.

"No," he told us and I felt instant relief. "I knew you would save me, you're my guardian."

I blushed. "We all saved you. In fact, it was all thanks to our new teammate Zeal."

Kyan shook hands with Zeal. "Thank you," he said.

"My pleasure," said Zeal.

"Even though it was invisible I could tell you pulled down the ceiling. How did you do that?" Ky asked.

"Well, truthfully I don't know. I mean I feel the electricity all the time but the power, it kinda just comes when I need it. Instinct, I guess, just ups my moves in a pinch." I ruffled Ky's hair. We would have to be more careful from now on.

I could hear Lucky on the phone communicating our success to Jage and Ari. He reported back to us that the couple wouldn't be returning to California but instead were going to stay here with us. Zeal, too, became a member of the crew. The three new members all moved into the hallway at the left of the solarium where my and Lucky's rooms were. There were six total rooms in the hallway, three on each side. I had the first room on the right. Jage and Ari chose to share the room next to me and Zeal took the room next to them. Our side of the hallway was full! These three rooms had a view of the backyard and in the distance you could see the beach. Lucky was the only one on the front side of the house. He had taken the middle of the three rooms. There were six of us now, Keith, Lucky and Ari for intelligence and Jage, Zeal and myself as infantry. Our first mission to rescue Ari and our second to rescue Ky had been resounding successes. I know we wanted to protect each and every synergy on Alexis' radar, but would that even be possible?

Keith, as always, was a step ahead of me. We needed training, real training. A daily regimen from experts of all types. We would go under the guise of a bodyguard squad protecting the Mal brothers and me. Keith gave me my first assignment when we got back to the office.

"We're going to call every synergy in these files and warn them about Alexis. Stephanie, you are going to be the one to call them," he told me.

"Why me?" I asked incredulously. I didn't think I was too good with people, especially strangers. My best friend in the world was only 12 years old, and I figured that was kinda where my maturity was at.

"You're the most famous synergy in the world, and the only one with credibility. Just get on the phone and be sincere," Keith ordered.

"Keith, this is serious. These people are in danger. If I mess up something terrible could happen." I was genuinely afraid of this responsibility.

"I'll help you," Ari piped up. "I've read all the files, I feel like I know these people. I can help." I could already see a wonderful friendship forming between us.

"Some of these synergies will listen to you and stay safe, others we may have to ask to come here for their protection. I'm even anticipating having to go and get some of the ones that are higher on the list," Keith instructed. "At this point we can only worry about those who speak Japanese or English. We'll figure out how to get the others in time. Let's break so we can get started."

Ari and I took the files into the room next door that I'd been using for my studies. Since the Miss New York pageant I had been a little too preoccupied to do my schoolwork. I pushed the books aside without a second thought.

Ari had ordered the files with the most powerful synergies on the top and the weaker ones toward the bottom, I picked up the first file. "Will Dave," I read aloud. The picture showed a handsome guy with red hair and a bushy red beard. According to the file he was 10 years older than me and he had a sort of wisdom in his eyes. Oh, and it says he's a radio DJ! Cool! I love music!

'Here goes,' I thought as I dialed the number in the file. As soon as the phone started ringing I got really nervous. What if he didn't believe me? What if my call had the opposite effect and actually put him in danger? He was on the phone too quickly; I still didn't know what to say.

"Hello," he said questioningly.

"Um, hi Will. Don't hang up!" Oh man, I suck! He's going to hang up for sure.

He chuckled "Strange girl calls, I'm not going to hang up. Who is this?" Well at least he was nice.

"This is going to sound weird; you don't know me, but..." I want to protect you. I want you to know you're not alone, that you've never been alone and will never be alone. I don't want you to suffer the way I've suffered. I want you to know if you ever need anything, I will be there for you, right or wrong, no matter what the sacrifice.

"...so you're a DJ, right? For fun or are you serious?"

"I'm always serious and it's always fun," he responded. I liked him.

"Maybe you could spin a set for me; I want it to tell a story..."

"I'm listening," he sounded intrigued.

"It's about a boy and a girl. They've never met but the girl finds out that the boy is in trouble and she tries to tell him, to protect him."

"And what kind of danger is this?" he asked with a smile.

"The serious kind," I told him. "The kind you get in but can't get out. The kind you want to avoid."

"Very mysterious. Who is the villain?" He asked in a more serious tone.

"A woman," I said breathlessly. "A lovely older woman. Someone who pretends to help but has sinister plans. Her MO is the internet."

"Yeah, I think I can imagine such a woman, but it is hard to believe she's harmful." He sounded dubious.

"She lures the kids in with a house of gingerbread but if they defy her they'll end up in the oven," I warned.

"Ok, so why does this girl care so much? So what if some kids she doesn't know get eaten?" He was looking for answers. I wanted to say the right thing, to do the right thing.

"They're cut from the same cloth. The boy and girl and many others. They think they're alone, shrouded in darkness. Maybe one girl who cares is enough to bring them into light," I said with a voice full of hope.

"Why not? We've lived so long in darkness, maybe all we need is that spark," he said with absolute seriousness. Wow, he said it all. He understood what I was trying to tell him and he let me know that he knew it was me.

"I'll get to work on this set. I have a lot of friends who might be interested. A lot of...talented friends. I'll grab your number from the caller ID and touch back if there's a problem." Will paused. "I...I thought you were a joke. I thought you came forward just to win a beauty pageant. It's nice to see I was wrong. You're more than a pretty face. Thanks for the warning. It was an honor just to have this conversation."

"The honor was all mine," I responded and hung up the phone.

Ari had been listening on the extension. She dropped the phone and ran over to give me a hug. "You did so good!" she screeched. "I think you really saved him!" I hoped she was right.

"It was weird though. He said 'spark.' How could he know my code name?"

"Stephanie Park. S. Park. It's not that much of a stretch, girl." Ari patted me on the leg. She dropped down Indian style on the floor next to me. "One down, 15 left to go!" she said excitedly.

"He seemed like such a normal guy considering he was supposed to be the most powerful. I wonder what number 2 will be like. I mean think about it, he's potentially the second most powerful being on the planet. What do you do with yourself?" I finished musing and began dialing the next number. An older woman answered. "May I speak with Hiten Shaw please?" I asked sweetly.

"Who is this?" the woman questioned suspiciously.

"Just, a friend of Hiten's," I responded.

"No girls!" she shouted into the phone. "Suddenly girls start calling my Hiten. One girl, she calls every day and then last weekend my Hiten never came home. Do you know where he is? He's not a child anymore but that doesn't give him a right to scare his mother, you know. He's with that girl, I know. She doesn't call anymore, number like yours from New York. You know this girl?" she demanded.

I was silent with shock for a moment. "I really don't," I replied. Without another word Hiten's mother hung up on me. I shakily returned the receiver.

"What happened?" Ari asked with concern. The celebration from the first call was immediately forgotten. Ari threw her arms around me again, this time for comfort. I held tight to her and nestled into her silky orange hair. Thoughts raced through my mind. That phone call had scared me and scared me good. I pulled away from Ari.

"We need to find the guys." I scooped up the files. "Everyone of these synergies is in danger of disappearing just like Hiten. The next three: Al, Dimitri and Chad are all incredibly powerful. We need to rescue these guys as soon as possible." With that Ari and I headed to Keith's office.

When we arrived only Jage and Zeal were there. Keith and Lucky had taken Ky home. The rest of us headed for home as well. I was following Jage and Ari down the stairs to the garage when Zeal grabbed my hand and pulled back.

"Why don't we get to know each other better?" he started.

"We're just teammates, nothing more," I told him.

"But there is so much chemistry between us," Zeal argued.

"Well, with me...it's always like that. Electricity, you know." I felt bad telling him but it was the truth. "Can we be friends? I'd really like us to work together."

Zeal sighed. "Of course we can work together. These synergies, they need us. I'm not gonna let some little crush get in the way of that. Just, understand that I've always got your back." I reached up and put my arms around his neck and pulled him in for a hug.

"Thank you," I whispered.

"And Steph, if things don't work out with Keith, I will be right down the hall waiting to score you on the rebound." He smiled a giant grin and the two of us cracked up.

When we got home we found Lucky and Keith in Keith's lab. They had navigational charts spread out everywhere and several computers were on. It amazed me that with no formal education, Lucky was able to keep up with Keith, a recognized genius. They worked together as equals too, one of the few partnerships where Keith didn't bark out orders.

I knew they were making plans to recover these synergies spread all over the world. I started tearing inside thinking of that last phone call and that poor frightened mother. I pulled it together and stepped inside the room. I could feel my static spread out across the area and over the two guys. Did it make them aware of what I was feeling? They both stopped what they were doing and turned to me. I had no idea what to tell them. My mouth opened and words just seemed to fall out.

"We're doing this tonight," I said and folded my arms.

"Whoa, whoa WHOA!" said Lucky. "We haven't even tested this shit out. You could kill yourself, or someone else."

"You could kill a lot of people, out of the question," Keith said matter-of-factly.

"Figure this out," I told them defiantly. "Ky is upstairs making up his class work from school today. When he goes to bed, I'm going to get these guys whether you help me or not."

Lucky knew me well enough to know when I was taking a stand. This was it—we needed these synergies and they needed us. I wouldn't take "no" for an answer.

"Steph, just give us a few days. You've never really flown before. Usually you just go straight up and come back down," Lucky was interrupted by an excited Keith.

"You're a genius Luke. We'll just design this so she can shoot up, redirect herself and shoot back down. It will be easy and manageable. Steph I think we can get this together, enough to make one trip tonight. There is a guy name Al in Saudi Arabia. He will probably be the hardest synergy to get by conventional means, you know with visas and passports and such. If you can touch down in the area and then sneak into the compound he's on then all that's left is for you to persuade him to join us." Keith made it sound pretty simple. I let the guys get back to their work.

I helped Ky with his homework, then we played some video games and ate junk food. Keith and Lucky didn't come out of their lab once, not even for dinner. After I tucked Ky in, I ventured into the study to find the guys but they were gone. I was looking over the work they had done. One desk was piled over with calculations and drawings while the next was like a workbench of metal parts.

"They're out back," Jage said, peeking in the room. "You know it is incredibly likely you'll kill yourself or these synergies, Stephanie. Even if Alexis gets them, we can always save them later when we're stronger."

"No," I said, forming my resolve. "No day but today, right? If I do this today, tomorrow I can work on getting even stronger. I swore I would never feel helpless like I had in that cage in the orphanage, but today when Kyan was in danger I felt more helpless than ever. These synergies are at risk and if I can save them they will make perfect guardians for Ky."

I turned and walked out the door to go find Lucky and Keith. Jage blocked me with his body. I looked up angrily and saw his eyes were full of admiration and concern. He wrapped his arms around me and squeezed me tightly. "You are rash, reckless, short-sighted and pig-headed but if you weren't I probably wouldn't be here today. Be safe, ok? Go change some other unsuspecting guy's life." He smiled. I smiled.

I headed out back where Keith and Lucky were experimenting on the equipment. They saw me and waved me over. As soon as I reached them Keith put a helmet on my head and started buckling it. Lucky was fitting me with a parachute. Ari helped me slip on some chain metal boots, much like the aluminum foil ones I had worn that first time with Keith. They fit me with an oxygen mask and hooked the plastic tank to my side. A backpack with a helmet/parachute/oxygen tank was hooked to the front of me to outfit the new guy I would be bringing back. They had also packed some bottled water, an international phone card and some other provisions in case things went wrong.

The global navigation system was just a big white plastic oval with two number counters on it. The guys had taped on it the coordinates I would need to use. The idea was that I would head up into the sky until the right numbers appeared. When I saw them, I would then head back down at that angle.

"How is it that you were able to put this together so fast?" I asked Keith and Lucky.

"Well, we didn't need to create a power source, so all we had to do was a little physics and a little tinkering," Keith sounded humble but his eyes burned with pride. He and Lucky checked me over and then backed up to look critically at me.

"What do you think?" Keith asked Lucky.

"I think we're f'n geniuses," Lucky announced.

"Time for a test," Keith said.

The guys went over exactly what I needed to do. Keep an eye on the dial, don't pull the parachute too soon. I think they wanted me to go up and down a few times, but I just wanted to get to this. I put on the oxygen mask and started breathing deeply. Everyone backed up. I sent an electric charge through the boots and started rising off the ground.

Before I got too far, gravity started pulling against me. I charged the air around me with electricity and pushed harder and faster. I kept pushing harder, faster, harder, faster, fighting against gravity. It started getting cold, freezing cold. I looked down at the navigation bar. Holy crap! I had blown completely past my target! How can that be? I've only been up here for less than a minute. I struggled to figure out which way I needed to go. Every tiny motion sent the dial spinning. I was freezing to death, gravity was dragging me down, I started to spiral and in seconds I thought I was going to vomit.

"Get it together!" I shouted in my own head. I have to keep my eye on the prize!

I let gravity drag me down a bit so I didn't freeze to death. I kept my eyes glued on the dial, noticing which movements triggered the change in numbers. I hung in until I matched one of the numbers, then tried desperately to match the other. Ok! I've arrived at my trajectory. All I needed to do was let gravity pull me in.

As it turns out, gravity wanted me to come a lot faster than I wanted to go. Trying to fight back after it had me was a joke. I was heading down way too fast. I tried to charge my boots but at this speed it didn't make a difference. I might be able to bounce my electric pulse off the earth but I would have to get in really close. I'd done it a million times before but nowhere near this speed. This might really be it, I might have pushed it too far.

Suddenly things were starting to take shape in front of me. I could see lights, then land, then I crashed.

I impacted hard on the earth below me. I folded my legs under me to avoid breaking them, but they still hit the ground solid. I bounced a few feet and then hit hard again. I dropped all of my equipment. I skidded in the dirt a bit and finally slowed to a stop. I didn't even know I'd lost consciousness until I came to with a start.

According to the file my target was a guy named "Al" who lived on an American compound in Saudi Arabia. My crash landing had alerted the guards. Did I really think I was just going to waltz in here, steal this guy and breeze out? You know, for a minute I really thought I was.

There were guards pointing guns and barking dogs on top of me before I could think. How many? Six? I could magnetize and steal their guns in seconds. My hand to hand would easily defeat theirs; in a big group like this you pretty much make them fight each other. I had a strategy and the ability, only… my legs wouldn't move at all. I was trapped. Uhhhh, better turn on the charm.

Turns out the guards were American and apparently they'd heard of the mutant Miss New York contestant. The story had gotten more out of hand then I realized. Somehow the guards bought my story about shopping in Dubai and then coming here to visit a friend. It is amazing what you can get away with just by having your name in the paper. They even escorted me to find Al. It didn't matter that I had no last name for him, they all seemed to know who I meant. When I asked to see him they were immediately concerned that he had hurt or stolen from me. I started to get nervous, what kind of a guy was this?

The guards led me past some beautiful homes in the compound. Ritzy American families living in style. I couldn't hide my surprise when they led me past the pretty homes to a shoddy shed with no plumbing or electricity. There were a dozen people sleeping on mats on the floor and huddling under blankets.

"Al," one guard yelled and shined a flashlight on the faces of the group. A tall, sleepy Arab stood up. I had just assumed he would be American. He had smooth copper skin and shoulder length black hair.

"Can I help you miss?" he asked when he saw me.

"I need you to come with me," I told him. "I need to ask you some questions." The guard let me borrow a room to talk in. It seemed more like an interrogation than a conversation. "I'll be blunt. I think your life is in danger." He handled that pretty well, didn't even ask about it. "My mission is to bring you home with me tonight. Would you be willing to leave everything behind and come with me to New York?"

"Yes," he said as if he had never been more certain in his life.

"You'll have a job."

"Yes."

"And a nice place to live."

"Whatever you ask of me, the answer is yes. Before you, I thought I was the only freak. The only one in the world. I thought that was why my parents abandoned me. I thought that was why I suffered. It hasn't been very long since I read about you in the paper, but they've been the best days of my life. I'm not alone. I want to be with the other freaks! Only…I don't have a passport or any papers," he told me shamefully.

"No worries," I said. "We're not going that way anyway. Tell me, are you ludicrously brave, 'cause I was sort of banking on it." He nodded his head vigorously. "Good," I told him.

Al knew a weak spot in security where we could hop over the wall. He meant that literally, he just jumped from the ground to the top of this 9 foot wall effortlessly. He helped me climb over. We found the equipment and strapped it on.

"We're going to fly?" he asked.

"Yes. No. Kind of. It's more like rebounding." He looked at me blankly.

"Don't worry, you'll love it," I reassured him.

My first trip with a passenger actually went very well. There is something inside me, I don't know what it is. A special power I experience when I'm protecting someone. It makes me smarter, more capable. Protecting Al allowed me to think of and plan for a bunch of different things I'd missed the first time around. We even touched down kind of smoothly.

I had enough strength to introduce Al to Zeal, Jage, Ari, Lucky and Keith before I passed out. I wanted food and a shower but I could barely stand. I knew the gang would show Al the ropes.

While I slept, Lucky and Keith had convinced another synergy over the phone to come and join us. By the time I woke up the next day Lucky was already back from the airport with this guy. Chad was a quiet, unassuming guy but you wouldn't know it by looking at him. Was this guy for real? He had the coolest hair I've ever seen! He had the surfer cut, a little thicker on top like the Beatles. It was jet black and parted down the middle. In the center of the right side was a thick white zigzag! Damn! Coolest hair I've ever seen. My hair worship didn't score me any points with Chad though. He didn't say a word to me. I was worried he might be shell shocked.

"Nah, he's fine," Lucky told me. "He grew up homeschooled in Minnesota, didn't have any friends or siblings so he was pretty isolated. Played a lot of video games, when online gaming was born this guy became a champ! I named him 'Hand-Eye' cause he has killer hand-eye coordination."

Keith had flown out last night to pick up another synergy from Russia. He hired a translator to meet him at the university this synergy was attending. He called late in the day to tell us he had made contact.

"He speaks English!" Keith shouted in victory. "His name is Dmitri and he is our newest recruit. It was easy as pie picking him up, he was happy to join. He was the captain of his college rugby team, which shows he's tough. Looks good I guess, kinda non-descript. He's nice and tall like me, brown hair that's a little curly and with sharp blue eyes. You're gonna love his power. He can actually hear people's thoughts. I'm calling him Eagle Eye because he doesn't miss a thing."

I wondered if I got to give Al a nickname because I brought him back. I liked Al a lot, I wanted to give him a kick ass nickname, but I wasn't creative enough to think of "Eagle-Eye." All the nicknames I thought of for him were like "Aladdin."

Chapter 17

It was truly amazing watching this thing unfold. A few weeks ago there were 3 of us, then 6 and now 9. I was so glad we had all those extra rooms in the house. True to his word, Keith had organized trainings with experts every morning. We trained for hours on martial arts, lifted weights, went running on the beach. We were getting in peak physical condition and we were learning to work together as a team.

Every morning we had a chance to address the group before the workouts. One morning Keith showed up with a mannequin wearing a very unique uniform.

The center of the uniform was that shiny metal vest we had worn on our first mission that looked like snake skin and slipped over the head protecting the chest. The coat around it was a floor length trench coat with a very large, open collar. The exterior was flame retardant and had a shiny dark blue color. It was lined with Kevlar, bullet proof and able to stop a knife. The inside of the coat was silver and that color peeked out from the sleeves and neck area. Between the two colors was a bold orange piping. Large buckles across the front of the coat could be used to close it in tight for protection or stealth. Protective pants in that same orange lined dark blue and black buckled boots finished off the outfit. It was durable and lightweight but protective and filled with all sorts of pockets for weapons, travel documents, you name it. Keith announced this was to become our uniform and a tailor took all of our measurements.

It was so frickin' cool, I couldn't wait for mine to be ready! I ran my fingers over the metal chest plates.

"We're going to look like snakes," I announced to the gang.

"With those collars we're going to be cobras," Al said.

"How about Sidewinders," said Jage.

"Copperheads," Ari giggled.

"Vipers, let's be Vipers," suggested Lucky simulating a snake bite with two fingers.

"The Vipers it is," said Keith and just like that our gang had a name.

Time starting moving in a blur. Christmas came and went. The Mals went back to California to visit their mother and Jage, Ari, Chad and Dimitri went home to their families. That left Lucky, Zeal, Al and I alone at the house. As a Muslim Al didn't celebrate Christmas and the rest of us didn't really have too much experience with holidays so we drowned ourselves in video games and sugar. We got pretty bored so Lucky and I taught the guys everything we'd learned about gambling from our time in Las Vegas. Now that was fun! The four of us started betting on everything: cards, sports. We started inventing contests to place bets on like arm wrestling and hand stand races. Just like that gambling became part of the Viper culture.

When the holidays were finished and everyone was returning to town. I got contacted from the office of the President. The President of the United States!

I realized when I met Al that the story of synergies really had traveled around the world. The President wanted America to publicly recognize the existence of synergies in front of the world. I was hoping the President's speech would clear up some of the sensationalism I'd been running into about synergies being superheroes and villains.

We took off for Washington DC. Keith got us a big hotel suite with rooms for everyone to stay.

I had never been to DC so I was thrilled for a chance to look around and hit up some historical sites. Keith and Lucky needed to do some company stuff so the Vipers and Ky and I hit the town. We walked up and down DC, making our way across the mall and to the Smithsonian. I couldn't believe how many people stopped to gawk at us. I didn't realize I would be so recognized out on the street like that. At first people just stared, but then people started approaching us. Were they synergies or just curiosity seekers? As it turned out, thousands of folks were arriving in DC just to hear the speeches tomorrow. Wow, this really was bigger than I thought. I just needed to make sure the right message was sent.

I ended up not sleeping that night. Keith never sleeps anyway so he was there to keep me company. He pulled me into his arms and kissed my hair. "Steph," he started, reading my mind as usual. "These synergies have lived their whole lives up until now. They are just fine. Sure what you say may influence them, but you are not responsible for them. Don't worry so much. Be happy that they care enough to come together out here in the open like this."

The Secret Service arrived at our hotel in the morning and asked us to remain inside. There were already thousands gathered by morning and they were expecting more throughout the day. I wondered how many were synergies. I wished I could meet them all.

After just a few hours I was dying to get out of that hotel room and spent most of the day pacing. I took forever getting ready just to kill time. Finally it was time to get out there. The Secret Service guided us the entire way. Still I felt vulnerable and made sure all the Vipers were guarding Ky.

There wasn't enough time to really meet the President but I got a quick handshake and that was exhilarating. They had me say a few words at the beginning. I pretty much just reiterated my Miss New York speech. I had never seen such an enormous group of people and I was definitely intimidated. Nothing prepared me for the sound of their applause afterwards. I hoped they were cheering for a bright future for synergies.

The President's speech was brief and vague. At the end the President grabbed my hand and raised it high in front of the audience.

Wow! This was so unbelievable: thousands of people shouting, helicopters, and flashing cameras. Security led the President in one direction and led the Mal brothers and me out the back to a secret location where our car was waiting.

We walked down a dark narrow hall. With the security guards in front of us we couldn't see anything. Suddenly they became agitated. One started shouting out orders in code and everyone drew their guns and ran forward, leaving us alone in the passageway.

The Mal brothers and I rushed ahead (without thinking, as usual). We wanted to see what was going on.

We emerged from the dark passage into a rush of light. I immediately stepped in front of Kyan to protect him. It took a few seconds for my eyes to focus. What I saw shocked me to my core. The security guards had already been disarmed and disabled. A pretty brown haired girl in a shimmery purple dress was locking them in their own handcuffs.

About twenty feet away another teen with short, spiky, dark blonde hair was removing the ammunition from the guns. He was throwing the empties into an already enormous pile of guns.

The two were at the base of a flight of stone steps. At the top were at least a dozen more guards, equally disabled and handcuffed. A giant, muscular young man with a ponytail that was waist length and the color of straw looked to be keeping guard.

The three jumped up when I entered. They abandoned their posts and dropped to their knees in front of me. The biggest guy addressed me. "Miss Stephanie," he said without looking up. "I apologize for the scene here today. Please understand no one was hurt."

Were they here to fight? Kidnap me? I wished the Vipers were by my side. All in all I didn't sense any malice coming from them. I was certainly intrigued.

"Why did you do all this?" I asked gesturing to more than a dozen helpless and struggling guards.

"We wish to be of service to you. We are talented synergies and we have braved trials to get here in the first place. We will be loyal, dedicated, valiant servants, if you would just give us a chance."

Before I had a chance to answer them, secret service guards came out from everywhere to attack the assailants and rescue their own.

"This way!" shouted Keith, grabbing Ky by the hand and leading us up the stone steps. He made a sharp right and we continued until we reached a road. Keith paused for a minute and looked around. "There!" he pointed to a limo halfway up the block. Keith got there first and held the door for Ky and me. I couldn't believe he was gesturing for the other 3 to get in. Once we were all inside he jumped in himself, calling out for the driver to "hightail" it.

We were supposed to go back to the hotel for the night but Keith instructed the driver to drive straight home to New York. He then made a call to 911, telling them about the disabled security guards. He stressed that he was worried it had something to do with me and rushed me out of there to safety. Not once did he mention the mutants who had caused all the trouble in the first place and were now in the car with us.

Ky stared at the three across from us. They all looked at the ground. I found both guys to be handsome (Lucky had started saying I had "synergy goggles" and found all synergies attractive.) The girl had a great, lean, muscular body and pretty short brown curls over violet eyes.

"I'm Kyan Mal," sweet Ky introduced himself. "What are your names?"

"We've given up our 'human' names," the big guy started. Just like Zeal? He stared me down with his piercing clear blue eyes. "Our synergy names are all you need to know. I'm Talon, a natural weapon," he said and pounded his chest. "The path between selfish and selfless is pretty narrow. I am constantly on guard to keep my moral compass pointing in the right direction?" He looked up as he turned the attention to me.

"Ky's welfare is all I care about," I told him truthfully. "Whether it's moral or not, I will do what I must to protect him."

"And we are willing to put our lives on the line to protect him too. Please give us a chance…" The spiky blond haired guy broke in.

248

"What's your name?" I asked him. Suddenly his cheeks reddened, his dark blue eyes also betrayed his nervousness. "They've been calling me Sky Walker. I kinda, well my power is…I can move things. I'm not sure how exactly, maybe it's psychokinesis or just a manipulation of molecules, but I can move stuff. I know you can move things too, that's why I'm here."

"Why, so you two can start a moving company?" Keith interjected snidely. I was amazed he had stayed quiet this long. I hadn't realized but he'd been banging away on his laptop the whole time.

"Sky Walker you said?" Keith laughed. "How about Tyler Marshall from Portland, Oregon? How does that strike you as a nickname?" The three strangers gasped.

The one calling himself "Sky Walker" was visibly upset. "We worked so hard to cover our tracks and you uncovered them in a matter of minutes."

"That's why my brother is the boss," Ky said proudly. "You'll never find anyone smarter than him."

"He is a full on genius," I agreed. "You can be confident taking orders from him."

"Wait…him?" Sky Walker asked incredulously. "I thought this was your gang?" The three new comers started shifting in their seats and whispering to each other.

"I'm the voice," I said bravely. "I'm the face of synergy. I'm the sweetheart who holds your hand and says you don't have to be afraid of synergies." Wow, I had really accepted the idea of my role. "I can't do everything by myself. If you thought I could, well then why did you come?"

The three were quiet for a minute or so.

"Violet Hardy," the girl said boldly offering her hand for Keith to shake. "Please call me Alice."

"A proper introduction and a heartfelt request, how can I say no to that?" Keith reached forward and shook Violet's waiting hand. "Alice it is...Alice in Wonderland?"

"That's right," the girl smiled. It's no wonder where her birth name came from, violet was the very color of her eyes.

Keith went back to pounding away at his computer.

The muscular figure with the long blond hair turned to look intensely at Alice. The two stared hard, clearly having some sort of silent conversation. Ky and I just watched wordlessly. Finally he broke the silence. "Russell Mc Kendrick," he stated to no one in particular.

"Russell Mc Kendrick," he repeated mimicking Alice and reaching his hand out to Keith. "I'll do whatever I have to, to ensure our group joins your service Mr. Mal." Keith hesitated for a moment. I couldn't blame him, this guy had practically introduced himself as a traitor – now he wanted to live in our house and work side by side? I didn't think Keith would go for it.

Keith still looked hesitantly at Russell's outstretched hand. "Why?" he asked plainly. "Why is it so important that you join our group?"

Russ started to speak right away, then stopped and thought a second. He let out a giant breath, dropped his hand and looked upwards, imploringly to Keith. "We've reached the potential of what we can safely learn on our own. We need a place where we can grow our powers without constantly worrying about being found out...and..." he trailed off.

"And?" Keith pushed.

"And..." he started again hesitantly when Sky Walker cut him off.

"We want to protect Stephanie," Tyler said, swelling with pride. Violet nodded vigorously and even Russell looked over and smiled weakly at me. Wow, I thought. These guys had traveled across the country to help me? I couldn't believe it, a look of shock registered across my face.

"What's more important than protecting Stephanie is protecting the things she is willing to fight and die for. Are you willing to do that?" Keith asked them. I know he was talking about Ky, but it was too soon to let them in on that. He turned his computer around and showed us the screen. On it was a wanted poster, a photo of a younger Russell with a shaved head and the words "Aggravated Assault with a Weapon."

Russell looked down at the floor in a flash, his cheeks aflame with shame and something else, rage? Well that was it, there's no way Keith would let an ex-con sleep a few doors down from his baby brother.

"I'm guessing you're here because you have no place else to go?" Keith asked Russell. "I assume you've already done your time for this," he gestured at the wanted poster. Russell nodded and said nothing.

"Someone reading this wanted poster would assume that you are pretty familiar with the use of a weapon, huh?" Why was Keith torturing the guy like this? What was he up to?

"Yeah," Russ said. He sounded defeated.

"The people that work for me usually call me sir," Keith delivered. I was a little slow on the uptake, but Tyler wasn't. "You mean you're going to gives us the job?" he asked incredulously?" Ky and I sat up in shock too, I guess we were both expecting Keith to blow them off.

"Well, we need a weapons expert badly," Keith started explaining his actions. "You're all in good shape so I'll take it that you are hard workers. You feel some kind of internal loyalty to Stephanie which I can use to my advantage and none of you are hideous looking so I can have you standing in the back of pictures. I'm assuming you have no place else to go or you wouldn't be here so you need us more than we

252

need you. As I see it, it works out for all of us." Keith folded his arms behind his head and leaned back in the limo. "There is one matter first, a new rule. Before you can join the Vipers you have to defeat one of the charter members in a fight. Russell, you and I will fight. Violet, you'll face Jage and Tyler will fight Luke. I'll give you a few days to get settled and then you can show us what you've got."

I liked the new rule and looked forward to the matchups. I was confident they would all do well. Ky and I spent the rest of the car ride from Washington DC to New York chatting with our future Vipers. The conversation fell silent and Ky fell asleep cuddled up next to me. I kissed his forehead. With all these protectors I was starting to feel like nothing could ever hurt him.

As the car was pulling up to the house Keith said one last thing to the group. "I know she's young but Stephanie has been through a lot. You can always talk to her if you need someone." The group murmured then left the car.

"Why did you say that?" I asked.

"On the internet I found out why they didn't want to tell me their names." Keith hesitated. "I don't know how to say this...they were all victims of synergy hate crimes." I gasped. I never even thought of such a thing. Keith continued. "Some synergy protest group set fire to Russell's car. Someone spray painted "Mutant Trash" on the side of Violet's house and Tyler...Tyler spent 6 weeks in the hospital after being physically assaulted." Oh My God! It was almost too much to believe. I chatted with them all night like it was no big deal when all the while they had gone through so much.

"I don't want you to mention it to anybody," Keith instructed. "They came here to forget, I suggest we let them do just that." I wholeheartedly agreed. They deserved that much.

Keith woke Ky and the three of us headed inside.

Chapter 18

When I returned home I was surprised to find an envelope on my bed. I opened it expecting to find some well wishes from one of the Vipers but found something decidedly different instead. It was a series of directions to a hidden spot in Central Park. It told me to arrive tomorrow morning at 6. It was signed "I will reveal to you the very nature of existence – Lord Eric." Eric? The guy who tried to kill Ky? It was impossible to know if that guy was a friend or foe. I was very eager to meet with him and find out the truth.

The next day I snuck out, I didn't want anyone trying to follow me. There was no telling what Eric was up to. I followed the directions on the card exactly. It was so early in the morning dawn was barely breaking. The card from Eric led me through the park and over a pebble walkway up to a little red cottage. It was quite unexpected to find a house like this here in the middle of a park in New York City. There were a few little bistro tables filled with breakfasting couples out back. The last table in the corner was a lone man bending down to feed some pigeons. I walked over to him and he stood to face me. This was Lord Eric. He looked noble with his solid brow and such a strong jaw line. Fair skin, short brown hair parted on one side and kept perfectly trimmed. His eyes were just as prominent as the Mals' but a lighter shade of green, like bug guts or Frankenstein green. He was looking curiously at me.

"What are you thinking?" he asked me.

"Your eyes are the color of bug guts," I told him, still hypnotized by his eyes.

"Uh…thank you," he said, clearly not sure if that was a compliment.

Eric pulled out my chair and I sat down. He sat across the table to face me.

"Do you have enough money for us to eat here?" he asked me. "I'm sorry but I don't carry money."

I was always ready at any given moment to run away, so my purse carried every penny I had.

"Sure," I told him. "Order anything you want."

The waitress came by and took our order. A small lady, bent over with age, slowly puttering about in her slippers making her way around the tables. She stared at Eric as if she'd seen a ghost.

"Do you know her?" I asked, smoothing out my white dress with the green polka-dots and tucking a stray blonde lock back into my hair barrette.

"No, but I get that a lot." He smiled. He was acting like a regular guy, hardly like the lunatic he was when I met him, hell bent on killing my sweet little boy.

We spent a moment in very awkward silence. Finally he began to speak.

"It's hard to know where to begin," he started. "A history lesson could take forever so let's just establish a few facts. Do you know how you synergies are born, or where you go when you die?"

"Uhhhh, I don't have the first idea." I know I sounded like an airhead. Eric didn't seem to mind. He set about educating me with alacrity. "Ok, so all humans get two lives, pretty much. When they are born, they are made of flesh and bone; essentially chemicals of the world around us combine to make the creatures. It is these chemicals and processes that create life, and essentially create your physical body. In addition to those earthly chemicals, there are also compounds made of ethereal chemicals. These create your soul. In your first life, your body and soul are attached. You are vulnerable to disease and aging this way and your body will eventually die. When this happens the particles regroup the same as before and you exist just as your soul. Your soul has a life too. The particles combine strong enough to give you sense and feeling. When you die the second time, your particles finally split apart. They recombine with other particles to form new souls. Are you following me so far?"

"Wow, uh, I'm trying. So what happens when you die?" I asked.

"Once your *body* dies, it's the density of your soul that decides if you go to heaven or hell. If your soul is very dense, you are pushed up into heaven. If your soul elements are loosely packed you are dragged down to hell," he stated.

"Wouldn't it be the other way around? Denser materials would be

257

heavier and dragged down," I told him.

"It is the exact reverse when we are talking about soul bodies," he informed me.

"Wow!" I yelped.

"Yeah," he agreed. "Back in the old days people knew that happened. They sort of assigned rising up to heaven with living a life of goodness and being sucked down into hell for those who were evil. I mean for a superstition it makes sense."

"I'd never heard anyone refer to the basis of all morality as a 'superstition' before."

The woman came and brought our food. She stared at Eric like a former lover begging to be reunited. Could she tell he was an Angel? He made sure not to make eye contact. As soon as she was out of earshot I pounced on him for more information.

"So even if you live a good life it doesn't mean you'll go to heaven?" I found myself scared to hear his answer even though I'd never imagined myself going to heaven.

"Well, your life choices can alter your particles for sure. You cause them to evolve and change through sports, meditation, stress, what have you. Your soul elements can grow denser or more loosely packed during your lifetime."

I understood that you could alter your destiny, but what was the path?

"So what do you have to do to get denser particles so you can go to heaven?" I asked with innocence in my hopeful blue eyes.

Eric reached out for my hand and threaded his fingers through mine. This was the first time he had touched me and it seemed rather intimate. He wasn't making eye contact with me. I felt like there was something he didn't want to tell me. I realized for the first time that he had been alive for thousands of years and he had seen and been through more than I could ever understand. When I thought about him, he seemed like this enormous entity filled with knowledge and power unimaginable. But when I touched him, he felt like any living, breathing mortal man. I wondered about his past.

"Have you come to earth before?" I asked cautiously.

"As a person, you mean?" he asked sadly. "I don't see any reason to lie to you. Yes I came to earth, but I was never human. I was born an Angel. My cousin who was my best friend was always trying to figure out a way to get out of heaven and down to earth. One day he found a way. We didn't know if he'd ever be able to get back or not so I went with him."

"Did you find a way back?" I asked incredulously.

Eric laughed. "Kind of. My adventure had just begun when my Dad showed up and dragged me back to heaven. Even now I have to pretty much sneak out just to come down here."

"Dad?" I asked. I hadn't thought of Eric as anyone's child. He seemed so wise and in-charge.

"We are not talking about my dad," Eric said matter of factly.

"Well, what about your cousin? Did your cousin ever come back?"

"No," he said, sounding defeated. "When you're an Angel or a human you can travel through heaven and earth and hell. Remember, there are only 3 levels of heaven, one level of Earth and 28 levels of hell. Theoretically, everyone from every dimension can hang out on Earth. It's the place to be, like existence's hottest dance club. Once you die though, you are confined to your resting place."

"So your cousin is off traveling all those planes of existence and you're confined to these few." I stated. When I said it out loud it sounded like a lonely life.

"Well, over time I developed a system of teleportation that you saw with the green glowing door. With that I can travel to any level of heaven, Earth and the first few levels of hell. "

"It sounds like you have a lot of freedom," I said encouragingly.

"Sounds like," Eric scoffed. He changed the subject. "Why don't we go for a walk?" he asked. Neither of us had touched our food. I left a generous pile of money and stood to go. Eric was holding my hand. He didn't show any signs of letting go so I said nothing.

We continued up the path and over hills until we reached a rock wall with water lapping at the stones. There was a small inlet and the ocean water poured in to greet the park. It was beautiful.

Eric turned and looked at me. "You know I've been watching you, right?"

I sighed. "You've said that, but I don't even know what it means."

"All Angels have a sight, a way of viewing remotely. The elite are able to focus in on whatever we want, whenever we want. We keep an eye on anything that might cause trouble on Earth or in heaven. I tend to keep an eye on the synergies."

"Keep an eye on us?" Was he some sort of absentee boss?

"I monitor them and make sure they don't get out of control," he said, sounding like he thought he was the boss. "And if they get out of control..."

"You send your goon squad to kill them, I get it. Why don't you just kill them yourself?" I asked spitefully.

"I could never kill anyone. Call it compassion or what have you but it's something I could never do. That's why I was so helpless in the hospital the day you met me. But when a high level synergy is killing the people around them only my team can stop it; human forces would be powerless. If I don't keep a balance, the synergies will take over, probably destroy humanity and then Angels and Fiends will flood the Earth." He sounded genuinely concerned but I was pissed. Synergies are people too. We are not his lambs to slaughter!

"Why don't you just kill us all right now and save yourself the trouble!" I spat the words with venom. He seemed shocked by the question.

"It's not my intention to kill anybody..." he started but I cut him right off.

261

"Just like you tried to kill KY!" I shouted.

Eric dropped my hand and pushed away from me. His cheeks were flushed and his bug guts eyes were flashing. I was fuming too. Angel or whatever, he tried to take away from me the most special person I had ever known.

"Kyan Mal is a special case," he started.

"He's a little boy!" I shouted. "His life has barely begun!"

"STEPHANIE!" he screamed and grabbed my shoulders holding me still. "Shut the hell up and let me talk." He was right, I came here to hear him out and I needed to listen.

"Kyan Mal isn't just a special case, he's THE special case. He is the man of legend, of prophecy. Kyan Mal will one day be the most powerful being that has ever existed. He is the Envoy. The prophecy says he will unite the dimensions and bring peace to heaven and hell."

I couldn't believe what I was hearing. My legs trembled. What a huge destiny to befall an unknowing little boy.

"You have no idea what I've been through just to keep him here on earth. The people in charge want the Envoy in heaven so they can have their influence on him. As long as he stays here on Earth he is a target. The Fiends of hell are going to come after him. Angels may even come after him..." he trailed of not sure how much to tell me.

"If he is in so much danger why did you leave him on Earth? Why not take him to heaven and protect him?" I asked impatiently.

"I left him here to be with you," he said.

It felt like the world was spinning. With me? I'm nothing, I'm no one. Why leave existence's most precious package in my care? I opened my mouth to say so much but only "Why me?" came out.

"Well, it's like this," Eric explained. "If I left him in heaven he would be influenced by the same Angels I've known all my life. If I thought any of them had the first clue about uniting existence or bringing peace to the dimensions, then I would bring Kyan to them. I don't think any of them have it figured out. Here on earth Ky can figure things out for himself. Let him evolve a little, let him learn the things that existence needs."

"I couldn't agree more," I told him. "I understand the need to keep Ky protected. The question is, why did you choose me to do it?"

"You really want to hear the truth?" Eric asked in a tone that implied I really didn't want to hear the truth.

I nodded.

"You have what is called an 'inferiority complex.' It happened to you at the orphanage. The other children ate first; bathed first. They were allowed to go outside and attend school. People worried about their futures. No one worried about you. You were raised to think those kids were more important and eventually you thought that anyone who wasn't locked in a box was more important than you were."

"After you escaped the orphanage a normal psyche might repair itself and learn to focus on self preservation. You never did. Do you know

263

how I command a team like Jenni, Sam and Steel? I select people with predictable natures and then I use them in situations that I know they will excel in.

I can tell you right now, if you saw a child you didn't know playing in the street and a truck was coming, you'd push the child out of the way, even if it meant you'd get hit by the truck. Jenni would get herself out of the way, Sam would scream to the kid to move and Steel would probably jump on the hood of the truck and put a sword through the driver. He'd get the truck to stop, eventually."

I shuddered. Steel's a madman.

"Trouble is, that Kyan kid has a target on his chest. Keeping him safe is going to be the main focus of your life. Training, preparing, raising an army..." Eric's voice trailed off. He turned away from me.

I didn't miss a thing. "Raising an army? What are you talking about?"

Eric started walking towards a playground over the hill. Surprisingly there were no children playing, perhaps too early in the morning for them. Eric took a seat on the swings. I sat on the empty swing next to him.

"The legend of the Envoy is the biggest, most famous legend in all of existence. You'd be hard pressed to find an Angel or Fiend who doesn't know the story. Although it is a story of peace, many see it simply as a story of power. Most think if they can get their hands on the Envoy, they can turn the tide to their side. Are you following?" he turned to me and asked.

"Sure, everyone wants Ky to listen to them, to further their selfish interests," I answered. I hope we had plenty of time before anything like this ever happened.

Eric turned away from me and gazed into the distance. "I don't know how to say this, but the danger is already upon us. As we speak an army of tens of thousands of Fiends is digging a tunnel to emerge on Earth to capture or kill the Envoy. They've been working on this tunnel for generations, but only recently were they able to locate the Envoy. Now they are planning on tunneling up right into the Mals' backyard."

My breath caught in my chest and my heart started pounding in my ears. This wasn't a hypothetical, this was really happening. As we were speaking there were Fiends digging a tunnel to the surface, ready to attack when they arrived.

"Can't we just hide Ky somewhere?" I asked in a panic.

"No Stephanie, I told you. If I take him to heaven he's in a different kind of danger. The best solution is for Ky to stay here on Earth and for you and your friends to protect him. There's one more thing..." Eric stood up and walked to the edge of the water.

I let him go. I started swinging on my swing, getting as high in the air as the swing would take me. I slowed down and started playing in the dirt beneath the swing with the tips of my shoes.

"If these Fiends get their hands on Ky, well that won't be the end of it.

They will pour through that tunnel and take over the world."

What! I thought I was going to vomit! "What do you mean, I thought they wanted Ky! Now you're telling me it's the God damned apocalypse!"

"Stephanie!" Eric shouted and walked over to me putting his hands on my shoulders to keep me from falling right off my swing. "These Fiends have been digging this tunnel for over a century. The Envoy has only been on earth for what, a dozen years? They were digging this tunnel for one reason and one reason only: to take over the Earth. Now they recognize their good fortune that the Envoy turned up on Earth and they are going to go after him as well. You have to protect Ky, but you have to save the Earth too."

"How the hell do you expect me to do that?" I asked, feeling defeated already. "I'm a 17 year old runner-up beauty queen. I don't know the first thing about fighting a Fiend, let alone fighting a war against Fiends. What am I supposed to do?"

"Train," Eric said with certainty. "A week from now I will bring you down to hell and you will train with Steel. It will be the most demanding and excruciating time of your life. When you return, you will use your popularity to draw out all the synergies hiding on Earth. You will train the strongest ones for battle. When the time comes you will be ready."

"Eric," I said with disbelief "Training to do what? Mixed martial arts? I have trouble believing that's going to win us a war."

266

"That is your role. Do as you're told. Train yourself and then train others. Keith Mal will take care of everything else. He's a brilliant strategist and spends his days working through military situations. He will be a perfect general."

Military situations? Those are video games! God, I sure hope Eric knows what he's doing. We talked for another hour, Eric giving me more details and answering my questions. This Steel guy sounded like a maniac. He was a killer who lived by his own code. For some reason Eric trusted and even relied on him and Steel did Eric's dirty work. Finally I said goodbye to Eric and headed for home. I had one week before I had to meet him again, one week before I started "training," whatever that entailed. I skipped the limo ride and ended up walking home, which took hours from the park where I was. I truly had the weight of the world on my shoulders.

Chapter 19

When I arrived home I had missed a very active morning. First the three new synergies had fought the charter members and passed. That meant three new Vipers! I had bet on all the new guys to succeed so I had some winnings to collect. I was also informed that Lucky had received an emergency call in the morning and that he and Keith had been holed up in the lab all day. I needed to talk to them but was afraid to ask. We could hear shouting through the door. I hoped they weren't killing each other. Around dinnertime my cell phone rang. It was Keith.

"Are you okay?" he asked with genuine concern after learning about my meeting with Eric. "That lunatic didn't lay a hand on you, did he?"

I swallowed hard. How could I tell Keith his sweet little brother is the cause of the end of the world? "Can I come in to the lab?" I asked. Keith agreed and a moment later I knocked on the door. Lucky opened it and pulled me into a full body hug. It was comforting, so familiar, but not appropriate in front of Keith. As I suspected Keith got a little jealous and pulled me away from Lucky. Then Keith leaned in and gave me a long devoted kiss. Suddenly I didn't feel so frightened.

"Take a seat," Keith said and pointed to a desk chair. The two of them proceeded to pace back and forth in front of me sighing a bit, clearly trying to decide what to tell me. I started worrying that their news was going to be worse than mine.

Without warning Lucky started giggling. "Surprise," he yelled flinging his fingers in front of my face to imitate an explosion. Of course this made Keith crack up.

"It's a boy!" A boy? Was someone pregnant?

"Did someone have a baby?" I asked, clearly puzzled.

"No!" said Keith while Lucky said "Yes" at the same time.

"We're getting a new kid," Lucky informed.

"He's coming to live with us," Keith clarified. Who, what, where, new kid?

"Do you remember my stories about Jack?" Lucky asked. Jack, sure. He was just a few months older than Ky.

"His mother was a prostitute, right? Never knew his father. Hung around with your gang?" I couldn't remember anything positive about the boy.

"That's right," Lucky told me. "His mother passed away two years ago and he dropped out of school to join the gang full time."

"Foul mouthed, belligerent with a blazing temper. And we want him in the same house as Ky, why?" I'm sorry but one child in a house full of synergies exploring their powers was more than enough.

"Well it's like this. Jack is really good with a sword, I mean really good. He's been practicing with the SliverSwords since he was about 6 years old. He really knows how to use his body weight to balance the blade. Watching him, well it's like art." Oh great, Lucky was starry eyed. Lucky slowed down abruptly. "I got a call this morning…last night Jack was in a fight. A really bad fight with a rival gang member, a Blade."

"Oh my god, is he okay?" I don't care how badly behaved he was, he was still a little boy.

"He's okay…for now. See, he actually won the fight. Sent the other guy to the hospital, ICU and everything. He'll live, but they don't know if he'll walk again."

I gasped. A 12-year-old boy did that much damage to a grown man? What kind of monster was this kid? "So why in the world would we want this kid? Sounds like your gang's problem to me," I huffed.

"Steph, shut up for a second. I know you want to protect Ky, but hear Lucky out." Keith seemed very much on Lucky's side. I guess I was about to find out why.

"They put a hit out on him, Stephanie. That guy Jack took apart was the rival gang leader's brother. This isn't a joke. The Blades don't care that Jack is a kid, they are going to kill him. The SliverSwords can't protect him. That's why they called me. This kid has nowhere else to go." Lucky was dead serious.

I didn't like anything about what I was hearing. "Isn't the gang just going to hunt him down here?"

Keith spoke up. "The SliverSwords don't think so. They think as long as he's safely out of sight the bad guys won't pursue."

"I'm sorry, which ones are the bad guys? Who's carving who up with a sword?"

Lucky laughed and looked over at Keith. "Pay up dude, I so totally called this."

"Called what?" I demanded. They were betting on how I would react?

"I knew you'd freak out. Keith said you'd want to help 'cause Jack's a poor orphan mixed up baby boy. I said you'd protect Ky even if it meant a bullet between little Jack's eyes."

Lucky wasn't right. Or was he? All I thought about, cared about was protecting Ky. I think I may have been obsessed. Did that harden my heart to the plight of another forlorn little boy? He was just Ky's age too. Maybe he just needed to be given a chance.

"Okay, we'll give it a try. Jack can come here," I told them.

"So glad you approve but we're not asking you, we were telling you."

Keith's words were biting. Why in my fantasies was I the leader of this group? In truth Keith was the leader. Lucky was probably next, damn I was third! "So when is this kid going to be here?"

Keith looked at his watch. "Probably in another two hours. We wired the money this morning and the SilverSwords got him on a bus. Lucky is going to pick him up from the bus station pretty soon."

Wired the money this morning? They really didn't care what I thought. I guess it would be that much easier on them when I left. For some reason I just couldn't tell them the news. I guess it wouldn't make a difference waiting one more day.

I left the lab and headed upstairs. Dinner was already served and everyone was at the table eating hungrily. They looked up when I entered.

"Everything go ok?" came from a chorus of voices.

"It's a long story," I said truthfully. "I'll tell you all tomorrow." Everyone seemed content with that and went back to eating. I noticed that no one sat in the chair I was fond of. I guess it was kind of "my chair." It had been a decade since I was allowed to sit at a long table with others. Tonight I decided to enjoy it. I looked down at the motley crew bent over, stuffing their faces. Mutants, monsters, freaks every one of them. Two years ago I never even imagined that there was one other person out there like me. Now a dozen of us had found each other. I'd fight for them too. They deserve a world to feel safe in. Maybe I wasn't their leader, but I could certainly be their champion.

After dinner I decided I was going to make this night super special for Keith. I went into my room and pulled out the red lingerie I'd been saving for a special occasion. I showered with pretty scented body wash and blew out my hair to make it look sexy. I put on my robe and snuck into Keith's room to wait for him. I sent him a text message that there was a "surprise" waiting in his room. In less than a minute I heard him bounding up the steps. I didn't even have time to light any candles.

Keith slipped through the door and ate me up with his eyes. You didn't have to ask if he liked it, his whole body conveyed his approval. He peeled off his clothes like they were on fire. I wanted to play and tease a little bit, but there was no time, Keith was already ready.

Actually, Keith was always ready, and not just to make love to me but to jump on me and pull my hair and kiss and bite everywhere. He turned the stereo on and cranked up the dial without taking his eyes off me. Then he charged on me, sweeping forward and knocking me down on the bed behind me.

This was exactly what I wanted! We were really moving together now, everything felt like magic. The song on the stereo changed and in the silence between songs we heard a ringing. Must have been Keith's phone from his pants pocket on the floor. Keith pulled away from me. "Red phone," he said. As Vipers we had all gotten red cell phones and had made a pact to always answer the red phone, no matter what. I knew he had to get it and I was worried as to what was on the other end.

"Slow down," Keith said into the phone, followed almost immediately by "What the F__K! When was the last time anybody saw him? Did you find the bus driver? North Carolina, oh dear god! Give me a minute, I'll call you right back." Keith grabbed his clothes and started getting dressed. "You get dressed too," he ordered me. "I need you to suit up. We're going...wait I don't know where we're going."

"Jack wasn't on the bus?" I asked, my voice filled with alarm.

"No," Keith told me. His voice was filled with anguish. He opened the door and leaned out. "Ky!" he shouted. "Get in here." He turned back to me. "Jack disappeared as soon as it got dark. The enemies must have been tailing the bus. The SilverSwords haven't heard anything yet. God, I have no idea if he's even alive and if so where he is. All I know is if they took him…"

There was a light knock and Kyan peeked his face in. Everything about Keith's demeanor changed. "Come here," he waved to Ky. Kyan approached and Keith pulled him into a hug. Ky didn't ask any questions. He understood Keith's suffering better than anyone. All I wanted was to be a part of their group. As if he heard me, Keith backed up a little and beckoned me to join their hug.

Keith called all the Vipers into a meeting. He explained the plight of little Jack and let everyone have their say on what we should do.

Lucky arrived home from the bus station. "We found him," were the first words out of his mouth.

"Alive?" Keith asked.

"Yeah. He uh…he got off the bus. He hitchhiked back to Atlanta. The SilverSwords have him now." Lucky sounded ashamed.

We all looked at Keith. He has such a temper, no one knew what he was going to do. Keith was silent for a minute. "Lucky, you'll take the first flight to Atlanta. Pick him up. Get him on the bus and get him here."

Zeal spoke up as usual. "Look, if the kid doesn't want to come, don't make him. We're better off without him."

"Maybe," Keith countered. "But he's one of us now. We'd do the same for any one of you and I'd expect the same for me."

"Is this guy even a synergy?" Tyler asked.

"He's a fighter. Same as all of us." I was surprised to hear my own voice.

"If I was a little human kid I'd certainly be scared to go live in a house full of freaks. It's no wonder he jumped ship," said Jage, his blue eyes looking up at us through his light brown locks. "I'm in, what do we do to get this kid?" He smiled. Jage was so compassionate. I sometimes couldn't help thinking Jage was pretty much perfect.

"Lucky, do you think you can handle him yourself?" Al asked. Now the team was pulling together!

The next 24 hours passed quickly and Al, Jage and Zeal all went to the bus stop to pick up Lucky and Jack. Lucky was gone so that gave Dmitri the chance to follow Keith around like a shadow. I ended up hanging with Ari, Chad and Violet or as Zeal called them "the mutes." We all kind of hovered around the front door like we were waiting for Santa Claus to come down the chimney.

We could hear some yelling coming from outside. We all stood up but Keith gestured for us to stay put. Finally the door opened and in walked Al. Behind him came Jage and Zeal; the three of them looked pissed. Lucky came last, pushing a little kid who was screaming and flailing around. This must be Jack! He came up to Lucky's throat, so he was a few inches taller than Ky. His skin was a creamy brown and his hair was straight and silky. We knew his mother was black but we knew nothing about his father. It was good to see his dark brown human eyes.

Back to the screaming. Yeah, he was shouting so loud you'd expect him to make himself hoarse. His face was contorted with anger. He started kicking the table in the foyer next to the door. With his foot he turned the little stand into splinters. Still screaming, he turned and ran towards the coat closet and started kicking that door. All this while keeping his hands behind his back. Wait...did they have him handcuffed?

I ran down the stairs. "Did you handcuff him?" I demanded.

Lucky was immediately on the defensive. "It was for his own good."

"No wonder he's acting this way!" I turned to Jack. "Jack please calm down. I'll take those handcuffs off. This is your home now."

Jack stopped kicking the door long enough to look at me. He was breathing heavily and sweating profusely. I couldn't tell if I'd gotten through to him.

"Whore!" he shouted. "Stupid g—damn whore try to tell me what to do? I'll never listen to you! I hate you! You make me sick!" Ok, so maybe I didn't get through to him.

"Jack listen to me for a second." I reached out to steady his shoulders. He leaned in and bit me! Bit me right on the forearm! I screeched. There was blood!

Lucky rushed in and grabbed me, pulling me away from Jack. "Just let him get it out," he said. "He'll calm down in a bit."

I don't know what quantifies as a bit, but Jack didn't calm down, not in the least. After about an hour everyone had lost patience. Some of the guys tried taking him out back and there was even talk about pushing him in the pool. Finally they dumped him in the little room next to Keith's. The room that had been mine when we first moved in.

Jack didn't stop screaming or kicking. We listened to him break every piece of furniture in that room, from jumping on the bed to knocking over the dresser. Jack was very thorough.

I wanted to cuddle with Keith but it was kind of hard with Jack rioting in the next room. We turned on the radio but Jack started kicking the adjoining wall and Keith's room started shaking. I'd had enough.

I walked out of Keith's room and right over to Jack's. Jack had kicked holes in his bedroom door so it was easy for me to see what was going on. He was still flailing and screaming and kicking. I opened the door. Jack hesitated for one second and then lunged for me. I let electricity

277

flow from my fingers and stopped him in his tracks with static. Then I lifted him off the ground and used my energy to press him against the ceiling.

"You're a freak, you're a witch, you're a whore," Jack screamed from the ceiling. "Put me down you whore!"

"Or what? Put you down or what Jack?" I admit I was taunting him.

"I'll kill you. I'll kill you. I'll find my sword and I'll cut you into a thousand pieces!" He was starting to sound hoarse now. "I hate you! I hate you!"

"I hate you too buddy," I figured I'd level with the kid. "Ask anybody, it wasn't my idea to have you here. Everyone thinks we'll get along because we're both orphans, we're both fighters, and we both come from the streets. But that doesn't mean anything to me. I'm a hero; I surround myself with other heroes. What use do I have for a rogue?"

Jack began to quiet down. "You think I'm a rogue? That's kind of cool actually. But you don't know nothing about me! I'm from the streets..."

"Been there."

"I have to steal so I don't starve..."

"Done that."

"I practically killed a man..."

"Yeah, I heard that one," I yawned. "Have you ever been shot? Have you ever been in love? Have you ever been famous all around the world?" I slowly let him down. "I mean, you're already here, why not just take whatever you can get. You might learn something and if you're not careful…you might even have some fun." I used an electric charge to free him from the handcuffs. He rubbed his wrists. He spoke again and I could hear the trace of a southern accent I hadn't noticed while he was screaming. "I still hate you," He told me.

"I hate you too buddy, I hate you too."

I thought I woke up early the next morning but everyone was already at breakfast. As I walked past the table to find my seat, I noticed that almost all of the serving plates were empty. Huddled in the middle seat was Jack. His plate was piled high with food and he was very obviously guarding it. Everyone was rolling their eyes or ignoring him.

I stood behind Jack and raised my forearm above him so that everyone could see. My whole forearm was swollen and there was clearly a dark red ring left by Jack's teeth. Everyone gasped. No one realized how hard he really bit me. "This," I said, pointing to my wound, "this is tenacity."

"We brought Jack here not just to join us, but to train us. Russell, as our weapons expert, I hope the two of you can work together." Russ nodded, his long blond hair pulled back in its trademark ponytail.

"Jack is also a hunted fugitive and he is going to need bodyguards 24/7," Keith piped up. Everyone groaned. "I know you all love Jack already," Keith said sarcastically, "so I will be deciding on who gets that job."

Everyone went back to eating nosily. "There's more," I said in a voice barely above a whisper. No one heard; no one looked up. "There's more!" I shouted. Now I had their attention.

"In a few days I will be leaving."

"Leaving for what?" Zeal asked.

"Training," I told him.

"Why can't you do your training here?" Al asked. "We'll all take turns fighting the new kid!" Al joked.

Jack heard that and immediately stood up on his chair. "I'll kill you where you stand!" he shouted. Al just continued to laugh which continued to get Jack steamed. The whole thing was pretty funny.

"When are you coming back?" asked a sweet timbered voice from the corner. It could be none other than my Angel Ky. I turned to look at him. He was out of his seat and standing next to Keith. The older boy had his arm slung protectively over the younger one.

"I...I don't know." I...didn't know what to say or who to say it to. I felt a hand on my back. I turned around to find Dmitri behind me. Was he reading my thoughts?

"Just tell them the truth. Tell everyone the truth. They can handle it," Dmitri whispered quietly in my ear.

I looked up at the Vipers. The whole group had quieted down completely. The only noises were Jack's enthusiastic slurping and munching.

"Eric seems to think…Well Eric told me…" I wish I had thought this through.

"Out with it!" Jack shouted, food tumbling out of his mouth.

"War," slipped out of my mouth. "Eric is preparing me for war."

Everyone started murmuring loudly.

We were all surprised when Chad opened his mouth. "How long do we have?"

"Months at best. Eric told me when I return from training I needed to recruit and train an army." Again everyone burst into noise. Some laughing, some sighing. Ari had tears in her eyes.

Zeal stood up. "I didn't come here to fight a war." Everybody nodded in agreement. "I came here to stand by you," he said, his ice blue eyes staring hard into mine. "Now, I guess, I'll stand with you." Tears sprung to my eyes.

"I'm with you too," said Tyler jumping to his feet.

"So are we," Russell and Alice rose.

"Sgt Al reporting for duty," Al said, standing up and saluting.

"I'm not going back to Minnesota," Chad joked as he stood. His first joke!

"I'm not a fighter, but I'm a hell of a spy," Dmitri stood up and told us.

Jage and Ari had been whispering to each other. I didn't expect either of them to stand. Ari made eye contact with me. "I know I can help!" she shouted and pulled away from Jage. She held her head high as she stood. "I know I can help," she sounded determined. Jage stood up behind her.

Lucky was the only one left seated at the end of the table. His arms were crossed but he had a very amused look on his face.

"Lucky?" I questioned.

"I'm going to wait until you beg," Lucky laughed. Tyler reached down and hit him in the back of the head. "Ow!" Lucky cried out. "Well, it can't be any worse than the things I've already endured for you." That was probably true.

"Jack?" I questioned next. He was leaning across the table to steal a sausage from Jage's plate and got that deer caught in the headlights look when I called his name. "Leave me out of this!" he shouted.

The only people behind me were the Mal brothers. It was time to turn and face them. Keith was looking hard at the table. "Tell me this war has nothing to do with Ky. Tell me it's not about Ky and I'll do anything you ask."

I reached down and put my hand over his. "This war is about all of us," I said.

"I'll take him away. Take him far away where no one will ever find us. There doesn't have to be a war." Keith was shaking.

"Eric led me to believe there would be a war either way. He was willing to take Ky himself but he thought he was better off…" I was embarrassed to say it.

Keith jerked his head up to look at me. "What? What did Eric say? Ky is better off..."

"With me,' I finished. "He said he would hide Ky in heaven but he thought he was better off with me."

"But why?" little Ky piped up.

"I don't know," I said truthfully. "Maybe because I love you so much?" I laughed, a little bitterly. "I once said I'd fight an army to keep us together. Remember that?"

Ky nodded somberly.

"Now I get to prove it." I smiled and reached forward to tousle his hair.

As I pulled back, Keith finally stood up. Everyone applauded.

"I really can't thank you enough," I said to the group.

"Just remember who said it first," Zeal pointed out.

"I will," I promised.

The week was passing by fast. I managed to get in some personal appearances as Miss New York second runner-up. It was starting to seem like photographers were jumping out at me everywhere I went. I couldn't for the life of me understand why.

I didn't know what supplies I would need for my training so I bought a durable backpack and the Vipers helped me pick out some gear and clothes to take along.

When we got home from shopping we found that the Mal brothers were in a fight. They had been screaming at each other for hours. Only once had I seen Keith lose control when dealing with Ky, and Ky, well I'd never even heard him raise his voice.

Ky's suicide attempt took us all by surprise. If we had stopped to think about it we would have realized there was something raging inside the little boy. His temperament always seemed so calm, so even that we just assumed that was all there was to him. We were dumb to think that the rebellion which drove him to suicide would never surface again.

I went upstairs and climbed into Ky's bed to wait for him. I must have dozed off because Ky was waking me.

"My baby," I said and wrapped my arms around him.

"Not now," he said wiggling out of my arms. Ky had never pushed me away. "Are you ok?" I asked with concern.

"I just need to be by myself," he walked into his bathroom and slammed the door.

I got up and went across the hallway to Keith's door. It was locked.

I went back to my room to go to bed. It seemed so big and empty.

The next morning I dressed and headed downstairs and out back for training. I was surprised to see the Mal brothers were already there. Lucky was in charge of training today. He was calling our attention to an obstacle course he had laid out the night before and giving us instructions. While he was talking Ky left the group and walked over to Lucky.

284

"Something wrong, bud?" Lucky asked.

"I want to challenge for a spot. I want to be a Viper," Ky said with conviction.

"Absolutely not!" came the roar from Keith. "Kyan Mal, you get back in line and we'll forget this ever happened."

"I second," came a voice from nowhere, cutting Keith off. Keith whirled around and gave the look of death to Zeal.

"You're willing to put my brother in the line of danger?" Keith asked Zeal incredulously. I was terrified a fight was going to break out between those two.

"The kid works as hard as any of us," Zeal pointed out. "He deserves a chance to prove himself."

"Doesn't matter anyway. To become a Viper you need to defeat a charter member, and no one's going to fight you." Keith looked back and forth from Lucky to Jage. Neither of them wanted to get involved in this family brawl.

"I will," I said, raising my hand. Everyone looked at me in shock. Not only was I willing to defy my boyfriend, but I was willing to pound on the very boy I had sworn to protect. Keith marched over to me and grabbed my shoulders.

"If you do this we are over, you hear me! Over!" He looked at me to make sure I was afraid of his threats, but I wasn't.

"I'm sorry Keith, I love you but…" I turned to the younger Mal who was holding his breath waiting to hear what I would say. "My duty is to Kyan. I can't let *your* fears hold him back." Keith's jaw dropped. He backed away from me without saying a word. I walked up and took my place next to Lucky.

Lucky stumbled on his words. We all knew we were witnessing history in the making. "Spark will challenge…um Ky, ok?" Lucky was asking. It's true, we hadn't given Ky a codename. We never bothered to ask if he wanted to join, we never treated him like a member of the group. Poor Ky, we all work so hard to protect him but it means nothing if he gets lost in the process.

"You're not really going through with this?" Keith demanded of Lucky.

"Dude, I don't really have a choice," Lucky told him. "I mean, they are *your* rules."

Keith was fuming. Lucky started announcing the rules of the fight. "We will have 2 five minute rounds. After that the contest will be decided by the Viper squad. Jage and I will referee. You can use any ability or weapon. Let's head over to the dirt mound on the other side of the pool. Once there the fighters will shake hands."

We all headed to the dirt area. There was already a circle in the ground left from the last fight. Ky and I met in the middle to shake hands. "I'm going to hurt you," I said. I wasn't talking smack, I wanted to make sure he realized what he was getting into.

"Good," he said. "I want you to bring it. I want one of us to go to the hospital." Wow, he might just get his wish. "Steph, you're the one I really wanted to fight. Everyone here is scared of you, but I'm not. When you fight someone, really fight as hard as you can – you start to understand them. You know them in a way no one else can. I want to know you in a way my brother never can."

Wow. Crazy to think this was a 12 year old kid talking. When he spoke it was so intense it made me a little nervous. "I want to know you too, pal," I said with an uneasy giggle. We shook hands and backed away from each other.

"Begin,' Lucky cried from the sidelines.

Immediately Ky turned away from me and took off running. What the hell? I raced after him. He ran closely around the pool. I was right at his heels. Suddenly he dropped to the ground and did a swift sweep, crouching down on one leg and spinning around with the other leg outstretched. I was right behind him so the sweep knocked me down and right into the pool. What a genius kid! Now I was soaking wet and the water would disable my electricity for the rest of the battle.

I pulled myself out of the pool and raced back to the dirt mound. I saw Kyan and ran straight at him. As I approached, the boy dropped to the ground and began rolling his body like a pencil towards me. He timed it well and I didn't have time to stop. I tripped right over him and fell hard to the ground face down. I spun around so I was on my back, but Ky

287

was already climbing on me. He got me in the full mount position (straddling my waist) and proceeded to pound into my face with his fists. I tried desperately to get out from under him. I couldn't believe this way my little Ky hitting me hard in the face. He opened up my eyebrow and suddenly my right eye was blind with blood. I punched him hard in the sternum and knocked the wind out of him. I was able to push him off of me and get to my feet. This was not what I had expected from Ky. I was amazed at his aggression and precision. There was no trace of the boy I tickled and kissed.

We were now facing each other at opposite edges of the dirt ring. He had gotten me on the element of surprise so far, but now I would be able to see everything coming. I didn't want to but I pushed forward. As I raced towards Ky with my fists raised for striking, he bent over to do a hand stand. He used the momentum from leaning down and pushed off the ground with his hands. His feet were still in the air and they crashed right into my face as I charged towards him. The impact knocked me right on my ass. The fight was over, Kyan had beaten me. The Vipers reacted like it was like a championship football game. As soon as Lucky declared Ky the winner, everyone swept up and hoisted him onto their shoulders! It was amazing to see them rally around him like that. I was so glad. This would inspire them to protect him.

There was one Viper who wasn't excited. Keith still stood at the edge of the ring, his back to everyone. I was in a lot of physical pain, but I made my way over to see him.

"Keith," I said. "I'm sorry that I disagreed with you," I told him gently. He kept his back to me.

My legs gave out on me and I slumped to my knees. Did he hate me? Why did he stay my boyfriend all this time? Did he think it would keep me around so I could protect Ky?

Al and Ari took me to the hospital. We were gone for hours. When we got back, Ky was sitting in the hallway outside of my bedroom door waiting for me. How long had he been waiting?

Ky's eyes widened like saucers when he saw the cast. "I broke your arm?" he asked in horror.

"Don't worry, it's just overextended. I just have to wear this sling for a few days."

With that I opened the door to my room and he followed me in. I grabbed some pjs and changed in the bathroom. When I returned Ky was already curled up on the bed. I lay down next to him and pulled his little body close to mine.

"It's my fault," Ky said as tears formed in his eyes. "I hurt your arm and you lost the man you love over me. I talked to Keith but he is being completely unreasonable. I didn't mean to break you guys up." The tears were free flowing by now.

"Ky, your brother sacrificed everything his whole life to take care of you. He was 7 years old when he started raising you. Can you imagine what that was like? Being in the 1st grade and raising a child? He has become very protective of you and rightfully so. The difference is that Keith sees the two of you as a unit. He thinks he can protect both of you. I know that is not true. Had I not lucked out by meeting Eric and been given the chance to fight for you, you would be dead right now. Eric would have crept into your hospital room and pulled the plug."

"I appreciate everything Keith has done, but you're becoming a man soon, you need to stand up on your own. I was never more proud of you than I was today. Deep down inside I know Keith feels the same way."

"Really?" Ky asked in surprise.

"Oh yes!" I said with certainty. "You proved yourself to everyone today. You're a Viper and you've earned it. Did they give you a codename yet?"

"No one mentioned anything," Ky told me.

"How about Able? So that no one forgets how capable you are."

"I love it! Able," Ky buzzed with pride for a moment but then his face darkened again. "What about you and Keith?" Ky questioned fearfully.

"I guess it's over," I said, filled with uncertainty and pain. "I always knew it would be a conflict of interests between me and Keith. I was hoping it was something we could sort out, but I guess it wasn't meant to be."

"He loves you, I know it!" Ky argued.

"I love him too, baby, but this was his decision, not mine. Now I only have two nights left before I leave so why don't we get some rest and we can eat breakfast in bed and watch cartoons in the morning."

Ky scampered under the covers. He was still wearing his regular clothes but I just let him be. I waited until he drifted off to sleep and then I began to cry. I loved Keith and wanted to be with Keith. He was never going to respect my opinion or treat me as an equal. Keith's megalomania was always going to keep me at a distance. Still, I couldn't help but love the way he smelled and the way he kissed. Maybe there was a way to win him back?

The next two days passed quickly. I didn't see Lucky or Keith at all. I was told they were staying in the city with Harlan, entertaining some models Harlan had worked with in Europe. I cried myself to sleep both nights. Keith was such a pig. At least he could have waited until I was gone.

Chapter 20

The week was over and I was already hugging everyone goodbye. Lucky and Keith had returned from whoring or whatever they were doing. I let Lucky, Keith and Ky take me to the park where I would meet Eric.

"Are you guys going to be okay without me?" I asked.

"Uhhhhhhhhhh," said Lucky, while Keith replied, "I'm really not sure."

I turned to face them. "Is something going on?" I demanded.

"Well when we get home we're going to..." Keith started but Lucky gleefully interrupted.

"Tell Jack we enrolled him in school!" he squealed. The two of them started that giggling that they only do when they're together. Wow, sending Jack to school. That took more bravery than fighting a war.

"Are you sending someone with him?" I asked.

"Yes!" Lucky choked out. He was laughing so hard his face was red. Keith couldn't seem to stop laughing either. After about three tries Lucky finally managed the name "Zeal."

Oh my god poor Zeal! He had just been taken off Ky duty a few weeks ago. He was going to have a fit when they put him on Jack duty. "You guys know Zeal is going to kill you in your sleep one day, right?"

"Oh God I know, I know!" Keith choked. I secretly wished he would really choke. Then Ky slipped his little hand into mine and suddenly everything was right in the universe.

"I'm sorry I'm going to miss your birthday Ky," I said of the upcoming celebration. "I know 13 is supposed to be a big deal but after the way you handled yourself in that fight, well you're already a man in my eyes." He squeezed my hand tightly.

When we arrived at the park Eric was already there. He shook hands with the Mals and Lucky.

"When will she be back?" Ky asked.

"When her teacher decides she is ready," Eric told him. God I hoped that was soon!

Eric turned away as I took one last look at the boys. Despite our current problems, they were still the 3 most important people in my life. I wanted to remember everything about them, their hair, their eyes the way they smelled and felt.

"Do your best," Ky told me. I squeezed him so tight.

"I promise," I promised with my heart and soul.

The glowing green door opened and in a second the boys, the park and my world were all gone.

Lord Eric and I found ourselves on a green mountaintop. Hills spread out in all directions. There was a dirt roadway and a few scattered trees.

"Are we in hell?" I asked incredulously. I had expected molten lava and caves. Not blue sky and fresh air.

Eric paused at my question as if thinking of something to say and coming up with nothing. "Yes. Technically we are in hell, but you are in no more danger here than on earth. This dimension is populated by many humans and Fiends in human form. They tend to be less destructive and violent than other Fiends."

"Except Steel, you mean." I wanted Eric to know that I knew the truth about his friend. "I heard Steel was scoundrel and a murderer."

"That may be true, but his deeds, wicked as they may be, have saved the lives of countless innocents. Not everyone is born an Angel." I sensed there was more to that statement but lately Eric seemed more characterized by his silence than by his words.

"Steel will be here any minute," Eric told me. "If he gives you any trouble, tell him…tell him you're a Legacy." He seemed like he wanted to say more but instead gazed off in the distance. A flash of green appeared and he was gone, leaving me alone here in hell.

I stood at the top of the hill for a long time, just gazing out in different directions. When I grew tired I sat right in that spot. Travelers would pop up on the road and I would hide myself in the trees. Night fell and I tried to balance myself in a tree so that no one could get the jump on me. I couldn't sleep a wink and when morning came I was tired and grouchy. I was amazed to see that the sun rose and set in hell. I figured it would be all caves deep inside the earth. Instead it seemed to be a world all its own. Did it exist simultaneously on earth while we did?

Again I waited all day. I was getting furious. Who the hell did Steel

think he was? It's not like I wanted to do this, I was drafted!

Finally his unassuming figure came over the ridge. He was dressed in

black pants and a sleeveless black vest. He wore a grey cloak and

carried a large grey sack over one arm. Across his chest was a braided

blue and purple cord. The cord connected to the scabbard of his

sword, which was slanted across his back. He seemed like a warrior

but still looked like a teenager with that spiky royal blue hair and

matching fingernails. I rushed down to meet him.

"Blondie?" I guess he was talking to me. "You're the one I'm supposed

to train? Oh dear God what a waste of my time. I thought Eric was

bringing me someone with potential. Well forget it, I'm not going to do

it. You can just wait here until Eric shows up to take you home." He

washed his hands of me and turned back in the direction he had come

from.

"Wait just a damn minute!" I yelled, well, to his back. "I came here to

train and we're gonna train. There's a war about to happen. I didn't

come here for nothing."

"Looks like you did, sweet cheeks. I've already fought you, destroyed

you and I can tell you right now you'd never ever survive the training."

"Destroyed me?" Was this guy insane? "As I remember it, Eric

interrupted seconds before I finished you!"

"As if," Steel countered. "I was just toying with you the whole time.

You're pathetic as a fighter. Believe me, I've seen your best and Honey, your best ain't good enough."

My best. I promised Ky I would do my best. Whatever kind of wicked Fiend Steel was didn't matter. I needed to learn whatever he needed to teach me. Bickering was going to get me nowhere. I ran to catch up with Steel.

"Steel, sir, you are right. I am weak and worthless as a fighter. Teach me to be better. Teach me how to fight a war. I will listen to anything you have to tell me."

He continued to storm off. I started realizing this could be really bad for me. I knew no one in hell. What if Eric didn't come back? I remembered what he told me to say. "I'm a Legacy," I called out to Steel.

Steel froze. He turned back to me. He looked me over from head to toe reaching out to feel my muscle tone.

"Impossible," he said aloud. He grabbed me by the chin and looked at my jawbone then drilled his blue eyes into mine. I had no idea what a "Legacy" was but it seemed to have changed Steel's mind.

"On your knees," he ordered. I shakily knelt before him. He drew his sword. Maybe he was going to knight me?

"The girl you were on Earth doesn't exist here in hell. Here you have no friends, no lovers. You have nothing but the things I give you. The things I teach you." He was running his fingers through my hair. He reached up with his sword and *slash* a large clump of my hair fell down before me. Steel moved with blinding speed, racing around me attacking and hacking into my beautiful blonde tresses. In a matter of minutes all my hair lay in a circle around me. I started to cry. Steel laughed.

"Yes! This is a beauty queen without beauty! A female without femininity. You're not even a girl anymore, you're an 'it'" Steel laughed at my tears. "This is the last time you shed tears in hell. You show weakness like that and even I won't be able to protect you from the awful things that will hunt you down."

Steel started down the dirt path again. I wiped my eyes and hurried to follow. I took one last look at my beautiful hair lying on the ground and reached up to feel the monstrosity he had made of my head.

Steel and I walked in silence until it was too dark to see. We slept in shifts to guard each other. In the morning we were off again walking a dusty dirt road over emerald hills. We turned at a fork and found ourselves at a brook. We walked alongside the brook for a few hours and stopped when we reached the base of an enormous tree. "This is where we'll train for a while," Steel said, carefully taking off his bag and placing it on the ground. "Don't touch my bag and don't EVER touch my sword," he instructed. I nodded. I hated Steel. I hated him with every fiber of my being. He was evil and Eric had no right to put us together. I hated him for cutting all my hair off and making me look like some boy. I prayed that this training would pass quickly.

"So what do I call you?" I asked, trying to make conversation.

"Steel," Steel responded coldly.

"Is that even your real name?" The Fiend was silent so I pushed on.

"You're instructing me so can I call you Teacher? How about Mentor or
Guru or Maestro or Sensei?"

"How about "Master?" Or Overlord, Controller…how about God?" he
snickered. "'Steel' is good enough. I don't talk just to make
conversation so if you've got something important to say, say it.
Otherwise keep your mouth shut." Oh yeah, this was going to work out
great.

The next morning and every morning after began with brutal assault.
Steel managed to wake up before me and would proceed to hit me,
kick me, push me or throw something at me to wake me up. I tumbled
out of bed and into battle every morning. No, wait "brutal" didn't even
begin to cover it. Steel was stronger than me, smarter than me and
faster than me. He had taught me nothing and spent the weeks beating
me up every way possible. Everything I said was wrong, every move I
made was wrong. Every second we spent together was a waste of
Steel's time. If he wanted to make me feel worthless, he was doing a
great job.

Steel forced me to attack him with my static electricity. I went after him
every way I could think of, but could barely hit him. Even when I did

make contact he seemed to brush off the attack with no injury. I even tried to use the move I had gotten him with the first time we met but this time he easily and effortlessly evaded it. He shouted to me while I flailed around trying to hit him.

"Do you even know what your center of gravity is? You manipulate static. You should be able to push and pull at the ground to keep yourself stable and standing at all times. The way you move now, a child could knock you down," Steel shouted. Thank God he didn't know I lost my fight to Ky.

"Do you know where your power comes from?" Steel asked in a tone that indicated I should know.

"Um, magic?" I responded. Steel stopped what he was doing.

"Oh no. You did not just tell me that you not only believe in magic but that you think that's where the electricity comes from. Magic? You idiot! You're even dumber than I thought. How do you dress yourself in the morning?" Steel covered his eyes and shook his head from side to side.

"There's no such thing as magic, you fool. Your abilities are just natural long term adaptations to the environment."

"But, I was born this way," I explained.

"Right, and your parents probably lived in a place with a lot of storms or something and adapted to conduct the electricity so as to live in harmony with the environment. All abilities are just adaptations. God, you've been believing in magic all this time? Maybe that is why you are so weak, so pathetic as a fighter. You think the power is within you, it's not. The power is all around you."

I looked around myself. I was standing on a broken log on the edge of a babbling brook. I was about as far away from electricity as possible. "I can tell from your vacant eyes you don't have a clue what I'm talking about." Steel dropped into a seated position on the ground. He picked up a handful of stones and tossed them one by one into the brook. "How serious are you about this? Training, fighting, launching a war?" he asked me earnestly. "Have you really thought what all of this entails? You're going to watch the people you love get ripped apart by monsters. Have you thought about what that's going to sound like? What it's going to smell like?"

He had a great point, I hadn't thought of that. I hadn't thought about that at all.

"C'mon," he said rising from the ground and slipping his sword over his shoulder. I jumped to my feet and followed after him.

For the next two days we walked. Steel said nothing. When we stopped to rest he foraged for food and brought it back to me. I ate anything he gave me. After a few days of eating bark and bugs you can pretty much stomach anything. I thought about this war. I thought about losing my friends, what that would sound like, smell like.

On the third day we walked a few more hours. I had been silent so long

I started to feel brazen. As afraid as I was of Steel, I found myself muttering "All this time, you could be teaching me something." I regretted it the instant I said it but there was no turning back. In a flash Steel was on top of me, his blade to my throat. I was frozen in terror. Steel's a loose cannon and he clearly hated me, this could be my end.

"I *am* teaching you something, you dumb bitch. God can't you just shut up for a second!" Steel screamed.

Clearly he wasn't going to kill me so I didn't hold back. "I've kept my mouth shut for three days now and I don't see how you've been teaching me anything!"

He lowered his sword and backhanded me across the face. It was so quick I didn't have time to react. I fell hard to the ground, blood poured from my mouth.

"The next time you make a sound without my permission, you die. Am I making myself clear?" his blue eyes narrowed.

My face was swelling with pain, but I nodded furiously to show him I understood.

Steel reached into his bag and pulled out his cloak. He dropped it on the ground in front of me. "Cover yourself," he told me. "I don't want anyone to know you are human and especially a girl. Where we're going I don't know if I can protect you. Stay covered and for God's sake stay silent."

I was starting to think maybe Steel wasn't such a loose cannon after

301

all. It seemed like there was a method behind his madness. He kept me silent the last few days so he could sneak me past danger up ahead. It certainly is a lot easier to stay quiet after you've been quiet a while. I needed to get past myself and start listening to what Steel was telling me. There must be a reason why he was Eric's go-to guy.

I bundled up using my clothes and Steel's cloak. We started heading in the same direction we'd be going for days. After a few hours we found ourselves at the top of a hill.

I couldn't believe what we were seeing. From the top of the hill we could see an enormous bustling city below. There were no phone lines or power lines, just thousands of tiny cottages lined up in rows. The main road in and out was bustling with carriages, people pulling carts, riding horses, you name it. Steel had very carefully taken us the long way around to avoid them. At the edge of the city was an enormous mountain. Workers were laboring intensely removing rocks and dirt from a giant hole at the base. Clearly they were trying to get through, but what was on the other side? It was impossible to tell from where we were standing.

It didn't take me very long to realize this was no human village we were staring at. Although several of the creatures had a human appearance, the majority of them were clearly inhuman. There were Fiends everywhere with skin of every color, purple, orange, green, gray. Some of them had spikes jutting out of their skin, others had multiple arms or legs. There were Fiends that were huge, 7-8 feet tall, and others that seemed only a foot or two tall.

I didn't have a lot of time to look. Steel was already making his way down into the village. I followed him closely and tried to be as silent as possible. Our sneaky way in kept us off the main road but we still started passing creatures on our way. A pair of large Fiends stopped to check us out. The two were covered from head to toe with thick orange hair. They were both 8 feet tall at least and hunched over, carrying shovels that were about the size of Ky. Both of them were filthy and smelled like a sewer. One wrapped a (paw?) around me and pulled me in close. He started sniffing me. Steel drew his sword. I stayed completely silent. Whatever Steel wanted to show me was in this town and getting into a fight here would ruin our chances of sneaking in.

"Working on the tunnel?" Steel asked, nodding to the shovels.

"Yeah," said the one furthest from me in a deep bellowing voice.

"Who's in charge?" Steel asked.

"Grimm," the oaf told us. "Grimm in charge."

"Excellent," Steel said in a voice that was uncharacteristically cheerful. He turned to me. "Grimm. That's who we report to." He reached forward and grabbed my arm, pulling me quickly away from the Fiends. When we were far enough away from them we stopped rushing and went back to our innocuous silent walk.

"Aren't you glad you stayed quiet?" Steel asked me. I nodded. I realized Steel had a plan and that I better obey every command so as not to upset that plan. It was more than that. I wasn't just following Steel, I was trusting him, too. We were walking into an enormous Fiend village. All Steel had to do was yell "Human Girl" and point in my direction and I would be dead or worse within seconds. It's not that all Fiends were dangerous or that all of them hated humans but there was a dark shadow cast over this village and its enormous tunnel...

Oh my god!!! My breath caught in my chest. I must be the dumbest synergy alive! This wasn't a tunnel, this was *the* tunnel, the one that was leading to Earth. I was dizzy. My feet faltered and I tumbled to the ground. Steel was upon me in an instant.

"Get it together," he hissed, pulling me to my feet. "You don't have time to think, you need to act. Push it out of your mind," he commanded. He was so right. Any number of small weaknesses could give us away. I had to hold it together for Ky. Steel never showed fear. Was he pushing it aside like I was?

We kept walking at a brisk pace and arrived at the mouth of the tunnel in no time. The tunnel opening was as tall as a sky scraper and a seemed as long as a city block. On looking in I could see for miles. Tens of thousands of Fiends were breaking rocks and carrying them out the entrance in buckets, wheelbarrows, whatever they could carry. The pace was slow but steady.

After peering into the tunnel, Steel gestured for me to follow him. We walked into the tunnel and went up the steep side until we reached a landing. Steel started rummaging through his bag. He pointed at the ground and I sat down.

"A few days ago I asked you how serious you were about this. I need your answer."

"What do you mean? I'm completely serious!" the question pissed me off. I wasn't fooling around out here. "I love Ky more than anything. I'm willing to die for him."

"Yes," Steel agreed with a hint of sadness. "But are you willing to kill for him? Dying is the easy part. Killing, that's the true test."

Killing, right. I knew that was why I was here with Steel. No matter how much sparring we did back home it could never prepare me to actually kill someone. Fiends were someones too, right? I mean I was half a Fiend myself.

"You have to look inside yourself and find a reason to kill. I mean, these guys are trying to take over Earth and stuff, that's pretty bad." Steel sighed as made his point. "They will probably rape and murder and burn like you've never imagined. This could truly be the apocalypse for your world. That's enough motivation for anybody."

"No," I said with conviction. "I mean, yes that is horrible, but that's not the reason why I'll kill. I'll kill to protect Ky."

"You really believe he's the messiah, huh?" Steel asked with amusement.

"I don't care if he is the messiah or not. I'm not protecting what he might be, I'm protect what he is. He's an incredible little boy and he deserves the right to grow up."

"What about the Fiends, what do they deserve?" Steel countered.

"I don't know them, but they make their own choices. None of us are busting into their backyards trying to kill them."

Steel was enjoying this conversation. He challenged, "What if the Fiends are really the good guys? What if killing Ky is the key that will unlock a thousand years of peace through all dimensions? What if you are on the wrong side?"

I didn't really have an answer, more like a feeling. "Battles this big can't be quantified as easily as good or bad. There are no real sides. I will protect Ky. Not because it's right or wrong. I will protect him because I have the power to do so and only with power comes choice."

Steel chuckled a bit and patted me on the arm. "There's still hope for you, Park. A slim glimmer of hope." What Steel then took out of the bag looked almost like a foam 6-pack of soda. "This is plastic explosive," he told me in his most serious voice. "It's a very powerful and very deadly weapon. We can't stop the tunnel but we can slow them down and buy us some time."

So that was his plan! We were here to slow the tunnel! That would give everyone more time to prepare.

"An electric charge is needed to detonate. You'll need to place the explosive and this blasting cap. Then get as far away as you can but stay close enough to detonate it. Hit it with an electric charge and fly out of that cave like a bat out of hell! Do you understand?"

Place the plastic, trigger the explosion, escape. I nodded yes.

Steel reached forward and squeezed my arm reassuringly. It was weird, a murderer showing me compassion. Wait, in a matter of moments I'd be a murderer too. Things really weren't so black and white.

Steel hopped down from the landing and turned to me to follow suit. He was wearing black clothes and the limited light in the cave made his blue hair look black too. His cerulean eyes were bright and alert. He didn't look like some scary killer, more like a teenager going to a party with his friends.

"Steel, in case we don't make it I just want to say," I didn't get to finish my words. Steel's boot came flying right at my throat to crush my windpipe. I actually reacted in time and pushed back catching his boot with my hands and knocking myself down in the process. I think both Steel and I were surprised.

Steel recovered immediately. "Don't jinx the mission. If you don't think you can do it, you tell me. If you can then just shut up and do it."

We headed in to the giant mouth of the tunnel trying to blend in with all the Fiends that were busy laboring. We walked for about an hour. Steel started a conversation with a Fiend that looked almost human. He was a withered old man with grey hair who was bent over from age.

"Been working here long?" Steel asked.

"I'm third generation," the Fiend told him. "My father and grandfathers all gave their lives to build this tunnel. I wish they were here now that we are so close to completing it."

"Really?" Steel seemed impressed. "How close are you to finishing?"

"Oh it won't be long now. Two, three moons at best." The old timer seemed wistful. "I really believe it's fate, you know. We've been building this tunnel for so long to get our hands on that kid. Now we're going to come up right underneath him and wring his neck. His bloodshed will bring honor to every generation of my family." For an old guy this Fiend sure seemed passionate about killing my little boy.

"The soldiers will get him you mean. When the tunnel is done the king will send his army, right?" Steel asked.

"Pshaw," the old man said with impatience. "There's no army in these lands. The workers, we're the ones that will seize the boy. We're the ones that will live in fame and glory forever!"

"And if the child isn't there when you get there?" Steel questioned.

"Well we'll have free reign to destroy the Earth searching for him." He put a comforting hand on Steel's shoulder. "Don't worry my friend, we'll get him. We'll get him and we'll torture him and we'll sell his pieces to the highest bidder, just you wait and see. This town will be famous in every dimension!"

Steel thanked the guy for his time and hurried me deeper into the tunnel.

"So that's it?" I asked when we were far enough away. "Money and fame? That's why these Fiends built this tunnel? It just doesn't make any sense."

"Moron! It makes perfect sense! Money and fame are what everybody wants," Steel told me.

"Not me," I said matter-of-factly.

"Of course not," Steel agreed. "You don't want them because you already have them. We only ever want what we can't have."

"What do you want?" I asked Steel innocently.

"I want you to shut up and do your job. You missed the important part of what that Fiend was saying. The ones coming through the tunnel will be laborers, not soldiers. That's a definite advantage." Steel stopped walking and surveyed the passageway. "This seems as good a place as any. I wanted to find a narrower part of the tunnel but I think we could walk for days in here and not find anything better. At least we are alone here, for the moment. Just blow the charge and get out. Oh and give me a good head start." Suddenly his voice softened. "Listen kid, don't wrestle with your conscience too much, ok? I know it's barbaric but beings like us, it's what we have to do."

"Beings like us," I spat. "You mean Fiends? Villains? Killers?"

"Guardians. I meant guardians." His words game me the chills. "We make the sacrifices to protect great people who affect existence in ways we never could." Steel said nothing more and headed quickly for the exit. He really knew exactly what to say to motivate me. I was ready to do what I must.

The tunnel opening was so gigantic. I don't know what kind of explosion this plastic would give me, but I couldn't see how it could make a difference in this enormous cavern. I started planning my escape.

In a rush it came to me. The greatest impact would be on the ceiling. That would surely cause a rock slide and bury countless Fiends while trapping many in the later stages of the tunnel. I didn't think I'd be able to place the explosive without being seen, so I decided to do it from a distance. I used my power to gently lift the bomb off the ground and floated it as far away from me as I could while holding it steady. I carefully controlled the static to raise the explosive up to the ceiling, delicately so as not to set it off. I didn't know what else to do. Detonate and run, right?

I didn't waste any time. The bomb was only 100 feet or so away so I got my body ready to flee. It was going to take all my cunning to escape. I took a deep breath and sent a strong electrical charge straight from my hands. Instantly the bomb detonated and there was a massive explosion! I was already in motion trying to fly my way out of that cave. The force of the blast threw me forward several hundred feet. I caught myself riding the explosion like a surfer riding a wave. Rocks and dust spewed everywhere. I got hit several times with larger rocks and was pelted with pebbles and silt. One of the larger rocks tore right through my left arm, blood spilling everywhere. I felt an overwhelming surge of pain first and then nothing, like I could no longer feel my arm at all. The rocks were hitting hard and only motivated me to push faster. In no time I could see the mouth of the tunnel.

Fiends were fleeing the channel in chaos. I soared over them, looking for Steel. I found him standing on a rooftop watching everything from a safe distance. I made my way over to him and collapsed in his arms.

"How did we do?" I gasped. It had only been seconds since the bomb was detonated. To me it seemed like a lifetime.

"You did good," Steel said, holding me tight. "The rockslide was colossal. We bought ourselves a few months at least. You did real good, Steph."

I started losing consciousness. Steel shook me to keep me awake.

"This isn't over yet, half-breed! It's not going to take them long to figure out who did this. We need to get out of here!"

"Leave me," I told him without considering the consequences. "I don't have the strength to go any further. Save yourself. Help Ky."

"Ok I know you're delirious so I'll just ignore that. I might be able to get us both out of here, but if I do, you owe me…understand?" Steel asked almost menacingly. "Whatever I ask, you'll do without question – got it?"

"Yes Master," I said and everything went dark.

Chapter 21

When I awoke I was in a bed in a strange wooden house with a high vaulted ceiling. I sat up like a shot. My chest and left arm was wrapped heavily in bandages. I wiggled my fingers. Steel must have figured out a way to save my arm! From the impact it took I thought I'd lost it.

A door opened at the other side of the room and a woman entered. As soon as I saw her I knew we were still in hell. This woman seemed to have a human form, but it was a mangled disfigured version at best. One of her legs had a second foot that seemed to sprout from her calf and failed to reach the floor. The other leg had at least five or six feet, all sprouting from the knee. Her pale white skin was covered by a long calico dress with lace at the neck and wrists. Her hands mimicked her feet. Several hands and even more extra fingers on her right side. On her left she had two complete arms. The one on the top had a singular hand and looked like a completely normal arm. The second arm was completely disfigured with extra hands and fingers. Her hair was in lovely tiny brown curls and she had warm, shy blue eyes. Her face was something so shocking it was almost incomprehensible. She had two eyes and one mouth just like any other human. The edges of her cheeks on both sides were covered with malformed, disfigured ears. She had 4 ears on the right side jutting out in a circle from her original ear. On the left side there were twice as many ears. They seemed to spring from every available patch of skin. She had one normal nose in the center of her face. On the right side were two smaller noses a third jutted out to the left. If I had seen a creature like this a month ago I would have screamed or ran. Now here in hell I was taken aback, but not really frightened.

"You're awake!" she shouted, surprised. She hurried to the side of my bed. She had a bowl of cool water and a dampened rag. She breathlessly blotted my forehead.

"Steel?" I asked.

"He'll be back this evening. They left before dawn again this morning to go hunting. At this rate I'll have enough meat to last for 10 winters," she laughed. "I'm Genevieve. The man that patched you up is my husband Mac," she told me and pointed to my bandaged arm. "Mac and I weren't sure you'd make it. You lost so much blood. Mac wanted to amputate your arm but Steel wouldn't hear of it. I'm glad we were wrong, you look like you're going to be just fine."

It was reassuring to hear I was going to be okay, even if it was from this unusual looking stranger.

"How long have I been here?" I asked.

"Just a few days. Steel has dumped people here before to get patched up. He's never waited for them to heal though. He must care about you." The last words were said more like a jilted girlfriend than a friendly caretaker.

314

I practically choked just hearing that. Steel doesn't just hate me, he completely loathes me.

"Have you known Steel long?" I asked.

"Oh yes, a few hundred years. He gave me the name Genevieve. I owe everything to him." She sighed and settled in on a stool next to the bed. Her eyes clouded over.

"When I met Steel I was called by another name, ReGen. As a child I lost a finger in a carpentry accident. Over the next few days a new finger grew in its place. My parents chopped off the new finger with an axe and sure enough another grew in its place. I had a gift."

"It wasn't long before word spread about my abilities. In less than a year my parents sold me for a very high price to a man from another hell dimension. My parents were people of means, high society. They didn't need the money, they were just tired of all the attention my ability to heal myself was bringing."

Her parents sold her? Somehow that seemed way worse than my parents abandoning me.

"I was taken to an enormous house and locked in the basement. My new 'owner' would take me out and parade me in front of guests. They would take turns burning me with pokers or cutting me with knives, only to watch my skin repair itself. Trust me, Stephanie, just because your body fixes itself, the pain doesn't hurt any less." I gasped, the poor girl!

"After a decade or so of this, my owner began getting creative. He hired men who experimented on me day and night. That's how I got all of this," she said and gestured to the ears on her face down to the extra hands and feet. They learned that removing a part would make it regrow, but that splitting a part would cause both halves to grow. They began clipping and selling parts of me, and not just parts on the outside; they started removing and regrowing my organs too. All I wanted to do was die, but my awful body wouldn't let me. I lost all hope and fell into despair."

"The boss would still parade me in front of his guests. Steel showed up one day. I noticed him only because he looked like a child, a new low for the boss. He sat at the end of the table and looked at me with cold piercing eyes and didn't move or say a word while everybody burned and cut on me and had their fun.

"Later that night Steel came down to the basement where they kept me. He asked 'Is there a person left in that body, or is it only monster now?' I said 'Little boy, get out of here. Forget everything you've seen. Never involve yourself with people like these. It's never too late to start over.' He turned and left without a word.

"Several hours later Steel appeared at the door of the basement again. He was breathing heavily and he was covered in blood. I didn't say a word; I knew what he had done in order to rescue me.

"We stayed together for many months as we traveled to find a friend of his. Steel decided that 'ReGen' was never to be spoken again and instead gave me the name Genevieve." Her voice cracked a bit with emotion. "I fell deeply in love with Steel, he was my...hero."

"Steel brought me here to this very house. Mac is a brilliant doctor and Steel hoped he could help me. The two had known each other from centuries before. When Mac was a child he had seen Steel fight and was overwhelmed. He followed Steel everywhere for more than a century begging to become Steel's apprentice. Steel had it set in his mind what kind of apprentice he wanted and Mac didn't make the grade. That didn't stop Mac from trying to prove himself to Steel every chance he got. In one of his battles, Mac was wounded heavily in the shoulder. Steel jumped into the battle and saved Mac's life. Sadly, Mac's injury meant he would never swing a sword again. Steel stayed by his side until they found a nice town for Mac to settle down in. He studied to become a doctor and even patched Steel up on a few occasions. Mac wanted to thank Steel for saving his life, but Steel only said 'you owe me one.' When Steel arrived at Mac's door with me he said 'We're even now.'

"Mac did everything he could, but every time he removed an extra piece of me, it would grow back again. I guess they're all a part of me now." As she said that I took a better look at her. Even with all the extra parts, she didn't seem scary anymore.

317

"Mac and I fell in love. I think Steel was a big part of that; it was just great to have someone who understood how great Steel was." Just like how Keith and I love each other for loving Ky so much!

"Of course I begged Steel to let me repay him for saving me. Again he said 'you owe me.' When he showed up at the door with you in his arms he told me 'I'm here for that favor you owe me.' At first I thought he just wanted Mac to tend to your injuries but when I saw how badly damaged you were I realized what he really wanted."

What he really wanted? Genevieve opened the collar of her dress. She had a bandage on her chest identical to mine. "Mac performed the Xxixxa," she told me.

"Ziza?" I tried repeating. "I've never heard of it."

"The Xxixxa is the death technique. It is the only way for Fiends to gain each other's powers. There must be two participants. They stop both hearts, then extract blood from one heart and inject into the other. During the procedure we were both dead."

I died? My knees felt week. I looked down at myself and my body didn't seem real.

I jumped out of bed on wobbly legs and bolted through the door. I found myself in a pretty, rural home. I made my way toward the kitchen. I reached into the knife block and pulled out a knife with a smooth edge.

"Don't!" Genevieve shouted, racing after me. "We don't even know if the operation was a success!"

"Only one way to find out," I told her. I raised my forearm and sliced into it with the knife. It f'n hurt like hell! My arm started bleeding like normal. I stood and watch the blood spill, then slow, then stop. Was I invincible now? My knees buckled and I fell forward, catching myself on the kitchen counter. Genevieve helped me back to bed and I fell asleep immediately.

I awoke when the hilt of a sword came down hard on my forehead. Steel!

"How much longer are you gonna take to recover?" he asked impatiently. "We've got a lot of work to do and very little time. And when I think about your skills..." he shuddered. "We've got a LOT of work to do." With that he turned and left the room. I don't know why, I guess I expected him to be nicer to me. Genevieve had said that Steel cared about me. He certainly had a funny way of showing it.

I was up and about but took my time over the next few days. Steel had taken off right after waking me. He returned a few days later to fetch me. I had taken a great liking to Mac and Genevieve. They told me countless stories about Steel. It seemed that Steel had always been a hard hearted and ruthless scoundrel. I guess that's why his rare acts of kindness seemed all the more special.

Steel didn't waste any time putting me back into training. He was swiftly moving me from place to place each day. I was too worn out to gawk at all the strange Fiends I was passing by. It was certainly a good tour of the first level of hell.

My teacher didn't take it easy on me. Night after night I slept on the ground or at the foot of a tree and every morning I'd be awakened by Steel hitting me or jumping on me or kicking me. The weeks passed this way, training past the point of exhaustion and collapsing into sleep each night. Steel took advantage of my new regenerative powers. He caused more pain to my body than I ever thought possible, cutting and stabbing me just to watch me heal up.

"I don't think you're immortal," he told me one day after cutting me open so severely you could see some of my guts. "I don't want that to affect your performance, though. You need to guard your weak spots, but your offense is your strength. You protect by getting rid of the threats. Let someone else guard the body."

"It's not a 'body' it's a little boy and his name is Kyan Mal. We've been training forever, when do I get to see him?" I was way past physical and emotional exhaustion.

"Well that depends on how long you're planning on spending with him. If you just want to spend a few months with him we can go right now," Steel said. I was nodding my head vigorously. "If you want to see him grow up, you'll stay here until you learn how to protect him." Damn. I knew Steel was right.

Days, then weeks, then months continued to pass until I could no longer remember exactly how long I'd been gone. Every day I gave my all to learning how to fight and how to kill. Steel took some odd jobs and were hired muscle, fighting strangers to get paid.

One morning I opened my eyes as Steel was about to hit me in the face with his scabbard. I only had a second but I reached up and grabbed the end. I placed my palm at the bottom and pushed up hard. The scabbard hit Steel square in the chin and knocked him down.

"Ha!" I shouted jumping to my feet. "How do you like it?"

Steel stared fiercely up at me, his blue eyes flashing. "'Bout time," he told me. "I had almost given up on you. Go down to the river and wash up, I'm taking you home."

Chapter 22

Home! I couldn't believe it! I couldn't get ready quick enough. We began the journey back to the place where Eric had dropped us off. I hummed and sang and twirled around during the whole walk. Finally we were there.

We waited nearly a day and a half for Eric to arrive. Steel kept me training the entire time. I didn't even notice the glowing green door or Eric's arrival. I was sweaty from training and retreated to clean myself up before heading home. The guys started talking.

"So what do you think?" Eric asked nodding in my direction.

"In a few hundred years she might be something. As for now, I did the best I could with what I had," Steel sighed. I guess I was just a big disappointment to him. "She'll live, and if she's protecting that boy with her life, then he'll live too." What, was he saying he thought I could win?

"What about Armageddon?" Eric asked.

"Whoa," Steel laughed. "I taught her how to fight, not how to win a war. Isn't Kaden's other son like some brilliant strategist? Leave Armageddon in his hands." Kaden? How did they know Keith and Ky's father? Well Eric kinda does watch over the world, I bet he knows a lot of things. Maybe he knew who my father was? Now wasn't the time to ask, Eric was about to take me home! I joined up with the guys.

"Ready?" Eric asked, smiling. I looked over at Steel. He wasn't coming with me.

"I can't thank you enough for everything you've taught me. Everything you've done for me." Steel didn't make eye contact. "Will I ever see you again?"

"You owe me a favor, right?" Steel asked.

"Absolutely," I said with certainty. Steel had saved my life. I would do anything he asked.

"Good, then someday I will come to collect."

"I'll be looking forward to it." That might have been an exaggeration but I did want to repay Steel.

Eric opened up that glowing green door right in front of me. I took a few steps forward and suddenly I was standing in the backyard of the Mals' house!

I was far enough away to watch for a minute before anyone noticed me. Kyan and another little boy were swimming in the pool. Was that Jack? I thought he would have gone back to Atlanta after a couple months. Some of the Vipers were splashing around the pool as well. Ari and Violet looked like sisters with their stylish hairstyles, both wearing white bikinis showing off their lovely bodies. Jage was by Ari's side but still dressed head to toe in full Viper gear, including that huge coat. Would we ever break him of his shyness?

Al and Zeal were sparring with the pool cleaning poles, using them like staffs. Lucky and Tyler were cheering them on while Russell was trying to teach the guys something useful about the staff as a weapon. I think his words fell on deaf ears, the two just wanted to pummel each other. All five were just in swimming trunks and I all but drooled. It made realize how long it had been since I had sex. I couldn't see Keith anywhere but he was going to get very lucky tonight.

I didn't know how to approach the group so I decided just to run straight to the pool and do a cannonball! I dropped my things and started running. It seemed like the pool was under me in seconds. I grabbed hold of my knees and made a gigantic splash when I hit the water.

The Vipers were on top of me in an instant! I guess they were always on guard in case some evil doers were after Ky. As soon as they realized it was me, everyone backed off for a second, but then drowned me in a sea of hugs.

Everyone started talking at once. "Hang on," I told them. In the shallow end of the pool was Ky. I slowly and carefully made my way over to him. Poor little guy, he looked so vulnerable. "What's wrong?" I asked, trying to catch his gaze. He dashed into my arms and squeezed me with such force it took my breath away. I know how you feel, buddy. I held him so tight.

Everyone started again with questions. I held up my hand to stop them. "Please no questions tonight. Tomorrow I will answer everything."

I let go of Ky. He looked up at me, wondering if I was really here. It was amazing; he looked exactly the same as I remembered. It was like time had stopped for him.

"Shower,' was all I could eke out. Ky nodded and took a step back to let me pass. I walked dripping wet out of the pool and into the house. As I entered I passed Keith. He looked exactly as I remembered him. I thought about walking straight past him but when I got up next to him I paused. "I've got all new muscles in all new places," I whispered in his ear. Let him stew on that while I was in the shower!

I walked in the back door and headed to the foyer with the winding staircase. Was this house always this glamorous? With a marble entrance way, an imposing front door and an elegant, sweeping staircase. It's hard to believe that just over a year ago I called this place "home." At the top of the stairs was the beautiful round solarium, outfitted with couches. I looked up and through a thousand tiny windows I could see the stars.

I turned down the hall on the left and entered the first door on the right. This had been my room. Little had been changed since I left but someone had clearly been using the room in my absence. The blankets were rumpled and there were articles on the bedside table.

Whoever was here could have the room, I would be happy to sleep on a couch somewhere. I was, however, going to use the shower.

I entered the private bathroom attached to the bedroom. There were no personal effects here, it looked exactly as I left it. I went to the closet and picked out pretty scented soaps, gels and shampoos. I turned on the shower and basked in the steam for a moment. I stepped into the hot water. It was every bit as divine as I remembered.

I spent the better part of an hour in the shower. It was the first time in more than a year that I was able to feel completely relaxed. When I was finished I went to my old closet hoping that there was still something of mine in there. To my surprise my clothes were all untouched. I looked through them. Wow, silks and satins, I dressed like a princess when I lived here. I put on a silky lavender dress and brushed my hair until it shone. My hair was uneven but had grown back. I doubt any of the Vipers would even notice a difference. I was glad; I never wanted anyone to know I had been hideous and bald.

I walked to the window and looked out. Everyone was gathered in a circle talking. No doubt they were all surprised by my sudden return. I went out back to join them. Keith immediately intercepted me.

"Let's go for a walk," he suggested.

We started taking the long walk down to the beach.

"Before you say a word, I have some concerns," I told Keith.

He looked at me and nodded. "I'm listening," he said.

"It's Ky. When I saw him in the pool...when I hugged him. Keith, there's something wrong. He looks exactly the same as when I left. It's as if he hasn't aged at all. And Jack, what is Jack even doing here? I thought he was staying for a few months at most. I definitely never thought he'd survive a year in this house."

"A year?" Keith asked. He seemed very confused, which may have been a first for Keith. He stopped walking.

"Stephanie, how long do you think you've been gone?" he asked grabbing me by the shoulders. I turned my head away; I wasn't ready to look in his eyes.

"I know how long I've been gone. Sixteen moons uh, months. I've been counting the days. Well after the first year I just started counting the months. When all you do is train your mind drifts off to listless nothingness. Remembering my loved ones, well it kept me sane."

Keith had his hands around my shoulders and he started shaking me a little. "Look Steph, I don't know what went on where you were, but here you've only been gone a month."

A month! You've got to be kidding! My knees felt weak. I felt like that guy in that old Christmas movie, I just got my life back!

Keith was yammering on about space and time and temporal distortion. I couldn't hear a word he was saying. It was like the whole last year of my life was one big dream.

I grabbed Keith and shut him up with one big kiss. He responded immediately and we began kissing franticly and devotedly. I wasn't really concerned that Keith had broken up with me before I left. All I wanted to do was show him how much I'd missed him all these months. Or days in his world, I guess.

Our connection in the woods was very passionate. I wanted to keep going but Keith thought we should go back and check in with the Vipers first.

Hand in hand we walked back up to the house to join the Vipers.

"Hey," Zeal shouted. "I thought you two were broken up."

"Reports of our demise have been greatly exaggerated," Keith announced as he dipped me backwards and kissed me like a hero in a movie.

When I regained my balance I asked how preparations for the upcoming war were going.

"Surprisingly good," said Lucky taking the lead. "Supplies, training, tactics all on schedule. We've even come up with a cover story for recruiting. 'Stephanie Park's synergy camp.' We'll set some tents up in the front yard and test their skills."

"We're not really going to charge people to come to this camp are we?" I asked, turning to Keith.

"No," he paused. "We'll say they all got scholarships or something. The important thing is that you're back. You need to do the recruiting."

Never a dull moment.

Recruiting was presenting a clear challenge. None of the Vipers had been recruited, they had all volunteered. Most of the synergies existing were underground, trying to give the illusion of being regular folks. We had very little success finding them on our own. As far as we knew there was only one place that synergies regularly gathered around – the DJ Phantom show. From what we could tell, hundreds, possibly thousands of synergies tuned in to his regular Saturday night broadcast. DJ would spin modern rock tunes and speak coded messages to his synergy audience. There was even a chatroom where synergies could go to talk safely with one another. Any casual observer would just see it as any other radio show.

The mastermind behind this synergy safe zone was the highly charismatic DJ Phantom. Known just as "DJ" to us, he had been one of the first files we followed up on after stealing the synergy intel from that villainess Alexis. We knew we'd never have a chance without his support. It was decided unanimously that I would be the one to call him and convince him to join us.

Saturday night came quickly and we all sat around the living room listening to the DJ Phantom show. After we listened for a bit, the Vipers were getting antsy for me to make the call. Everyone in the room was watching and listening as I dialed. The phone rang a few times and then DJ answered it himself.

"Hey DJ Phantom, long time listener, first time caller," I said, trying to sound as casual as possible.

"It's great to hear from you listener," DJ answered cheerfully. "But I think I remember you calling before. Your voice sounds kinda familiar." Wow. The shock registered on my face, everyone shifted in their chairs. He knew it was me. This was big. I needed to get DJ on my side. I remembered back to our last phone conversation. He had been so hard for me to read but it seemed like he could read me so easily.

"So you remember my voice from my awkward last call?" I hesitated.

"Oh sure, it's what I do. Also I might have heard that voice on the news, TV, radio, internet. Your voice kinda gets around." He was right, my voice was everywhere. I hadn't thought about that until now. "Also, who could forget your Eric Stuart Band obsession?" He was laughing.

"I mean when I started getting sixty to seventy requests a week for 'The Remedy,' I knew you were behind it." Now I was laughing too.

"Hang on for a moment." He put the phone on hold and I could hear him on the radio talking about the next song. Wow, it was cool to get to hear a DJ in action. Suddenly I felt a chill down my spine. This plan wasn't going to work. DJ would guard his listeners. They believed in him. He would hear everything I said through protective ears. He would tell me he needed to think about it and he would hang up the phone. If that happened, the war would be lost.

I looked around the room. All the Vipers were anxious. They would make a fuss if I told them what I was thinking. There would certainly be an argument and Steel taught me to act, not to waste time. After the radio show went off the air there would be no surefire way to get a hold of DJ and this couldn't wait until next Saturday. I moved out of the living room and ran down the stairs and across the hall to the TV room. Jack and Ky were arguing over a video game. It was my job to keep them safe. I needed to build an army. I took a few dizzy steps backwards. The cordless phone slipped from my hand and smashed when it hit the ground.

Without thinking I turned and ran as fast as I could towards the back door. I knew the Vipers would be right on my heels so I leaned in with my shoulder and broke through the door. I ran straight through and turned a sharp right towards the garage. I connected my static charge with the garage door and pushed it open. Everyone was confused at best and was gathering in front of the dark garage. I made enough noise starting up Zeal's bike to make sure everyone moved out of the way. Then without another thought I peeled out of the dusty garage and took off into the night on Zeal's motorcycle.

I didn't have time to explain to my friends what I was feeling. All I knew was I needed to get to the radio station before the show was finished.

DJ was going to make me tell him the truth and I thought he deserved to hear it in person.

I hadn't really thought about it before but the studio was actually less than an hour from my house. Good thing too, because (except for some fooling around) I'd never actually ridden a motorcycle myself, I'd only held on as Zeal drove. I was doing pretty good; well I didn't crash. Steel had taught me how to hone my center of gravity so I just extended it to the bike. It was about midnight on a Saturday so I didn't hit any traffic. I hadn't worn a helmet though, so my hair was a mess. I stopped when I entered town to buy a hairbrush and ask for directions to the studio. The folks at the store had a vague idea, but no one knew exactly where the studio was. I rode around for a bit trying to track it down.

I finally made it to the studio with only a few minutes to spare. I didn't want to interrupt the show so I just paced back and forth in front of the door. I was excited to meet DJ in person, but nervous too. I was hoping he couldn't read my mind and then secretly I was hoping he could. I needed to forget myself altogether. No pressure, I'm just responsible for the future of existence.

A couple people came and went. Finally, DJ Phantom himself stepped out. He was almost exactly as I pictured him. My height, a redhead with some red facial hair and dizzying brown eyes. He looked at me with disbelief. "What are you doing here?" he asked.

332

I felt stupid but I nodded. "I need to talk to you. It's extremely important."

"Yeah, I gather that." He didn't sound so sure that he wanted to talk to *me*. "I have work in the morning and I have very little time to sleep so we'll have to do this some other time."

"The people I love are in danger," I told him fiercely. It was up to him to believe me or not. "Look can't we just get some pancakes and talk for a bit?"

He was uncharacteristically silent.

"Where's Holly?" I asked about his teenage on-air assistant. I had seen pictures of her on his website. She was adorable and her antics were often the highlight of the show.

He laughed. "Holly's bits are prerecorded. She actually lives in Arizona."

Damn. I had a feeling Holly would be on my side and I could tell DJ had a big brother weakness for her.

"This concerns her too. It concerns everyone you care about," I ventured.

"Was that a threat?" DJ questioned in a tone that frightened me.

"No, God no! I'm the good guy! I want to save the world and I need your help." How many times does a mutant beauty queen drop a bomb like that at the front door of your job at 2am? I wouldn't blame him if he turned away and never looked back. I tried to catch him in my big blue puppy dog eyes. It worked! He chuckled.

"Pancakes, right? All right, follow me." Without giving me a hint of what he was thinking he hopped into his car and I trailed him to a diner.

We asked for a booth away from everybody. I let DJ order for me and waited eagerly for my coffee to arrive. I didn't have the faintest clue how to start this conversation.

"So," DJ said rather charmingly. "Spill it."

Deep breath. "In approximately a month Fiends from hell are going to rise up and try to take over Earth." I laid it all on the table. "I need you and your followers to help us create an army to stop them. They have been digging a tunnel for some time now. We've been told that if we can hold them back at the mouth of the tunnel we can collapse the passageway and crush their invasion." I was using my hands to illustrate and I pounded my closed fist against my open palm to simulate the "crushing." The woman arrived with the coffee.

"That's an interesting idea you have for a movie, there," DJ Phantom said loudly in front of her to cover my tracks. "Sounds a little far-fetched to me." The woman left and I tried a different approach.

"How much do you know about synergies?" I asked.

"Nothing really. Everyone is different. It may be linked to radiation levels the mother is exposed to during gestation. The usual," he said rather coolly.

334

"The truth is way more simple but very strange." I said, trying to feel out if he was ready to believe me.

"Lay it on me," he said, leaning comfortably back in the booth.

"Ok, it's like this; life on earth subsists on 32 planes of existence. They all line up in a specific order. The one that we live on is, well, number 4. The three above us we refer to as 'heaven.' The 28 below us we call 'hell.' These terms are huge oversimplifications." I tried to make eye contact with DJ to see what he was thinking but he was staring hard at the table.

"There are Angels in heaven and Fiends in hell. Some of them can move about freely in other dimensions. When they come into our world and mate with a human being, the resulting child is a synergy. This is the truth behind our so-called 'mutation.'" He still wouldn't make eye contact with me. He was playing with the wrapper from his straw.

"DJ," I started, laying one of my hands down on his. "What I'm telling you is very real. Fiends will attack and unless we hold them back, they will kill and destroy." He shook my hand off of his.

"So you want me to what, hand over my listeners? I won't let them be casualties of your war!" He was pissed. "Just so you know, the people on my website and in my chatroom aren't just random people. I care about them. Most of them are young and scared. They have these strange abilities to deal with and they don't know how to handle them or what they're for."

"Stop and think, DJ. Maybe this is what it's all for?" The tension was painfully thick. "Movies, comic books, TV, they all show us the same thing. Horrible things happen and a tiny group of superheroes rises up and saves the world. Well, we're the heroes and guess what, the world needs saving."

I continued, impassioned. "I don't think you know it, but you are the world's greatest synergy leader. Hundreds of synergies follow your shows and chatrooms. They know you and they trust you. I can't do this without you!"

The woman arrived with our pancakes. The tension was so thick she just wordlessly set the pancakes down and walked away. I chowed down, at least food in my mouth would stop me from saying anything stupid for the moment. Will nibbled in silence.

DJ spoke first, and without hesitation. "Did you hear the song I played for you tonight? After you hung up the phone?" he asked earnestly.

"No." I wish I had. "Was it Eric Stuart Band?"

"It was Devil with The Green Eyes by Matthew Sweet," he told me. I gasped.

"You know that song isn't about synergies. It's just a metaphor for jealousy," he said knowledgeably. "Still, it bears an uncanny resemblance to your synergy beliefs." I had always thought that when I heard that song.

"Yeah, but he got the eyes wrong," I protested. "It's the Angels who have the green eyes, the devils have blue."

"What greater devil than a fallen Angel?" he mused. I thought for a moment.

"Does that mean you believe me?" I was skeptical.

"Let's pretend for a moment I do. What's your big plan?" he asked.

My cheeks started getting pink. "Well, we thought we'd create like this camp for synergies and test their abilities. Those that passed we would tell the truth and let them decide if they wanted to join us. Then we'd break our asses to get them ready for combat."

"Who's 'we?'" Will asked.

"Oh, well, the Vipers of course," I responded somewhat happily. "My bodyguard squad."

"You mean those kids," he said and gestured with his fork through the window at a group sitting in the parking lot.

Yikes! They must have followed the GPS on my phone. They could see I was ok so they held their distance.

"Yes, that motley crew in the parking lot. And we're not children. We're the fate of the world. We are going to hold the front lines. The rest of the synergies will back us up."

"And you're sure this is really happening? Fiends are going to attack Earth, it really is Armageddon?" he questioned.

"My intel is solid. It comes from above and below." Take that!

"I can already tell you're going to want me to be present," DJ said grudgingly.

"Well yes, you're the one that everyone looks up to," I reminded him.

"Anyway, you can't have a great party without a great DJ." I smiled.

"Fine. I'll come to your camp, but I won't play reveille in the mornings, I won't make lanyards or paddle a canoe." Yay! This was the DJ we all knew and loved! We both dissolved into giggles.

I tried to talk while still laughing. "Just make sure you bring all your friends so we can…"

"…turn them into Stormtroopers?"

Oh, man my sides were hurting.

"Just as long as you let me hide in the back. *You're* the face of mutation," he pointed out.

"Yeah but, *you're* the voice."

DJ gave me his digits and paid the tab, generously tipping the waitress he said we probably "scared to death." As we were heading out the door, I stopped. I turned around to face him and ask one final question.

"How do you do it, DJ?" I asked him earnestly. "How do you inspire? No, how do you lead an entire race of people?"

He smirked. "I depend heavily on the ignorance of others to make me look good," he laughed.

We headed to the parking lot. The Vipers waved but nobody came over so DJ got into his car and left. I headed over to Keith's jeep.

Keith was standing in front, his arms crossed. He was waiting to hear the fate of my recruiting efforts. I threw my arms around him and kissed him.

"Mission accomplished," I told him. "He's ready to work with us and I think we became super best friends as well!" I laughed.

"So DJ is completely on board? He knows about the war? He's going to help us recruit his listeners?" Keith sounded skeptical.

"Yes," I reassured him. I took his face in my hands and looked into his eyes. He was definitely troubled.

"It's just, the whole thing seemed too easy. I think there's more going on. You don't get a following like his by accident." Keith seemed a bit in awe of DJ.

"So you think he's hiding something?" I slowly questioned.

Keith suddenly acted like he wanted to forget the whole thing. "We're all hiding something," he said. I smiled.

"Do you want to take the bike home?" he asked and nodded towards Zeal's motorcycle.

"Yeahyeahyeahyeahyeah!" I bubbled. "Wait, is Zeal going to let us?" I looked around at the crowd but I didn't see Zeal's dirty blonde head anywhere.

"Oh, um, he's at home," Keith confessed. "Babysitting!" He barely got the word out before he choked on his own laughter. I myself had a short burst of hysteria. Damn, that never got old.

"You know one day Zeal is going to rise up and kill us, right?" I asked.

"I know, oh, I know," Keith answered, trying to catch his breath. He picked me up and threw me over his shoulder, my legs kicking fruitlessly, then tossed the jeep keys to Jage. He carried me over to the motorcycle and placed me on the back.

"Are you tired?" he asked and I shook my head "no."

"Let's go watch the sunrise somewhere where no one will find us." The motorcycle roared to life. I wrapped my arms around the man I loved and for the moment we left everything behind.

Chapter 23

Keith called the Vipers together the next morning before training. There were a lot of things we needed to get straight before these campers arrived.

Lucky spoke first. "We know everyone who participates in this 'camp' thing is going to bring a different set of abilities to the table. We would like to get away from calling these abilities 'powers.'" The term 'powers' implies something supernatural, even magical. Stephanie's teacher, Steel, says there is no such thing as magic, and I tend to believe him. All these 'powers' are ability techniques made possible by the Fiend or Angel bloodline of the synergy. Let's remember that and call them techniques or techs. I'll expect to hear 'What's your tech?' rather than 'What are your powers?' Are we clear?" Lucky finished. Everyone murmured in agreement.

Keith spoke up next. "I want to make sure we all understand who the key person in this whole camp scenario is."

"Stephanie, right?" Zeal piped up.

"No, Stephanie is the key person for recruiting," Keith responded. "The key person for camp is…"

"Kyan?" Tyler interrupted.

"OK everybody just shut up," Keith snapped. "The key person is Ari."

I think every one of the Vipers gasped or murmured. I mean aside from being attached to Jage, Ari never said or did anything distinguishing. Nobody looked more surprised than Ari herself.

"If any of you idiots remember, Ari can see auras around synergies in colors that directly relate to their power levels. It follows the visible light spectrum. White auras are the weakest. They may indicate a synergy who has not yet tapped into their tech. They may also indicate a human who is trying to pass themselves off as a synergy, so be cautious." Keith began to break down the different levels we were about to encounter.

"Red is a step up from nothing but nothing to be afraid of. Orange is next, probably someone who is aware of their tech but doesn't have much control."

"Now yellow is where it gets interesting. Russell is a yellow. He is clearly a synergy with increased strength, speed and mental acuity but he hasn't shown any signs of a tech. Al is the same way. The next level is green. Chad is a green. His tech is hand-eye coordination and it is top notch. I dare say he has the best hand-eye in the world. Beyond this he shows no other signs of being a synergy. Blues like Jage and myself have control of our techs and are in touch with our synergy traits. Violets are the same, only better. Right, Steph?" Keith looked at me and I blew him a kiss.

"Anything greater than a violet shows up as black. I want you to consider any synergy or Fiend with a black aura to be extremely dangerous. Do not confront them by yourself, that is why we train in teams," Keith finished. "Any questions?"

"How can we tell who is who when Ari isn't around?" asked Al.

"We've devised a system of pins," Keith explained. "On day one Ari will approach each person with a pin the same color as their aura. She'll also assign them a codename to protect their identities from each other. During the training stages she will change out the pins if any of the campers' auras evolve."

There were more questions, but I tuned out.

Finally the intelligence people left for the office and the infantry gathered outside. I was surprised to see Chad had stayed behind. Usually our afternoons were pretty intense and Chad could hardly keep up with the regular workout.

"What's with the square?" I asked Russell, nodding my head to Chad. Russell turned to me, his eyes like ice. "Mind your business," he said with no nonsense. Kinda harsh I thought, all I did was ask.

Russell gathered us up. Zeal, Tyler, Violet, Jage, Al and myself. Ky and Jack were at school. We all piled into the big limo and took off. No one knew where we were going. When the limo finally stopped Russell started speaking.

343

"I've brought you to a gun range. I know Keith won't allow any guns on the property but that doesn't mean you shouldn't know how to use one. Chad and I will take our time, teach you slowly and make sure you understand. If anyone wants to back out, I'll understand." He looked directly at me. Everybody turned and looked at me like they expected me to freak out.

"I will do anything to help Ky. If that means taking another bullet then I'm glad to do it," I said matter-of-factly.

Zeal put his hand on my head and ruffled my hair. "Everyone, repeat after me," Zeal started. "Don't shoot Stephanie."

"Don't shoot Stephanie," the Vipers repeated, all giggling.

"It's totally ok to shoot Zeal though," Tyler announced.

We piled out of the limo and went to work learning about guns. When it came time to the actual shooting, Russell went first and hit the target right in the heart exactly every time. Everyone was silent with amazement.

While we were still speechless Chad got up in front of us. While he faced the group he reached his loaded gun behind him. Without even looking he hit the target even more precisely than Russell had. We were shocked out of our silence. Everyone jumped up and ran to Chad, all talking over each other.

"Dude!" shouted Jage, giving Chad a high five. "Who knew we had an Army Ranger in the house!"

Violet pulled Chad into a big hug. "No more intelligence, baby. You belong with us, you're infantry now!" Wow, she was usually as silent as he was. I was the last one to shake his hand.

"Your little speech at the pageant was the answer to my prayers," he told me, looking in my eyes for the first time since I met him. A lot of the synergies had told me such things. We all grew up believing we were alone.

"Well, you be the answer to mine and we'll call it even," I told him. For the first time, he smiled at me.

We all rushed across the range and practiced our shots. Most of the guys and Violet were phenomenal. Me, Jage and Tyler not so much. Well, we would stick to the physical attacks.

The next day Chad went back to work with the intelligence crew and Russell took the more talented part of the team back to the gun range. Jage took over for the day and trained Tyler and me. Tyler had the ability to affect things at a distance, but we couldn't quite figure out how. Whether he manipulated the wind or heated the air or manipulated the molecules of his target, we just weren't sure. The only thing we did know is that his tech and mine could accomplish the same thing when it came to distance manipulation. All we needed was to master control.

Jage set up some chess pieces at a distance. The idea was for Tyler and me to knock the pieces down. Then we would learn to push and pull them. Finally we would learn precise control by playing a game of chess at a distance.

This proved to be harder than it seemed. I managed to blow my chess piece about 20 feet away, while Tyler pitched his straight in the air. We worked our asses off, pushing and pulling trying to figure out how to control our techs. Tempers were short, frustration set in and we all started yelling at each other.

After the first few hours Jage announced he was going to get a drink and took off into the house.

Tyler and I both sulked. Steel's teachings had been more on power than control. I didn't have the techniques and I didn't have the patience for training like this. I turned back to tell Tyler that I quit but he had already disappeared.

I heard some noises coming from the house. I looked up and saw Tyler climbing the roof. When he got to the top he sat down Indian style, closed his eyes and made circles with his index and forefingers. I climbed up next to him and asked what he was doing.

"I'm meditating," he said. "When I was younger I had no control over my tech. I'd get pissed off and suddenly things would smash or fly around the room. I would end up in a straight jacket or a padded cell."

"They locked you up?" I asked him. He nodded. Before this Tyler had forbidden any discussion of his past.

"Mr. Byrnes was an instructor at the institution. He was the first to treat me like I was gifted, not unnatural. Mr. Byrnes taught me to meditate and to focus. I hadn't thought about him in a long time. Maybe this can help us?" he looked at me with wide, open eyes.

"Absolutely," I agreed. "Tyler," I said. "We're in this together, from now on." I smiled. He smiled.

We spent the rest of the afternoon on the roof meditating. Then we concentrated on using our techs to find the chess pieces, pick them up and place them on the chess board.

Jage watched from a window. "I never would have believed it if I didn't see it myself," he told us later. "You two are dangerous together!" We giggled.

Chapter 24

I started waking up every morning to press releases and public appearances. The next few days were all about promoting this synergy "camp." The team stayed home and prepared for the crowds. The days passed quickly and suddenly it was the night before everyone would arrive.

I stayed up late helping the team put up tents in the front yard. We had gotten more than a thousand responses so even accounting for no shows, we still had to prepare almost 300 tents.

When I woke up the next morning, the house seemed empty. I dressed quickly and went to check on the boys.

Ky was already gone but Jack was still in bed, covers pulled over his head and snoring loudly. I sprung from the doorway and jumped on top of his sleeping body yelling "catch me!" The force woke him immediately. He seemed to fly into a rage on impact and I just couldn't help but laugh at him. He calmed himself down but still shot me a dirty look for waking him.

"Everyone's outside already! Don't you want to see what's going on?" I asked.

He hesitated. As much as he was against this camp thing, I knew he was curious.

The two of us made our way down the hall to Lucky's room. We figured the view would be the best from his window.

Jack pushed the bed over to the window so we could sit down. I pulled open the curtains and the two of us were stunned into silence by what we saw. Already there were hundreds of kids milling around the tents. Dozens of busses were lined up to drop off even more synergies. The Vipers were checking everyone in as they got off the bus and showing them to the tents and around the grounds. There was a giant buffet table set out in the back to feed everyone and porta johns set up to accommodate the enormous crowd.

This sight, all these synergies coming here for answers, it was overwhelming. My legs gave out and I fell on the bed, crouching forward, staring blankly in front of me. What were we playing at? In a matter of weeks I would be asking these strangers to fight and maybe die to protect Ky.

Jack slid across the bed and next to me. I was worried a little human boy like him might be overwhelmed by the arrival of all these synergies.

"Is it weird for you and Lucky sometimes?" I asked gently.

"Oh? You mean because we're the only SilverSwords? Nah. We try not to look down on anybody. I'll bet some of these synergies have fantastic techs. I'm looking to learn some things," Jack said with a smile.

Gotta love him. I was concerned he was feeling inferior and here he thought I was calling him superior. Yep, that was Jack for you.

We sat in silence. I was so scared to look out that window again. All those people were waiting for me.

Suddenly Jack turned his head toward the window. "Oh my God it's a porcupine!" he shouted and giggled. I had to look up and see what he was laughing at. Sure enough, there was a guy with spikes sticking out of his skin everywhere. We had made room in the house for a few special cases and he was definitely one.

The next few hours passed this way, mostly with Jack making fun of everybody who got off the bus. We kept an eye on all the Vipers. Little Kyan followed behind his big brother Keith like a shadow. I was actually glad that Keith was the leader and not me.

The tents were getting full. It was scary how many synergies were gathered. If anything went wrong this could easily be a dangerous situation.

There was some commotion going on in front of one of the busses. A crowd had gathered and the Vipers had pulled together in a huddle. They stayed that way, strategizing until more Vipers arrived. The new arrivals started pushing back the crowds while the Vipers in front started boarding the bus. About 5 of them piled on. In less than a minute the 5 were pushing their way back off the bus.

The Vipers were all lined up and watching as a guy got off the bus. He was wearing a green "Jets Football" cap and toting a big blue backpack. Reality seemed slightly out of order around him. Whatever his tech was, I think it was dazzling my senses, even from a few hundred feet away and through the glass between us. I was instantly fascinated with him. I wondered why they had made such a big deal over him.

As I continued to watch, this new guy backed up a bit from the bus himself. Apparently this guy wasn't the one causing the stir. There was something else on the bus, something dangerous.

Jack and I had our faces pressed up against the glass window. Everyone from the camp seemed to be gathered, all waiting for this terrible creature to materialize.

From the steps of the bus a pair of little black shoes became visible, followed by some red tights, an olive jumper and a red and olive striped shirt. An adorable teenage girl with dark brown braids and dark brown eyes appeared. She bounded down the stairs and gawked at the enormous house in front of her. The Vipers made a circle around her and guided her past the crowds up to the front door of the house. Only a few kids had been chosen to stay in the house and those were a danger to themselves and others. Who was this girl? Was she really so dangerous?

Trying to keep pace was the guy with the glasses who had been on the bus with the girl. He was getting knocked about as he tried to stick with the bodyguards. His hat got knocked off his head, revealing a shock of red hair.

DJ! I knew it immediately. That man was the famous DJ Phantom and the girl must be Holly, the beloved harlequin whose antics were legendary with radio fans.

I know I was forbidden to leave the top floor of the house but I had to greet these two. I bounded down the stairs and into the foyer where they were just arriving. Holly screamed as soon as she saw me.

"Oh Stephanie," she cried. "I'm your biggest fan!" she was jumping up and down.

"I'm your biggest fan!" I informed her. "I never miss a show and your stories are hilarious!" I told her truthfully. I reached in to give her a hug but the red haired guy stepped between us.

"DJ" I shouted turning to greet him. "It is an honor to have you here." I placed palm over closed fist and bowed a little.

Russell had been standing next to Holly this whole time. He sighed and started to speak. "Steph, you can't touch Holly. No one can. Her skin secretes a poison. For humans it's dangerous but for synergies it's deadly. I'm sorry, but you will have to keep your distance."

He uttered just a few words but my breath caught in my chest. The poor girl, unable to have human contact. Not so long ago I was her. Things had been all about Ky lately, I guess I'd forgotten where I came from, how hard I fought to get here. I looked towards the open front door. There was a sea of synergies on the front lawn. Younger, older, every race, color and creed. All of them seeking answers, all of them trusting in me, letting me be their voice. None of them knowing the truth about why I had brought them here.

I turned my attention back to Holly. "I was just like you, Holly. I couldn't be touched either and I needed a lot of help to get where I am. Take a good look, help is all around you. We're going to beat this, Holly. And when we've got this thing figured out, I would be honored to reach my hand out for yours." As I spoke I stretched my hand out towards her. She was still encircled by bodyguards, but she reached her hand out to me. Our fingertips were nearly touching but both of us knew that the distance between them was an eternity.

The rest of the Vipers headed back outside to deal with the crowds while Al and I took Will and Holly to the spare rooms on the north side of the house. The spiny guy we had seen from earlier was already there, as was a bleached-blonde skater punk I hadn't seen before.

I took a few steps into the room and the skater let out a low whistle. "Very cute," he said, looking me up and down.

"I agree," I nodded, checking him out too. About 6 foot tall and muscular. He was wearing oversized jeans with suspenders hanging down, a plain white T and an orange hoodie. "*Very* cute."

I introduced myself and DJ and Holly too. There was a private area for Holly to sleep in, but the four would pretty much be roommates.

I tried to talk to DJ a bit but I just couldn't get a read on him. When I saw him after his radio show he seemed trusting, even happy. Now

353

standing in front of me, he seemed like he'd rather be somewhere else, anywhere else.

I said "goodbye" and was walking out the door when something caught my eye. On the skater's hoodie was a green pin with the word "Jag" written across it. I turned and walked back to ask him about it.

"It's my codename," I let him tell me. "Some red haired chick was walking around giving them out. She said we couldn't trade them for any reason." He seemed proud to be teaching me.

"So what does Jag mean? Do you own like a super nice car?" Holly piped up.

"Nah," the skater said suddenly looking shy. "I'm a shapeshifter. I can turn myself into a jaguar, only..." he sighed. "Only I don't have a lot of control over it. Sometimes I change all the way, sometimes only part of the way and sometimes I can't control it at all and it just happens. That's why they put me inside, so I didn't hurt the kids out in the tents."

"That sucks," Holly told him.

"Not really," Jag responded. "Have you seen those tents? Heh heh, my stupid brother's gonna sleep on the floor while I have a nice bed and air conditioning. Oh yeah."

I was so excited to see a green button! "Did your brother get a green button too?" I tried to sound nonchalant.

"Nah I think his was yellow. They wrote 'Onyx' on it. He thinks he's so cool because he's African American." Jag had an obvious chip on his shoulder.

"Are you adopted?" Holly asked, trying to make sense of the situation.

"I wish," he told her. "It's worse than that, we're twins. He's such a tight ass because he's four minutes older than me. Four minutes! Like that means anything."

"Okay so you are white and your twin brother is black." Holly was still trying to puzzle this out. "Are you sure you're brothers?"

"Are you sure your skin makes poison? Look synergy girl, having a black twin is not as weird as having poison skin," the skater pointed out.

"Okay," Holly said. "I can live with that."

I turned around and left them to talk. Wow, it's all happening!

I rushed out of the room and upstairs to take a shower and put on some party clothes – a white dress with purple straps and trimming. The day had passed quickly and all of the busses had been emptied. The tents were full and the property was buzzing!

I peeked outside from my bedroom window. The opening disc jockey had already started playing records and a bunch of folks were dancing. More were milling around the giant buffet table. Even from this distance I could see a lot of the pins the kids were wearing. There were many reds, a lot of whites and I even spotted several orange and a yellow! That guy Jag was still the only green I had seen.

There was a sharp tap on the door and Keith entered without waiting for me to answer. Kyan tagged behind him but brushed right past Keith to run right into my arms for a hug. As usual, neither of us wanted to let go and Keith had to clear his throat to break us apart. He began speaking to me like a general preparing me for battle.

"Now tonight is going to be your first official appearance at this thing. We have 1044 synergies down there between the ages of 18 and 27. You have to maintain a semblance of control at all times. If these kids start a riot, we will not be able to control them. We have some tear gas but the best protection is to not let them get out of control in the first place." He gave me a pointed look, then raised his eyebrow to question if I understood.

"Sir, yes sir," I said and saluted. Ky cracked up laughing. Keith looked furious for a moment then broke into a smile. "C'mon guys, this isn't easy for me. I'm trying to build an army out of skateboarders and DJs."

"If anyone can, it's you," I told him confidently.

"Look, just stick to the script when you get out there tonight. We'll play it by ear for the rest of the week but tonight, you make a speech, you mingle a little and then you excuse yourself." Keith paused. "Um, I don't want any jealousy raring up so let's just keep our relationship under wraps this week."

"Sure," I easily agreed. It's not like he was super public about it in the first place.

"Oh, before I forget..." he reached into his pocket and pulled out three pins. Our codenames were already on them, a violet pin for me, a blue for Keith and a white one for Ky. I leaned in to pin it on him. He looked at it and sighed. "A white pin with black letters," he said sadly.

"Oh no!" I cried, "That's just on the outside. It's all backwards. On the inside you're a black pin with white letters!"

Ky giggled a bit at what I said. Keith reached down and ruffled his brother's hair affectionately. I stepped forward and pulled them into a three-way hug. I squeezed my eyes shut and hoped I could preserve this moment forever.

We broke the hug and headed downstairs to the party. We ran into Ari, who was running upstairs to shower and change. I was eager to know how many of each button she had passed out.

"Oh well," she thought for a moment. "I passed out a handful of yellows, a couple dozen orange and a couple hundred reds and whites. I did pass out at least one of each of the others," Ari explained. My disappointment must have registered on my face because she was quick to reassure me.

"Just so you know," she giggled. "When I first met Jage he was an orange, now he's a blue. The colors only tag power, not potential." With that she reached forward and poked Ky's white pin. "I rest my

357

case," she smirked. Ky smiled and I smiled. "Anyway I put buttons on all the Vipers so make sure you check them out when you see them." Ari told us. She was wearing a Violet pin that said "Spectra."

Ari headed upstairs to get changed and we headed downstairs to join the party. Before heading out the back door to join everyone, I charged downstairs to the basement where I knew Jack would be hiding. Sure enough, he was playing video games in front of a giant TV.

I came up behind him and put my hands on his shoulders. "Why don't you just check out the party…"

"Nope," he cut me off. He didn't pause his game and he didn't look up.

"Jack, maybe if you gave it a chance…"

"Nope," he snapped. "All I have to do is train and go to school. I don't have to fight in your stupid war and I don't have to hang with your stupid groupies." He paused his game long enough to cock his head and give me a dirty look.

"Always a pleasure, Jack." At least he didn't curse at me, maybe we were making progress. I tapped him on the shoulder and left him to his devices.

When I got back upstairs the Mals weren't waiting at the door. I figured they had gone out but I couldn't see them from peeking out the curtains. I decided to head upstairs and look for them from the balcony. The music was pulsing. I opened the French doors and stepped out into the fresh air.

"There she is," someone from the crowd cried out. The music stopped and suddenly hundreds of synergies were racing to gather at the base of the balcony.

I felt a lump in my throat. Below me were hundreds of people, kids mostly. People I would be asking to fight and maybe die for my cause. It was all too real. Who was I to ask this of them, who was I to make this request?

As my self-doubt mounted I started to feel my legs give way. Before I tumbled to the floor a pair of strong arms reached out and caught me. Keith! He pulled me up and stood next to me, his arm wrapped around my shoulders.

"Hello Everyone," he shouted into the crowd with a smile. "Wave," he snapped at me. The two of us began waving like madmen at this now screaming crowd. Keith very gently released me. "You can do this," he whispered and guided me forward towards the crowd.

Suddenly I could do this. We were asking these kids to save the world and we needed to prepare them.

"I'm so happy to see you all here tonight," I shouted. The crowd roared back. "This week will be difficult. We are going to push all of you and ourselves very hard to find out what we are all capable of. Don't be afraid to ask questions, don't be afraid to try new things and don't be afraid to push yourself passed your limits. This week all bets are off. Shake off the ideas of what you should be. Leave behind your human identity. Here we only exist as synergies. Wrap your mind around that. I want you to give everything you have, in every way. When it's over you won't be the same old you walking out of here, you'll emerge as something new!"

The crowd was screaming and my heart was pounding so loud I couldn't even hear what I was saying. "Synergies. Why are we here? What's our purpose?...I don't know. I honestly don't know, but we have the future to figure these things out. This week we are going to answer one question...what are we capable of?" The crowed thundered. I said "thank you," and nodded out, taking a big step back away from the balcony.

Keith grabbed my hands and steered me right in through the French doors and down the hall right into my room. He turned to me his green eyes sparkling with excitement and pleasure.

"I knew you could do it," he said and immediately swept me up into a kiss. I surrendered to him completely, so glad to be away from the crowd and safe in his arms. He kissed me so passionately when he was proud of me, it certainly made me more eager to please him. A few more blazing kisses and Keith pulled away.

"Awww," I pouted.

"Not tonight," Keith instructed. "I have to make sure these mutants don't destroy our house."

"They're SYNERGIES," I corrected. He was right; such a big crowd did need close watch. I thought about staying inside so as not to excite them but then I remembered Ari saying she had passed out buttons of every color and I wanted to go find who they belonged to. I know that some people would be like Ky, hiding tremendous power behind a white pin Those with the colored pins, they weren't potentials, they were the real deals.

I decided to make my way out to the sound booth first. DJ Phantom was getting ready to go on. His assistant, Holly the poison girl, was warming up the crowd with crazy stories about her adventures. The crowd was already screaming when they heard DJ's signature song, "How Soon Is Now," by the Smiths. He went on to play a series of tunes and I made my way over to talk to Holly.

"How is everything going?" I asked her, noticing her blue button.

"Great!" she shouted jumping up and down. "I think I'm going to be perfect for this, and I'm already making friends!" Holly was in long sleeves and gloves but still she had to stay in the sound booth to make sure no one touched her accidentally. She had explained to the audience how she and the prickly guy couldn't be touched, but her poison was so lethal, we really had to keep her confined.

I waited until DJ had started another record before interrupting him. He turned to me with a wide smile and asked me if I had a special request. I didn't get him, sometimes he seemed so nice and sometimes he flat out ignored me. I asked him to play Matthew Sweet's "Devil With the Green Eyes." He told me he would and then turned back to his soundboard. I waved "goodbye" to Holly and then headed over to where I saw Zeal and Tyler. They were wearing the pins Ari had given them. Zeal's pin was violet, Tyler's pin was blue. I was impressed. Blue was very high and violet, well Zeal's level was higher than Keith's. The two were clearly talking about me as I approached. Tyler handed me a red plastic cup full of soda.

"So?" Zeal asked.

"What?" I asked back.

"Nice wardrobe on DJ, right?" he questioned.

I wasn't getting it. I looked back at DJ. He was wearing blue jeans and a black T-shirt that said "DJ" over the pocket in little white letters. It was fine but not overly nice. I looked back at the guys quizzically.

"Having a dumb blonde moment?" Zeal asked.

WTF? What are they talking about? I looked back over at DJ. I didn't see anything spectacular. Scuffed up white sneakers, baggy blue jeans and a black t-shirt with…Oh My God! I dropped the full cup of soda as I did a double take. DJ was wearing a black pin! My pulse started racing.

"How many black pins did Ari give out?" I asked the guys without looking back, my eyes were locked on DJ.

"Oh, I don't know Tyler, how many black pins did she give out?" Zeal teased.

"Well, black is all the rage these days, she must have given out dozens," Tyler declared.

"Hundreds," Zeal chimed in.

Without breaking my stare at DJ, I reached back in an instant and grabbed Zeal by the throat, cutting off his air supply. Zeal gagged and choked for a moment as Tyler looked on, worried, but not sure what to do.

I let go of my grip on his throat and he fell to his knees and gasped for air. You don't f with me when it's something serious. Black pins were stronger than any other and there really wasn't a way to measure how strong. They could be gods.

Tyler bent down to see if Zeal was okay. I knew I hadn't grabbed him hard enough to damage him so I wasn't worried. I turned around to look at Zeal myself. I gently grabbed his blonde hair and pulled his head up until his blue eyes met mine.

"How many black buttons?" I asked again.

"One," Zeal choked out. "Only one."

"Hey, it could be worse," Tyler pointed out "at least DJ's on our side."

I nodded but my mouth was dry. "On our side," what did that mean? Sure, he seemed nice enough, but we really didn't know him.

My eyes fell on DJ and studied his every move. He looked over at me and waved, probably letting me know he was playing my request. The opening bars of the song sent shivers down my spine. As I listened to the lyrics I became more afraid. I was surrounded by dangerous strangers. How could I trust any of them? Just one of them could be our undoing. All our plans, all our hopes were resting on the shoulders of total unknowns. It was too much for me to contemplate.

Zeal came up behind me. He wrapped his arms around me, pulling me close to him. He leaned his head in and spoke quietly in my ear. "I know you're worried," he said.

"Of course I'm worried," I snapped. "Our lives are in the hands of strangers. I don't know who to trust."

"You never would have escaped the orphanage if you hadn't put your life in the hands of a stranger," Zeal said.

"That was different!" I said emphatically. "I didn't have anything to lose back then. Now I do."

"And so do all of these kids, Stephanie. Don't worry, the ones with bad intentions will make themselves known, they always do."

Zeal squeezed me like a hug from behind. He and Tyler took off towards the crowd. I watched them for a moment then retreated into the house. On my way I passed Violet and waved. The girl's name was Violet but her pin was blue. For some reason that made me smile. You're practically violet, Violet.

I headed into the basement to check on Jack. As soon as I opened the door I heard lots of voices shouting over the loud video game noises. I entered the basement to see Jack, the Mal brothers, Chad, Dmitri and two strangers pounding on the wireless controls and yelling at the TV screen. The group completely ignored me until their game was finished.

"Oh good," Keith said as he handed me a controller. "This is an 8 player game." He gestured to the two strangers, both were wearing white buttons. "This is Chase and Drew. They are more intelligence than infantry."

Chad's pin was green and Dmitri's was violet. The new guys Chase and Drew were wearing white pins. I reached forward to shake hands and welcome them. All the sudden I realized one of them was familiar. Drew! Mr. Gerard's nephew! I hadn't seen him since before the pageant. No wonder Mr. Gerard was so interested in synergies, his own nephew was one.

Jack knocked me out of my thoughts with an irritated "Are we gonna play, or what?" We played video games and talked trash to each other until it was time to go to sleep.

Chapter 25

The next day was insane. We had more than a thousand "campers" so it was really difficult to coordinate. We divided them up into 4 groups. They ate in groups and participated in activities in groups. We had 4 different activities for them to participate in and they would switch off for the next 4 days. We just needed to filter out this group to a much smaller group that could survive in a Fiend battle.

The groups would do one activity each day. Group one would go skydiving. That's it, just skydiving over and over all day long. Jage and Zeal would monitor how many times a camper jumped and how they handled themselves. The first two jumps were tandem and the rest were solo. If a camper wasn't willing to do the solo jump...well, we assumed courage was an issue. It wasn't enough to rule someone out, but it seemed like a good test of nerve and durability.

The second group was to learn self defense. In all truth they were learning battle moves, but we couldn't tell them that. Keith had invited a girl to teach the campers. She was a spunky black chick with short, curly hair and a wicked grin. She had taken second place in the women's martial arts world championship and she was aching with every muscle to beat the champion and take that title. She was kind and understanding when teaching moves to the campers but merciless when running them through practice drills. She was a much needed addition to our team.

The third group was split in half. They spent half the day learning about weapons from Russ and Violet and the other half, well, hanging out with me and Ky. Yep, hanging out – that's it. The Vipers thought it would humanize our cause if everyone got to know me on a personal level. Trust me, hanging out with 125 people in 4 hour blocks was less personal than planned, more like a question and answer inquisition. The final group would spend the day demonstrating their techs. This was the real deal right here. The remaining Vipers would test, discover and uncover the essence of every unique technique. This above all would decide who would be asked to stay and who would go home. The next four days were an absolute blur to me. I met so many people, heard so many stories, I had no chance of keeping it straight. The Vipers made their selections: 265 people were pulled aside and asked to stay. The rest piled on busses and headed for home. I hoped they had gotten something out of this, even if it was just the chance to be themselves without fear of rejection.

Keith gave everyone who stayed a day off. He piled them all on busses and sent them to Six Flags for the day. Where was he getting all this money? Was MalAdjusted really doing that well?

I got a day alone with my boyfriend! We didn't even make it out of bed until Kyan got home from school. We took Ky and Jack to the boardwalk that night. There were some autograph seekers but no one really bothered us. Jack only called me a "dumb bitch" three or four times, which was a record low for him. Keith threatened him with all kinds of retribution but I don't think it scared him in the least. Jack was fearless, I admired him for it.

We got home and tucked Ky into bed. It was time for a group of us to gather and put together a game plan for tomorrow.

I went down to the basement where they had assembled. From the old Vipers there was Jage, Zeal, Russell, Al, Chad, Dmitri, myself, Keith and Lucky. I noticed a yellow pin on Russell and a blue pin on Al. Joining us were DJ, Chase, and Drew.

Keith was the leader, he was always the leader. "You all know why you're here, right?" Everyone shook their head and murmured.

"We are on the eve of war. This is the intelligence council. There will be two generals, General Luke and myself. I will lead the smaller group who will fight inside the mouth of the tunnel. General Luke will command the bulk of the troops who will battle outside the tunnel. It is this council that will decide where everyone will fight. I don't want to separate groups that work well together. For example, there are 7 of DJ's followers who have made it this far. I would like DJ to be a captain and to lead this group." DJ said nothing but he nodded.

"We will meet every day from now until war breaks. We must plan the battlefield, the medical tent, supply issues, everything," Keith concluded.

Everyone settled down and Russell raised his hand to speak.

368

"We need Jack," he said gravely. "Twelve years old or not, he's the best sword handler I've ever seen."

"We'll talk," Keith replied.

The rest of the conversation was about how to break the news to the new troops. We thought it was better if we didn't tell them about the Envoy. I was uncomfortable that so many people knew already. What if one of them decided to make a deal with the Fiends? They could steal Ky out from under us. I had to have faith. These were our allies now. It was decided we would tell the group all at once, let them lean on each other for guidance.

In the early morning light we assembled the group together. There were 265. That's a pretty serious crowd. We started by telling them the story that Eric had told to me about who synergies were and where they came from. We fielded a lot of questions. By the time we were finished it was time to break for lunch.

After lunch Keith told them the truth about why they were there. Fiends are building a tunnel to Earth. They will sweep over and destroy the world like locusts. We are Earth's only defense.

Some of them didn't take the news too well. I saw one guy run to the side of the house and throw up. I looked at his name tag. It was green. "Mend" it said. "Mend, huh. What do you do?"

He looked at me, still gasping from vomiting. "I'm a healer," he choked out.

"Pretty safe in the medical tent," I told him. "Wouldn't want to lose a guy like you," I patted him on the back and moved on.

There were a lot of confused and frightened synergies. I looked over the yard. Holly was already leading an enthusiastic group in some cheers. I saw a couple of boys arguing loudly and went to see if I could help.

As I got closer I could see that one of the boys was that blond skater I met. The other was a tall, stiff black kid with silver rimmed glasses and a button down shirt. This must be the "big" brother. I interrupted their fight.

"Hi, I'm Stephanie Park," I said to the new guy. "Spark," I said pointing to my purple button. His button was yellow and said "Onyx."

"You guys okay? You know none of you have to do this."

"It's not that," Onyx said and kinda trailed off. "It's just..."

"Why'd you have to pick him too?" Jag piped up. "Why couldn't you just pick me?"

"Is that how you feel too?" I asked Onyx. He shrugged, but then he nodded.

"Well here's how I see it. You guys are pretty competitive, right?" They were both nodding, this was a no brainer. "That means you are probably both very good. I mean, if I was going to fight a war, I'd definitely want someone good fighting with me, you know. Rather than someone who sucks." They weren't really going for it. I needed to

370

change my strategy. "It's not like you're going to see each other anyway, you're on two completely different squads. I mean General Keith wanted to keep you two together but Jage just insisted on having Onyx and Al wanted Jag so they had to split you up!"

Jag raised an eyebrow. "Yeah?" he asked.

"Absolutely!" I totally lied. "I guess we'll just see who is better on the battlefield!" Oh, they liked that! They had their competition and we had two willing soldiers!

For the rest of the day the Vipers tried to smooth things over as best as they could. In the end roughly 80 soldiers packed up and left. It was heartbreaking. We would just have to do the best with what we had.

The next day we broke them down into teams and started training. I got the group with the special attacks like sound waves or heat blasts. I trained them all the very same way Steel had trained me (only I was lot nicer!)

The top guy on my team was Latino, codename Ace. He had straight black hair that always seemed to have wind rushing through it and killer brown eyes. Ace had some sort of control over the movement of air. He was already able to move objects with his tech and knock people down. I immediately made him my assistant.

I had this kick ass guy codename Quake, in my group. He had smooth dark skin, friendly brown eyes and a cool British accent. He could shift sand. No one really knew how to use that as a weapon. We were working on trying to create a quicksand pit.

I had a Native American girl with long, silky black hair. For her tech she was able to create force fields. They weren't very strong and they didn't really last but I still thought she had "front lines" written all over her.

Sapphire could freeze water into ice. She was the shortest person in our group and she was very conscious of this. She had pale white skin and long brown hair. I kept catching her staring off at Dmitri's group of psychics. We were having trouble making the most of Sapphire's ability. To turn water into ice she needed the water first, so we had to figure how to get it to her. We tried a supersoaker and that worked okay. She was able to drench the person and then turn the damp clothes to ice. Still, I didn't know how to weaponize that.

Solara could absorb sunlight and then radiate it almost like I did with static. Because her tech was so similar to mine I taught her how to redirect the power to her own body to make her physical attacks more powerful just like Steel taught me. I loved her dark green hair and she was tanned bronze from hanging out in the sun all day.

I had about a dozen others in my group, all with different abilities. I realized that everything I was teaching them somehow related to the things Steel had taught me. I was gaining a new appreciation for the man who pushed me to new limits.

We broke for lunch and the captains gathered up to talk about their troops.

Girls were fighting for a spot at the psychic's table. It didn't take long to see who Sapphire had been watching.

"Who's the stud?" I asked Dmitri, pointing to an older guy with long black hair surrounded by a bevy of beauties.

"That's the height of synergy popularity," Dmitri informed us with a smirk. "Formidable martial arts skills for a psychic. Get this, he can erase memories."

"Ladies man who can erase memories, sounds like the recipe for a date rapist," Zeal quipped. Dmitri and I cracked up.

"What's his codename?" Zeal wondered.

"Well it's Style, but the gang calls him Doggie Style!" Dmitri laughed. Oh man! I cracked up again.

"I'm never going to remember all these names and techs," I announced.

"Don't try to," Dmitri told me. "Just meet everyone. The important ones will make themselves known, you'll see."

Dmitri started telling us about the rest of his psychics. "The one with the long brown hair is 'Miss Direction.' Her tech is amazing. She can enter your mind and distract you. She can only hold it for a few seconds but she's getting better as we train."

"So her power will become useful in time," Zeal commented.

"Oh no," Dmitri defended. "She's indispensable now." Dmitri interrupted the poor girl's lunch and called her over to show us. I really couldn't see how that ability would be useful in battle. I mean I guess it could, well, huh.

"I'm sorry, did you just say something?" I asked the group. They were already laughing at me. "Wow, she's better than I expected." I blushed. "I guess a few seconds distraction is enough to knock any warrior off his game. I'm glad you're with us," I told her.

Dmitri dismissed Miss Direction and went back to showing off his troops. "That one sitting by himself is codename Hiss because of that big tribal snake tattoo down his right arm. His tech can create illusions. He's the child of two synergies and has been training his whole life. That's an advantage, but he has never gone to school or been around kids his own age. Socializing him has been a challenge." We looked over to the table where Hiss ate alone. He had a kind face and more black tribal tattoos on his neck.

"Actually the tattoos are all over his body, head to toe," Dmitri said, reading my thoughts. I didn't mind it when Dmitri peeked into my head. I'm sure a lot of people were bothered by that but I thought it was cool.

"What about his hair?" Zeal asked. "Is that natural?" Hiss' hair was black but in the sun it looked completely purple.

"Don't know," Dmitri replied.

I'd seen that Jack had agreed to participate and had himself a team. I headed over to congratulate him. He was chatting with some of his subordinates. He noticed me approaching and started speaking loud and exaggerated. "It's nice that they put everyone useless on one team so that they don't waste our time. Oh look, here comes their captain," he said and looked up at me. My team, useless? I couldn't think of a thing to say. My cheeks flamed up and I turned to get away.

After lunch we had a question and answer period. It was the first day and none of these kids had even seen a Fiend so we thought we better explain a bit.

The first question came from on Tyler's team. "If Fiends are just as fragile as we are, why can't we just get guns and shoot them?" Russell, our weapons expert fielded this one. "Here's the problem with guns," he told us. "If you aren't really great with yours, somebody bigger than you can take it and then use it themselves. We will have a team of experienced gun users inside, but beyond that we can't take the chance that the guns will do more harm than good."

Solara from my team raised her hand. "I don't know if I could kill someone." It wasn't really a question and it shocked the crowd into silence.

I was about to speak when Jack piped up. "It's not about killing. It's not about right or wrong, us or them, any of that. It's about protecting what's yours. Earth is my home. If someone kicks me out, I have nowhere to go. I've been homeless most of my life, people. Now I live

375

in a mansion, eat rich food and play video games all day. You think I'm gonna let all that go because some Fiend wants to rape me, eat me, and burn my house to the ground? If we don't hold these bastards back here, they are going to destroy everything and then take everything that's not destroyed. There is no one else. Believe me, I wouldn't be standing here if there was."

Holly jumped to her feet and started applauding. The entire crowd started cheering. You've done well, Jack.

Everybody went back to training. I put Ace in charge of my team and continued walking around to see what the other teams were made of. Tyler had a small team of kids with special abilities like his telekinesis. There was a handsome, older Latino guy codename TNT, who could expand particles rapidly in a burst. On its own his tech didn't do much but try to place that power in the center of something and the whole thing explodes.

Tyler introduced me to a younger, Chinese guy named codename Ocs.

"Ox? He's not that big a guy" I pointed out.

"His tech is X-ray vision," Sky Walker said. "Ocs is short for oculars."

"I am never going to remember that," I told him.

"Just go with Ox then," Tyler said slightly exasperated.

"Tell me about your tech," I turned to Ox. "X-ray vision sounds pretty cool."

"It's really just thermal imaging!" Steven told me anxiously. "I don't want you to think I'm looking through girls' clothes." I laughed. I hadn't thought that until he said something.

Every one of the Vipers had their own team. Even Ari had two girls following her around. A freckle-faced brunette beauty who could see synergy auras like Ari (though not nearly as well) and another girl with shorter brown hair and lovely eyes who had some sort of animal communication.

I realized I could spend all day checking out the teams. I decided to stop and see Jage before returning to my own team.

Jage's team fascinated me. They were the group with physical mutations. Jag and Onyx were there, the black and white twins who morphed into jaguars. The guy with the spiny skin was there too. Everyone who had horns or a hunched back or hair growing in the wrong places was here. I felt the most comfortable with this team. Looking as perfectly human as I did was awkward for me after my stint in hell. I knew that part of me, if not all of me, was Fiend, and part of me longed to be Fiend and leave this human existence behind. I know Jage's group had it the worst in the real world. I was lucky I could hide in this human shape.

"Hey Captain," I said to Jage. "Maybe it was wrong to give you a nickname like Rue. I know the guys were just poking fun at your tail."

"Yeah I knew that," Jage smiled. "An insult is only as powerful as you allow. I've turned the word around, taken their power away and kept it for myself. Now 'Rue' isn't an insult, it's an honor." I was stunned into silence for the moment. What an enlightened frame of mind.

I went back to my team and we went back to training. Every day was long and tough. We would all exercise in the morning, break into our groups and train all day.

For the past few days DJ's team had been getting a lot of attention. I went by and met a dozen smiling faces. DJ introduced them all but only two caught my attention.

"My assistant Holly." He gestured to the young, beautiful brunette standing to his left.

"Her skin secretes a deadly toxin so even a touch from her can be fatal." Holly turned to DJ and blew him a friendly kiss. Her power sounded horrific but it was hard to be scared with her standing there grinning ear to ear. She noticed me and gave a quick little wave.

DJ familiarized us with the rest of the team. He seemed reluctant to introduce us to the last member of his group, a beauty with long dark hair and gentle eyes. He put a hand out for her and she took it, coming shyly forward. She wore a violet pin. "This is Kitt. Kitt lends her energy to a partner to enhance their abilities. We call this tech 'Amplify.'"

My breath caught in my lungs. It was clear from looking at the shy, unassuming girl that Kitt had no idea just how valuable her power was.

378

I turned to the crowd and most of them seemed to be drooling and sizing her up like a piece of meat. The idea of multiplying your power was seductive to anyone. Few of them realized that the greater power would require a greater measure of control that none of them possessed. I was thankful she was on DJ's team. I knew he would protect her from the power hungry.

At our next assembly, Russell addressed the teams with some battle info. He showed an egg-shaped package each one of us would carry. When you popped open the package there were three fabric flags. If you were hit in battle and needed immediate attention you were to drape the green flag over yourself. The yellow flag was for someone who wasn't going to make it so not to waste the medical attention and the red flag...well the red flag would be draped over people who had died. The entire conversation was pretty sobering.

Afterwards I tried working with my group down by the water. Sapphire was unable to freeze the ocean waves so that meant her power dispersed. If only I could figure out what that meant. I felt an enormous presence looming behind me.

I turned around and came face to face with Steel. Steel!

"What are you doing here?" I asked. My face lit up.

"You are an odd duck," Steel said but he sounded amused. Intensity lit up his blue eyes (and it kinda lit up his blue hair and fingernails too.) "If I'm here you can guess it's not for a good reason." We took a couple steps away from my group. I noticed there were two guys following Steel.

"Who are the guys?" I asked pointing to them.

"Oh, I found them in hell. They were synergies living in a city of Fiends. They thought aliens had landed and taken over the Earth. This is Lix and his apprentice Barry. They're your problem now." Steel said washing his hands of the two.

They could be my problem any day! Both were a little older than me and very well-muscled. Barry was good looking, black skin, strong jaw, gentle brown eyes. Lix had a full head of silver hair! Not grey, silver, sparkling and everything. His eyes were a piercing blue. The two of them had swords at their waist. I pointed them over to Jack's group.

I turned back to see Steel working with Quake. I don't know what he was telling him but suddenly Quake released a burst of power I'd never seen. It actually did quake the ground. It shook in a straight path all the way until it hit the ocean. I rushed over to congratulate Quake. He and Steel hadn't moved from their spots. I opened my mouth to speak and Steel held up his hand to silence me.

"Wait for it," he said. I turned and watched what they were watching. Quake was shaking with exhaustion. I think his eyes had turned yellow. All of a sudden a huge tremor hit us, knocking everyone to their knees. Off in the distance an enormous rock was rising in the middle of the ocean. It was pushing up like a mountain range created by an earthquake. The thing was huge, like a quarter mile in diameter. I couldn't believe it! Steel was here for minutes and he managed to unleash the power inside this guy.

"You had him shifting sand?" Steel drawled like I was the dumbest girl alive. "And never once did you consider the seismic waves he was emitting to do that? You are a silly girl. You needed more training."

"Stay,' I said immediately. "Train me more. Help these guys. We need you."

"Begging is never attractive," his eyes flashed in anger. "Aren't you the least bit concerned why I'm even here?"

"Well I just assumed…"

"Assumed? Just shut up and let me speak, you moron. Did you see a green glowing door anywhere?" Well no, but to be fair Steel did come up behind me. "Answer the question!" Steel demanded.

"No, I didn't see the door." Jeez.

"Then how did I get here?" Steel asked impatiently. Steel didn't ask questions for no reason; there was a very specific answer he wanted from me. If Eric didn't bring him here…

"No! No!" I shouted, realizing what he was here to tell me. "No, it's too soon, we're not ready!"

"Ready or not here they come!" Steel had come through the tunnel. He passed through the tunnel which means it was up and completely functional.

"How long do we have?" I asked, afraid to hear the answer.

"Days."

"Will you stay and fight with us?" I pleaded.

"No," he answered coldly.

"Will you stay and fight with *me*?" I begged.

"I can't. Don't you think I would if I could? I've invested so much time and training in you. You're my investment. I protect my investments." Steel was cold and mean on the outside but I knew enough that his heart was somewhat good. Every time he said the word "investment" I know he was really saying "You're my concern."

"Why won't you stay? We need you. I need you." How can I win this battle without him?

"I have a responsibility to Eric. Someday you'll understand."

"Sure, if I live that long," I spat. Steel hit me across the face so hard it took me straight down to the ground. Everyone jumped to their feet to defend me. I held my hand up to hold them back.

"It's her teacher," Lucky yelled out to explain to everyone. "It's her teacher."

"I don't want to hear the bullshit, understand?" Steel's eyes were on fire. "You are going to lead these people and you are going to win this battle. You owe me that much." I nodded.

"Anyway, you won't be alone. I'm sending Sam and Jenni to join you," Steel said, consoling me.

"So Eric can spare them but he can't spare you?" His blue eyes met mine. "I get it. I do."

"Barry and Lix can't go back. We killed a couple Fiends on the way here. They'll be dead meat if they try to return." Steel didn't sound concerned but I could feel that he was.

"I'll take care of them," I assured him. "They're my problem now, right?"

Steel nodded. "So when you say you killed a 'couple', what does that mean exactly?" I smiled.

"A couple…hundred, give or take." Steel smiled too. "It's bad manners to arrive at someone's home without a gift."

Steel turned and I knew he was about to take off. "I'd say good luck, but given your training you won't need luck. All I can say is…don't mess this up." With that he bolted.

Now I was left with the chore of telling my Vipers that war was upon us.

Chapter 26

I assembled the team right away. I called together everyone from the old squad plus the new ones from the intelligence group. I brought in Barry and Lix and I called in Jack and Ky as well.

Everyone was shocked.

"You came through the tunnel?" Lucky asked Barry and Lix. "Can you show us?"

The two led our group to the very edge of our yard. The land ended abruptly with a steep cliff. Lix went to the edge and peered over the cliff. We all tentatively followed.

I craned my neck to see. There it was, the opening. It looked like a fissure at the bottom of a rock, but the opening was more than 8 feet tall. The cliff wall was massive. If it was opened up it would be big enough for dozens of Fiends to pour through at once.

We all needed to see inside. I grabbed Keith and Ky and used static to ease myself to the ground. Everyone else started to climb down.

"Number one, create a way for soldiers to get to the battlefield," Lucky said, making an audible check list.

We arrived at the fissure. Barry and Lix went first, I followed with them. What we saw was really quite remarkable. As soon as we stepped inside we were in an enormous stone room. It was a giant cave, almost circular, with stalactites and stalagmites everywhere. The cave had a vaulted ceiling and the stone was reddish brown. Across from the crack we had entered through was another large crack in the cave wall. This was where the Fiends would come through.

Everyone was standing in the cave by now and Keith was addressing us.

"You see the crack in the cave wall is twice the size of the one we entered through. I would estimate about 2-4 Fiends could enter at a time. Only 1-2 can get through the opening to the outside world at a time, thus creating a bottleneck. This would allow the inside team more time to slay these beasts." Keith surveyed the landscape. "I think about 30-40 bodies on the inside team would work. It would give us enough room to move around and fight. That leaves about 150 troops for you, General Luke. Can you handle that?"

"No problem," Lucky said.

Jack piped up. "So let me understand; there's going to be 40 of us in a cave flooded with Fiends and our only escape route is this little crack in the wall. We're gonna be trapped like rats. Get some dynamite and make a bigger door!" He had a good point.

"Number two, dynamite the door," Lucky said.

"Number three," Chase said, verbalizing along with Lucky. "Um, floodlights. Hello, are you expecting people to fight in the dark? What if these Fiends have night vision?"

Everyone on the team had suggestions for improving the battle conditions. They spoke and then put their thoughts in order of importance.

We returned to the house. The intelligence team went directly to the basement to make plans. It was up to the rest of us to tell the troops. It was up to me. They trusted me to be honest.

As I expected, the news caused a lot of commotion. Crying, screaming. Some of the troops declared that they quit. Most everyone said they hadn't had enough training.

"It doesn't matter if we trained our whole lives," I told them. "You're never ready to take another life. This is Earth's desperate call. We are the chosen few who hear it."

I tried to reach out to the strongest ones, the ones that would make a difference if they stayed or went. I wish I could say they were all important, but this was the end of the world and I needed all the green, blue and purple pins. We split into our teams. I told my team there was no dishonor in stepping down. No one stepped down. I was truly proud of them. I assigned Sapphire to medical duty. Her powers were too undeveloped for battle. The rest would all be on the front lines.

Everyone was divided into teams for guard duty. We didn't want to leave the mouth of the tunnel unguarded for a second. We went in 4 hour shifts so no one got too tired. We needed everyone on guard.

Generals Keith and Lucky thought it was best if we kept the teams training and kept them focused. They seemed to work twice as hard, desperate to refine their skills before the actual event occurred.

The troops started digging foxholes, setting up traps and putting together the medical tent. The medics were gathered where the medical tent was going up. There were boxes of supplies everywhere. How did Keith manage all this? I knew his brain could process multiple what a human brain could, but I was still amazed. He seemed to think of everything.

I checked out all the recruits from medical. One of them caught my eye, a preppie with a pale complexion and a standard short, brown hairstyle I seemed to recognize. I waited until the lecture was finished, then I pulled the guy aside.

"Mend, right?" I asked. His blue eyes seemed very surprised to see me. "I'm happy you decided to stay. After the other day…I wasn't so sure." I was referring to the tears and vomiting he did after finding out about the Apocalypse.

"You're happy?" he asked incredulously.

"Uh, yeah. Why do you seem so surprised?" I narrowed my eyes. I was always on my guard.

"It's just, you know. I thought you would think I was a coward," he admitted shyly. "All the Vipers are so strong and brave, I don't think I'd ever fit in. And you, you're so…"

"Judgmental?" I questioned.

"No, no! I was going to say…incredible." Mend's cheeks flushed.

He was the right choice. His loyalty to me would be total. I needed an ally in the medical tent and I think this boy could handle the job.

"I need you to do a job for me. It might go against everything your squads and your captains and your generals ask of you." I broke off. I admit I was being a little dramatic but I needed him to buy into this. My friends' lives depended on it.

Mend's eyes were wide as saucers. "I don't know that I'm the right one for the job," he said clearly lacking confidence. He reached behind his head and scratched the base of his hair nervously.

"I picked you. That makes you right for the job. Mend, what I'm about to tell you no one else on this earth knows. It is the biggest secret I've ever kept and you are the only person I trust with it. But before I tell you, I need you to swear to God that you will take this mission. That you will do what I ask whether it is right or wrong."

Mend hesitated. "Will I have to kill anyone? Because I just don't think I could do that."

"No, you won't be killing anyone. In fact you'll be saving lives. Whichever lives you choose. I'm going to give you the power of a God." I waited a moment to let that sink in. "All I ask is that you save this power and only use it on the people I tell you to."

"I can do that," he agreed.

"Mend, my blood has the power to heal. You are going to find the EMT, learn how to draw blood and then you and I are going to draw and store as much blood as possible from now until the battle. Once the war starts you will administer this blood to everyone on my list who gets wounded. Under no circumstances will you administer it to anyone else unless I directly order you. Do you understand? Can you do this?"

"It would be an honor," he said his eyes shining with pride.

"You know my secret now. We're bonded. You know me in a way that even Keith and Lucky don't. I've trusted you. Don't let me regret it. If you tell my secret or use any of the blood," I sighed. "I don't think I need to threaten you but if one of my friends dies because you weren't doing what I asked - I will kill you." I said with ultimate seriousness. He gasped but I could see it in his eyes that he would come through for me. I sent him away and stood there watching him go.

"It's a little late to be out here all by yourself, don't you think?" mused a sweet timbered female voice behind me. I turned to see Ari emerging from the shadows.

"You didn't hear any of that, did you?" I felt I could trust Ari but the fewer people who knew the better.

"Just arrived,' she reassured me. "I did want to talk to you in private. Specifically, I wanted to talk to you about my Mom. I've put some money aside for her. If I don't make it through this battle, I want to make sure she's taken care of."

"That's great, really, but why are you telling me? I don't know anything about money." I truly didn't.

"Yes," Ari agreed. "But I know you're honest. I know you won't let a couple hundred thousand go missing."

"A couple what? Ari, are you joking?" How did such a simple girl accumulate that kind of sum?

"Nah, I went to work with Keith and got it all in one good day," her smile was almost wicked.

"I'm confused," I started. "You worked in software for one and you made, what a quarter million dollars?"

"It was half a million to be exact and no, I didn't work in software. What, you think I made half a mil working at MalAdjusted Games?" Ari laughed and looked over at me. I was clearly confused.

"Steph," she started gently. "I'm thinking you know nothing about business?" I shook my head, Ari continued. "A video game startup like MalAdjusted takes years before it even turns a profit, let alone makes big money. Keith has single handedly financed this entire war. You have no idea where that money comes from?"

I shook my head "no" again. I had wondered but Keith had never mentioned anything so I assumed he was just good at business.

"You've heard of Wall Street haven't you? People trade stock certificates all day. They try to buy them at a low price and sell them at a higher price to make money. Chad has the fastest hand-eye coordination on the planet. On his computer he can buy and sell faster than everyone else. Traders are always reading the papers and talking to each other to try to find out what the brokers are thinking. What if you could hear what the brokers are thinking?"

"Dmitri!" I shouted.

"That's right! Mix in Keith's business sense and you've got a money making machine!" Ari shouted.

"Where do you fit in?" I asked.

"Well," she chuckled. "I caught them doing it and I blackmailed them into cutting me in. I only did it for one day. It was cool but..." she sighed. "It wasn't what I wanted."

I laughed. "Half a million dollars wasn't enough? What did you want, their first born?"

"I wanted enough for Jage and I to live off of in case this war goes the wrong way. I wanted to pay back my mother for raising me on her own. My father left me a trust that supported us until I was eighteen. My mother doted on me and my mutation all my life. Suddenly now she has to get a job. I wanted enough to support her. When I found out that Keith had money put aside for all of us I put the whole $500,000 aside for my mother."

"So Keith became a millionaire from the stock market," I mused aloud.

"Oh, Keith isn't a millionaire. He spent every penny he made on this war. Except for that old jeep, he's broke." Ari told me.

391

"But what about his fancy office? And what about the limo and our house?" I asked.

"Why don't you ask him sometime," Ari suggested.

Our conversation seemed to end. Ari turned to look back at the medical tent. We stood wordlessly for a few moments. "My mom was human and had no idea the man she fell for was a Fiend. I just hope with all this warfare, the human race doesn't become a casualty."

"It's the human race I'm fighting to save," I choked on the words. I felt like I couldn't breathe. Ari's words were weighing heavily on me. Suddenly the gravity of the situation came crashing down on me. I was fighting to save the human race!

She opened her arms and I rushed into them for a hug. In disbelief I found tears falling from my eyes. I had hidden them from the other Vipers and Keith, even from Ky, but something about the openness of this girl allowed me to open up as well. Ari held me tight as I cried. After a few minutes Ari gently "shooshed" me to stop crying. She stepped back and took both of my hands in hers. "Steph, you're going to see a lot of people get hurt. You can't worry about all of them. Keep fighting the good fight. I'll be right behind you saving them all. You believe in me, right?" Ari looked to me like the big sister I'd always wished for.

I shook my head "yes."

"Well I speak on behalf of the whole world, and we believe in you."

Chapter 27

Three days passed and nothing happened. Everyone started to relax. It was late evening; I was cozied up in bed with Keith when both of our red phones went off. Emergency!

We picked up the phones and listened desperately. "Get down to the cave, NOW!" Jage's voice was shaky.

Keith and I made a break for it. Most of the other Vipers were flying out of their rooms as well.

Lucky's crew had built a wooden walkway to get down to the cave. It would still take several minutes for them to reach the bottom. I grabbed hold of Keith and lowered us instantly with my static.

Jage was standing at the fissure, the entrance to the cave. His team was sitting out front. Jage turned and slipped inside the cave. Keith and I followed. About 40 feet away, across the cave and at the mouth of the tunnel was a body. It was twisted and contorted with blood pooling underneath. The floodlights were so bright I couldn't tell who it was. We crept forward slowly until we recognized it.

Oh my god, it was Holly! "No!" I screamed! Oh God not Holly, she had barely lived and yet she was liked by so many.

"I tried…I tried to save her," Jage whispered. He was holding up his palms. They were lacerated with acid burns.

"Jage needs a doctor!" I screamed to Keith. Forget it, I was the fastest.

"No," Jage protested, falling on his knees next to Holly. "I won't leave her!"

I grabbed the underside of his hands and shoved his destroyed palms in his face. "You're no good to me like this!" I screamed. God, I was just like Steel. I grabbed his arm and started pulling him from the cave.

"Wait!" he shouted. "Lix! Lix chased the demons back into the cave. He grabbed Ox, the guy with X-ray vision and they bolted. Lix said the Fiends were a scouting party and he was going to kill them all so they could never brag about killing Holly." Lix. His heart was noble but he should have waited for backup. Why did brave always seem to equal stupid?

I let Keith handle Lix and I took Jage to the medical tent. It was staffed with EMTs and would have a team of doctors round the clock as soon as war was declared. This show of Fiend aggression meant the declaration of war.

I entered the medical tent with Jage. Most of his team was here getting patched up from their scuffle with the Fiends. There was a hush when they saw me leading their captain in. I took Jage straight to the back and pulled a curtain to separate us from his troops. Two doctors had been called in and were washing up.

"Do you want me to call Ari?" I asked.

"Not yet. Let's see what the doctors say. I don't want to scare her unnecessarily," Jage told me, but he and I both knew his injuries were

394

far worse than we wanted to believe. The doctors arrived and asked me to leave. I exited the medical tent and went to get Mend.

When I found Mend he was asleep inside his tent. "It's time," I told him. We raced back to the medical tent together. I returned to Jage. The doctors had already left and Jage was staring listlessly into his mutilated palms.

"The doctors can't do anything. No sense, no feeling. I'll never touch Ari again," he said, his voice full of pain.

Mend arrived with the equipment. We were going to do a direct blood transfusion from me to Jage.

"Jage, I need you to trust me," I started. He had nothing left to lose. "Your hands have already started healing. We need to open them up again, remove all the damaged tissue. We're going to give you a transfusion of Fiend blood. It has the power to regenerate."

"Right," Jage laughed bitterly. "Where are you going to find this magical Fiend, and why would he give his blood to me?"

"I'm the Fiend, Jage. My blood is going to help you," I told him reassuringly.

"Since when?" he scoffed. "I've watched you get beaten up by a 12 year old."

"Well you'll need to trust that a year and a half in hell can change a girl!" My blue eyes burned into his.

Wordlessly, Mend performed the transfusion. When it was through I pulled him into a long, strong hug. Jage was passed out. I would return later to see how he was doing.

I left the medical tent and went back to the cave. They had removed Holly's body but were still standing around discussing everything. The chatter quieted down when I approached.

"How did DJ take the news?" I asked. He and Holly were so close. "Is he okay?" I tried to make eye contact but everyone seemed to look away.

"We thought it would be better if you told him, you're closest to him." Keith said.

"You're all cowards," I scolded and turned and exited the cave. I made my way immediately to the house and into the private rooms, where DJ had stayed to watch over Holly. I found DJ sleeping soundly. I hesitated in waking him up. Holly. DJ had known her since she was a girl. She had taken such delight in his radio shows and the music he played. He had adored her so much that he made her a part of his show, and the audience loved her.

I shook the man awake. I blurted everything out at once. DJ screamed and smashed his hands hard on the wall behind him. With tears in his eyes he asked me to explain exactly what had happened. I explained what little I knew. DJ wept openly. I've never lost anyone I loved. I had no idea what kind of agony he was suffering.

After a time, DJ composed himself. He asked to see the body. I led him down to the cave and over to where the team had placed Holly. I left DJ alone to grieve.

At this point the Vipers had been rounded up and were sitting on the cave floor discussing strategy. Although some seemed scared, no one looked like they were going to back down. I felt proud.

Lix and Ox showed up about two hours later. Both were out of breath and covered in blood. Lix had slain the entire scouting party, Ox backed him up. Through the layers of rock Ox's gifted eyes had seen the Fiend army. They were mobilizing and there were thousands of them. Thousands of Fiends and roughly 200 of us.

I grabbed Ox by the arm. He was covered with blood and holding a short blade in his hand. "Are you doing okay? I didn't peg you for a fighter," I told him.

"They killed Holly," he said looking down at the spot on the floor where we had found the girl. "I'm not going to let them take any more of my friends."

I gave his arm a sympathetic squeeze and started walking away.

"There's more," he yelled. I turned back to hear. "I've seen inside these things. The Fiends that aren't shaped like humans, they have vital organs in different places. I can tell you where to hit them."

I reached out and squeezed the hand that was still clutching the blade handle. "You're very brave, but do you really think you can handle the front lines? Your tech isn't going to protect you."

"I will," came a voice from behind us. Lix came forward and put a bloody hand proudly on the Chinese guy's shoulder. "He's proven himself to me, I'll stand by him."

"What about your apprentice Barry? Don't you need to protect him?" Keith asked.

"Oh please!" Lix started laughing. "You guys have no clue. Barry's a better fighter than any of you. He's my apprentice because he's not better than **me**." He slapped Ox on the back. "Welcome to the team."

"Yes! Inside Team gets all the chicks!" Ox celebrated.

"It's not about the chicks, it's about the power. The inside team will make all the impact in this fight," Lix instructed.

"Is that why you came here? To test your power?" Al asked.

"I came here because I wanted to see The Guardian in action," Lix answered.

I felt my cheeks blush. I knew he was about to reveal something about my trip to hell that I hadn't told the team.

Lix turned to me. "Steel told us about your adventures, *Guardian*. About how the two of you went to towns being ravaged by particularly nasty Fiends and how you carved them up to save the day."

"It was no big deal, they were just training exercises," I was hoping he would let this go but he was only just beginning. Lix turned to the group who were now surrounding him with rapt attention.

"So across our lands this rumor starts spreading about a guy with blue hair and a girl with golden locks who are covering the countryside defending the weaker Fiends by destroying their murderous tormentors."

"The story that made them famous was that of the Goblin. Picture this, a tall mountain peak and all around it lush valleys, fertile and beautiful. Beyond that were hundreds of miles of scorching desert in every direction. Right in the middle of this oasis was a mountain cave and in the cave was a huge round, pasty white, nasty Fiend. For hundreds of years he had lived there picking off the lives of the townspeople like he was picking fruit. You never knew when he would strike or how awful it would be. The townspeople tried everything, smoke, fire, diseases. They raised an army, they built elaborate traps. Nothing so much as slowed this creature down. Desperate, they sent out a distress call for any warrior willing to travel the several hundred miles over desert to defeat the beast. Heck even I tried myself when I was younger. The thing beat me up pretty bad, gave me this scar."

Lix held up his arm and showed a scar that ran from his elbow all the way up to his shoulder.

"But I bet Steel didn't tell you any of that before you faced the creature. He just pushed you into the cave and told you to fight." Lix looked at me for an answer.

I shook my head yes, that was pretty much it. I arrived at the cave and fought the Fiend. Only one of us walked away.

"The woman who defeated The Goblin became a woman of legend. No one knew her name. I think Steel started calling you 'The Guardian,' and it caught on. You'd be surprised how fast a rumor travels through hell, our world anyway," Lix explained.

"What level of hell are you from?" Dmitri asked.

"We've been living on what you would call the 6th level for a while, but where exactly I'm from I'm not sure. My family was killed and eaten by Fiends when I was small. I swore I would avenge them. I could barely walk and I was already learning to fight. I've traveled up and down the levels of hell improving my strength. About 2 years ago I met Barry. His uncle kidnapped him when he was six years old and sold him as a slave to some Fiends. He told Barry that aliens had landed and that was why everyone looked so strange. It's a good theory and who knows, maybe its right. I've seen some crazy Fiends in my day."

"So Barry, do you know where you came from originally?"

"A place called Orlando."

Everyone started murmuring. "Orlando! Florida?" I shouted. That's here on Earth. When this war is over we'll take you there and help you find your family."

"You don't have to do that," Barry said shyly. "My family was killed by the aliens or the Fiends or whatever you call them."

"No Dude wait," Lix started thinking out loud. "Maybe your uncle lied. Maybe your family is out there."

Barry was stunned. I stepped forward and pulled him into a hug. "Now you have something to fight for," I whispered. Lix, Barry and Ox all started talking amongst themselves.

"All I know is that he better be as good as he claims," Keith snarked to the Vipers gesturing towards Lix.

I left everybody to go check on Jage. He was still passed out in the same spot I had left him. I woke Jage to see how his hands were doing. As we removed the bandages I had to bite back tears. There were scars to be sure but all the sense and feeling had returned to his palms. Jage was overjoyed.

"Tell no one of this," I instructed. He nodded.

Keith announced that all the Vipers would gather in the basement in 15 minutes. I ran to find Kyan. Keith had kept him away from Holly's body but he knew the girl was dead. No one had seen him and I started to get worried. Finally I tracked him down. He was sitting in the empty bathtub in his room just like we did the day we bought the house. The little boy was despondent, his face pale when I found him.

I climbed into the tub behind him and pulled him close to me, wrapping my arms around him. "Ky," I said his name aloud. I wanted to feel him relax into me but he was so stiff I worried he was catatonic.

"I didn't just learn offense. I learned some amazing defense. I know you're scared but I *will* protect you. I'll protect you." I repeated trying to reassure the boy.

Ky was silent for a long, long time. Finally he spoke. "I'm not worried about myself. I'm worried about everyone else. If anybody dies it's my fault. It's because of me."

"Don't say that. Everyone here is a volunteer. They all know what they're getting into."

"Everyone on our side, maybe. What about the Fiends? Do they really know what's waiting for them?" Ky turned around to face me.

I looked deep into his quivering green eyes. He was the most caring and compassionate being I'd ever encountered.

"Sweetheart, I've been to the other end of the tunnel. These Fiends have been building it for decades. Long before you were born. They were going to come whether we were here or not. The only difference is us. If it weren't for you, none of us would be here, prepared for battle. Do you understand? You are the ONLY reason earth has a chance."

My words seemed to pull him together.

"There is one more thing…I'm worried about you," Ky told me. "When this war is over, and we win what will happen to you? I don't want to see you get by on just your looks anymore."

His words shocked me to my core. "Is that what you think I do?" I asked in disbelief.

"Um, Steph, that *is* what you do." Ky said matter-of-factly. "It's not like you have a job. Where do you think the food in the fridge comes from or the clothes in your closet? People give you things because you're pretty. People follow you because you're pretty."

"People follow me because I give them hope," I said defiantly.

"True, that you do. But they listened to you in the first place because you were pretty. Look I'm glad you're pretty Steph, but you rely entirely on that to survive. That could change in a flash. You could have an accident or an illness or maybe just grow old. Your looks could leave you and where would you be?"

I couldn't answer him. "What do you want me to do?" I asked.

"Finish school. Graduate. You started studying for the SATs but you gave it up over the stupid pageant. Graduate high school, go to college. Become a senator or something. Change the way the world sees synergies but do it the right way." Here I thought I was looking out for him but he was really looking out for me. "There's one more thing," he began. "But we'll talk about it after." That was the most reassuring

403

thing he could have said, as if he had no doubts whatsoever that we would sail through this. "We'll talk about it after."

Keith had gathered up all the Vipers and we met them in the basement. We went over the plans, and then Keith addressed us. "Listen, I know none of you would be here if it wasn't for Stephanie. Face it, I wouldn't be here either. We all have a common goal, which is saving the world, but before all that we were all united in protecting my brother Kyan. I spent my whole life protecting Kyan, because of that I didn't really have a chance to do anything on my own. This team is...well...you're the first real friends I've ever had. In the past year I've moved across the country, made and spent a fortune, bought a house, fell in love and made friends with some wild and crazy synergies." Everyone started to holler. "Tonight we fight for our lives. We're going to win and it is because everyone in this room is right here, right now. Thank you." The Vipers burst into applause.

My head was spinning. Did he say "fell in love?"

Keith took Ky and Jack with him and departed, leaving the rest of us in the basement.

"We've got about 20 minutes," Zeal announced. "Let's play Truth or Dare."

Everyone giggled. That would break the tension for sure.

Zeal went first. "Stephanie, if you could get with any Viper besides Lucky or Keith, who would it be?" he asked clearly hoping I would choose him.

"Jage," I answered matter of factly. I looked over at the guy with the soft brown hair and the prehensile tail. His arms were wrapped tightly around his girlfriend Ari.

"No offense Ari," I said.

"None taken," Ari giggled. "I'd get with Jage too!"

"Ok my turn. Violet, truth or dare?" I challenged. The girl picked dare and I dared her to kiss one of the Viper boys. She picked Russell, the tall guy with the long, light blonde ponytail. I expected it to be just a peck but Russell pulled the girl into a long and very passionate kiss. After that the crowd went wild, daring each other to kiss and touch and all kinds of wild stuff. Tyler chose Lucky and Lucky chose "truth." Tyler asked, "What is your deepest, darkest secret?"

Lucky got quiet and the whole room went silent. We sat like that for what seemed like an eternity.

Finally Dmitri spoke up. "You don't have to answer, Luke."

"Yes, I do," Lucky said with absolute seriousness. He was staring hard at the ground.

"Can you leave me and Stephanie alone, everyone?"

The Vipers shook their heads and murmured as they all filed up the stairs and out of the basement until it was just Lucky and me. I was a little nervous.

"Steph, I want you to take off your shirt," Lucky instructed.

"I thought this was a truth, not a dare," I teased. Lucky didn't respond. He seemed so upset, I didn't even ask any questions I just pulled my olive tank top over my head. Lucky walked over and put his hands on my hips. He didn't look me in the eye; he just stared down at my stomach. He took a fingertip and started tracing over the lines of my bullet scar.

"You could have died," he said slowly, like it was painful to discuss.

"I didn't," I reminded him.

"You could have. And if you did…it would have been my fault." His faced flushed with shame.

"Lucky, what are you talking about? You were attacked just like I was. There was no way you could have taken out all those guys to protect me." Poor guy, blaming himself for something he had no control over. Suddenly his face twisted in anger. "Are you stupid?" he screamed in my face. "The whole thing was my fault. *It was my gun. I'm the one who shot you!*"

Oh my god could that be true? My knees went weak and I thought I was going to vomit. Lucky continued.

"I got scared, you know? There were two gangs in the alley that night. The ones that jumped me the night before for my money and Camino's guys trying to get back the gun he sold me. The gun was actually the weapon from a homicide. Camino sold it to me with the intent that I would take the fall for the crime. His gang decided it would be best to get rid of the gun instead so they gathered together to take it from me." Lucky was speaking so fast I didn't dare interrupt him, besides I wouldn't know what to say.

"As soon as I stepped out the doors the gangs started beating on me. I couldn't see anything. One came down hard on my right leg and broke it. I knew I couldn't fight these guys. I was hoping somehow you had escaped. When I saw those guys attacking you, I knew I couldn't protect you and I panicked. I grabbed the gun I'd bought and fired a few shots into the air just to scare everyone. One of the guys tried to grab the gun out of my hand and it went off. That was the shot that hit you. Everyone fled the alley and there you were, unconscious and bleeding. With my broken leg it was hard to move but I dragged myself over to you. I pulled you in my arms and told you how sorry I was. I told you how much I loved you." He was still staring at the bullet scar. My head was spinning.

"Someone at the hotel had called the police. I should have stayed with you, I should have held your hand. I heard the sirens and I saw

407

everything we worked for just falling apart. You would go back to the orphanage, I would get deported."

Lucky took a long and heavy breath. "I thought…I thought as long as I stayed in the country I could rescue you somehow and we could be together again. I never meant…"

I couldn't let him go on torturing himself like this. I grabbed his arm and cut him off. "You did the right thing. You absolutely did the right thing. I *was* rescued and we *are* together. You made the right choice. I know how hard this must have been for you, how scary."

Lucky looked up to meet my gaze, his eyes brimming with tears. Through all the things we'd endured I'd never seen him cry. He looked at me with disbelief.

"Just like that? I betrayed you, I almost killed you, I got you locked back up in your orphan prison and you just forgive me?"

"Nothing to forgive, Lucky. Everything wonderful in my life is a gift you gave me. How could I be mad at you for making a decision I agree with? You were doing the best you knew how to protect us. As bad as you think shooting me was, it could never undo any of the incredible things you've done for me. You were my salvation. I was a princess locked away in a tower and you were the prince that rescued me. I could never stop loving you, this I promise you." I pulled him into my arms. Poor guy, he must have tortured himself all this time. I wonder…

"Lucky?" I asked and he fought to regain his composure. "Is this the reason why you let Keith be my boyfriend? Is this the reason you didn't fight for me?"

Lucky weakly shook his head "yes."

"Keith figured it out. That first night at the hospital he asked me if I had come back to tell you the truth. He said if I wasn't honest with you that he was going to take care of you instead. I could tell he was a good guy and that he really cared for you so I backed off. I thought you'd be better off. I figured once I told you the truth you wouldn't want me around so I've lived in a lie all this time." Lucky seemed completely defeated.

"Wow. I guess that's what I deserve for letting you make my choices for so long. You just make the decisions without asking me or informing me. Well, I've changed. I'm stronger now. I can't let anyone make my decisions for me anymore. You decided I would be with Keith and it's working out. Keith has been great to me and I love him and Ky very much. I'm very happy here."

"See, it all worked out. I knew you would pick him," Lucky conceded.

"You're right, in that it did work out, but you are so very wrong." I looked intensely into Lucky's eyes. "I wouldn't have picked him. I would never pick anyone over you."

I had said all that I wanted to say. I put my shirt back on. "We have a war to fight."

Chapter 28

Lucky and I turned without another word and headed up the basement

stairs and out the backdoor to catch up with the rest of the Vipers.

Immediately something was wrong.

"It's DJs team. They're gone, all of them," Russell reported.

"You've got to be kidding. They are an inside team! They are vital to

the success of this mission!" I cried. "Are you sure they didn't just go

off somewhere to grieve?"

"Well if they did they took all their stuff and one of the busses with

them. Face it, Stephanie, they fled."

Keith and Lucky paired off and spoke franticly to each other. They had

created backups and fallbacks for everything, so they knew how to

handle this. When they finished, it was time for them to become

generals. It was time for them to declare war.

Generals Keith and Lucky addressed the troops. They told everyone

exactly where to be, what to do, how to get medical aid. We were

ready to go, but something didn't feel right. Everyone was scared.

Everyone was scared to death.

I jumped up on a picnic table where people were resting their

weapons.

"Some of you have been saying we're not ready for this. That you think

we need more people. The Fiends will have greater numbers, yet we

will prevail."

"Let's be honest. Some of us won't make it. These aren't soldiers we fight. They are brutal, powerful Fiends. They will fight us ferociously and unmercifully. When they fall they will take some of us with them. But those of us who live, those true heroes, just think about it. What will it be like to look each other in the eye and know what we survived. What child hasn't dreamed of becoming a superhero? Today you are that hero. How many of you knew when you woke up this morning that today was your day to save the world?"

Today we make history. This is the story we will tell our children at bedtime and it will be so fantastic they will never know it's the truth. Anyone who learns of what happened here will rue the day that **we** stood for liberty, **we** stood for justice, **we** defended the human race and they will wish to God that they had that glory."

"Let's get this party started!" came an enthusiastic shout from the rear. Eric's troops: Sam and Jenni! They must have snuck in while I was talking. Oh I was so grateful to see them. Last time we met we were enemies, this time they brought me hope.

"Where do you want us?" Jenni asked. Her strawberry blonde hair shimmered even in the darkness. Had she always been this beautiful? A huge sketch pad was under her arm and Sam was holding an easel.

"On the front lines?" I questioned.

"Now you're talking," Sam said, his brown eyes sparkling. These two weren't afraid of combat, in fact they were excited by it.

411

"Has anyone seen these things?" Jenni asked. "It would make things easier if I could get some preliminary sketches." I directed her to Barry and Lix. Sam grabbed Jenni by the hand and they ran to the fighters who had faced these Fiends and lived to tell about it. The rest of us started getting in position and not a moment too soon, the ground started trembling with the movement of the Fiend army in the tunnel.

I made my way into the cave. The teams were arranged in three triangles with the tip facing the Fiend's entrance. Sam was the first in his triangle and closest to the tunnel entrance. Behind him were Jenni and Lix and behind them were a lot of our best combat fighters. I was the front of the second triangle. Directly behind me was Ky. We figured that was the safest place for him. On the left side of Ky was Keith, on his right was Zeal. Directly behind Zeal was Jack and the rest of the crew were the team I had been working with.

The front of the last group was Jage. Russell and Tyler were right behind him and the rest of their group was a mix of combat fighters and psychics. It was supposed to be DJ's team but we needed to improvise.

"We're counting on you, Guardian," Keith snarked.

"Do I get a kiss?" I asked my boyfriend.

"Sure," Keith responded. "After." I sighed.

The Fiends came at us immediately. They burst from the mouth of the tunnel like an explosion. We thought the opening would keep them

412

flowing at a steady pace but they flew right through it. I was able to stop and electrify the first 15-16 that emerged. Everyone saw that and everyone cheered. It set the tone.

The Fiends started moving too fast for me to control. Suddenly everyone was engaged in hand to hand combat. I shielded Ky as Keith shouted orders to everyone. I was amazed how level headed he stayed and how clear and precise his decisions were despite the chaos that surrounded us.

It was definitely Armageddon! It was just as loud and bloody as you can imagine. People started to fall and I saw green flags everywhere, then I saw red flags. My team lost two fighters in the first hour. Other teams were losing their members too. I squared my shoulders and faced the entrance to the tunnel. I needed to do my best, I needed to protect everyone.

Jenni had hung dozens of sketches on the rocks around her. When a Fiend she had drawn emerged she dowsed his picture with red paint and the creature dropped to the ground in pain. Lix and Barry were twirling their swords around slicing through dozens of Fiends. Sam had started lifting rocks from the cave floor and bashing them over the Fiends as they streamed out of the tunnel.

A large, round, orange Fiend rushed out of the tunnel and bowled right into me. While I was winded it made its way past me on the right. I turned my head away from the tunnel to watch the beast. It pushed

413

Zeal out of its way with extreme force. The blow forced Zeal back into Quake and knocked the two men down. As the Fiend hurried past them, Jack drew his sword and slashed the infiltrator across the belly. His unusual guts rushed out onto the cave floor. With his sword raised, Barry rushed forward to help Jack. Running through the creatures spilled guts, Barry slipped and got knocked on his ass. Lix appeared behind him and slashed straight through the orange Fiend's head. He reached down and grabbed his apprentice by the hand and hoisted an embarrassed Barry back to his feet.

While I was distracted, a tall thin Fiend with green skin and many arms emerged from the opening and began battering me about the head. Sam ran to my rescue and swung one fierce uppercut to the Fiend's chin. The blow knocked the green guy into the air where Sam hit him again from above. Wow, Sam was lightning fast! The second shot seemed to jam the Fiend's neck and he fell helplessly to the ground and twitched.

I went back to electrocuting whom I could when they were entering the cave from the tunnel. There were hundreds in this first wave and they were all big and strong. I managed to electrocute another six while the teams behind me struggled to defeat the monsters that were already in the cave. By now many of the beasts had made it out of the cave to the troops waiting outside. I could only hope things out there were going well.

A Fiend emerged from the tunnel and I stepped forward to blast him with a static charge. My power had no effect whatsoever on this beast. He was at least 7 feet tall, a brownish color with huge arms and knuckles that dragged on the ground like a gorilla. He lifted one giant fist and swung at me, catching me right in the face. I tumbled backwards my heels over my head and somersaulted a few times. My head hit the ground hard and I was immediately dizzy. As I strained to lift my head off the ground, I saw the monster charging toward me. My brain was too dizzy to think. I was about to have my face smashed in. At the very last possible second I saw something rush in front of me. Jage!! He drew a knife from his waist and held it at eye-level with the Fiend. The Fiend's momentum was too great for him to stop. He crashed full on with Jage's knife. The force of the crash was enough to knock Jage off balance but he managed to hold on to the knife with all of his might as it stabbed deep into the Fiend's head. The enraged Fiend shook his head from side to side trying to shake the synergy off. I felt helpless, frozen on the floor looking up at them.

Al appeared from the left. He grabbed the hand of the Fiend and jumped up on its back, twisting its arm as he did it. The arm snapped and dropped helplessly to the ground as the creature was now trying to shake off both Jage and Al.

The monster was badly hurt but it only made him more angry and ferocious. With his good arm he grabbed Jage and threw him with all his might. Jage flew back more than a dozen feet and crashed into the stone wall of the cave. He was immediately knocked out and crumpled to the ground in a heap.

Al was left alone hanging on to this monster, trying desperately to slow it down. From behind me sprung two giant cats. They were panthers, no, jaguars. One black and one tan. It must be Jag and Onyx! They leaped onto the Fiend and started tearing into it with their jaws.

I shakily managed to get to my feet. If the creature's anatomy was similar to mine I knew exactly where the heart should be. As the twins and Al distracted the beast I built up a static charge like a lightning ball in my hand. I'm pretty sure I couldn't do that before. I ran straight towards the menacing creature and released my tech right into his chest.

The static seemed to make the creature implode; its enormous chest seemed to cave right in. I watched the creature tremble and seize as it drew its final breaths. It collapsed to its knees and its eyes rolled back into its head. Blue eyes. Just like mine.

It's hard to tell time in a battle, but we were into the fourth or fifth hour when the Fiends unleashed a new tactic. Out of the tunnel came an enormous creature, a giant woolly beast with Fiends riding on top. The first one took us by surprise. We were busy avoiding getting trampled and no one noticed the Fiend on his back wielding a sword. The Fiend swung his sword to deliver a fatal blow to Zeal. Zeal jumped back and narrowly missed the cut. When Zeal jumped back it left Jack exposed. The sword slashed diagonally across his body spilling his guts. Jack just stood there looking down at his wound.

"Medic!" I screamed to Zeal. He scooped Jack up and ran right out the opening towards the medical tent. The whole thing freaked me out. I made eye contact with Keith.

"We need to get Ky out of here," I shouted.

Keith nodded. "Get Lix," he told me. I turned to find the soldier with the silver hair and found myself in the thick of battle. Lix was close to the mouth of the tunnel, slicing clean through Fiends as they tried to enter the cave. I fought for a good twenty minutes before I even got near the warrior. When I returned Keith had gathered Jage and Russell. He didn't need to tell me why he picked them, Lix was the best fighter on the team and they were the two soldiers Keith trusted most. I was glad to see that Jage was unfazed from being knocked out earlier. I already knew Keith would instruct the guys to take Ky straight to Lucky.

I turned back to the fray. The guys were mobilizing Ky when I heard him ask, "Don't I get to say goodbye?"

I turned my head sharply towards the boy while my body stayed ready to engage. "This isn't goodbye," I snapped fiercely. They moved him quickly out of the cave and to safety, I hoped.

The battle was hitting a frenzy and it was becoming dangerous for all of us inside the cave. I tried to communicate that to Keith when

417

suddenly Quake made his big move! He shook the ground with a seismic wave that hit everybody. It knocked the Fiends to the ground, but it knocked our team down too. The quake also loosened the rocks that made up the cave ceiling and walls. Pretty soon dust and rocks started to fall all around us.

If that wasn't bad enough the Fiends were starting to come quicker. The Fiends we fought seemed to be pretty mindless but someone on the other side was leading them, and it was likely a master strategist.

"We need to get out of here," I shouted to Keith.

"No way!" Keith told me. "We need to hold this ground."

There was an immense burst of rocks as the tunnel started to collapse. The mouth of the tunnel was now twice the size. The Fiend forces were pushing through rapidly, but the cave was crumbling even faster. More stones were falling everywhere, landing on the Fiends that were now pouring through the opening. The enlarging mouth was a menace to Keith's strategy. I turned back to look at the troops. Everyone was dodging the falling rocks. I saw a large boulder fall and knock Dmitri down. Violet threw herself into Russell to keep him from being hit by another rock. The falling stone hit Violet hard in the leg and even from a distance I could see it smash the bone.

The noise created by the falling rocks made it impossible for anyone to hear General Keith's orders. The team was scampering every direction trying to avoid these rocks and trying to deal with the new influx of

Fiend attackers that were now streaming up from hell.

I turned to look at the mouth of the tunnel, now dangerously wide, dozens of monsters all pushing their way through.

I heard screams behind me. General Keith had sounded the retreat. Everyone scrambled to pull back to the next lines where we would try desperately to stop them. I stood frozen. Already more than 100 Fiends had gotten past us and through the door. I was confident that General Lucky's troops had defeated them, but no doubt they were tired and weary. Everyone from the inside team seemed to have been wounded somehow, some of them gravely. The Fiends, on the other hand, were arriving at the mouth of the tunnel hungry with excitement. They were battle ready and had no qualms about killing.

The Vipers were fighting fiercely just to get out of the cave. Earlier, when everyone was facing the tunnel, ready for battle they seemed invincible. Now as everyone rushed to get out of the cave they left themselves very vulnerable to attack. Fiends were coming up behind my friends and getting the jump on them. One of the Fiends had blindsided Al. Sam ran to help. Once he was out of the way an extremely large, muscular Fiend with white skin and a single horn on his head attacked Jenni. Without Sam for protection and with no way to reach her sketch pad or paints Jenni was defenseless. I watched in horror as the Fiend lifted her up and placed her on his head, her hands grasping his horn to keep from falling. Several of the troops had turned

419

around and were trying to battle this Fiend, but the creature was more than nine feet tall, and they were afraid if they pushed too hard the Fiend would drop Jenni.

As I watched in horror I felt someone squeeze my arm. I turned my head and came face to face with Tyler. He didn't have to speak, I knew what he was thinking. He held my arm and with our free hands we raised them towards Jenni and used our techs to lift her off the Fiend and high in the air. With strict concentration we brought the girl toward us and placed her on the ground in front of us. As soon as Jenni was out of danger the fighters charged forward and took down the Fiend. We helped Jenni up and she pulled us together into a three way hug. "You two are dangerous together," she praised. Tyler and I smiled. Sam finished saving Al and ran to find his girlfriend. He put his arm protectively around Jenni and the two made their way to the exit.

It seemed like the entire cave was now filling with Fiends, making retreat almost impossible. Keith was shouting to me to head for the exit. I shook my head "no." This was the end. As soon as my friends were safe I would release whatever energy I had left.

Suddenly from behind I was pushed to the ground. I looked up. DJ? When did he get here? He was running straight toward the mouth of the tunnel, pulling Kitt by the hand. In a second I was back on my feet. I speeded right past them and started taking out Fiends in their way. I pushed and shoved and struck out wildly in every direction. Suddenly

DJ grabbed me painfully by the hair.

"This is my fight, get out!" he shouted to me. I looked over at the exit and DJ followed my gaze. The cave was filled entirely with Fiends all trying to force through the exit. There was no possible escape. DJ and I looked back at each other, his brown eyes full of sadness. "I should have never let it get this far. I'm so sorry."

"We're in this together," I told him.

A Fiend from behind me lunged for my head and knocked me on the ground. I rolled onto my back and looked up. DJ had his hand under Kitt's chin pulling her gently to look at him. He seemed to be talking softly to her and tears were running down her face. He pulled her tenderly forward and drew her into the sweetest, most caring hug I'd ever seen. He wrapped his arms tightly around her, drawing all of her power into him.

Seconds later an explosion of sound came rippling off of DJ's body. The shockwave destroyed everything around it. Rocks burst, the ground shook and any Fiend in its path was ripped apart by his sonic power blast.

I stayed down until the riot moved past me. I guess being on the ground I had missed the ribbon of the blast. I was using what static I could to keep the rocks from falling on me.

Now the tunnel truly began to collapse. Suddenly the Fiends were trying to pour back into the mouth they had been so eager to spring from. There was no time. The tunnel collapsed almost immediately, trapping the fleeing Fiends under a landslide of rock. The cave itself was collapsing too. Earth and dirt piling on top of everyone. The Fiends who survived the collapse were scared. They would be easy to dispatch for the troops waiting outside.

The ground was still shaking like an earthquake. I could see DJ a few feet in front of me protecting Kitt from the collapsing cave.

Suddenly behind them rose up out of the rubble the biggest Fiend I had ever seen. He was at least 12 feet tall with blue skin stretched tight all over his body. It seemed as if his brilliant red veins were on the outside. He had a long bony face, almost like a rhino with no horn. He swished his colossal tail. It was like that of a stegosaurus only blue with enormous red plates standing upwards. The lash of the tail sent a spray of rocks right into the crowd causing immense amounts of damage.

I knew I had to get this beast away from everyone before he buried them in rubble. The only ones between me and the creature were DJ and Kitt. I ran to protect them. DJ blocked my path!

"Take Kitt to safety," he ordered me. "This is my fight."

"Why do you keep saying that DJ? I'm Ky's guardian. This is *my* fight!"

"This was never about Kyan Mal," he screamed. "It's me they're after!"

DJ stopped for a moment, unsure if he should continue. Shamefully he confessed "I'm not a synergy at all. I'm all Fiend and both of my parents are Fiends. When I was young I ran away and came to this world. I never wanted to return to my old life. My parents will stop at nothing to get me back. They are very powerful down in hell, royalty. They built this tunnel and recruited all these goons to capture me."

DJ! Could what he's saying be true? Ky was never in danger? I felt relief wash over me and renew my strength. As long as that beast was around, everyone was in danger.

I thought about what Steel had taught me. I took a deep breath and matched up my static with the vibe given off by the beast. Slowly I lifted the two of us off the ground. He began to thrash but I ignored it and concentrated on his core energy. I managed to get us about 20 feet off the ground. At this height the creature couldn't hurt anyone, but slamming him into the ground wasn't going to do much damage either. In the wake of the earthquake DJ's tech had caused, the entire cave had collapsed. All that that loomed above us was sky. I needed some strategy. I looked for Keith. He was pointing towards the water. Of course, that small island Quake had created in practice!

I wasn't taking any chances of letting this thing go. I slowly moved the two of us over to the water. Now my abilities are useless above water. I have no idea where or how to bounce anything off of anything. I looked at my captive. He was thrashing about. His giant claws were ready to rip my poor friends apart, his jaws ready to chomp on them. I changed my plan. I stared to rebound against gravity and shot me and my monster right into the sky. I pulled us both up as high as I could get us, which it turns out was pretty high. I could no longer see the island, or the water, or New York for that matter. I thought about dropping the creature but realized if it didn't die on impact it could cause great destruction wherever it landed. No I had to keep it contained, the little island was my best bet.

I tried to let us down slowly. My plan was to position us over the island and let him fall. Unfortunately that meant letting myself fall too because we were connected by static. Then I'd have to try to catch myself before I hit ground which was never one of my strengths.

We closed in on the island and I let him go from a few stories up. The beast impacted hard on the ground. I only had a second to feel smug. Without warning, I began spiraling out of control. I was lost in the freefall, nothing I did would slow me down. If I couldn't regain control I was going to hit the ground and splatter.

Suddenly I remembered the ball lightning I created in the cave! That much energy compacted would surely keep me alive. I put my hands together but it was no use. I didn't have enough energy left to create. Stupid girl! There was energy all around me. If I couldn't create it I would just have to harness it. It was now or never, the ground was rapidly approaching. I used what energy I had left to draw in all the static energy in the surrounding environment. I channeled it through my body and up into my arms. A small ball with lightning trembling inside it took shape in my hands. Not a minute too soon! I reached the ground, the ball in my outstretched arms hitting first. The impact was just enough to knock me a few feet up then letting me crash to the ground. Whew! Talk about cutting it close!

I caught my breath then walked slowly over to the Fiend to gauge its injuries. As I got near it, it moved its front paw and batted me away. I flew nearly 20 feet, hitting the ground twice. I nearly toppled over the edge of the island into the water. I was literally hanging by my fingers. The falling motion actually created friction between me and the stone face of the island. Without missing a beat I used this friction to catapult myself up in the air.

My legs were all scratched and bruised but they were still my strongest feature. I pulled myself high off the ground and let gravity bring me in - steering as much as possible. I was on target to hit this monster straight in the face. The impact might be strong enough to take him down for good. When gravity has you, it's never easy to control. I bent one knee and left the other leg straight out to give him a good hard bash.

I was inches from his face when the creature dodged! I missed his face entirely, impacting on his shoulder. The force was enough to knock him down but it took me with him. The creature was on his back and I was sprawled out on his chest. I took a moment to gauge the placement of his humongous claws; I didn't want to get struck by them again. I was about to make my escape when I felt razor sharp spikes piercing through my shoulder. He bit me! I don't know why I didn't think of his mouth as a weapon. The beast bit down hard. He grabbed onto my right arm just below the shoulder and took about a 9 inch bite right out of me. The pain was maddening. He bit right down to the bone. I wasn't going to survive this. The creature stood up and I clattered to the ground. He turned his back on me to savor the meat he had just pulled off of me. I looked at my injury. I had minutes left on my life. I needed to come up with one final strike that would finish this monster and leave my friends in peace.

I started focusing all my energy on my left hand. My fingers and palm began sparking immediately. I remembered my teaching and started pulling the static from everything, the land, the air, even the beast himself. I used every muscle in my body to get this shot together. After this I wouldn't have enough strength to go on. I prayed. 'Lord Eric who art in heaven or wherever, let this shot be enough to end my enemy and protect my loved ones.'

I released the blast from my palm. A giant sphere of electricity flew straight from my body to his. The blast looked exactly how I always imagined my soul would look. Maybe this was the greatest way to die, as a hero defeating a Fiend with my very soul. The blast hit the monster and burst into a flood of light.

It wasn't enough! The creature wasn't even pushed off the island, he was only knocked back. I failed. Everyone I loved would suffer and die. I prayed the creature would eat me first and spare my friends. I looked at the beast. For some reason it was hardly moving. Did I paralyze it? Blood was pooling underneath it. But how?

I looked closely and could see a sliver of metal entering from behind and piercing through the creatures heart. I saw the blade being pulled from the monster and Steel stepped out from behind the beast. The monster crumpled forward, expired.

Steel! What was he doing here? Saving my butt, as usual. The monster was slain, the tunnel destroyed. I closed my eyes for the very last time.

I was trying to die in peace but Steel wouldn't let me. I opened my eyes seconds later. Steel was striking me hard in the face. "Stay alive you stupid bitch!" he yelled. "I need you to bounce us back to the shore." He turned my face so I could see what he was talking about. I didn't have the strength to do as he asked.

"I can't," I whispered. "I'm sorry."

"No!" he screamed and started shaking me. "You owe me you dumb bitch. You owe me!"

I did owe him. If the last thing I could do in this life is repay Steel for all his kindnesses, then I could die happy. I strained to get my scrambled thoughts together and Steel scooped me up. I mustered just enough energy to bounce us from the island back to the shore.

Steel hit the ground running and in a moment we were in the medical tent. I was dizzy and exhausted but I struggled to stay conscious. The doctors saw my wounded arm and immediately tried to stop the bleeding. Mend brought the cooler of my blood transfusions. The medics hurried to move things around to tend to my wounds. All around me were brave friends of mine lying on stretchers.

In the back corner was a stretcher with a yellow flag. Oh God, another companion who isn't going to make it. I saw a head bent over the cot crying. Was that Zeal? Wait, on the cot…it couldn't be…

"JACK!" I cried out. Zeal stood up and looked over at me, tearstained. "He's not going to make it Steph. The doctors said there's no hope." Zeal turned back to the tiny little boy dying right in front of him. "He was my responsibility and I failed him."

Oh my god, I'm the one that failed him! Jack, I hadn't put him on the list to receive my blood. I was only thinking of the Vipers. I forgot about this little boy that lived under the same roof and shared our meals. If Mend had gotten to him in time, we might have saved him. Now my mistake was going to cost him his young life. Lucky once predicted I would protect Ky even if it meant putting a bullet between little Jack's eyes. That couldn't be true, could it?

"No," I said as the doctors came to move me for treatment. I tried again, louder "No! I don't want you to treat me!" Everyone froze in shock. "I want you to prepare us for the Xxixxa. I want you to give my

428

heart's blood to Jack."

"They can't do that, Stephanie. No one on Earth has even tried that before. They don't know the procedure," Steel huffed.

"You do," I turned my head to Steel.

"In theory," Steel said shaking his head.

The head doctor made his way over to me. "You've lost a lot of blood Stephanie. We don't even know if we can save you. It's very sad about Jack but we've done everything we can. This hocus pocus treatment isn't going to save him. Even if I can stop your hearts, there is no guarantee I can get them started again. You'll both die."

"Why are we still arguing this? Get Jack ready for surgery. His fate will be the same as mine." I collapsed into Steel's arms with exhaustion.

"Did I make the right choice?" I asked my teacher as things grew hazy.

"You never do." Steel's words were the last things I heard and then darkness.

Chapter the last

I was asleep, I knew that much because I was dreaming. It wasn't anything tangible, I think I was dreaming about electricity.

I opened my eyes. For a moment I had no idea where I was and I was disoriented and scared. I sat up like a shot.

"You're okay," a voice told me. "Don't move." The voice, I thought I recognized it.

"Al?" I questioned.

"Right here," Al answered. "Keeping watch. You've been asleep for three days, we were starting to fear the worst."

I thought I was in a hospital room, only I seemed to be in a king size bed. I was connected to all kinds of IVs and beeping machines. Wait, this is my room. The war must be over, and if we're not hiding underground, that means…we won!

In a second Al was on the phone to Keith and in another second Keith was coming through my bedroom door.

Al stood up and exited as Keith rushed into the room. "Bring the doctor straight here," Keith ordered as Al closed the door behind him. Keith turned to me and jumped up on the bed, clamoring over the wires and machines to reach me. He grabbed my face in his hands and gave me an excited kiss. The heart monitor I was attached to started beeping like mad and we both broke the kiss and giggled. He slipped his arms around my shoulders and pulled me into a deep hug. I didn't need to ask, I already knew everything was okay.

"How are you feeling?" he asked as he drew back to look at me. His green eyes were clouded with concern.

"Jack?" was all I asked

Keith smiled. "He's fine. In fact he's probably in better shape then you are." Keith opened the door asked Al to go get Jack. Then Keith pounced on me. "When did you acquire healing powers like that?" he demanded.

"In hell, with Steel," I explained.

"Why didn't you tell me?" he asked, clearly hurt by my keeping the secret.

"I just thought it was better to keep that one to myself, you know?" I could tell he didn't agree. "Speaking about keeping things to yourself, before the battle you mentioned being in love with someone. Did you maybe want to tell me about that?" I asked sweetly.

"Uh, I don't remember that." Keith totally lied.

"You were speaking to the Vipers," I tried leading him.

"Well a leader has to give inspiring speeches."

"So it wasn't true then, just part of your speech?" I asked looking hurt.

"I didn't say that." Keith just looked at the floor.

I decided to go first. "I love you Keith," I said with sincerity.

Keith continued to look at the floor. He took a breath with a long exhale. "Yeah, I knew you did," he said.

431

Well at least you could always count on Keith to be Keith.

"Here's the little cretin," Keith changed the subject gesturing towards the wheelchair Al was pushing in. Wrapped in bandages and looking like crap was a very much alive Jack.

I ran my hands over my bandages. I looked down and verified they were the same as his. The Xxixxa was a success. When I had my first operation, Genevieve's Fiend powers merged with my own giving me that incredible healing ability. Jack was alive - that meant the healing ability had been shared with him.

"I'm glad you finally woke up, I've been waiting to talk to you." Jack began. "The guys told me how you put your life on the line for me and I just wanted to say...I never asked to be saved and I don't owe you anything." Wow. That's gratitude for you. Jack continued. "Now the doctor said I might develop my own synergy abilities, which is just great. I was perfectly happy being a human but you had to drag me down to your level. The only thing I don't get is why you saved me. I mean it's not like we were friends or anything. I definitely wouldn't have saved you."

I felt emotional remembering the moment. "I just saw you there and I thought how you didn't want any of this. You didn't want to live here, didn't want to be a Viper, you didn't want to fight in this war. I thought I should be the one dying, not you. That's why I did what I did."

"So you did it to spare yourself the guilt? That's stupid. You are so stupid. There are a lot of reasons why I don't like you but being stupid is at the top of the list," Jack said smugly.

"You could try being nicer to me," I said glumly.

"Where's the fun in that?" Jack asked spitefully.

"Enough," Keith interrupted. "Get out of here Jack, let Stephanie rest." Al walked around behind the wheelchair and started wheeling the little boy out.

"As soon as I am better I am so out of here," Jack was saying loudly to Al. "I'm going to meet up with Luke in Atlanta."

"Did Lucky leave?" I asked Keith. "Is he okay?"

"He's fine," Keith said in a rather disconcerting way leading me to believe Lucky was anything but fine. "He left for Atlanta when the battle was over. He's gone back to his gang, The SilverSword Alliance. I was finally able to get him a visa so he doesn't have to hide underground anymore if he doesn't want to. He said he would send for Jack as soon as it was safe, but Jack's not going anywhere for a while." Keith paused, trying to decide what to say next. "Lucky was a brilliant general. Without him there would have been so many more casualties. He didn't sustain any serious injuries, but he just seemed to lose heart. I think living without you finally caught up with him."

I heard Keith's words about Lucky but something bigger was on my mind.

"How many?" I asked with cold detachment. "How many casualties, Keith? How many people did I lure to their deaths?"

"Steph, you pretty much saved the world. You can't blame yourself…"

"How many?" I cut him off.

"There were 31 casualties on our side,' Keith answered quietly.

"Thirty-one!" That was far more than I had anticipated. I started to tremble. Keith held me but I felt no comfort. "Thirty-one of our friends. Who were they?"

"I'm not so sure we should even talk about this. You just woke up, rest yourself." Keith tried to soothe me.

"Who were they Keith? Who followed me to their death?" I demanded.

"Of course you know about Holly," said a voice from the doorway. Standing there was DJ. He looked like he hadn't slept in days. "We lost two more that I knew."

"Kitt?" I asked remembering the weakened girl in his arms.

"No. Believe it or not Kitt's just fine. She was more of a fighter than I ever saw in her." DJ forced a weak smile. He reached out for my hand. As his hand slid out from his sleeve I could see slash marks all up his arm. I didn't need to ask, I already knew I'd find 31 of them. "All these deaths are my fault. The Fiends were here for me. If I had just let them take me then no one had to die."

"No," I told him. "They weren't going to stop at just you. If we hadn't held them back here who knows how much damage they could have

434

caused. Anyway, you're one of *us*, DJ. I would never make you go somewhere against your will. If we could fight to protect Ky, we could just as easily fight to protect you. We just didn't know we were doing it."

"You're saying you would have done all this, staged this whole war to protect me?" DJ's voice quivered when he spoke.

"Sure, why not?" I asked. "You deserve freedom and happiness as much as anybody. Just be honest with us next time."

DJ kneeled down next to my bed. "Thank you, thank you for everything. Our friends will not have died in vain, I will make sure of it."

"I have every confidence that you will," I told him. I was about to continue my conversation with DJ when a figure appeared in the doorway. Kyan! DJ and Keith both got up. Keith kissed me on the forehead and the two exited leaving Ky and I alone.

The boy stood silently in the doorway and looked at me. I looked around myself at the bandages and wires. I must have looked downright scary. I started ripping wires and tubes from my arms and chest.

"Stop!" Ky screamed, running in to stop me. "You might need those!"

"Nah," I said. I scooted over to make room on the bed. Ky laid down next to me. I lay back and the two of us stared at the ceiling. "So, what happened," I asked.

"Not much, really." Ky began. "After I left the cave Jage and Russell took me to the top of the hill, away from the fighting. I had a good view of everything. Lix was cutting through every Fiend in sight. I saw DJ's team return. He and Kitt ran into the cave and a few minutes later his sonic blast leveled the place. Everyone watched as you rose from the rubble with that giant Fiend and brought him to the island to battle him. We really thought you were done for. If Steel hadn't shown up when he did... Then they get you to the medical tent and you would rather save Jack then yourself. That was pretty amusing."

"Are you okay?" I asked. "I mean you don't have a scratch on you, but how do you feel?"

"I didn't have to kill anyone, that was good. Finding out that this whole war had nothing to do with me, well that was the best feeling in the world. But there's something else I wanted to ask you, something big." This must be what he was waiting to tell me. "The legend of the Envoy, I want to know what it is. If I have a destiny, I need to understand it."

"Absolutely," I agreed. "I'll talk to Eric."

"That's just it. This whole war, the Envoy thing – all of this came from Eric. I want you to go to hell and find out the truth on your own. Until then I don't know if we can trust Eric," Ky said cautiously.

"It's not Eric you have to worry about, it's everyone else," came a deep male voice from inside the room. Ky and I sat up and looked for the intruder. Standing outside the bathroom door was Eric. He must have

436

materialized in the bathroom and snuck in. "I am always on your side, both of you. But I can't watch you every second and I don't know everything."

"Did you know this war had nothing to do with Ky? Were you using us the whole time?" I looked at Eric in skepticism.

"I couldn't allow Fiends from hell to take over the Earth. Protecting the Earth and heaven is my priority and anything I do will be for that purpose. I assumed that the Fiends were after the Envoy. I guess I didn't have all the facts. I didn't lie to you, that you can believe." Eric sighed. "Honestly, even if I did know the truth I might have done the exact same thing. You were the only one I knew who could save this world, Stephanie. I mean there might have been hundreds of folks that were better suited than you, but I only watch over a small group and out of that group you were the best choice."

Huh. I wasn't the best in the world, I was just the best that Eric knew. I guess that should make me feel less significant, but it didn't. Maybe there was more help out there.

"Why us?" Ky asked Eric.

"Well, Stephanie, I watch all Fiends of your race. Kyan, your story is very different. You see there are 3 worlds that make up heaven. One world is for all the spirits of deceased humans that are able to go to heaven. Above that is a world that is restricted to Angels. At the very top of all existence is a world that is only inhabited by the most elite

Angels of heaven. This is where your soul materialized when you had your brush with suicide. In all of recorded history a human soul has never reached the highest level of heaven. That's how I knew you were special." Eric paused to let that sink in. "Right now I think I'm the only one who knows. You were dead for such a short time, seconds only. I know everyone on the highest level felt your presence, but I think I'm the only one who knows your identity."

"Well couldn't there be Angels watching us right now?" I asked.

"Sure," Eric answered. "There is always that possibility, but I highly doubt it. Your Fiend race is a personal interest of mine, Stephanie. I don't know anyone else above that cares about it. And Kyan, well let's just say your dad's not too popular in heaven. No one up there cares what his kids are up to."

Ky was immediately defensive. "What do you know about my dad?" he demanded.

"The Mal? You know mal is Latin for 'bad,' right. Kaden Mal was the first bad Angel. He was the first Angel ever to turn against God and escape from heaven."

"My dad is an Angel? Did you know him?" Ky asked in wonder.

Eric sighed. "It was not my intention to tell you any of this, but yes, I know Kaden Mal. My father, Lord Ruin, is a very busy man. Too busy, in fact, to raise me. My uncle Lord Kyr had a son that was just my age. He raised me and my cousin Kaden like brothers."

"I remember you mentioned a cousin. You said he was your best friend. Is that Ky's father?" I asked.

"Yes," Eric nodded. "Keith and Kyan's father is Kaden Mal, my cousin and my best friend."

"So that means we're related?" Ky asked Eric in astonishment.

"Yes, we are related," Eric confirmed.

"Does that mean you and I are related too?" I asked Eric.

"No Blue Eyes, there are no Fiends in my family. At any rate I didn't come here to chit chat, I came to warn you." Suddenly Eric was all business. "This war you fought wasn't about Kyan but that doesn't mean the next one won't be," Eric warned.

"Next one! How many wars are you expecting?" I exclaimed.

"Stephanie, the legend of the Envoy has gone on for millennia. Now that he's appeared we really don't know what to expect. I will promise you this," Eric took my hand and looked into my eyes. "I'll do whatever I can to protect you both," he said with complete sincerity. "Now get some rest, I know Steel is anxious to get you back into training. He'll be back for you in six months."

"Six months! Didn't I just save the world? Isn't that worth something?" I shouted.

"Yeah," Eric laughed. "Apparently it's worth six months. You can ask Steel for more but he's just gonna say you owe him."

I groaned. "Why six months?"

"In case the other girls drop out, you're next in line for Miss America."

"Miss America! Oh no way! I'd rather fight another war!"

www.ingramcontent.com/pod-product-compliance
Lightning Source LLC
Chambersburg PA
CBHW021122260626
47169CB00005B/1400